I0630673

John Ballou Newbrough

The Fall of Fort Sumter

Love and war in 1860-61

John Ballou Newbrough

The Fall of Fort Sumter
Love and war in 1860-61

ISBN/EAN: 9783337267957

Printed in Europe, USA, Canada, Australia, Japan

Cover: Foto ©Andreas Hilbeck / pixelio.de

More available books at **www.hansebooks.com**

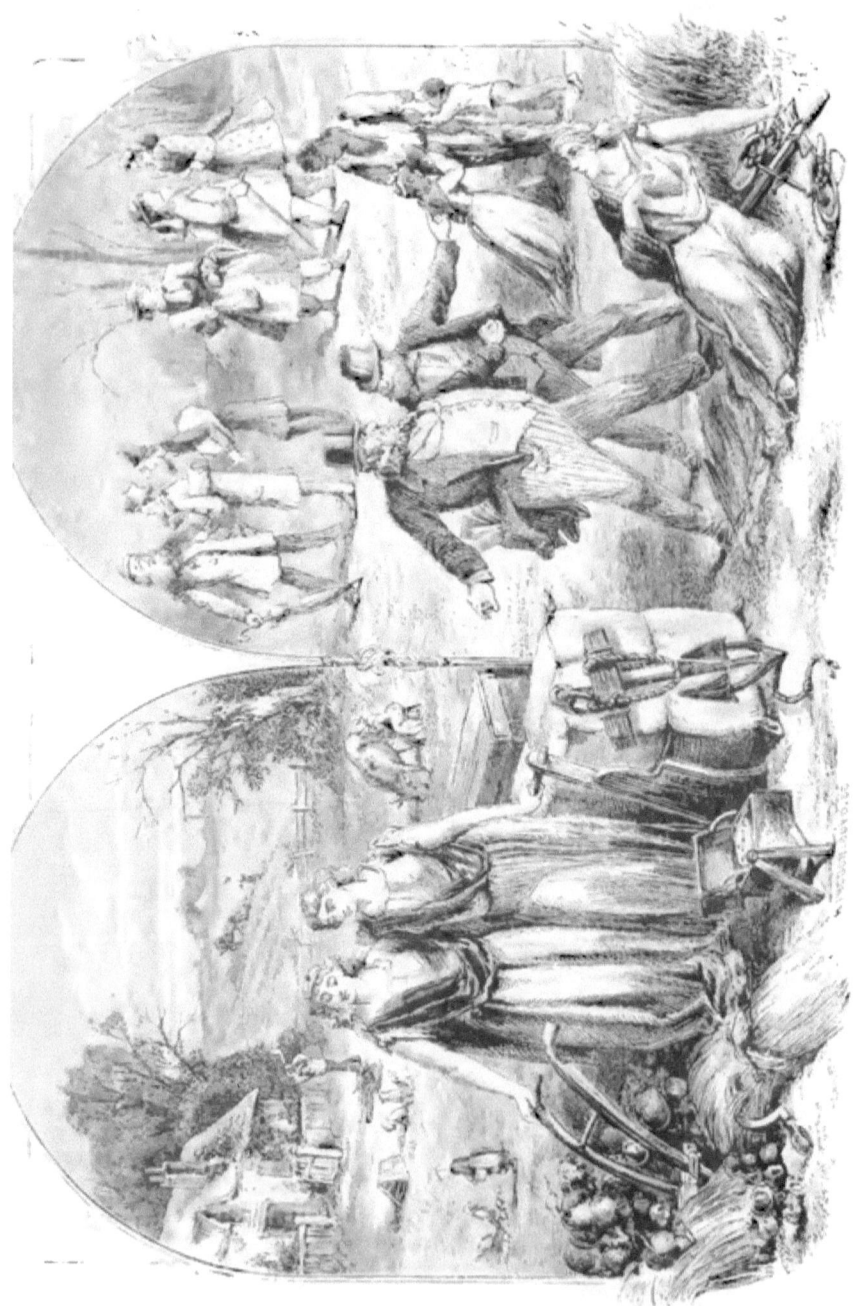

Commerce and Agriculture had, on the one hand, made the country prosperous and great; but had, on the other hand, opened avenues for idle fanaticists and politicians, who, for party issues, trampled Justice under foot.

THE FALL OF FORT SUMTER;

OR,

LOVE AND WAR IN 1860--61.

"BY THE PRIVATE SECRETARY TO ——, ETC."

NEW YORK:
FREDERIC A. BRADY, PUBLISHER,
No. 22 ANN STREET.

Entered according to Act of Congress, in the year 1867,

By J. B. NEWBROUGH,

In the Clerk's Office of the District Court of the United States for the Southern District
of New York.

THE FALL OF FORT SUMTER;

OR,

LOVE AND WAR IN 1860.

A SORT OF PREFACE.

JUST before the war, our country was almost without news. We were obliged to make the most of everything, in order to have excitement enough to live on. Many cultivated, rich, and ease-loving gentlemen used to spend their time in the National Capitol, and, to while away that time, as the over-full enjoyment went on, they were put to many straits for something to talk of.

In the summer of 1857, a party—myself among others—established a select court, criminal, civil, and *élite*. The whole object and end, however, of this court, was to amuse and interest ourselves. We had a definite organization, and seldom varied from the established rules of an ordinary court. We had for our judge a portly man of about fifty—the most eccentric, good-natured, well-informed kind of fool you ever saw; more of a gentleman than Falstaff—less a drinker; more of a wit—less a knave: and, as Jenkins says, about the same to America that Falstaff was to England.

Jenkins, whose real name was Rumor, and who fashions the bulk of this history, had been for many years a reporter; but, having recently come into the possession of a fortune, no longer followed his pursuit, except for amusement. Rumor had it, too, that about the time referred to he was in love with the Judge's niece, afterwards well known by the battles in the neighborhood of Loudon Heights.

The other members of our court constituted the jury, plaintiffs, defendants, witnesses, et cetera. As you will perceive, if you read this history far enough, our court had also to do with courtships and marriages, and did really have contact with the outside world as much as was generally supposed at that period. I continued a member of this court until the war broke out, and then, being a Northerner, I withdrew, taking no further interest in the matter, only so far that I always remembered with great joy the pleasant hours I had passed. During all this long war, I was left entirely to my own conjectures about my former companions, and of their whereabouts. Neither did I know who, since that time, had taken charge of the marriages and courtships that were the life of Washington.

One day, not long ago, Jenkins, that is to say, Rumor, came into my office, and I was right glad to see him. He said he was broke—dead broke—and indeed he looked a good deal discouraged; but I gave him wine, and he rallied rapidly. When he was himself again, he said I was the cleverest man he ever knew, and that I might as easily get a monument to my greatness as any one, if I would only fix up his notes and publish them: for, he said, they contained not only the full history of the rebellion, but all the fashions, marriages, and courtships during the whole four years. I gave him more wine, and he said I was a good-looking man, and that no other should have the privilege in so great a work as that he was going to offer me, and that was, that when I was dead and gone my picture should be in the frontispiece. He unfolded a large bundle of papers and handed me a large basketful beside. "Good Lord," said I, "must I rewrite all these, in order to be great?" But he smiled, and said, "You, sir, that have read all languages; that have travelled all over the world; that have studied and labored for thirty years in literature; that know all men and value them so highly; that look from your aerial position; (I am very tall) you, to talk of all these?"

When he tumbled out the basketful, I saw that the manuscripts were in phonographic characters, and told him I could not decipher them. But he said he would furnish me an interpreter, and all I had to do was to write. I thought I would give him another glass of wine, which, when he had finished it, he pronounced excellent, and then he went on,

"Who wrote the best history of England? Shakespeare. Who the best of Scotland? Scott. And we all know who wrote the best history of knight errantry. They dealt in love affairs, and you know we prize them first. Now I will venture to say that there is not a man or woman this side of Jersey who does not feel a tingle of joy on learning the finale of some spirited amour; and, for that reason I want you to salt these things down."

With that he tossed them into my arms, saying, "You know one of the rules of the club was that no member could refuse to do what was ordered by a superior." I took them, and he immediately translated a portion to me, beginning with the session of the Chicago convention. Now if you will be kind enough to read what follows, you will learn the things that Jenkins wrote.

CHAPTER I.

ABOUT twenty of us were waiting in the office, and about forty others outside. We were waiting for news from the Chicago Convention. I did not know at that time who Rhett was, but was told afterwards that he was editor and proprietor of the Charleston *Mercury*. Whilst the talk was going on in the office, I heard a Mr. Jones ask how far it was to Chicago. The conversation turned on politics, and a Mr. Smith became engaged in angry words with Jones. The latter said he was in favor of freedom in the Territories, and the former thereupon accused him of saying "a nigger is as good as a white man." It was like all political rows, beginning in calm argument, but ending in violence and shame. Then came the flourish of weapons, knives and pistols.

At this instant Rhett and Johnson rushed upon them. Rhett said, "Gentlemen, what would you do? Must such trifling words incite you to deeds of blood?" He took Smith, and Johnson took Jones, and they were bearing them back, when Smith said, "What, shall he deride my native state?" Jones replied, "I did not." "You did!" says Smith. "You cast a slur on Breckenridge, and he and I are Kentuckians." "That is too far-fetched" said Jones; but thereupon Smith tore himself away from Rhett, reiterating, "Coward, you say a nigger is as good as a white man." He flew at Jones, but the crowd interfered and forcibly ejected him from the office.

As soon as quiet was restored, Rhett said, "Did ever man take offence so easily; did ever man so hastily come to a base conclusion. A dozen words, and then to knives and pistols." He then called Johnson, and Johnson said, "Well sir." Rhett being old, and somewhat excited, leaned on Johnson's arm, his hand on his shoulder, and he facing the crowd, "This is indeed approaching war," he continued; "all men, and on all occasions, meet now, but to discuss North and South. Brooks bled poor Sumner for this, and for as trifling a matter as this between Jones and Smith. Sumner spoke, Brooks took offence —not for what Sumner said, but for what he himself inferred might have been spoken. Brooks loved offence more than even justice, and so do we all. We have had no war for fifty years, and we have become chronic. The Creator designs that there shall be a grand upheaval in this nation. We have not learned to govern ourselves with moderation and reason, and the scourge of war is already in embryo in every man's breast. These trifles which we behold, are but its leakings; outbreaks preliminary to a mighty revolution."

Now, when Rhett began to talk, we were all silent; for the wisdom of his words showed us that we were in the presence of a superior man. Up to this time I did not know Johnson, but was told who he was. He replied to Rhett by saying, "This is through politicians, and, like their fellows in all countries, they have their hobby for electioneering purposes. Like the Prussian king, who told his subjects that the savages of England and France were coming, and that they should at once invest him with absolute power; and he promised that if the country would give him his desire, he would fill every man's purse with gold, and his stomach with beer. The opposite party, however, wishing to retain the parliament, often came to blows with the king's party, who invariably retorted to them: "So, you say a Frenchman, or an Englishman is as good as a Dutchman." The king's party however succeeded, and this style of argument is still the basis of all politics. In England, a candidate electioneers by saying he will fill the stomachs of his constituents; or by cautioning him that the infidel French are coming; or, that the barbarous Americans need watching. In the South, we say slavery is wealth, give us more; and our opposite party says a "negro is as good as a white man." Now this is all nonsense. These are extreme and ultra views which no sensible man of either party endorses. They are political fabrications. False, for villainous party purposes only. What we want, Mr. Rhett, is concession."

"Concession! dogs!" said Rhett, "for

thirty years we have conceded all to the North; but, sir, till they get our slaves, or we get the government, I swear by heavens, as I am a man, this agitation shall never cease. Men like you are as detrimental to the whole country as to the South." "Why, now, look you," said Johnson, " you are like Jones and Smith; like Brooks and Sumner. Because I said that one word, concession, you infer that I am on the opposite side, and might say some ugly things."

"No, sir," said Rhett, " I infer nothing, though the South shall have her rights. We have done nothing but concede. We have been battling like dogs for thirty years to obtain even a decent footing in the West. Sir, the Free States are usurping everything. The tide of these affairs will soon rise, till three-quarters of the States will be free, and then what becomes of us? We can thank our stars for poor Pierce and James Buchanan; but—suppose a devil with some shrewd sense be elected from the North? That is the gist of our forebodings. I tell you, Johnson, sooner than have this country overrun with abolitionism, I would have every man, woman and child in it annihilated." *

Johnson replied that he considered him one of the greatest agitators in the country. Rhett denied it. He said he only wanted the rights of the South guaranteed, though ere he replied in full, the place was thrown into some confusion by the entrance of Toombs, Floyd, Thompson, Wigfall, Davis, Slidell, Mason, and Yancey, and immediately after them came Gen. Scott leaning on the arm of Prescott. Johnson said, good humoredly, " Here are your disciples, only for Scott and Prescott." When he said this, Rhett leaned over the railing to look at Scott and Prescott, and he asked who that was on whom Scott was leaning? "Prescott," said Johnson; " young Prescott, the son of a washerwoman." "The son of a washerwoman!" said Rhett, and he drew down his eyebrows and scowled. "The son of a washerwoman! Well, it is well that poor men do well in this country; and it is ill that they do ill in others. But there is a tide in the affairs of nations, and when it is at the flood, why, it gets no higher.

" Cæsar rose from nothing, but the gods were insulted, and so great Cæsar fell, and with him his country. Cæsars rise out of

every dunghill in America, and they will prove the death of us."

Johnson turned to him calmly and said, " I, sir, am a tailor. I understand the fashions of a cut. A goose, well tempered, may smooth a thing, but if it be too hot, it burns. I know also there may be sharp things in a poor garment, and even a goose may be made to feel the prick of them."

Rhett was thrown completely off his bearings, and he looked at Johnson, surprised at him; but Johnson walked away. Rhett stood for some time looking after him, and then he said: " A tailor, a washerwoman's son; a pretty pass in this our great republic. Am I, that am a fair gentleman, bewildered with the things I see, seeing double, both the false and true, as truth; or is my native country mad? Mad! It follows now an ape—a common ape must rise and set its nose for Congress, learn to take offence and mimic gentlemen. O heavens! shall never beam the star of glory on our fair land, and wills majestic rise to consummate the Southern Parliament? Shall not my thirty years of constant prayer reach up to Him who notes a sparrow's fall, and answer bring imperative—no North, no South, but one united whole: a country's laws for all; not one the sole inheritor, nor property devoid of bond up North that is down South employed? No, never. Low ambition rules the land. The loudest clamoring politician sways the universal mob; villainous poison is secreted under the name of Liberty. O Liberty! I sicken at thy oft repeated tale; from my very soul I hurl thee into endless chaos."

I think he said more, but, at this time, some bustle occasioned in the office by a report coming from Chicago, I heard Cobb say, " You are right, Mr. Rhett." I have known Cobb for many years. He is a stoutish man, and often repeats what others say. He boasts a good deal for a man of his worth. " You are right, Mr. Rhett," said he, " those are my sentiments;" and then he added some oaths that I do not like to mention. Afterwards he shook hands with Rhett, and continued, " Our few heads are more powerful than were all the warriors and philosophers of the Roman Empire. We need but to rise and shake our fists in the face of the world, and we shall be the mightiest of nations. No one dares oppose us; only let us stick together and get loose from these dolts and plebeians that are eternally robbing us of our rights under the sickening name of Liberty. They tell us we dare not secede, what say you?" and then he made oath, adding, " It is all gammon,"

* These words were thought to be too good to be lost, and afterwards appeared editorially in the columns of the Charleston Mercury, and were copied into the New Orleans True Delta, and with even worse threats attached to them.

using such language that even Rhett and Davis looked ashamed.*

Despatches were now coming from Chicago announcing Seward's rejection, and the news interfered with the conversation. We observed two persons, Madame Ponchard, and a man called Orsini entering the place. They were a mysterious pair. She was apparently a woman of great wealth, and he a man of neat and plain attire, as if he might be only an attendant. Yet both were reserved, secluded, diffident. She recognized by nearly all of the great men present by a polite bow; he unnoticed. As soon as they had passed indifferently aside, as if to await the news from Chicago, we were still further interested by the entrance of another person— a woman of strange and noticeable mark: a tall, serene person she was, and of an age no man might question. She came in so boldly, and looked around with such commanding mien, that we all stood still as if awaiting our doom. "Gentlemen," she said, "why this silence? Methought this bustle and these murmuring voices were indicative of something terrible, and that within this noble structure, I heard oaths so abominable, that the very foundation of my woman's nature trembled in my delicate form. But, lo! how soon is peace and quiet. How majestically sweet and humble is man's nature, turned by the presence of modest, unassuming woman. I thank my stars, gentlemen, that I have been the innocent means of assuaging this raging tumult. These missions are my errands. I am to redress the wrongs of woman, and to reform the uncultivated faults of man's nature. My name is Miss Lucy Tabiatha Stimpkins."

Thus saying, she drew from her pocket a bundle of papers and distributed them amongst us, giving every man one. Some said it was Donna del Don Quixote; but she heeded nothing round her, and went on speaking. "You will perceive, gentlemen," she said, "I am just starting a paper to be entitled 'The Journal of Progress,' and I am to be the editress. I have long beheld the down-trodden condition of my sex, and am prepared for the direst slurs you may heap upon me for my apparent boldness. I have heard lectures by our eminent women on this subject, and I have resolved to devote the balance of my days as the champion and adjuster of our wrongs. You see, too, like the knight of the Lion heart, as some one of you has been good enough to compare me, I pitch into all places of danger, that all men may

learn my power—my woman's power. But not like that knight do I invoke the power of my lover; for I tell you frankly I love no man, having been thrice married and thrice divorced; but I speak to Him who has power to give to the meek and lowly according as their just rights demand. Though prayer is nothing without work. I have put my shoulder to the wheel. My talents are my arms; my sex is my shield; my cause is my Rosinante. By this prospectus, gentlemen, you will see that I am the champion of freedom for all men, and for all women too. You are thankful for your freedom; but you undoubtedly remember the women of the days of Lycurgus, how they bared their breasts and demanded the liberty of their husbands and brothers, or death. Then came the republic—the first republic. You thank those women, and some day your children and your children's children will thank us. Not, sirs, that we will bare our breasts;" (here some of the crowd said, "got none to bare;" but she heeded not, going on,) "we take a more noble method of action, and, we trust, more powerful than the sword. My object will be in the 'Journal of Progress' to show you that the abolition of slavery is near at hand; to show you that if it be done by war instead of peace, you have everything to lose, and nothing to gain; to show you that Elihu Burritt, the learned blacksmith, has demonstrated that you can sell your slaves into freedom by the sale of western lands; to show you that woman comes among you as a ministering angel, to carry out the great principles of human liberty. Now, gentlemen, with this brief statement on my part, allow me to ask, will you subscribe for the Journal?"

We all laughed loudly, but she went on, "Three columns shall be devoted to news and letters, one to advertisements, twelve to temperance, sixteen to the abolition of slavery, and twenty to woman's rights." When she had got thus far, the whole office joined in roars of laughter; but she was still as calm as before. As soon as quiet was restored, Rhett replied, "It is strange, madam, that every person North runs on these same topics—slavery, temperance, and woman's rights. As soon as a woman learns to read, she mounts the rostrum with adjectives numerous, and topics worn threadbare, not to elevate or beautify rude man, but to disgust him with the presence of woman. Miss Lucy Tabiatha Stimpkins, I pity you. You have harped upon these subjects until you are mad. You are indeed like Don Quixote. These subjects have made you crazy, and

---

* From Cobb's speech at Mobile, 1861.

the result of your crazy-headed lecturing (a great deal of exaggeration mixed with a little truth) will make many, very many unhappy persons, especially females. If anything makes me hate the North more than abolitionism it is your species of women. We have none such amongst us in the South."

"Exactly so," said she, "and to educate you to that higher sphere of life have I come among you. I come to bear the brunt of your reproaches, and I am happy that my modesty and delicacy do not quail before you. I belong to that class—I may say race—of unselfish beings who can view slavery, temperance, and woman's rights from a holier point of view. Sir, you pity me, allow me to reciprocate the sentiment on your revered head."

This was so easily spoken that the crowd set up another laugh, and some of them clapped their hands. Rhett rallied, although he showed an inclination to turn away. "Pity devil," said he, "but, since you have a face bold enough to argue, let me tell you one thing as a principle in philosophy—and that is, that so much boldness of Northern women is proof positive that man's nature up there has cked out into woman, and hence the dastardly, cowardly character of all the members they send to the national Congress. It is also the best assurance in the world that in a few years the South will be entirely the master of the country."

"I don't argue sir," said she, "I maintain my rights. I am champion for others. You may fight and conquer us, you may extinguish an army of women, but, sir, our doctrines, our woman's rights, shall finally vanquish you. Little girls shall be taught to know their rights, and, coming to majority, they will maintain them. They will make men sue, oblige them to stand trembling, to know and do their pleasure. I look far ahead, sir, to the time when woman's voice shall ring in yonder Capitol, and, too, when the black man, if he has talent, shall grace the Senate with his brilliant tongue."

Here a roar of laughter set in again, and the poor woman turned and left, protesting at the top of her voice, that she was but a poor helpless woman, but that she would meet them again in after times, with such editorials as were never put to paper.

As soon as the laugh was over, Rhett, somewhat excitedly, shouted out, "Welcome war, thrice welcome bloody war, Our land is stagnant with peace. Folly is in the vision of Northern millions, and welcome, welcome war!" Cobb rejoined, "That is my prayer too. This country is rotten," as Hamlet says, "it is rotten, sir. Fanatics grow out of washtubs. Dyspepsia is called a medium, a seer of spirits; a foolish tongue is loosest hung, and random gab is set down for sound philosophy. My heart is bent on war, as Shakespeare says, 'for bloody war.' I want to see every Southerner, like Coriolanus, 'all smeared with smoke and blood,' emerging from the putridity of these vile scenes to bequeath to coming generations a purer and holier stock of men. These are my sentiments, Mr. Rhett, give us bloody war." He then stalked about the telegraph office like a king, and said he had seen that day the Prince of Wales, and he thought the British government better than ours. "For," he said, "there their snobs and bootblacks have their ambition checked, nipped in the bud, and it keeps them in their proper places."

But, when he had got thus far he was confronted by Prescott, Scott having previously gone out. "Why, how is that, Mr. Cobb?" said Prescott, "you would not quell ambition?"

"Yes I would," said Cobb, "I would wipe it out of human nature."

"Then," said Prescott, "I am happy that you did not construct mankind. Ambition for wealth, knowledge, ease, or even luxury, has lifted the common people of this country to a higher point of excellence than in any other."

"At the expense of people of higher birth," said Cobb.

Prescott replied, "I cannot deal with theory—only facts. But, sir, I never knew before the cause of your own deterioration in moral and mental acquirements."

When he put this witticism upon Cobb, the latter said, "Do you say a nigger is as good as a white man? Must I stand and hear a man blackguard my own State? You should know, sir, that we have such a thing down South as chivalry, and it loves liberty."

"Liberty!" said Prescott. "Oh Liberty! how much men ask in thy poor name. Why, sir, you have liberty. You make your own laws, and you unmake them at your pleasure. Even have you liberty to enslave others and to use them at your pleasure, and yet you plead for liberty. You are indeed very chivalrous. You come up North and make us catch your runaway slaves and carry them to you. You killed Northern men who entered Kansas, because they brought no slaves with them; you killed John Brown, and he was merely the foolish champion of the rights of others. Now, sir, for you are no child, you know that there is a crime amongst you, and it is this that makes you sensitive."

"So then," said Cobb, "you have turned abolitionist too. Now I swear that of all we most desire down South, the greatest wish is for Abolition blood. We have endeavored to abide by the constitution of our land, but now are we sworn that whoever meddles with our slaves shall die."

"Why sir, look you," said Prescott, "Abolitionists are so plenty you might drown yourself in their blood."

"A pretty boast," said Cobb, "and one for which I'd have thee whipped in Savannah," and Rhett added, "or in Charleston either;" but Prescott said he was glad he was in Washington, for such conduct as theirs was the result of the accursed institution amongst them.

When he said this Rhett and Cobb came near him, and Rhett said, "Gentlemen meet as gentlemen, but when a cur comes in their company he must be kicked out," and therefore some of the bystanders did kick at Prescott, but the crowd cried "Shame," for Prescott was a small man with a pleasant face. When he had withdrawn a pace, he added, "Behold this blood;" for in the scuffle some one had touched him on the nose, and it bled a little. "These gentle drops do rush to the view of modern chivalry appalled, and registering each a score of Southern widows, as the debt to come of your weighty arguments; and you, sir Cobb, for a little, I would punch the pith out of you." And then he seized him by the shoulder and shook him until Cobb was nearly frightened out of his wits. The crowd however interrupted at this instant by crying, "Shame! shame! can we not meet as gentlemen without these eternal political rows?" We were also greeted at this time with news from Chicago, and in an instant, were as silent as a house of mourning. The operator read aloud, "Abraham Lincoln of Illinois unanimously nominated." This was cold water on the whole assemblage of us. The Southern men were dumb with astonishment. Rhett's eyes were set in their sockets. Davis hung his head in silent wonder. Yancey—straight-haired Yancey, was more like a weather-beaten statue than a living man. Cobb tossed his hands aloft, and, trembling in every nerve, his bloodshot eyes were riveted upward. The die was cast. The great republic had thrown its challenge to the world to stand or fall for human rights. Not Northern rights, nor Southern rights, but human rights, and, sectional be the slur, still the issue was begun.

A fearful thing, oh, my countrymen! to oppose those who had always wielded the power and who held ever their awful threat against a Northern President on freedom's platform. The North had now but one object in view; that hereafter there should be no more slave territory admitted into the Union, and the South had at stake her ordinary interest. The North stood for principle merely. These ideas all ran through every man's mind quicker than they can be spoken. Every one knew what the others were thinking in this assemblage. Rhett first broke the silence, without sign or gesture; for he stood there as frozen as the poles, and as pallid.

"Abraham Lincoln!" "The freedom of the Territories!" Again all was silent for a moment, and then he went on: "Wealth and refinement, against the plebeians. Which is most powerful, the North or the South? In England, wealth rules; in France, monkeys; beggars, in Italy; ambition with a rag on its back is king of Germany, Spain, and Ireland, and now, do their descendants ascend over us. The descendants of these emigrants, these plebeians, have overpopulated the North, and they have raised their heads to demand that we of the South shall be subservient to them. Indeed, then the North is our enemy. I know this Lincoln, this boatman, this rail-splitter, this hewer of wood and carrier of water. He is to hold the poniard to our hearts and say, 'your slaves or your life.' We must knuckle to him. We must sit and see these vermin undermine our houses, because we have comfortable beds. No, no, by heavens!" and then he moved around. "In God's name strike out; put all your wits to work, in secret, in public, anywhere, everywhere, meet, combine the elements of your power. Live in constant effort. Let slumbering fires within your breasts flame up. Strike out! We must, we will accomplish it! We struck on the tariff, but that gave way. We struck on native Americanism, that lost. It might have given us the balance of power for a short period. Then came Mason and Dixon's line; then Douglass and the Missouri Compromise. But all, all have failed. We have no more allegiance to the Union, and must secede. We will go by ourselves. Peaceably if we can; forcibly if we must." He then said Lincoln was an unknown man, and consequently, that his platform was his strength; that the whole fight would now turn on the platform of the freedom of the Territories, but not on the man. "This," said he, "makes his election sure. This is the whole reason the Republicans have taken an unknown man, and it is this will be the death of us." He then said, "Davis, what shall we do ?"

Davis said, "We shall lose this election, God knows we shall lose it ; " and the tears started to his eyes, and he added, "Even the powers we now wield may be turned against us."

Rhett replied, "That power must be scattered to the winds beforehand," and Davis said "That might be."

Now, when they had said thus much, they looked at each other for a moment, as if there was a reflection going on in each other's mind. Then Yancey clenched his fist and said, "If they come against us "—(I thought he meant Abolitionists ; for he stopped there, and seemed to make oath toward the heavens)—" South Carolina will secede as sure as yonder sun goes down," said Rhett. Cobb said, " So shall Georgia," making a threat, and breathing an oath. " Mississippi will, I am sure," said Davis ; and then Yancey and Floyd both made oath that the South would secede.

" Now, then," said Rhett, "must we know the cue of Scott and James Buchanan. Davis and Cobb, will you go with me ? " And then they withdrew a pace, and the latter remarked with a low voice to Davis and Cobb, " This will be a dangerous business for us. We must send men to see them at once, and inform them of this nomination. Hark you ! I know a man, the most ingenious, sensible kind of tool that ever lived. He is so inquisitive, that he can ascertain every politician's secret thoughts, and they all the while heeding little what he says, and not caring. This man we will send to all prominent men, and ascertain what part they will play—particularly, Scott and Buchanan. You know him, I mean Judge Francis Underhill, of London Heights," and they all smiled and took their departure.

Floyd then took Thompson's arm, and whispered to him, " Our deadliest enemy lies in the nation's offices, and it should be scattered. I mean the specie, the Government securities, the national treasury, sub-treasury, customs, and post-office funds." And then Thompson said, " That is a great power. Let us lay our heads together in this matter," and they also departed.*

* The danger to the national treasury was anticipated by the New York *Tribune* and Cincinnati *Gazette*, and the scheme concocted and here alluded to was published prior to its transpiring, and yet no action was taken by the Government to prevent it.

During this affair, the strangest of all was that mysterious tall woman, who came in silk and diamonds, with the long-faced Italian Orsini. If you will be kind enough to recollect the circumstances of the National Hotel poisoning, nearly four years ago, when James Buchanan nearly lost his life, you will remember that at that time there were three foreigners in the Hotel. One of them died, leaving a widow—a mysterious person of great fashion, and that person was Madame Ponchard. She was said to own a large plantation somewhere ; but she so seldom spoke to any one, that no one seemed to discover who or what she was. She was so constantly in the society of Floyd, Thompson, and Davis, and anon of Governor Wise's son, and she seemed so greedily to devour the words of Floyd and Davis. Many rich men had made advances to her on account of her supposed riches, but had all been defeated. She had this day had an interview with the Prince of Wales, and now, during the scenes in the telegraph office, she had steadily watched all that was said—many of them looking at her to see if she seemed to make note of it, and which this deponent holds as evidence that she and Orsini had some secret connection with the origin of the great rebellion.

Summing these affairs together—the things which I had seen, and the things which I had long known to be talked of, I set myself about to look after the beginning of what actually did result in one of the greatest wars that ever occurred. Not to be thwarted, however, in my endeavors to search its most intricate purpose, I resolved to inform the different members of our private court of the points I had gained, and of the end I had in view. My object was, first, to acquaint the Judge of the determination of Rhett, Davis and Cobb to use him as their tool in the management of Scott and Buchanan. I had also in view the employment of Miss Lucy Tabiatha Stimpkins as an agent to expose and frustrate, what I deemed the villainous purpose of these would-be rebels. I also mistrusted the deep conniving and secret power of Madame Ponchard. She was so mysterious and deep ; so much watched by all parties, familiar with Washington life, yet, so little was known of her, that every person who knew her seemed to harbor a great suspicion of her.

With this important disclosure, I now close the first chapter of this important history, relying on you to proceed with the next for further information.

CHAPTER II.

When I had the foregoing history set down, I told Jenkins that he must not forget one of the most important rules of all great authors, which was that the leading characters must be introduced in the first chapter. But he replied by saying that this book would be unlike any other ever written, and not copied after anything extant.

"In the present age," he said, "most of us follow up a single narrative, and run it to the end; like a colonel in a battle managing a single regiment. But we shall do like great commanders, who divide their army into many parts, all intent on a general end, managing them in such harmony that the lesser parts shall add to the glory of the important whole." I told him that we would get too much egotism in the book, if we kept on at this rate. But he said "That also must be so to be in the fashion. Let us come to the work," and he immediately uttered these very words, to wit:

"I went, according to agreement today, to have another court-sitting at our Temple; for I was anxious to tell the Judge what Rhett, Davis and Cobb had proposed of him in the telegraph office. After waiting an unusual length of time, and no one else coming, I ventured to ask some good folks near by if they had seen Judge Francis Underhill, of Loudon Heights? And they answered no, that they had not seen him since yesterday morning. I concluded then that something of a serious nature must have transpired, and I immediately set out for the Jackson House, where he resided. When I arrived near, I heard him in the midst of a speech which he was discharging in the office to a promiscuous dozen of idlers. He is an elderly man, and very stout in the waist, always wearing rich but threadbare clothes. His low-topped shoes are always neat, showing fine silk stockings. He always takes off his soft hat when talking, and bows through every sentence he speaks. His politeness gains him hearers, and his egotism and general information make his superiors, even, listen to him with respect. He had been a Whig in the days of Harrison, and he still adhered to his doctrines, although the party was extinct. When I came up, he nodded to me, and I asked him why he had not come to the Temple? Said he, "Some persons of importance are to arrive soon, and I have been requested to remain;" but he refused to tell me who they were, and he bade me wait. He then resumed his speech, which was as follows:

"It is a fault in this country, as it is in others, that parents study more how to make rich matches for their children, than to teach them how to earn riches for themselves. I remember when I discussed this matter with Daniel Webster, he told me that the fault of all governments was, that they governed too much or too little. All the avenues should be thrown open to the people, and such branches of trade as are easily injured by foreign importation, should be protected by high duties on imports. This would give all young men and women useful employment. The factories would give them homes, and keep them at home, and the present migration would be knocked in the head. I do not mean to injure your hotel, sir, but while this country boasts of having so many and so fine hotels, and such a vast patronage to them all, it also boasts that such patrons are a host of idlers, and worthless beings, travelling from place to place to find profitable business. If we made half the goods we consume, these quack lawyers, and quack doctors, politicians, gamblers, clerks and idlers might have something decent to do, and it would open the road too for woman's services. Women, instead of being bartered off with their fits and infirmities to wealthy old bachelors, or instead of auctioneering themselves off in public speeches, would find employment in which they could be proud, independent, and happy. But all this physical and moral force is thrown to waste by lack of a wholesome tariff. The money of the country is sent abroad for goods, and our prodigal sons and daughters (the Judge is an old bachelor), living at the top of the fashion, fly from place to place, endeavoring to better themselves by marriages or strange adventures."

Here the crowd laughed so violently,

that he was in a measure interrupted, but he retorted :

"I know it all. It is all very well. If I have no sons or daughters, I might have had, or may have yet. For twenty years I have been chased by the women. Anxious mammas have come to me with no more concern for the welfare of their darling daughters, than I value the toss of a dice box, and they have told me how ardently their dear children admired everything I said or did. But no, as I said to Henry Clay, these things show that there is something wrong in this country. My opinion is that these hosts of idlers can never be exterminated but by a huge tariff or a terrible war."

The Judge then turned to me and asked if that was not the truth ? I told him yes, and urged him once more to come to the Temple ; but the clerk called out, "No, not yet, for here they come," and just then some new arrivals came to the hotel, though what the importance of it was, I yet knew not. There came in a carriage, an elderly-like man and woman, accompanied by a daughter—a fairylike belle of seventeen—who dismounted and entered the place. The gentleman registered his name as Mr. Edge, wife, and daughter Victoria. The clerk distributed them to their rooms, and we were left to reflect upon the apparent richness of their style, combined with their seeming awkwardness.

Some person present suggested that in-a-much as the Prince of Wales was in Washington, this Victoria might be some relation. The Judge and I moved up to the desk, and the clerk said to the Judge. "Ah, Judge! we have somebody at last you do not know, and is no relation of yours."

The Judge always pretended to know all great persons, or, that they were distant relations ; and this clerk knew his weakness.

"I am not sure of that," said the Judge.

"Then why are you puzzled at the name ? " said the clerk.

"Because it is a strange name. It seems to me, however, I knew some people by the name of Edge. Where are they from ? "

"From Ohio," said the clerk.

"Possibly I may know them," remarked the Judge. "Be not too sure."

"Indeed ! have you begun already ? " said the clerk ; and the Judge replied, "Ill fortune on your tavern, that I have supported for the last twenty years by a constant stream of fast marriages, if ere another day you do not tell this Edge family that I am king of Washington."

"And may, your stars forgive you," said the clerk, "for the big ones you have made me tell in order to bring couples together. Not a month since, you blew riches into the ears of a couple that could not pay their washerwoman. They really thought each had a fortune, until they were married. This you did, on a wager of a bottle of Bourbon."

"No matter," said the Judge, "I will lay the corn that this Edge has brought his daughter here to marry her off, and, what is more, we can have her at the hymenial halter in a month."

He had no sooner said this, than, on looking around, he saw entering the room the business man, Mr. Edge. The porters were carrying in his boxes.

"Now you shall see," said the Judge, "how I shall quiz this old man. Stand there boys. Be careful with those trunks. You think a man's boxes are made for battle, and you lam them and jam them until every nail comes out. It puts me in mind of a trip I took to Ohio several years ago, in company with Daniel Webster."

"Indeed !" said Mr. Edge. "Why, that is my native State."

"Ah !" said the Judge. "Then I suppose you are acquainted with my excellent friend, Tom Corwin."

"I have not that honor," said Edge.

"I used to know some of the Edges in Ohio," said the Judge. "They were literary people."

"Then," said Edge, "They were not my relations. I am only a railroad builder. But, if I am not too impertinent, what is your name ? "

"Francis Underhill, sir. I am called Judge of Loudon Heights."

When he said this, he stretched himself to his most dignified length.

Edge looked at him with astonishment, first, because he seemed so familiar, and next, because he had so accidentally fallen into the society of a man of such seeming high rank ; for he deemed him at least in possession of next to the highest office our country had to give.

"Excuse me, sir," said Edge, "I would not have been so familiar, only that I have been all my life with plain, blunt men. I was, sir, like Ben. Franklin, brought up a tallow chandler ; but I deserted my business. I have saved up a little, and now I seek to see and to know the world."

"I admire your frankness, sir," said the Judge. "I shall be most happy, at all times, to give you the benefit of my most distinguished acquaintanceship. Also, if you please, you may say to your lady and daughter that my carriage is at their service, and that I should be extremely happy to introduce them into the highest circles of society."

As he was going on in this strain, the three important persons, Rhett, Cobb, and Davis, came in and called the Judge, who joined them. They all went out to the sidewalk, where the three entered into their entreaty to the Judge to call upon Scott and Buchanan, which we will refer to in a moment. It was, however, a great mortification to me; for I had determined to acquaint the Judge with the designs of Rhett, Davis and Cobb, before they came together. Though for the present let us turn to the interior of the house.

The clerk immediately told Mr. Edge who the trio were, and Mr. Edge was more pleased than ever to think that he had already made the acquaintance of a man who was counsellor and adviser for the heads of the nation. He was yet busy with his baggage when the clerk winked to me. "Entre nous" said he, "he has brought his daughter here to marry her off. The Judge knows hundreds of young bloods, and we must fix this thing up. We will have a marriage in high life, good times, and plenty of champagne."

But I checked him for making so light of such matters, and withdrew a pace, and sat down to await the Judge's return; for, indeed, we were interrupted by the approach of Mr. Edge, who inquired what kind of a man the Judge was.

The clerk pointed out the Judge as one of the United States Judges, one of the greatest men in America—told Edge, in fact, that since the days of Jackson, no man else held so great a sway over the affairs of the Government. He had but to say this or that must be done, and the nation's treasury was at his service. The clerk even went so far in his enthusiasm in relating things of this worthless old judge, as to say that the nation's purse had got to be almost wholly his own. "Why, sir," said he to Mr. Edge, "The judge once said he must have some celestial curiosities for the national museum, and the next day a vessel sailed for China. He has, indeed, only to say Build me a post route to Oregon, or a railroad to New Orleans, and it is lobbied right through both houses of Congress, and the President signs the bill as a matter of course. Only get the Judge's friendship, Mr. Edge, and Washington is all yours."

Edge rejoined that he thought that the Judge was no ordinary man, and that he would be quite happy to have his wife and daughter get acquainted with so prominent a person.

The clerk told him the Judge was the most easily approached of any man in the world, and also that he knew everybody in Washington that was of any importance, which was, in fact, nearly true, though it was equally true that the Judge was tolerated in good society, mostly on account of his eccentricities and monstrous pretensions.

Edge was most pleased, however, to learn that he had found a man who could command money. He was himself a speculator. He liked to sell stocks; to get contracts put through; was interested in jobs that needed helping through Congress. He had himself amassed a great fortune by this kind of speculation, beginning with one single thousand dollars—and this thousand too, it was said, he came into possession of improperly. His father had placed it in his hands for safe keeping; but the son never returned it. The old man failed, and became grieved and the conduct of his son, endeavored to better his remaining days by life in California, but died on the way, thus giving the son full possession of the thousand dollars. This money the son had invested in building a railroad bridge on the Miami. He cheated the contractors in the grade of the bridge, and doubled his money. He took another job on another road; again took advantage of the contractors; bribed the inspectors, and doubled his money. By this kind of speculation, he had amassed a large fortune, until, as he said, he had now set out to see and to know the world.

His wife had coaxed him away to Washington, for the benefit of Victoria, their daughter. The mother was one of that good kind of women who are always called an excellent wife and mother for a common person. She was a farmer's daughter, and had been taught to read and write; had worked hard to help save her husband's money. For the past few years, she had been relieved from manual labor, and took to teasing poor dressmakers and milliners, and trying to learn to get into a carriage gracefully, instead of climbing in as she would into a market wagon. These things puzzled her wits so much that she resolved that her daughter Victoria should be better trained in early days. Vickey had been sent to school in Philadelphia, had acquired her education, and already acted as tutor of the fashions to her mother.

"Mother," she would say, "you always begin your letters in that way—now I take my pen in hand, et cetera. Do you know it was wrong? Why, I forgot, I should not have called you mother—I should have said ma! Now let me see, where was I? Oh! Dear ma, we always begin at the back of a letter in fashionable society." Here she would lisp a little, drop her chin, look interesting at her mother, and smile. She said a great many things about fashionable society, such as she had learned in the Philadelphia boarding school, always beginning and ending the sentence with "that is the way it is in Philadelphia." She was, indeed, as sure of how things were done in Philadelphia, as was the New England clergyman, who went to Paris several years ago, of the fashions and wickedness of the French nation. He only staid one night in Paris, and, in the morning, on looking out, he saw a red petticoat hanging near his window. This was enough for him. He construed it into some improper banter from a French woman, and thereupon left the country in disgust. On his return home, he wrote an account of French high life and immorality, condensed into two royal octavo volumes. People who have not been in France, say it was good. So did Mrs. Edge say of her daughter's stories about fashionable high life, and she had now made Victoria chief of affairs in the present adventure into high life in Washington. Vickey was so elated therewith, that she was continually showing her mother how things should be said and done.

"Do you see, ma," she said, as soon as they had entered their private parlor, "we are at once looked upon as persons of mark," and she drew her mother to the window. They looked out, and beheld on the sidewalk Rhett, Davis, Cobb, and Judge Francis Underhill. The latter at that instant happened to be looking upward, less heedful of the rebellion than of the pretty belle gazing out of the window. Just as Mrs. Edge looked out, Judge Francis dropped his glasses and smiled. Vickey playfully kissed her hand to him and ran away.

"Why, my child," said Mrs. Edge, "how can you do so to a stranger?"

"Pshaw," said Vickey, "that is the height of fashion—at least in Philadelphia."

Her mother was about to give her a severe reprimand, but just then the clerk appeared at the door to know if their rooms were satisfactory, to which they replied in the affirmative. The clerk then also approached the window, showing them the Capitol, the White House, and the Potomac, adding, "Here is Pennsylvania Avenue, where you can behold all the costly fashions, and all the great people of all parts of the civilized world." He paused a moment, and again continued, "Well now, even here, here is Judge Francis Underhill of Loudon Heights," and they all looked down to where the four were standing below talking. "That man," continued the clerk, "that old gentleman with the silver spectacles, is Judge Francis Underhill; one of the most remarkable men of any age. He is the boast of this country. He is a man of literature, science, fashion, and integrity, he is all that constitutes greatness."

"There mother," said Vickey, "you thought he was just some common person; but I know what it is to see people of rank."

"Indeed that is so," said the clerk.

"If the Judge were to have a procession to-day, it would be far more proper than a procession for the Prince of Wales; he is so free, so jolly, and yet so grand. His wealth too cannot be computed."

The ladies both expressed a desire to become acquainted with so important a person. Being informed that they could by passing their leisure moments in the general parlor, they both expressed a full determination to do so. After some trifling conversation about the Prince of Wales, the clerk departed, having precautioned them as to the style and character of Judge Francis Underhill; that it was through him they would reach the avenues to the good society of Washington. He also told them that the Judge was very eccentric in his style; that he used very highfalutin language on the most trivial occasions; but that they were to take no notice of it, and assume the same style towards him as much as possible.

"Trust that to me," said Vickey. "We did that to perfection in the Philadelphia boarding school. We girls compared ourselves to flowers, stars, rainbows, angels, and congratulated each other on our nonsense, in quotations that were never heard of."

"Why, my dear child," said Mrs. Edge, "how did you learn that stuff?"

"Learn it, mother!" said Vickey; "we made it in imitation of those beautiful novels I told you of. It is so easy. A tear in the eye is a diamond; a crony is a satellite; a love tickle, is an electric thrill; a plain compliment is an adamantine pavement whereon our duller sense trips in fear and trembling up to the genius of the immortal speaker; and then we sigh—thus—our bosoms heaving like a cataract, or the billows of the ocean. At least, that is the way we did in Philadelphia."

"Well, now, Vickey," said her mother. "I never heard you speak so eloquent, and I never until now felt so sure you could maintain the due distortion of our family."

"Discretion you mean, mother; but, you know, I always told you I never would be myself until I got into high society."

And then she laughed, as the clerk said, a mysterious laughter, and he further added, "When I left them to their toilet, I thought she was indeed the strangest girl I ever saw, and the prettiest."

But here let us refer to the Judge's interview with Rhett, Davis, and Cobb. Having myself been stationed so near that I could hear every word, and having also heard the forty thousandth lecture on Southern institutions, State rights, and all that sort of constitutional nonsense—secession, war, annihilation, subjugation,—and heard it with indifference to every threat; and as I said before, standing myself near enough to hear this party addressing the Judge in that manner, I quietly awaited the full development of their plots and plans with him. Now, when the Judge was informed by them that they had already organized, and that, as he considered himself a Southern man, and as he had frequently expressed the same sentiments that they held, they had selected him as one of a committee on very important business, he was not a little surprised.

"We must know," said Cobb, "the line of demarkation: who are friends and who are enemies," and his position in Congress gave importance to all he said. "We have known you long," he continued, "and the necessity of the case makes us plain with you in all we say. Now it is not wise to ask a man his sentiments; but by conversation we often learn what we desire to know. It is thus that we hope to learn who is for us and who is against us. You have the advantage of long acquaintanceship, and men will say in your presence what they would not in ours: and you in turn can say what you like without offence or suspicion. You have that faculty."

"Yes, I know I have," said the Judge; and he stiffened his lips like a member of parliament.

"Now then," said Cobb, "I want you, as the news of Lincoln's nomination is still fresh, to ply men well to the task, to know what they will do in case the South does secede. The whole thing must be done between now and the 4th of March.

If Buchanan does nothing, we are safe; if Scott goes with us, we are victorious."

"Ah! I see," said the Judge, "you want me to be a tool for you. Do you think I am the town's fool? You bellow and blow awhile, and then it will all end in smoke. It was so in Calhoun's time. They came to me then; but they would not stick. It is all bosh: though I will tell you this, if you would go in, as I used to tell Henry Clay, tooth and nail, I could take the administration whichever way I like. But, I will be no tool to go around peddling my opinions before such men as Scott and Buchanan. I must first see the coast clear, and then I will advise my friends as I think best."

Cobb.—"You misunderstand us Judge. I only want to know what these men's predispositions are—to know if the thing is so and so what course to adopt."

"Ah, well!" said the Judge. "Ah! I see. But, for that matter I can soon ascertain, but, I cannot lend myself to any scheme that might compromise my well-known principles. You know I have been a whig since 1840."

Cobb then assured him that they had organized on the evening previous, and that the most prominent citizens in the Capital were bound together, and he also pointed out the necessity of taking by violence if necessary, all the offices of the Government, and acknowledged also that if Scott could be brought into the fold, the whole thing could be fixed up in a week.

When he talked this way the Judge got a little frightened, and also a little puzzled; for he thought perhaps they were playing a joke on him. So betwixt the scare and the puzzle he abruptly withdrew, and afterward assured me he was up to the whole game.

The others were now in a perplexity to think that they had discussed so great a matter to one so heedless and unconcerned. It was evident that their position rendered it dangerous, as yet, to attempt any overt act against the Government. The magnitude of their intended attempt to dissolve the Union, made each one more backward than his neighbor, and anxious for a fearless leader; to know the position of Gen. Scott, was at this time one of the most anxious inquiries ever seated on a nation's heart. That the South would secede was now believed by all politically well-informed men in the country, but the agents of its success seemed to be depending mostly on Scott and Buchanan. The North was praying for Scott, but the South was ready with its vengeance on all who might oppose them.

Rhett, Cobb and Davis were at this period the head and front of the rebellion, and they were restless, moving from place to place, bent on every invention to further their ends. Immediately now Judge Francis had so equivocally promised them they resolved on another and more expeditious method of accomplishing it—though more of that hereafter. And again we will refer to the Judge, who had now made up his mind to treat the matter as one of second rate importance. At present he was interested in seeing me, and I am happy to say he found me in the office anxiously awaiting him.

"Come, come," he says, "those royal bloods have had me out in yonder burning sun, trying to cram me, and play some game with me for my everlasting good nature. But I understand the point of a joke, you know. I am too old for them. Wait, you shall see."

I then told him how they had spoken of him in the telegraph office, and of the tool they designed to make him.

"What!" said he, "do they rate me in such a manner? Then, indeed, this has been no joke. It was in earnest. They wanted to send me to Scott and Buchanan to make a fool of me. Indeed, this affair promises mischief. Well, let's have it. We need mischief and a grand surprise. As I am a judge, I say this country needs a surprise. It is the hardest up of any place I ever heard of. We have no characters, and no chance to make any. Our best novelists and poets are played out. Every body is a stick, a dolt, anything. Let's have a war. We will then have characters. For twenty years I have visited this city, and God forgive me, I have often been tempted to overstate the truth of things, just in order to have a bit of news; but now it may be, we shall have news sufficient to warrant us in speaking truthfully. Yet, I do not believe they will secede. It is all blowing. I am a Southern man, I used to blow. I learned that of John C. Calhoun, but, as for tricking me, or making me a villain, why let them go to Scott and Buchanan themselves. No. Mind you, I am almost resolved to go and tell them a barefaced falsehood; that I have been to Scott and Buchanan, and that Scott and Buchanan are both in favor of secession. But, wait. I must study this matter. We shall see who is fool for the other."

He then pulled me along, and we marched into the general parlor, where we had scarcely entered before we met Mrs. Edge and Vickey. The former was an excellent type of a plain, blunt woman, attired in silk satin and diamonds. She had a very substantial step. The daughter was a pretty blue-eyed girl, with black ringlets, and tall, thin, and straight up an down.

"Now let me," said the Judge,—and he turned toward them and bid them be seated. "Now let me"—and he spoke to me in a whisper. "I will show you how to make them at home,"—for really he was as much at home in this house, as if it were his own, having made it his stopping place for the last twenty years, and having also provided it with the choicest wines from his own plantation. He then turned toward the ladies.

"If I mistake not," said he, "this is Mrs. Edge and her daughter Victoria." They nodded assent. "Mr. Edge, the large railroad contractor, is well-known by name to myself, and, in fact, to every prominent man of the Capitol. But, I believe, fortune has not favored us with so large a knowledge of his family, further than that they are on a visit to lend the charm of their accomplishments to this city. Excuse me ; my gray hairs tell you that I am only speaking things that give me more pride than pleasure, and that I desire to make you comfortable while you enjoy the hospitalities of the place."

They smiled and bowed an affirmative, feeling confident now that they were indeed emerging into some of the upper circles. The Judge, pleased with his own style, went on.

"If you please, I will now take the privilege of introducing my excellent friend, Mr. Jenkins," upon which he smiled and bowed, and they in turn smiled and bowed to him, and Mrs. Edge, with a square plain voice, said, "I hope you are both quite well. I am glad to see you and get acquainted. It is a nice spell of weather."

Now I had indeed been astonished to see how the ladies were puzzled at the Judge's compliments, and I was still more puzzled when Mrs. Edge answered him so plainly, and we were both of us without anything to say for a moment.

Vickey, seeing our predicament, and bringing her boarding-school tactics to bear on us, now rejoined :

"If I mistake not, you are Judge Francis Underhill of Loudon Heights?"

The Judge bowed.

"The country at large acknowledge the past and present ruler of its manifest destiny. This other gentleman, whom I am sorry to have had the misfortune to have never known, I take to be one of the satellites of your important glory. I am indeed so happy with this adventure;" and again she smiled, she and the Judge alternately bowing.

I was puzzled to know if she were not poking fun at us, and I think the Judge was too; for he hesitated a moment as if to say to me that, for once in his life, he had found a more presumptuous fool than himself, or else one who understood him more than he had ever been before in his life. After a moment, however, he retorted:

"Too much honor you give to one who has ever esteemed himself scarcely better than a Congressman, and yet I accept it with more pride than had it been uttered by any of the queens or potentates of any other country under the sun."

He now thought he had sealed her up, but she came in as fluently as if she had been taught in a theatre:

"Not the compliment, sir," she said, "when its source could come back to me with so dear a fondness from the lips of none other than the clearest-headed philosopher that ever graced a nation. We have heard with unmistakable pleasure the power you wield, and of the admiration and brightness of your lustre in the society of our most devoted countrymen, and now chronicle it in our untutored hearts--this happiest of all human events —the meeting of one never to be forgotten."

I knew the Judge was nearly at the end of his string, and was in hopes, too, that I would get something to run on with him afterwards, for being quashed by a green country girl.

When I looked around to Mrs. Edge, I saw that she was breathless and seemingly scared by the eloquence of the speakers.

"Indeed!" said the Judge—the happiest of all human events to him, whose hoary hairs have sprung from the dire cause of its long withholding. "I am at loss, not for your ultimate joy, but for the part I am to contribute in every passing moment you may sojourn in our city of magnificent distances."

Again she replied. "Not so much your loss in that, as will be ours to accept and maintain with due discretion to our uncultured minds. You know, sir, we come from Ohio. You, I am informed, are of the first families of Virginia. We have come amongst you to behold the greatness of great men and women. Like pitiless housewives, we make but an unseeming part in the world of spectators around, praying that the dazzling glory may so gently fall on our unexpecting vision, that its radiance lift us into the winning paths

where the heart of woman dallies in her fondest dreams; where she lingers in the hope that some of her gentleness has touched at the fount, the reciprocating omen responsive to her far off sighs and endless melancholy."

The Judge was now almost lost. He had never heard so vast a strain before; but still he rallied:

"We hope," said he again, "only for the relict of other days standing between it and the consummation of an angel's wish."

"Not age, sir," said she, "but the heart within makes the mighty difference, if difference indeed there can be."

"Indeed," said he, "I tell you, young hearts often live in old men; but, in such as have been married, or taken to politics, in them the heart dies. By the by," said he, turning to me—for he was entirely played out, and longed for a change of the subject—" By the by, do you know, my excellent friend Buchanan told me this morning he cannot remember having ever loved anything in all the days of his life. Remarkable—'pon my word, remarkable."

"Indeed," said I, "he loves his party."

"Just as I told him," said the Judge, "and, had he pursued the even tenor of man's good nature, he had had a heart full of love to this day. But, ladies, I had forgot myself, not having the heart to withdraw, I promised the senior member of your family that my carriage should be at your service during your sojourn in Washington, and I shall take great pleasure in introducing you into the highest ranks of society."

He always offered his carriage to everybody that stopped at the Jackson House. He and his carriage, though both the worse for wear, had both become fixtures for the hotel—the carriage having for several years degenerated into a kind of public hack; still it sounded liberal to tender the use of it, and the ladies named now thanked him cordially. Mrs. Edge told me a moment afterwards that she had been so transported with the foregoing eloquence of her daughter and the Judge, that she "could hardly tell whether she was herself standing on her feet or on her head."

The whole affair was now cut short by the entrance of the mistress of Loudon Heights—Miss Ann Underhill, niece of the Judge. As she afterwards became one of the greatest solicitudes of the country, and as her perils, hardships, struggles, and sterling worth may long be remembered with kindly feelings by the whole country, I must here tell you about her, however much I may be moved in so doing.

Ann Underhill was an orphan, brought up by the Judge, and now in her twentieth year. She had received excellent advantages; the Judge having spared no expense to develop her naturally attractive qualities. He had her well educated, and had also favored her with the best of society in this and other countries: add to this a fun-loving, frolicking disposition, with due regard for reverence, backed by an inherited fortune, and say that she was a sweet girl with auburn hair, rosy cheeks, plump person, and real, innocent, pleasing beauty, who, seen but once, is ne'er forgotten.

As I said before, she now came into the room, running in and calling out "Oh! uncle, uncle, come to the window—come and see," and she flung her arms around his neck and dragged him hastily towards the street window.

We all looked out and now beheld a crowd of boys, worthless fellows, coming down the avenue. Whereupon we all drew near the window to see the attraction, and we did behold a thing; it had a head, and ears, and such a tongue! may the stars bedim our vision if ever was such a funny creature—a woman! Good Lord, a woman! Miss Lucy Tabiatha Stimpkins —in a bloomer! She came and stood on the porch near us, and began about her journal.

Some one outside the hall asked her if she was going to publish marriages in her journal, and she answered by saying, "Marriages, marriages in my journal? I hope I will fill it with better stuff." As there were many boys and idlers near her, we heard them laugh, and shout so that the half she spoke was not heard by us. In a little while, however, she told us she liked to see us merry; "but I am sorry," said she, "you don't cultivate your minds for more honorable ends."

Some one again shouted "Publish the marriages!" but she was becoming so enraged as to not answer with sufficient discretion to suit so base a crowd.

"I'll not publish such stuff!" she finally screamed out; when some one near said, "Call marriages stuff?"

"Yes," said she, "stuff," and she fairly squealed.

Again some one said, "Very important stuff!"

"No, sir, poor stuff," said she, and thereupon the laugh became so loud and boisterous, that she stood still and became immovable as formerly, angrily composed. "I have been married," said she, "I know what I say." ("Good! good!" from the crowd.) "Ah! indeed, you may laugh; but I say marriage is stuff. I go in for the cultivation of the moral and intellectual faculties. You may laugh. I am resolved that marriages shall never be published in my paper; it shall stand on fundamental principles. Reform, is my motto (Laughter.) Well, laugh on; I am not a laugher myself; nor do I mean to be the cause of laughter in others. When my journal shall have wiped out a thousand grog-shops, then you may laugh; when I have overturned slavery, then I'll laugh. Ah, go on! go on! You shall see me laugh then, and I'll make the whole country laugh on the other side of their mouth when I laugh. You and all your doctrines shall be vanquished then."

Of course we laughed, and in a moment she handed some papers to a sort of consort,—a thin-faced man, with long whiskers, who accompanied her, and whom she called Professor, and who was called by the crowd Pro-fusser Jackson; and then, with much sternness, she walked away, followed by the uneasy crowd.

The Professor remained, and somewhat abashed, approached our friend Prescott, and asked him to subscribe to the Journal of Progress. Prescott declined, and referred him to Judge Francis Underhill, and sure enough the Judge subscribed.

The Professor thanked him, whereupon the Judge said he was not aware that any one was associated with Miss Lucy. The Professor said in turn, "Neither there was until this morning. I was most miraculously thrown into her presence last evening, and we discovered such an affinity of ideas, as induced us to go into partnership."

"What," said the Judge, "are you married, then?"

"Yes, if you term the contract between man and woman marriage. Why, yes. But we are married with freedom, under protest, that whenever either is desirous of dissolving partnership, we can do so. We don't endorse the ancient scheme, 'for better or for worse,' but, for better only, and if we find it no better, why, like sensible creatures, we quit it." "An excellent doctrine," said the Judge, "and, sir, may I ask what the future name of our editress is to be?"

"The same as before," said the Professor, "Miss Lucy Tabiatha Stimpkins. We are not arbitrary. We keep our own names. The harmonial system gives us that privilege, especially when both names are euphonious."

We all expressed our approval, with which flattering indorsement the Professor took his leave.

GENERAL CASS.

"Now I will tell you," said the Judge, " the signs of the times betoken much difficulty to t'is country. In all countries—in all ages of the world, a long peace has ever given rise to these spurious philosophies. Wise and unassuming men keep in the background; but self-conceited, brainless, would-be philosophers, inconsiderate of the facts of history which prove the system of social and political life best suited to the elevation of mankind; and they start now with their foolish theories as the foundation of something holy. Spiritualism, free-love-ism, magnetism. Tut! Such folly; such nonsense. It racks my brain."

"Why, indeed, Judge," said Vickey, " you surely believe in magnetism ? "

"Oh yes; that of a fair lady, who can draw any man unto her."

"Yes," said she, "and that men can magnetize one another."

"Well, let them magnetize me; they will have a good time."

"Now I know a man," said Vickey, "a Professor. He came on the same train with us, and is stopping at this hotel. He besought me, if I found a man, a sceptic, to tell him of it, and he would magnetize him."

"Then I am his man," said the Judge. "Bring him on; let him put me to sleep. He shall put me into the magnetized slumber." Here the Judge recollected himself, and introduced his niece, Ann Underhill, to Mrs. and Miss Edge, and he and one of our friends, Mr. Prescott, whom we will notice hereafter, took their departure.

As the ladies had now turned to each other, I took advantage of the opportunity and withdrew to await the Judge's return; for he and I had an important charge in reference to the Prince of Wales' procession, which was set down to take place on the day following.

Now, it so happened that Vickey and Ann Underhill were favorably impressed with each other, and Mrs. Edge was not ill pleased either.

But, I must say here, in consequence of the many idle rumors afloat of the melancholy affair that followed, in reference to Miss Underhill, that up to this time I had never published any attachment to the Judge's niece, nor had I by word or gesture induced any one to think so. She was indeed a pretty girl; I had said the same to myself fifty times a day, but said nothing of it. I had seen now, for the first time, Prescott look at her with some earnestness, and he had also with as much fondness seemed to look on Vickey, whose greenness, or, in fashionable parlance, extreme innocence, together with so good, natural wit had surprised us; but that the Judge could be in love with Vickey—that was the novelty, and of its discovery you shall now hear.

On leaving the parlor, he called at the office, saying to the clerk, " I am done with all this nonsense. I have seen an angel; and I cannot be in any way accessory to a trick on her. We have given a lift to many stuck-up-faced young women, and we have done so with a clear conscience; but, to this one—never! No! never ! "

"Well, now really," said the clerk, " if you really are a great man, you have at last betrayed a weakness."

"No, no," said the Judge, " I bid goodby to all my folly. Yonder belle has spoken such words as only could come from the lips of Nature's queen; and I caution you, if you ever speak of her, to do it with such prudence as a well-deserved person may attain."

At that the clerk laughed, immediately saying, "Why, why don't you tell her that you love her, and not come to me ? "

"Tut," said the Judge, " I am an old man. I can admire beauty, intelligence, and noble qualities, and esteem the person, yet; but I prate of love no more."

At that he sallied out of the office, in company with Prescott—where, or for what purpose, was yet unknown to me.

While I sat there, I mused on the coming events of the country, and of the probable future marked out for myself, with anything but satisfactory conclusions. That there would be war between the North and the South, had been prophesied for many years by many men. Andrew Jackson had, thirty years ago, by a single message, set it off for an indefinite period. James Buchanan could do the same, but would it result in much ? Sooner or later, it must come. Then why not let it come at once ? Has not the great power that rules over the nations left the wayward clamor of politicians to sway the people, until the present imbecile President is the tool—the lowest degrading point of party love ? A thing to mark the zero of man's most ungodly weakness. Can these isms—these fanaticisms and follies go on, when they thus spring from the idleness of man, and from the corruptions of his mode of obtaining a living ?

An editress! A lecturer! Magnetism! Quack doctors! Quack lawyers! Behold what a host of idlers, contributing not so much as one poor potatoe to their fellows' existence. Idlers! and then I said to myself, what am I? A rich man's son, with nothing to do! Indeed, I am not so much in worth as yonder poor porter, who carries trunks and boxes for these care-worn travellers. And then I said to my-self, I should marry, and convert the balance of my days to some use; but ever and anon that hard-faced editress passed before my vision. Had not some poor fellow been once caught by her? and might not I be likewise caught? The sumach hath a tender, beautiful blossom, but when its fruit ripens, even its smell is death to the passer by. The sumach makes us dread the hyacinth; and one Stimpkins strikes us with dread at the approach of angels. Thus I mused, the while taking notes of what was passing, and which, in fact, interrupted me by the strangeness of the scene. But a moment before, the trio of ladies had been prome-nading the parlor, apparently enjoying themselves as all transient acquaintances do in our magnificent hotels; but now I beheld only Ann, the others having left, and she was seated near the piano, not playing, but idly touching the keys. Near her stood a tall and handsome young man, with such long hair as told me at a glance he was a Southerner. He looked on her, but she looked not upward, and I heard him gently going on in this strain. "We have such mild breezes from the ocean, and the vines and evergreen forests ever nestling above us, shielding us from the burning suns. Sometimes we rouse our-selves to certain action, to prove the genial things around be not in dreams but pres-ent are. Sometimes from active sports, we pensive train ourselves to mete out the deep devotion we owe for these endless blessings." And then she replied, "O! I think 'tis beautiful to dwell in such a place!"

"Not always beautiful," said he, "for even as we in the sunny South have that which only bounteous nature can bestow to make us appreciate all the joys and glories that man can attain, so does the contrast, with equal force, ply to soul, if the highest of anticipations be not achieved. The sadness then of an unap-preciated nature, and the woe of a disap-pointed affection, reverts upon his former dreams but to make all things desolate." From this on, his voice was inaudible to me; neither did I hear the frolicsome Ann say another word. She seemed to dally with the keys, as one absent in thought; her golden ringlets, like so much sunlight, shielding from view even that which their own beauty adorned.

Why did I not know this man? How

was it that the Judge had never told me? How was it that he seemed so well ac-quainted with Ann, and yet she had never mentioned him? Who was he, and what was his business? His language seemed fine, but I could not catch another word. Her answers were short, but only to give me more uneasiness. He finally drew from his pocket a splendid watch, saying, "The time is indisputable, and though a mo-ment is more prized than all the wealth of Cræsus, yet it flies from my grasp. To-morrow, at ten." She nodded, but said nothing; and then he bade her good-by and left. I was nigh rushing up to her to demand the meaning of this affair, but hesitated for a moment, and she trilled a little on the piano, and then up and ran out singing—

"A southern home 'n endless summer," etc.,

her voice so merrily sounding through the hall, that I almost forgot what had just passed. When he had said ten, to-morrow, I knew that was the hour the Prince of Wales procession was to begin, and I fully expected he had offered and was accepted as her companion for the occasion. I had previously resolved to be that companion myself, but now was fully resolved to say nothing about it to her. Thinking there would be no court to-day, I was about leaving, but on pass-ing out in the hall, that large, wide, out-side hall, I saw just before me that ever present Mrs. Lucy Talitha Stimpkins, and her new-made husband, Professor Jackson. They were rehearsing some-thing, and did not see me; I withdrew to play a sort of eaves-dropper. At the far end of the hall were Ann and Vickey, who were also playing eaves-dropper to the scene. "You know," said Mrs. Lucy, "it is the same eternal dread of woman's power that makes men unwilling to give us footing. But these things shall not continue. I am resolved to vanquish all our enemies. I will attack them in every place, and I will prove that mind, even if it be woman's, can and shall master all the rudeness in man. To-morrow is to be the procession in honor of the Prince of Wales, and you shall see; even boasting Briton's scion shall knuckle to woman. He shall stoop to know my will and pleasure; mine, even me, yet an unknown woman; and I shall so berate the down-trodden condition of the women of Eng-land to him, that he'll never pass another happy day on this continent. Now, I want to know if in your opinion it would not be wise to give him such a philan-thropic lesson?" "Certainly," said the

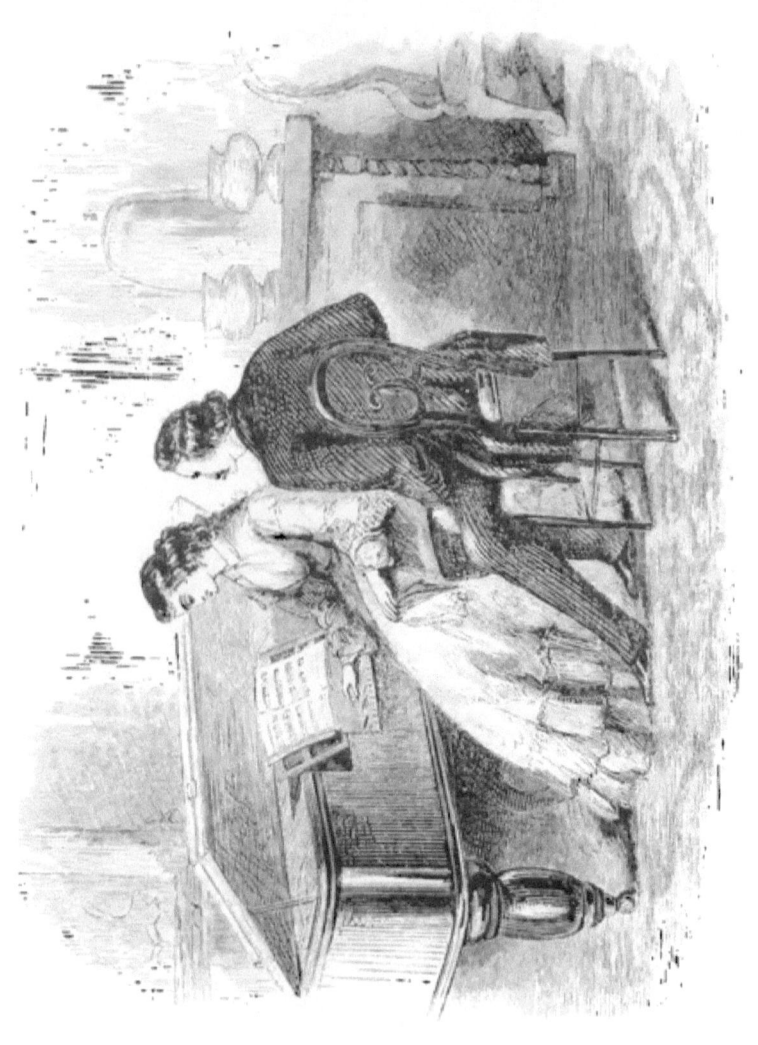

Professor, "certainly, it would be excellent. It would be a valuable contribution to the harmonial philosophy." "Well then, hark you," she said; "hear my plans. We shall station ourselves somewere near the route, in the midst of the crowd, and, as the Prince draws near, I'll rush forward and pretend to be knocked down by the throng; falling even at his feet. Of course, he'll pick me up, and I'll cry out, 'Where's the Prince! Where's the Prince! Let me his horns behold; that boy, so unlike all men and boys, can draw to the view of his august body this mighty throng of free-born Americans! Where is that Prince? Where's the Prince?' and thus I'll rate until he, forsooth, tells me he is himself the Prince, and then I'll scorn, saying, 'You! you the Prince? I thought you were a wandering country boy, whose legs outran the body, coming here alone with scarce a head to hold the two together. Proud scion of ancient Albion, I greet you with a woman's tenderness. Know, sir, that my name is Mrs. Lucy Tabiatha Stimpkins, the champion for the rights of down-trodden woman. In olden times you had in your own country knights errant to alleviate the horrors of her sphere; but now, alas! you, too, even as the men in this country, do seize upon the light avocations suited to her, and you drive her to the most wretched misery! And then I shall tell him such tales of horrors about the poor women of England, as shall vanquish all his remaining joys." "Most excellent," said Professor Jackson, "nothing could be more apropos. Its effect will endure for ages; it will teach the world to know that woman's rights must and shall be respected." "But now, mark you," said she, "you must be near, to see that when I throw myself at his feet, no harm comes to me; you know the English are awful ill-mannered, and only possessed of snail-like speed; now you must not let me be run over." "O! I'll look out for that; I'll see to it." said he, and she then showed him how she would do, and the part he was to play. I could not help smiling at such simple mockery, and was all on fire to acquaint the Judge and other members of our court with the contemplated scene. The girls at the other end of the hall were laughing, even so that I feared Mrs. Lucy would hear them; but she did not. As soon as the way was clear, I started. In the hall I picked up a slip of paper on which was written "To the most beautiful ——. Be happy!" I

dropped it at once, lest the fair ones might suppose that I myself wrote it. I supposed Prescott wrote it, and it was intended for Vickey; but I knew not. As I passed through the office, the clerk called me. "Do you know," said he, "there's going to be war? Every corner is blocked by men in cautious conversation? Such mutterings as I do hear, and every man has so much a bull-dog look. Even priests and other pious people, in company and alone, do clench their jaws; and from every man's mouth, even though he be silent, I do hear oaths terrible! Methinks the very air hath a solemn sound, and the drum and fife, and fierce rattle of musketry comes from afar off. Nor am I alone in these horrors; for e'en while you waited yonder, strange and active men have come and gone in this hotel, as never men did before. Every man has some great errand, some mission that needs be done at once. Prescott comes for Judge Francis; some one comes for Prescott, and while they whisper and nod, another comes, and they all hurry off together." When he told me this, I was being troubled lest the Judge might fall in with the seceders, and, of course, leave the city, taking with him his niece. With a somewhat heavy heart I ventured out, determined to go to every place but I would find the Judge. I fancied I had detected something of vast importance to the whole nation respecting Floyd, Thompson, Madame Ponchard, or the Prince of Wales. Just as I came to the corner of J Street, I met Judge Francis, who exclaimed, "O! such things as I have heard! Come, let us to the Temple; we will assemble our happy dozen to con over the strangest things ever heard of. Go, call our friends together; we've caught a hare!" Now I noticed, when he came near, that he had something concealed in his bosom, and it seemed very large; so I began to talk with him, drawing nearer the while, till I got a peep, and I beheld that it was a huge bouquet of flowers. Then I told him we should at once go to the Temple, but he said, "By and by; go you, I will come after." But I said, "Why not let us go together?" He hesitated a moment, and then told me he had a little business affair down at the hotel. I knew then he was going to take the flowers to Vickey; but I said nothing about it. So we each one set out to meet at the Temple, where I was to give in my testimony—the most important history ever heard of.

CHAPTER III.

AFTER I had finished the last chapter, I looked back to the place where Miss Stimpkins was saying she would make the whole country laugh on the other side of its mouth, and I also laughed. The consequence was, Jenkins saw me laughing, and he asked me how I liked the book thus far? I told him every one of his characters seemed to have a good deal of self-conceit; and that he himself betrayed it a little. "No matter," said he, "the book must be a true history of the country; if we do manifest a little self-conceit, why, you must remember that we are only two hundred years back descended from the English." I told him, too, that where Victoria used such fine language, I thought it was overdrawn; but he said that there are many country girls in his country as green in their public behavior as she was, and yet have all the brightness, fluency and innocence that Vickey manifested. He says, moreover, that the same country girls are the purest and best that can be found in any part of the world. I told him I would write it down so, though I feared it would not be satisfactory for them to hear of it. Then I urged him to tell me whether he married Miss Ann Underhill, and he said, "wait a little."

"No, no," said I, "before I write another word of this great history, tell me whether you or the Southern gentleman got her?"

He smiled a little, and then began as follows, to wit:

After returning to the Jackson House, several of our members urged the Judge to disclose his designs for our action, and when we had seated ourselves around for that purpose, he drew forth a paper, and then vainly searched for his spectacles in his pockets. Thinking they were lost, he at last exclaimed, "Is it possible I have lost my spectacles!"

I told him to never mind it; for he ought to be furnished with something better than silver spectacles.

"Silver!" said he. "Indeed they were gold; fine guinea gold."

Several of us shouted, "O, Judge!" and he replied, "Indeed they were; they cost me twenty dollars."

Some of us said, "O, Judge! twenty dollars!"

"Well, no matter," said he, "I'll get another pair; but I cannot read this paper."

"Please you," said Mr. Prescott, "I found a pair of spectacles in the entrance to the Temple. Will you try them?" and he handed them over to the Judge. We all recognized them as his, and they were silver, and had been broken and tied on one side.

When the Judge put them on, he said, "Why, most remarkable—why, I can see with these old things first rate." We all assured him they must indeed be his own, but he said, "Of course they are since I have them on. Mine had a flaw on one side, and might easily be taken by a casual observer to be the same."

"Now, Judge," said Prescott, "I am sure these are your original spectacles, and you are so much of a philosopher, you don't often notice the things you wear. You are like Governor Walpole of Kentucky, who did not know his boots from his wife's slippers."

"Well, I confess it is somewhat so," said the Judge, being anxious to change the subject. "What did you know of Governor Walpole? He was one of my most intimate friends."

"Governor Walpole," said Prescott; "I knew him to be a scholar and a gentleman of the first water, and he was undoubtedly one of the finest linguists in the country."

"He was that," said the Judge, "and I believe he was one of the most versatile men I ever saw. Indeed, they were a talented family. His father and my father both graduated in the same college."

As he was going on in this style, we began laughing, for we were posted in the matter.

"Now, Judge," said Prescott, "why do you make such pretensions? I do not know any Governor Walpole; there never was any Governor Walpole. I was only drawing you out."

When we ceased laughing, the Judge said, "Indeed there was a Governor Walpole, and I knew him.—No, I mean Governor Waldo.—Yes, Governor Waldo;" and he afterwards adhered to it that there was a Governor Waldo. That is the manner in which he would always get out.

We could never make him own up to the falsity of his great pretensions.

We then arranged our business, and, as the Prince of Wales' procession was to take place on the day following, you may well imagine the anxiety we had in making the necessary preparations. Previous to this I was to start out on my business, with reference to the action of Floyd and Thompson. This began business for me early on the following morning, while nearly all our members were allotted to their various parts.

Accordingly, as soon as it was daylight, I went to the Treasury to witness the result. I had, in fact, barely stationed myself, when Floyd and Thompson came up and halted even as the latter spoke.

"Hold, Floyd, I would reflect awhile."

Floyd.—" Wherefore ? "

Thompson.—" If here were sentinels, as are in France, passing to and fro to guard the nation's gold : or, if here were a dog —even a dog to watch it, some excuse could I find warranting this deep design. But it is like despoiling innocence unarmed, with arms equipped for thunderbolts. I do revolt at it."

"Ha, ha! read that," said Floyd, and he pointed to an inscription above the entrance, which was

"THE PROPERTY OF THE PEOPLE."

Thompson.—" And I behold in that short sentence so much eloquence, that I scarcely value less my own approaching tears, than the boon you promise. That is the nation's only guard, and must we murder it ? "

Floyd.—" And such a guard ! Why, sir, only a nation of fools would have such a guard. It is a safeguard while we are all fools, but only while we are fools. I tell you, Thompson, babies believe the devil's in the corner, and so behave themselves ; but we are men."

Thompson.—" Not fear, dear Floyd, is my incentive to halt awhile, but the thought that I do betray a trust most sacred—to rob my countrymen."

Floyd.—" Rob ! Ha, ha, ha ! Tell me a ship at sea is foundering, and that he who swims away with its gold to save the gold is a robber ! Our nation totters to the base ; it sinks forever ! Speed us, then, before the ruin comes, to save that which will found another on its ruins ! Out with its coffers, god-like be our deeds, that from this awful threatening, on the part of a plebeian race, we bring eternal harmony. Shall not we, who have, by Providence, been placed in the doorway to our own and to the nation's glory,

walk in ? or hesitate till the mighty trust evade our grasp, and worth despoiled forever censure our low-born conduct ? "

Thompson.—" But suppose this whole thing miscarry ? "

Floyd.—" It cannot. It cannot. But suppose it does, what of it ? Every way is our gain. Wealth at least is ours."

Thompson.—" But still, the trust betrayed ? "

Floyd.—" Why, see what Cobb has done —to you the keys and management. Now I take it, if I am not a fool, that Cobb is Secretary of this Treasury, and yet he is fishing in the streets."

Thompson.—" And yet no other act is done for benefit of the South ? "

Floyd.—" Nothing done ! Now, *entre nous,* as I am Secretary of War, I have, within two days, transferred one hundred and fifteen thousand rifles and muskets from the Springfield Armory and Watervliet Arsenal to five depositories in the South.* Governor Gist, of South Carolina, has called together his State legislature, and hath already advised the organization of an army. Is this not something done ? "

Thompson.—" I do remember now, Cobb said not a dollar shall remain in the National Treasury when he goes out."

Floyd.—" And yet you would parley even at the door-way. Come, I pray. I want the bonds."

Thompson.—" And shall we still remain in Washington ? "

Floyd.—" Amongst our friends, of course. Let us haste ; this day is the Prince of Wales' procession, and so, while fools to Britons bow, we'll count the gains the fools have hoarded, that they remember now our nation dies.

'Our pageantry is gone. We've naught to love,
Yet, here, alas! a foreigner's a dove.
Come, Briton, come—a country loving you
To human rights itself cannot be true.'"

After they had thus spoken, they entered the Treasury, and I felt sure now that the national funds were indeed at the mercy of robbers. I was about to turn away from the scene, when that very suspicious-looking woman, Madame Ponchard, was seen approaching. She seemed in trouble; wrapped in profound thought ; not noticing me until she was within a few yards. Whereupon she looked to the ground, as if searching for something, and then turned and retraced her course, joining, a little distance off, the dark-eyed Orsini.

Thus the great cloud of the rebellion was sending forth its scouts, its vultures, to nibble at the feet and envelop a great,

* This was afterwards boasted of in the Richmond papers.

unguarded, Christian people, and there was no law, no arm of power to stay the approaching scourge. We could but look at the great fabric and weep, as we stood so powerless to do it service.

Thus was I waiting, reflecting, and watching, when who should approach, but the Prince of Wales, and the Duke of New Castle, for their morning walk. When they had approached near me, they asked what building that was? I told them it was the National Treasury. The Duke said, "What! has this country a Treasury?" And the Prince said, "It seems so, and without soldiers to guard it. Let us halt a while and contemplate the novelty of this sign:

'THE PROPERTY OF THE PEOPLE.'"

"Quite interesting, is'nt it?" said the Duke.

"Do you know, my lord," quoth the Prince, "that that sentence is the only thing of all I have seen in this country, that I admire?"

"Really, I think it has some significance. Ah! but what significance; that's the puzzle—whether this property is all the people have got, and needs this sentence to prove the title, or whether this sentence is to show foreigners the extent of American enterprise, which is to say, this young nation has already saved enough to buy one house."

"My lord is jovial," said the Prince. "As for myself, I feel serious. Do you know there is not another country in the world that leaves unguarded its national bureaus? And this it is touches me. It is a kind of honor I looked not for; it is a glory outmatching all the armies of France; it is an inward strength and full composure; like Hercules, unmoved when the gods at common omens trembled."

"Indeed, so," said the Duke. "Why, you are a metaphysician. Now, I took it, the American boast was a fireman's parade, wide streets, and wooden houses. This building is something, to be sure; but where is that score of botanical gardens and botanical colleges—those zoological gardens, and their attendant lectures—where are those mineralogical and geological colleges, with their gratuitous instruction? where the astronomical observatories for the instruction of ambitious young men? And this is the nation's Capital! I declare, it is very amusing, very amusing indeed!" "I say, my lord," said the Prince, "this nation is very young; it boasts that it is very young." "Ah, but that is not so; only young in wisdom. It is nearly as old and nearly as

powerful as it ever will be. It has no noble type of character. For the lack of the places of instruction I spoke of, in its National Capital, there is no place for the wealthy and intelligent to assemble to form a model of Americanism; and, in consequence, those classes fly to Europe to unmake their nativeism by a smack of foreign airs." "But how, my lord, is it possible to have these great public institutions in a republic? The places to be filled, would open only a new source for politicians." "Very wisely said," replied the Duke, "very wisely said; and hence it is, a republican government can never raise the common people to a high state of civilization. The more elevated are constantly pulled down to the level of the great multitude. Nature gives genius to make it exclusive; but a republic will not sustain that which nature has designed should mark the difference. Hence it is, genius and refinement in this country is burdened with the contact of ignorance and slothfulness; it feels the burden; it inwardly revolts at it. And yet, a day since, did I hear some Southern gentlemen say that the national affairs are gradually falling into the hands of the common mob, and that the more elevated are determined to cut loose, and establish the supremacy they are entitled to. Add to this the fact that American offices pay just enough salary to attract common jockeys, and not enough to meet the demands of the great and good, and you have the weakness of the Government in a nutshell." Now, as it so happened, while he was speaking, Floyd and Thompson emerged from the Treasury and concealed themselves behind the pillars thereof, to listen. "If not now," continued the Duke, "it will soon follow that the men who come into power, will be little better than highway robbers. They will no more regard that inscription on the Treasury, than they would the morning dew. It was so in the Roman republic; men even violated their solemn oaths, and often took paltry bribes as an equivalent for their influence. Finally, they became themselves too great a corruption to live together; and there was a general scramble for the spoils, in the pretence, and in fact, of the necessity of founding another government." Thompson knew the Duke, and hated him, because he was English, and because he and the Prince refused to visit Richmond, on account of it being in a slave State, and he spoke to Floyd in a low voice, saying. "O, I am cursed! O, I am cursed! Heaven has sent my enemy to chastise me. Had I godliness in my cause, I would rush upon him and give him a good thrashing. These monarchical prophecies of our country are of long standing, and it makes my blood boil to see, alas, that they are true." "It is true, as you say," continued the Duke, "the things the Americans boast of are all foolish; and the honor and honesty you infer from the absence of soldiers, is indeed something worth while. That Americans never steal, and that Americans, in business habits, never tell untruths, are their only distinctions that are good." "And they are good things, indeed," said the Prince. "Such is the boast of other nations—Jews, of gold; French, of fun; Britons, of banks, and Americans of honesty." "'Tis well, indeed," replied the Duke, "that my lord of Renfrew cannot be heard in this country; he'd make the people vain."

Thompson.—"Great heavens! Must I, must I bear this!"

Floyd.—"Sh! sh!"

Prince.—"American citizen! Glory in the name! it has honor, justice, peace, and plenty; it is guardian to the needy of other countries; it is the trust of man as man; it is the banishment of the arms that menace thieves, and the welcome of fellowship to all men. Glory be to thee, O! American citizen!"

Thompson.—"I cannot, will not bear this!"

Floyd.—"Sh! sh! they go; hear me."

Duke.—"And yet these things will pass away. Envious politicians will break through this theme of glory; they, and they alone have despoiled every nation since the foundation of the world, and they will here. Even at present is the deepest infamy accused to the party in power."

Prince.—"No, no! I pray, don't persuade me so. Let me leave with the thought that yonder inscription is glory, the most hallowed of all my memories of this people; to think that I, with my own eyes, saw a nation without soldiers; saw people that trusted one another. And yet this vow I make; if ever Americans disprove their present honesty, no joy more will I take in seeing the face of man." When he had finished speaking, he and the Duke went their way, the latter admonishing him that it was Friday morning, and that whatever was done on that day, would prove a failure; alluding to the vow the Prince had made. Thompson thought he meant Floyd and Thompson's deeds, and he walked out and said to Floyd, "You see, we are damned in the very onset. A base robbery!"

Floyd.—"How now? Have I not said our ship of state is wrecked, and that we are merely saving that which would otherwise be lost? Why, Thompson, you yourself did first propose to Cobb to take this stuff away." He held up gold bags and paper bonds. "Is it better we throw it in the river, or leave it here to burn, or take it to our homes, or fly with it to Canada, or pout and grieve that we took it at all? Methought the founders of a new nation had more pluck. Is not the state dead? And—we the trustees?" "So the state is dead," said Thompson; "the state was our mother, and we have rifled our dead mother's pockets."

Floyd.—"Why, now, what frame of mind is this? Must we stand and parley till our very actions give warning to every passer-by? Come, let us go—;" he turned then to look if any one was near, the while holding on to Thompson's sleeve, and he saw me, and said, "Hallo, fellow! what are you doing here?" "Nothing," said I, "only halted to hear the Prince and the Duke." "Scoundrel!" said he, "you lie, you are an eaves-dropper," putting therein a fierce oath. Now I had, all the while the Prince and Duke were talking, been seated on the curbstone, making believe my boot hurt me, so I could hear what was said. Floyd and Thompson came up to me, even while I sat there, and the former caught me by the collar. "What would you do?" said I, rising; but Thompson caught me too, and I struggled to get away, fearing bodily harm. "You'll do no more harm to us!" said Floyd, and he swore again. They then pulled me over backward, my feet catching against the curb-stone. "You dog!" he continued, "I know you, you are poking your nose into everything." But while he was speaking, I seized Thompson by the throat with one hand, and shook him. He was very cowardly and broke loose, standing aloof; and Floyd instantly drew a knife.

I had, in the meantime, worked myself into a better position, and now sprung up. He was frightened—not daring to strike me with his knife.

"Sir," said he, "we are more than two hundred strong. Before two hours hence, you shall be a marked man; consider this as you please." I made no reply, and they started to walk off, and again he retorted, "You cannot arrest us. The very officers to whom you would apply, will put the seal on you."

I stood there waiting for some time, not making any answer, and, in fact, until they had disappeared. On my way back,

"Even when they had robbed the National Treasury, Floyd still maintained a brazen face."

I stopped at the market-place, near the outer posts thereof, where I heard a voice which I recognized as the Judge's. On drawing still nearer, I beheld him alone, with flowers uplifted, evidently contemplating a rich interview with his Victoria. In view of the novelty of the scene—to see and hear the Judge, with such a bouquet, and by himself rehearsing—I halted a moment.

"Beautiful!" said he, musing with a low voice, "beautiful flowers! Thou shalt deck a fairy form. Thou shalt grace a queen. Behold the lily and the rose, so fair, so sweet, outmatched by the lady I love! Aye, ye precious little diadems! precious warblers on that bosom! O! what tides in my emotion rise! Beautiful Victoria! Victoria! My angel of glory! Daisies, lily blossoms that warble on such fairylike bosoms, do I love thee? Oh thou fairest of the fair, behold the tenderness of these! inhale their fragrance! compare their exquisiteness with my fond appreciation! Old, thou hast made me a child! This heart, pure as adamant—it is thine, and thine only. Ah, dearest! thou hast fear of my quality, and dreamest that the tender of my love is but a dream! Dream on, blessed angel, these blessed flowers shall make thee dream forever! Come, sweet flowers! envious mortals! thou shalt play at the lips—press on the heaving bosom! Oh, that the glory of coming hours were here! Now, let me rehearse:—

"'Madame, my carriage waits at the door. Will you accompany us to the procession? We have a place. Oh! ah! shall I have the honor? Will you sit by me? Ah! allow me, my dear! Here are flowers. Take them, their natural perfume evaporating toward the great expanse above, like the lone heart never captured, giving love to the imagery of an unheard of beauty! Take them, I pray you! feed upon their sweetness; no age is there. Some of them are curled and wilted; but, ah! the perfume is even as sweet as from the infant bud. Ah, indeed, my lady faints; poor child! The fatal deed is done; the battle fought and won! Be happy, oh thou, my dearest dear!'"

As he was still rehearsing to himself and examining his flowers, and alternately bowing and cramming them to his nose, and then viewing them, I was myself so much agitated, that it was almost impossible to remain silent. On looking over the way, I saw Miss Lucy Tabiatha Stimpkins approaching directly toward the Judge, and I saw too, that she beheld him in his ecstasies with the flowers. Behind her, and at a little distance, came Professor Jackson.

When they drew near, she bid the Professor halt. The moment that she had approached near enough to the Judge to hear his folly, and see his antics, it was evident that she was enraged. After witnessing it a short time, she suddenly stood before him, face to face.

"Is it possible?" said she. "Judge Francis Underhill—a man of your years?" He started up, confounded.

"I am but a boy, madam," said he. "My hairs are white, it is true; but my heart is like an infant's."

"I venture to say," said she, "if there be war, your age would exempt you without a jury. More should you think of your grave than of a fair dulcinea."

> "More the sexton seek,
> Than this maiden meek,"

said the Judge. "Nay, Miss Lucy, you interpret from the frozen cinders of your own impulses. But who that has felt the genial flame, would not, for a single moment's glorious ease with the lady of his love, confront the cold philosophy of a frowning world. Oh madam! I mean Miss Lucy Tabiatha, when you feel and know the fervency of a dear sweetheart; to know that its recipient is touched by the same chord of matchless tenderness, and hath but craped this mortal part to make one's self reveal exquisite joys within its compliment—too much, too much for the nerves to bear—Ah! you smile Miss Stimpkins! Question you my love? If ever man for woman vowed, then I to mine am resident alway. Age is fire, and I have age, hence, I am warm; and these [touching the flowers] gentle emblems shall decorate her matchless beauty;" and thus saying, he walked away, not giving her a chance to answer.

Miss Lucy was discomfited at this sudden departure, and immediately addressed her consort, Professor Jackson. "Professor Jackson," said she, turning sharply towards him, "heard you that attack upon woman's rights? Will you stand and hear me vanquished? What right has he to meddle with the fundamental principles of human love? Where is the voice of his fair one? Is there none to warn her?"

The Professor suggested that there might be some misunderstanding about the congeniality of the two persons.

"No, sir. No, sir," she replied. "I neglected to be true to the rules of my own doctrine. I let my feelings move me. I was overcome. But yet, I shall vanquish him. I shall show him these boasted affections are but promptings of sin. I shall teach his fair one to rely only on moral and intellectual principles. I shall teach her that this thing called love, is all moonshine. Professor, I have more advantages than he ever dreamed of. Talk of reclining on bosoms, I shall recline on the Prince of Wales, and make my enemies bite their fingers; for I have enemies—so had Bonaparte, and so had Cæsar." "It is so," said the Professor, and they left together.

I had indeed been anxious to come forth and personally witness the past contest; but, having my clothes soiled as before mentioned, and being anxious to return for a change, I waited a moment so as not to be seen in my present condition. Scarcely was quiet restored, when I heard a noise as of some one weeping, and turning to look, I beheld there the identical man who had been conversing with Ann Underhill, on the previous occasion. He was leaning against the Jefferson Archway, twirling his little walking-stick in his fingers, his head leaned backwards, and the heel of his boot playing upon the other. Half-way between song and speech, he then turned and went on in this fashion:

"I will away, away to th' wild lagoons
Of my own dear native state,
The jeers I've suffered and the scoffs endured
From these people I'll there relate.
Glorious and free,
Happy in liberty,
I will away, away to th' wild lagoons
Of my own dear native State."

Diamonds glittered on his shirt bosom and on his fingers; he seemed like the kind, intelligent, and darling son of more than common folks. On the instant I regarded him as a rival, but when I beheld the deep solemness of his nature, I was won over to him. "My friend," said I, "I am moved with pity to the strangeness of this melancholy." He looked up, and when we faced each other, we recognized that we were brothers of the same society, though we had never before offered each other any salutation. "My brother," said he, "I am cast down. Such things run through my brain as would move a world to tears. I see the progress of events, and I know that all the glory and peace of our country is at end. Woe on me that I have lived in this scourging period." I took his hand and he rose up. "Though nations fall," said I, "and religions perish in envious broil, one thing alone will ever endure, whereby men can faithfully rely upon the confidence of each other. Tell me, brother, what is this that wears so heavily on your mind."

"This is the substance of my sorrowing," said he: "Peace and respect no Southerner now has, even in the Capital of this great country. Everywhere am I pushed into the pitiless storm; abuse is heaped upon me alway. This is a deeper grief than you premise. When first I came to Washington, I loved it as a Northern romance, and, much in hope, my joys were lifted up. Cares of home I banished, and the luxury of ease I sought out. In all concourse, I made free the confidence I did expect from others, oft dilating with right good will on my own good fortune. For, till now I called it good, and now I deem it not so. You may know, my dear sir, I was born of wealthy parents in Louisiana. My father was the largest planter in that State; he owned eight hundred slaves, and his wealth was the chief support in employment of three thousand men. When I was a boy of fourteen, my mother died. My father being young, married again; but, not content with a woman of his own country, took her from that ever-renowned land of the poets, Italy. She was my tyrant; often after she came did I wish that I had never been. These trials were not unknown to my excellent father. He had employed for my instruction the best English and foreign teachers, who became enamored of my future promise. My father desired that I and my step-mother should be kept apart, and he resolved to take her to Italy to live; himself to spend his time equally in the two countries. When he acquainted me with this fact, my sorrows knew no bound. My father was a great and a good man; he was all I had in the world to love; but I never said him nay. No, I never! Accordingly, when I was in my eighteenth year, my father having appointed all the necessary officers of his estate, came to tell me the time had come. The last words he said were: 'More, I desire, my son, that you be good than great. The good may be crossed awhile, but in time their joys will be eternal.' He folded me in his arms—we separated! I never saw him since, although I have since spent many years on the continent of Europe, and searched every conceivable place where such a man could live." When he finished speaking, the tears were fast falling on his cheeks, and I knew not in what way to comfort him. His appearance showed me that I was in the presence of no ordinary man, and one the most deserving sympathy I ever met with. "Indeed," said I, "this is worse than death; for it is the burial of all peace of mind. Heard you never a

word that could lead to the whereabouts of your father?" "Several times, and in several places were they seen together, and even for two or three years, all the way from Paris to Naples. The last I ever heard was that they left Europe for America, more than four years ago; but whether they ever arrived, I know not. I returned and took possession of the estate, and have since managed it. Now I have more grief to add to it, it is the threatened aspect of our country. As I said before, I had only a father to love, and when I lost him, I lost all. You must know, sir, the position I was enabled to take in foreign countries, and my most remarkable mission threw me into the best of society, where, alas, I received the severest blows ever dealt to man. People pitied me for the loss of my father, and while they pitied, they sneered at the slavery in my native land. They even insinuated the death of such a man as my father, was nothing more than the retributive justice of heaven. I plead my country's cause; its laws excused for the manner of its long-standing custom, estates descending with all appurtenances, and content and comfort amongst the slaves in full requirement. I could bear such goading sympathy, for I was in search of my father, until I had exhausted all hope of ever seeing him more. Then, as I said, I returned. O! what joys unspeakable within my breast when again I reached my native land! All the castles of monarchies, the arts and sciences of Europe, and all the elevated and noble people whom I could have loved but for their eternal sneers against this country; all, all I now gladly exchanged for my glorious land of liberty! I settled on my estate in comparative joy, my heart so full that even the greatest of Abolitionists would have found me a kind and honorable friend; so great was my joy to meet my countrymen; so much I hated the noble families of France, England and Italy for their abuse to me, for that which I could not help, nor were the cause. But my retirement could not last long; my ardent nature sought enjoyment. I came here to mingle with the choicest of my countrymen, and I have given many compliments. In return I am sneered at for the slaves I own and cannot get rid of. The conflict of two terrible parties is about to begin. Then will my former boasts of my country in Europe be turned to mockery." "Indeed, sir," said I, "you have touched something which would move all the honest and great men of our country." I then told him who I was, that I had been a long time a local reporter, but that having acquired a great fortune, I now amused myself merely going about taking notes, which I rehearsed before the courts of Judge Francis Underhill. "Underhill!" said he, and I told him yes. He then said, "I have heard Miss Ann Underhill speak highly of her uncle," but we thereupon ceased to speak more of the Underhills, nor did anything pass between us tending to show that either of us mistrusted the rivalry, and we then returned to the Jackson House to get ready for the procession.

CHAPTER IV.

I TOLD Jenkins I longed to hear more about Miss Ann Underhill, but still I was not forgetful of the fact that he had neglected to tell me whether he himself married her. Said he, "I was telling you as fast as I could, but you know it is the fashion of modern authors to tell anything except what they have to tell, in order to make a book as large as possible. I know one author," he continued, "who took up the waste papers that he had rejected from different books of his own writing, and when he saw what a huge pile there was, he said to himself, 'what shall I do with it?' So, wishing to make the most of his name, he sent them to a publisher, and had a book made of them, and it had a good run. Another man took his cue from it, got a history of the sewers of Paris, and some police reports, put them in a bag, shook them up a few times, then took the papers out and paged them for a book. Being at a loss for a name for his book, he turned to his publisher and said, 'Ah! Les Miserables,' and then he went home determined to abandon the project. But the bookseller went on with it, and it is said that many people read it, and never discovered the joke."

"Well," said I, "well, Jenkins, you will not try any such game as that?"

"Oh, no!" said he, "but, in the language of Falstaff, 'shall I not take mine ease in mine own book?'"

When he said this, I made no further argument, and told him to go on with the transcription. He told me to begin, saying:

"Having resolved to attend the procession, and fixed upon a ride with Judge Francis, I immediately repaired to the hotel to acquaint him with the determination. The Judge at once ordered out his carriage and horses, informing us that everybody was welcome in it. It was more than twenty years old, and so were his horses, and they were attended to by the same servant that had done so for more than twenty years. The carriage had had many breakdowns, and was pieced and patched in every side and corner. Many painters for many years had painted the various repaired parts, and it was of many colors. Some of the silver mounting was gone, some was loose; and the broken bolts had been replaced with monstrous nails, splitting the boards here and there, and bearing many gashes withal. One horse had turned old faster than the other; one very fat; the other lean. The reins and harness had often broken on a midnight ride, and been with ropes made whole. The cushions of the carriage had shed their stuffing, and the cover thereof had been gone for many years. And yet, to the Judge, the whole concern was as perfect as on the day he bought it. It had, like a wife, grown old by such slow degrees, that the owner never knew it. Every part of it too had a history; the Judge could talk a month on its scars. He would say, "Behold you that dash board? What a rent is there! That occurred one pleasant day in June, as I was going in company with Henry Clay to the races," and then he would fashion out how it was done. "See that twisted bolt?" he would again go on. "Daniel Webster had often urged me for a journey to Mount Vernon. I shall never forget that memorable day," and so he continued; in all probability not the quarter part was true. But he boasted so much of his great associations, that he at last believed them himself. So, when we had expressed our desire to go to the procession with him, not knowing he was to have many ladies, and when the carriage was ready, and while the Judge was yet in the hotel, not less than eight of our court members climbed into it, determined to have at least one more good time,

whether there be war or not. Now, while we were climbing in, there came by that everlasting Mrs. Stimpkins and Professor Jackson, and they thought it was some public conveyance, and that they might avail themselves of the opportunity of riding to the procession, where they could then dismount. Accordingly, she jumped upon the steps of the carriage, saying, "I think a gentleman would at least give a seat to a lady!" and we all cried out, "Certainly, madam, come in!" and in she came, followed by Jackson, the gifted Professor. We were all wondering in our own minds what the Judge would say when he came out and beheld no place for himself. What was our astonishment, however, at seeing him at last, with Vickey and Ann Underhill on each arm, followed by Mr. and Mrs. Edge. "Ah!" said the Judge, "nearly full!" and he smiled; for there was not room for the smallest thing more to get in. "Quite full, sir!" shouted Mrs. Lucy Tabiatha Stimpkins; "you can't get in here, sir! Go ahead, driver, crack up your old skeletons!" We, who had taken first possession of the carriage, were about to leap out, and yet trying to smother our laughter; but the Judge was too clever for us, and he said, "Keep your seats, I pray; I was never so pleased in my life. Here comes another carriage; we are provided." He bowed and laughed heartily, and so did many of us. In a few minutes, he and his party were in another carriage, and we were started on. "I told you, Professor," said Mrs. Lucy, "that the time would come when I should vanquish that Judge. He fancied he could overcome me on all occasions as he did at the market-place." Thus she went on for some time, but we were brought to a change by meeting Judge Walker, who motioned to me that he would speak a word. So he got on the step of the carriage and told me some important matters he had for me, and then he asked where we were going, and I told him. "Why, have not you heard that?" says he, "it's not to be to-day!" "How so?" says I. "Why," he said, "it is not consonant with the feelings of the royal family to go to receptions or any other place on Friday. They fear there will be no good come of it, and so the President postponed it until to-morrow." When he said this, he bid me good-day and left.

Now, Miss Lucy had been so earnestly talking all the while to the Professor, that she heard not a word of it. I told all my companions of it, and told them to say nothing; that we would give our Lucy a ride. We resolved at once to drive far out of the city, and then discharge her and the Professor, and let them have the benefit of a walk back to the Capital.

As soon as we were clear of the street crowd, I made the driver drive—(and he did drive). In a few moments we were out of the city, on the Georgetown road. Miss Lucy was alarmed, and shouted, "Where are you going? What is the matter?" But we heeded her not, and urged our driver to go the faster, the horses being kept at full gallop. Some of us would say, "Madam, you are right; it is a very fine day." "How far did you say you were going?" and such like, as if we did not hear what she was saying. Thus we flew over hill and dale in break-neck style, all of us laughing fit to kill. Mrs. Lucy and the Professor now began to look terribly afraid; soon, indeed, they thought we were playing a sad joke at their expense. After a while, we turned up Miller's Lane, where all was dust and hot sunshine; poor Lucy, quite enraged, shouted with all her power, "Where are you going? For heaven's sake, stop! This is the wrong stage? Let us out!" After we were half a mile further on, we succeeded in understanding her, and halted to let the pair dismount.

"Gentlemen, I thank you," she said, as soon as she reached terra firma; "you might have told us this was a country stage. We took it for a carriage going to the procession. You have no regard for helpless woman. You are very smart, gentlemen, I dare say. You can snicker, and play the nice gallant to doll-faced misses, but you don't see nor hear a woman of sense."

She then turned and looked fiercely at her consort, Professor Jackson, and stared him out of countenance.

"Professor Jackson, I am astonished at you! Have you, too, no regard for the rights of poor helpless woman?"

But ere we had time to hear her full lecture, and in the midst of our laughter, we turned our carriage and began to retrace our course. What then was her amazement; what her heart-burning anger when she saw and knew that the whole thing had been a joke on her and the Professor. Here lay several miles between them and the city, to be walked over in the burning sun, and amidst clouds of choking dust. We had little pity for her, though, because she had so rudely come into our carriage; yet, we were heartily sorry for the poor Professor, who now must needs withstand her storms all the way back. We also justified ourselves on the ground that the day was a holiday,

and we were entitled to have some sport.

What was our astonishment to find, on our return, that an equally important joke was being played upon the venerable Judge. The clerk and Prescott had laid a wager on the result of the Judge's being magnetized. The wager consisted of a dozen of sparkling catawba, and the nature of the wager was that no trick could be played upon the Judge, to make him acknowledge that he was beaten in a joke. The plan was, for the whole party, after the Judge was seated in the parlor, to withdraw and leave him sitting there. If the Judge continued sitting an hour, under the belief that the magnetizers were standing behind him when they were not, or if he would own up that he had been sold in the matter, then the clerk lost. The Judge knew nothing about the bet. He agreed, however, to sit to be magnetized; and at the end of the hour they were to fire a pistol, and he was to get up and show them that they had failed. The magnetizer was promised something handsome for his services, but he had to agree to the plans of the party.

So when all the party was in the parlor, the magnetizer opened the affair by a short lecture, beginning, of course, with the beginning of the world; passing through the old fogyism of man in not believing in magnetism, and blowing on its powers and usefulness. He then told us that everybody could be put in the magnetic state; that if it could not be done by one person, it could be done by a number of persons all acting on the same subject at the same time. He then informed us that, with this brief statement, he was ready to begin.

The Judge smiled, and shook his head to signify his disbelief.

If you never saw a magnetizer, I will tell you how he does it: he makes downward passes toward you and around you, until you go to sleep, as it were, with one eye open ; that is to say, some of your external senses are asleep, while your internal senses, or reflection, are in cognizance of the magnetizer; and so, losing consciousness of yourself, you obey him.

When several persons magnetize a single subject, one makes the passes upon the subject, another stands behind the one, withdrawing, as they say, the magnetism from one source. Its merits, however, and modus operandi, are generally described by its adherents to be the withdrawing of the electricity in the system. It is also said that natural sleep is produced in exactly the same way; that is to say, the daily toil and the contact with outside objects, withdraw so much fire from the system, in the course of a day, that the person goes to sleep.

With animal magnetism, it is claimed, the subject may be so reduced that there is no communication with the sensitive nerves, and that the motor system can also be made as rigid as a frozen corpse. One of the chief arts of magnetism is, therefore, to impress fully some startling facts upon the subject, before beginning the operation.

As stated, therefore, the present lecture of the Professor having partially frightened the Judge, and he being resolute to show us that he could not be put to sleep, became passive to our design. He was, therefore, placed in the centre of the parlor, his back toward the door. Behind him we stood in single file, and began the downward passes—the Professor being next the Judge. The Judge was told to sit still until we had him in the magnetic state, and that we would fire a pistol and see if he could arise at the end of the hour.

When we had given a few passes, we one by one passed out into the hall, until all of us were gone, leaving the Judge sitting in the parlor alone. He thought that we were still operating upon him, and he was waiting for the signal.

The gong now sounded for dinner, and if there was anything that the Judge hated, it was to be kept from his dinner; but still he was determined to sit it out, to show us that he had beaten us at our own game.

We went to dinner and made a good deal of merriment at the table. The doors were thrown wide open, and we could all sit at dinner and see the Judge in the parlor, where he could hear our noise and laughter. He envied the folks at the table undoubtedly—not knowing that so many of them were ourselves—being himself of a merry disposition, especially about the time the heavy wines come around. So for one whole hour we kept the Judge sitting there, and then, after we had finished our dinner, desired some one to fire off the pistol, and so make the Judge own up that we had played a joke on him.

Accordingly, the pistol was fired; the Judge rose up, turned around, saw us, and, of course, realized at once the true state of the case. We cheered him heartily, and in he came, saying:

"If it had not been for that pistol, I might have slept all day."

"Good!" said the clerk, "he won't own up; I have won!"

"Why, no!" said Prescott, "we magnetized him; so I have won!"

"Nonsense!" said the Judge, "nobody has won. I took my regular sleep, and when the pistol was fired off, I awoke. It was, indeed, my trick on you all. I only sat there to take my usual sleep while you were at your sports."

Although we knew he had not been to sleep, Prescott did not wait for the laughter to subside, but ordered in the sparkling catawba. In a few moments, however, we were aroused by the solemn realities of the great nation, of which we were yet happy members. One, two, three rapid shots of cannon rang in our ears. The decanters started, and the glasses, half raised, fell back. "What was that?" "What was that?"

Prescott arose. "Ladies and gentlemen," said he, "we are still free in our light enjoyment. It is not so in all countries, and it cannot be so long here. I hope that we may ever esteem these happy privileges, and never view the departure of our present enjoyment. We have no cause for rebellion, and yet this very city is in the hands of men projecting one; not against the city, but against the freedom of man. One man alone, out of so many millions, has the hardihood to oppose them—I mean General Scott. He foresees trouble, and yonder cannon are all the few he can scrape together. I think he is determined to keep the national Capital, though only himself do stand to battle. He has just had an interview with the Cabinet, and these are his messengers."

When he had said this, he turned and left, and I myself followed. Several of us who had charge of the Prince's procession, having been sent for to attend to the arrangements. But as the whole affair is related in the next chapter, the reader is referred to that.

CHAPTER V.

In order that you may appreciate our description of the Prince of Wales' procession, I must first introduce to you our action in the Cabinet, which was, however, an informal meeting; Prescott, myself, and several others being among the number. As you are all conversant with the general form of cabinet meetings, I will at once begin with the interview with James Buchanan. He was, when we approached, in the grounds in front of the White House, but with us, immediately retired within, when Prescott handed to him some Charleston papers, saying, " Here is something straight from Charleston; see, it smells something of gunpowder." He then handed the Charleston *Mercury* to the President, and added, " the Southerners, you see, want some British royalty here to sit on a Southern throne and wield their affairs of state, where cotton is king."

The President made no reply, took the papers, and then passed them around to several persons, Davis among the number. Davis, however, being cunning, was anxious, if possible, at that time, to make the appearance of the projector of the rebellion as insignificant as possible. He therefore replied to Prescott, " When we attempt to muzzle the gas of newspapers, we may suffocate ourselves. We have indeed more important business on hand than the discussing of editorials."

Mason.—" Something important from Charleston ? "

Prescott.—" Aye ! Beauregard has gone to the coast to survey the forts and plan out the mode of attack."

Davis.—" The merest balderdash."

Prescott.—" Assemblages throughout the State, add fury to the fire. Here in this paper is offered, by a planter, ten thousand dollars in gold for Lincoln's head ! and this advertisement is copied in many Southern papers."

Davis.—" A mere electioneering trick, I do assure you, Mr. President."

Prescott.—" But this administration should take some note of it. This crime, if it be a crime, is only to be accounted for in the State of the criminal, and his State, with all the Southern States, do uphold the villain's offer."

Mason.—" That is what the North have brought upon themselves by electing such a man."

Davis.—" Indeed, gentlemen, shall we not attend to more important business ? We protest that when our house is on fire, it is not wise to discuss its original cause. In all candor I would ask, Does any man suppose that there will be war, or even secession ? Agitation may be dangerous, but we have power, by concession, to heal all grievances."

Buchanan.—" I hope so ! Oh, I pray that it may be so ! "

Several questions were then brought up, not, however, relating to the most important affairs before the country ; and then, after a little informal conversation, some of the party left. Buchanan, however, stood there alone.

" Oh, the mystery of these things ! " he said, " the mystery and vague forebodings ; a word is spoken, and men appear and disappear but to fill me with unspeakable awe and dire confusion. Nothing in this country now has a head or tail. Men's actions are without meaning. They stilt and stiltify one another, making me their spectator for punishment. I am a very stumbling block where both parties come and break their shins, myself getting all the blows. Misshapen Richard complained that dogs barked at him, but I have all my countrymen, and yet I am President of the United States. What have I done ? Wherein is my fault ? That I love my country too well ? That I will not take sides ? Why, bless me, have I not explained the Constitution ? Will not my country understand me ? I do protest these things shall not be. I will write another message, and I will so illustrate the Constitution that no man may gainsay me more."

This he spoke, in a great measure, to himself, but somewhat toward Prescott and myself. Prescott was anxious to make a reply, but I checked him a little out of respect to the position we were in, and also because at this moment General Scott approached and entered the place. As soon as Scott had passed the salutations of the morning, he at once broke forth in plain English, telling him to re-

"Scott spoke for the nation; but Buchanan hung down his head and wept."

inforce the Southern forts; and telling him plainly that it must be done.

But Buchanan wavered in assent, suggesting that "it might at this time be unnecessary."

"It is necessary," said Scott. "A small force of men sent there in time, would save the country from shedding one drop of blood."

"I take it that that would only be a menace to the South," said Buchanan, "Davis says so; so does Cobb, and so does Rhett."

Scott,—"Of course it would be a menace. Jackson menaced them once before, and even for that the South, in the end, took sides with him. Wavering minds always choose sides with the Government. There are ten such wavering minds in the South, at the present moment, to one secessionist. If you keep silent, these minds will all follow in the beat of their leaders."

Buchanan,—"Have you any evidence that the South will secede, or that there will be any disturbance?"

Scott,—"Governor Gist is already arming his State. All assemblages in the South now gleam with swords and sparkling bayonets. To be even thought to be a Republican, down South, is now but to meet certain death. Everywhere South has the threat been made that if Lincoln be elected, secession shall result from it ; and, if need be, by force of arms. And yet we sit in silence, even countenancing the fall of our country by our inaction."

Buchanan,—"I find no precedent in history of reinforcing the forts; neither is there aught about it in the Constitution."

Scott,—"The Constitution!" And when he said this, he looked so fiercely at the President, that the latter turned pale. "The Constitution! I've brought down a few guns to this city, and I shall fight for it whether it is in the Constitution or not!" Scott rose up, and I saw he was filled with a deep, burning fire; his massive brows fell, and like a lion to a lamb, he gazed on the trembling President.

Buchanan,—"Do you think I could reinforce the forts with safety to the South?"

Scott,—"The South! The South! Is that your country? Are not the forts, the harbors, and custom-houses the property of the nation? Are you not bound to protect them, whether any section likes it or not?"

Buchanan,—"If I had the consent of the Cabinet—"

Scott,—"If you cannot get that, why, get a Cabinet that will consent with you.

This should be done at once. Toucey is sending the navy off to foreign countries, Floyd is sending the army to the western frontiers, and Cobb, through Floyd and Thompson, has sunken the treasury from eighty millions to twelve, and now they have stolen even the remainder. Really, sir, this is no time to be reading the Constitution."

Buchanan,—"Indeed, you are right. I am resolved to reinforce the forts at all hazards."

Scott,—"It must be done; only show a little spirit, and nine-tenths of the people South will stand by us."

Buchanan,—"I believe so too; and we will show them spirit. It shall be done. Every fort shall be crammed with picked men."

Scott—"But at once."

Buchanan,—"On the instant."

Scott,—"I hope so."

Buchanan,—"Oh, you can rely on it."

When this was concluded, Scott seemed much pleased, and took his departure.

"Mr. Jenkins," said Buchanan, after having hung his head awhile, and fingered his vest button, "Mr. Jenkins, I am going to write a message, and I want you to be my amanuensis. It shall be filled with the soundest arguments. Everything in the Constitution shall be laid down so plain a child could understand it. Moreover, I shall tell the South in plain words that the election of a plain man like Lincoln, is not cause enough to justify secession and rebellion."

Just then, when he got thus far, Floyd came in, and stood listening; Buchanan, not seeing him, went on :

"Fort Moultrie shall have two hundred men, and Sumter three hundred, and so shall I garrison every place in the South. And in some places I will put shrewd detectives, to keep me well informed on all dangerous doings among these fire-eaters. Indeed, it shall so turn out to my thankless countrymen that I am not only a peaceful man myself, but the cause of peace among other folks. Come, Jenkins, I will ask my Cabinet nothing; I am going to stuff the Southern forts."

Right before him now stood the unflinching Floyd, the man of oaths, the cunning Secretary of War.

"You will?" said Floyd.

Buchanan,—"Ha!"

Floyd,—"What now, Mr. President? Are you planning the death of the nation, and a gallows for yourself?"

Buchanan,—"Why, indeed, sir?"

Floyd,—"Fear not, I mean no harm, neither does any Southern gentleman. I am not only your friend, but the friend of my country. Intimidate the South, and all is lost. Compromise, give the South plenty of time, and all will be well."

Buchanan.—"In this extremity, what shall I do? There is a mill-stone about my neck, and I am to brave the ocean, or, in failing, die. Two elephants are pulling me in opposite ways, and I am half ripped in the middle by their powerful tension. I cannot go with one, for the other pulls me away. One threatens eternal execration, and the other death. What have I done that I must die? Not my life do I begrudge, though I don't want to die, but to go by the Constitution, that's my matter. Now, in truth, I have just promised Scott to reinforce the forts."

Floyd.—"You have?"

Buchanan.—"I have."

Floyd.—"And will you?"

Buchanan.—"Why not?"

Floyd.—"I have nothing to say."

Buchanan.—"I am aware that the Constitution guarantees Southern rights. I do not wish to menace those rights."

Floyd.—"And yet you will do what you would not do."

Buchanan.—"I hope not. No, I am resolved. I will not reinforce the forts. Go tell my would-be murderers I shall maintain the Constitution, though the whole country perishes. I will."

Floyd.—"That is the talk! Southerners are the hottest blooded people on earth. Reinforce the forts, and every man, woman, and child will be in arms. To intimidate such men, ay! but to raise a hand against them, is to destroy one of the greatest nations! We protest against force; we are sworn to the stand, to demand a guarantee for our institution, and we will have it, peaceably, if we can; forcibly, if we must. Blood, blood be on the head of him who dares transgress the rights of these Southern sons of chivalry!"

Buchanan.—"You are right! You can demand your guarantees, by the Constitution. The Supreme Court will uphold you, and so will all peaceable men. Come, Jenkins, I am resolved to write a message. I will show the whole country how the matter stands; that there is nothing against secession in the Constitution, and that there is no law empowering the President to make war against any section of the country. I will also employ Bishop Hopkins to write a sermon on slavery, to prove its right and holy origin. I will arouse the democratic party to rally round the Constitution, and, if chance be that Breckenridge be elected, this muddle will

all blow over. Come, I am in humor for it. Get me the decisions of the Supreme Court, and bring in the Constitution."

When he said this, he hobbled up to a mirror and did adjust his cravat, saying to us, "Excuse me, gentlemen, a moment," whereupon we withdrew, Floyd assuring him that his remarks were just the right sort of stuff for these times. In the hall we met Cobb, Rhett, and Davis, though when we told them Buchanan wanted to adjust his cravat, they did not enter, but, in company with Floyd, walked off. They went down the winding stairs toward the lower grounds of the palace, and even as they passed on the lower step, I heard a voice of a woman, who said, "Go; no more; go at once." I turned to look, for it had a sepulchral sound—dramatic and touching; and I beheld Madame Ponchard and Orsini, with the papers in their hands (newspapers), and I took them to be the same that Prescott gave to Floyd and Davis. The thought flashed over me in a moment that they were reading of the offer of ten thousand dollars reward for Lincoln's head; and when I mistrusted what country people they were, I trembled in breathless apprehension.

"That is short the mark," said he.

"Patience," said she, "patience, sir; in the name of all that is sacred, I charge you say no more, but go at once."

"But if the place was known?" said he.

"Follow them," said she. "I am off to the Senate. Remember, too, that admonition. Now, no more."

"I am yours to command," said he, and he bowed and left; but she came up and entered the mansion, and passed through the hall, but where, or for what purpose, I at this time knew not. These were the most words I had yet heard either her or Orsini speak, though I had known them by sight for several years, and had seen them so constantly in company with the most respectable people of Washington. They had, in fact, become to me like a cloud, coming and passing wherever good or great people were assembled. On this occasion I endeavored to follow her, but she soon mysteriously disappeared.

A few minutes afterwards, I heard loud rapping at a door—a most unusual sound there—and I sought for the cause. It was Prescott trying to get in Buchanan's room. I told him the old man was fixing his cravat, and that we had better wait awhile. Just then the door opened, and the man himself appeared before us. Prescott introduced his business at once, saying that news had just been received from South

Carolina that three commissioners were to be appointed to come to Washington to demand the State's withdrawal from the Union, and to settle for the National property within that State, and that, in the opinion of Scott, the men in Fort Moultrie and Fort Sumter should be at once reinforced, and furnished with supplies, as the men already there could easily be starved into a surrender.

Buchanan.—" Why, you astonish me ! You frighten me ! "

Prescott.—" 'Tis enough to frighten all men."

Buchanan.—" But I tell you, Scott's going wrong end foremost about the matter. He is a soldier, and he wants to fight; he knows no other way to settle anything. Tell him I have reconsidered the matter; that reinforcing the forts would precipitate us into war on the spot. Also, go and telegraph all over the country that I will not do a thing against the South. This will quiet them; it will satisfy them I am determined to stand by the Constitution at all hazards."

Prescott.—" But suppose we wait till they are in position to demand; they will say, 'Give us the forts, or we will starve the garrison ?' "

Buchanan.—" But they must give us time to weigh the matter; time to write a message."

Prescott.—" Shall I, alas, put forth this simple thing ? The watchman prays the thief to hold awhile—till he writes a message to justify the thief ! "

Buchanan.—" Sir ! "

Prescott.—" Sir ! "

Buchanan.—" Who are you, sir ? "

Prescott.—" A man, a citizen of America. I am one of the firm that has employed you as our watchman. Before we employed you, you made solemn oath you would take care of our common property, and we look to you to fulfil your obligation. You have no right, sir, to barter off the nation's things to any section, and yet your inaction is the doing of it. Therefore, to suffer it to be so, is to violate the trust we gave you—to violate your oath ! "

Buchanan.—" This is abuse. You take advantage of your privilege to enter here. But, sir, I shall not be ruled by any party. I go by the Constitution."

Prescott.—" If this is abuse, sir, you have it in a milder form than you will in five years hence. I am only one, but you are doing wrong to millions. You are plunging the country into war, and, if it once begins, hundreds of thousands will be butchered by your impotent criminality. Say not that you know not how to avert this dread calamity; for General Jackson showed you. Say not that you have no one to help you; for you can make your own Cabinet. Say not that you lack in money; when you put thieves to watch over it."

Buchanan.—" Would to God that you were President ! "

Prescott.—" In faith, if I was not that, I would, at least, be master of myself ! "

Buchanan.—" You would find that there were two powerful parties pulling at you, and that a great Constitution was stuck under your nose wherever you turned."

Prescott.—" Why, sir, the nation never reads the Constitution. It has the sense to tell what justice is, and it has feeling to tell what dismemberment would lead to. It is the bond of party, and the technicalities of law that have confounded you."

Buchanan.—" Indeed, you almost convince me; almost am I resolved to join the cause of bloody carnage."

Prescott.—" You have no chance. You are here to do the country's will, and we look to you to do it."

Buchanan.—" And I will. In fact, I was right with Scott. Go, tell him I will reinforce the forts at once; a ship shall be despatched to provision our soldiers there. Oh, our poor soldiers ! "

When he said this, Prescott seized his hands, and wished him many blessings, on which he took his departure. " Now this is the last time," said the President to himself, " the last time I will change my resolutions. I will be as firm as the everlasting hills."

I saw that his cravat was not on straight, and I turned him round a little, and fixed it for him. Just then Davis came in, but Buchanan kept on talking; not seeing the former.

" I will not move one jot from this, though the heavens fall. The bloody hand of Mars shall threat and cower these fire-eating Southern bloods, till they trembling pray me mercy. I will so engulf them round with soldiers and large cannon, that even a breath of wind will tame them. Then shall come my message, and Bishop Hopkins' sermon, like a clap of thunder——. Ah, Mr. Davis ! " And he saw Davis, the latter smiling at him.

Davis.—" Why, sir, what humor's this ? "

Buchanan.—" Ah, indeed, what humor is it ? "

Davis.—" To reinforce the forts ? "

Buchanan.—" I must; the curses of the country are on my head."

Davis.—" Why, now, indeed, you much mistake the country. To reinforce the forts, is to arouse every manly feeling in the South. It is to threaten with a straw that they may laugh to scorn such mockery in us. They are the 'embryo of a great nation, called into being by these woful threats from an unmannered and impotent people. They may be led or pacified; but driven, never! No, never! Reinforce the forts, and you, sir, ruin this great republic."

Buchanan.—"Woe, woe is me! The curse is on my head! Take me to my chamber. Send for Bishop Hopkins, ay, and Wigfall. Excuse me, gentlemen, I can bear no more."

Thus saying, he went out, having appointed a time for me to call and write his message.

"Poor old man!" said Davis, "he takes these things entirely too serious for any good. I'd lay a wager of fifty niggers at a slap there will be no secession, no war, nor no trouble of any kind."

I remembered that he had told Judge Francis that there would be secession, war or not; and that it was his determination to keep the thing a little quiet, till they had the cards shuffled. But I betrayed nothing, merely adding that I knew of no grievance nor any damage, either of principle or property, that any State had suffered, and that I could not believe men were so far forgetful of their country as to seek its destruction.

"Of course not," said he, "it is the merest balderdash, smoke, folly. But what hint did he drop about the message?"

"Oh, many, many" said I, and I told him how the President had been pulled about by the two parties.

"Good! good!" said he. "I hope they'll keep him at it; 'tis all we want."

Before he spoke more, Madame Ponchard passed through the hall, and he addressed her, and they walked off together. Now I was alone. I had attended a Cabinet meeting, and it was no meeting at all. More than ever was I forced to reconsider what the Duke of New Castle told the Prince of Wales—we had no government at all. Every Cabinet member came and left, as did any body else, and Buchanan was only tormented thereby. I threw myself into an easy chair to contemplate the apparent coming horrors of my country, and the real weakness of our government. How much we need a man of firmness for such an office as President, and how little do the people weigh his qualifications while he is a candidate. If he be indeed the chieftain put forth by some ignominious convention—the people

vote him in. But how could it be otherwise? Great men, that are well known, can never be President here. They would not put the convention into foreign missions, and fat jobs—and so, the convention will not nominate them. It seemed evident to me also, that if there be secession and war, it was not about slavery, more than it was about the spoils of office. I was familiar with the corruption of the privileged class in England, where a single landlord can interdict the privileges of a railroad company, and menace a whole county into his whims; and this disgusted me more than the other. But as for France and Germany, I had only the spectacle of Government living wholly on the extent of its robbery of the people's rights. With all these horrors before me, I still acknowledged in my heart one great advantage in our own government; that was, that a fool or a villain could only serve four years. But while I thus pondered over the affairs of State, I had taken from the table before me a copy of the Constitution, and the decisions of the Supreme Court, a fact, no doubt, that accounted for the nature of Buchanan's mind. On the margin of a leaf was the following curious poetry:

"Oh, so long and dreary pass the hours,
    When my Peggy's gone!
Oh, so cold and cruel seem these flowers,
    When my Peggy's gone!
I have a love so gay and fair,
    A love, an angel full of the glee
That charms the heart of an old man;
    A love, that maketh so merrily,
    What otherwise would not be."

The next verse explained it all:

"Long have I waited, O my fair one,
    Long have I stormed the batt'e,
Almost faltering, almost fainting,
    But you have come with your pretty prattle,
    To tease and to tussle,
    And now am I happy in glory,
    Happy in glory, happy Victoria!"

No doubt could be raised as to the author of the letter, and I knew also that it had been just written; for the Judge had occupied that seat when I entered the mansion. Hastily I tore off the scrap and pocketed it, intending it for further examination before our private court, which was to meet that very night. I then left, passing down the avenue. In a little while, I fell in with young Wadsworth, my expected rival, who greeted me with much cordiality and friendship, bidding me come and see an object of commiseration near by. He took my arm, and we passed down toward the Treasury, where we approached a man, indeed an object of pity. He was sitting on the grass, leaning over on one elbow, dusty, threadbare, and apparently wearied; his hat far down on his eyebrows.

We asked him if we could do anything for him, and what his misfortune was? He slowly looked upward, and I recognized him at once as Professor Jackson. "Alas, alas!" he said, "I do need pity. I am an object of commiseration. This, indeed, proves woman's greatness. She picked me up and married me in a day; but I am no more in control of her affairs than a thumb paper. She sets me down on a corner, or lugs me all day through different streets, and, moreover, since I find her out, she is quite old and ugly. Alas, alas! I have dreamed for many years of many maids, and now have I been snapped up by one whose face reminds me more of an abandoned tan-yard, than a woman. And yet, why do I grieve? Is this not the cause and effect—that our two genial natures ran together like water? Our money went the same way—all into one purse—and that purse is hers. She has my hard-earned hundred and sixteen dollars. Alas, the day!"

Even while he spake, his wife came upon him, hearing his last words, "Alas, the day!" and then she spake:

"Professor Jackson! you are indeed a perfect Sancho Panza. That famous squire was ever discouraged; ever fearful that the glorious promises of his master would never be realized. So is it with you; not that I am your master, for I only hope to stand on equal grounds with all men; but you, you cannot estimate what we have already achieved. If we were overcome at the market-place, did we not vanquish the same opponent in crowding him out of the stage? Then, too, shall we not to-morrow, at the procession, make the most decided victory for woman's rights that has been since the days of Lycurgus? Only a little while more, too, and the 'Journal of Progress' will be out, which will of itself strike terror to the heart of all oppressors. The down-trodden slaves of the country shall have their liberty; and the bondage of woman will be torn asunder."

When she began to talk, Jackson rose up, but still held down his head.

"I will tell you," says he, "as for vanquishing the Judge by crowding him out of the stage, my opinion is, we have been vanquished ourselves by that rascally driver. My eyes are so filled with dust, I scarce can see, and I am almost overcome with the heat. And for the 'Journal of Progress,' I know I am in a hundred and sixteen dollars, else I would go take a bath, and get a good dinner."

"Professor Jackson! Is that so? Now am I much mistaken, indeed! You told me you had been lecturing on woman's rights for seven years; and now, when we are near the pinnacle of fame, you needs must grumble for a dinner! I never eat but one meal a day, and that consists only of bread and water, at four o'clock in the morning. And this is itself a great triumph; it shows the ascension of mind over matter; it is the genius to which all men must knuckle. Only be patient, and you will have cause yet to be proud of your wife. Methinks, when I see these doll-faced women, that men chuck under the chin, and call pretty and sweet; what a work is yet before us! When man can behold the eagle-like vigilance of the woman of intellect, and love her for that, instead of for the face she wears, or for the idle love-talk she twaddles over, then can we glory in our cause. Man shall be taught to bow and smile to knowledge, without regard to the form and features, and woman, too, shall learn that a pretty face and gentle voice are but silly items in that greater day. But, sir, we have work to do; there are sufferers, whose wrongs are crying out to us, and we must not tarry here. There is a law in this land that taxes women, ay, widow women, women of wealth, and yet deprives them of voting. Shall we idly stand while these women suffer?"

He assured her over and over that she was right, and that hereafter he would complain no more till their great mission was accomplished.

As soon as they went away, we resolved ourselves into a committee to decide how nearly they resembled Don Quixote and Sancho Panza, and we found them to be nearly identical; so much so that it would be impossible to write down their adventures, without the writer being censured for playing a caricature on those illustrious personages. My friend Wadsworth told me also that this was an excellent illustration of the nature of the human mind. "When it pursues one thread of philosophy," said he, "it invariably results in monomania. This poor woman has harped so much on woman's rights, that she feels and sees nothing else, giving all her energies to carry out a mere phantasy; neither does she suppose for a moment that she is deluded. She imagines she can turn the tides of man's imagination, and make him love and idolize females of her appearance. She has not the face nor voice to gain admiration and love, and, frantic with slight, she blows her horn, to call man's attention to the attributes she does possess. I do really pity such a woman."

"But how is it," said I, "that such a man as Jackson, who is not devoid of knowledge, falls in with her and seems to appreciate her?"

"For two reasons," said Wadsworth: "Firstly, nature never afflicts with a malady, but she has also provided a remedy. You shall see; he will soon become displeased with her, and his displeasure will either drive her into such madness as will be her death, or she will behold the folly of her conduct, and so abandon it. Secondly, there is no one else for either of them to love; what he lacks in manliness, she has; and what she lacks in modesty and backwardness, he has, for he needs a leader; and so, too, are such people the end of the propagation of the species. They are the line where nature has set her everlasting seal. They feel this, and hence their wail and cry of anguish. They feel that they are a separate race, and hence their jealousy of rights and privileges."

I told him I coincided with his views, but ere I had time to say more, he interrupted:

"But, as I was going to add, this monomania is but a small part of that with which the whole human family is afflicted. What more is an Abolitionist? What else is a politician? They are all Don Quixotes. They harp on a certain topic, till they want to bring all the world over to their side. They take up their cudgels at the sight of every windmill. Why should the North meddle with the South? Or the South disturb herself about Lincoln? Lincoln could not harm the South if he were elected, even if he tried. And yet hereon are topics sufficient to drive a nation to war; to destroy a million men. This is all a monomania; a madness. It is the folly of man; he will not control the reason he has. And this is a weakness with which all men are afflicted; it extends from the highest to the lowest of the human race. Man cannot control himself. Of all animals, he is the weakest in this. God has given him reason, and it is an engine that runs away with him. Only one man in all the world is sane, and he it is who can govern himself; but who will find him?"

Now, when I beheld that my friend was inclined to reason, I felt that the strength of soul within me, which mostly lies slumbering in all men, received a new impulse of vigor; for it is good, amidst all humor, that the chords of sympathy are sometimes touched by seriousness. I replied:

"How can such a man be? Man loves that thing most which is most in his mind. He who has not travelled, values his house greater than a king's palace; and his neighbors, he estimates, are above all others. His house and his neighbors are his scales, wherein he weighs all things. So is it of sections and of nations. The North and the South have learned that their scales do not agree; but who shall say which is right? Let them exchange their abodes, and the light of humanity will be upon them. Glory be to him who has travelled, for his fetters are off, and he sees with a new vision. Wherefore is the prejudice of religion? and who shall say which is right, save Him who knoweth them all? Neither can any man say he is a philosopher, or a poet; for time, and the judgment of others prove all things."

Then he asked me how it was possible for man to be happy, and I answered:

"Only by doing all that he has power to do. He must work hard all the days of his life and do all the good he can; but most of all his essentials, it is required of him that he be not himself, and that he be himself also; for when he sees his fellows, he must forget himself in the sympathy he owes them; but when he sees the rain fall, he must remember himself in the law he cannot govern, rejoicing in the things he knows, and in the things he knows not of. When his house is on fire, he shall not grieve, remembering that not a hair of his own head was burned. When his wife is sick, he shall remember that he has willing hands and a good understanding; and he shall thank God that he has used them rightly, whereby he is enabled to alleviate her suffering. When he reads a tiresome book, he shall go to sleep; but when his boots pinch his feet, he shall sell them, for they are not worth a curse; neither shall he curse anything under the sun, for all things are of some good. When he writes a book, he shall not write to please others, but to inform them, and to please himself; for his vanity, as well as his stomach, loves a glorious feast—or no temptation. All these things he shall do, and as many more as there are stars in heaven, else he cannot be happy."

So, when I ceased speaking, he said I was more comfort to him than was any other man he ever met. He said he could almost be happy, were he always with such a man.

"I have a great plantation," said he, "in fact, I scarcely know how much I am worth; so vast are my possessions. But you have drawn a black mark across it all. You have, in a few sentences, shown me the vanity of all earthly treasures, and you have held up to my vision that priceless boon in the human soul, which can carry man over all the ills of life triumphant. Long have I been oppressed. I have neither mother nor father, sister nor brother. I have had not one to love. My heart is famished and broken. My grief has become the bulk of my observance ; I need to have it chased away. Herein is the superiority of wisdom over riches ; for the latter cannot comfort me. Now I pray you that you speak more, and that you teach me to forget my sorrows." Said I, " No, this thing could not be ; to stand and talk would not do." Then I told him if he had no objection, I would compare him to a lunatic ; and I told him it has been proved, by facts, that lunatics, put together, cure each other. The philosophy is, that the constant diversion of the mind, is its greatest strengthening power ; that in life, as in a book, constant changing scenery is the style to which all men pay homage. With that I took his arm, and we started down the avenue, but scarcely started, ere we beheld approaching Victoria Edge and Ann Underhill. They were clothed in the richest attire man could invent ; and their jewels were without number, blazing in the evening sun, so that we could scarcely behold their smiling faces. Two such gems of beauty never flattered man before : two such queens as auburn Ann, and rosy-cheeked Vickey. The latter swung in one hand a huge bouquet of flowers, and with the other managed her clouds of drapery, that her satin gaiters were seen to pat most saucily on the stones beneath her as she moved along. But Ann no fixture had ; a changing scene of mirth and good-humor, playfully hiding that deeply seated soul of sympathy, whereon but to gaze, is paradise to man. Only one thing seemed wrong—for Vickey to have so huge a bouquet, with nearly all the flowers scarlet. There could be no doubt in my mind who gave her the flowers ; I had seen the Judge with the same.

Now when two persons meet, they must turn aside a little, otherwise they cannot pass. So also, when two people meet two others, there are two pairs face to face. In this condition my friend Wadsworth came up to Vickey, and I to Ann ; and every one of us seemed reluctant to turn aside. Vickey said, " Behold the twin Apollos !" and Ann quickly added, " versus grace and beauty."

" Why not ?" said Wadsworth, " why not take upon ourselves that which the ancients did ; each one claiming to be some figurative character, so that, in after ages, visitors to Washington may say, ' here indeed, they were ?' Let this avenue be the loitering place ; let the Jackson House be the mansion, at the windows of which we sigh for the fair ones within. Then we have your uncle, who shall be a grave and jealous protector, and you shall at times steal from under his care, and we shall attempt to fly with you, but become thwarted in our endeavors."

" Now I do think that would be delightful !" said Ann, " only you might never be thwarted. We might be forever carried off, and our acknowledged protector might become despondent, and die of a broken heart. We, too, might hear of his misfortune, and we might grieve so much as to make you miserable ever after : to think that our protector had taken us in infancy, shielded us from all harm, and that he had taught us to love him in spite of all his oddities. It is a subject too sacred to jest upon."

Although she smiled, yet I had never heard her speak so seriously before, and I was thrown off my guard ; for I thought she intended it as a hint to both of us. On relating this afterwards in our court, to the Judge, he said of her : " An excellent girl, as I am a judge, she has no superior on the face of the globe."

I never gave him any definite answer as to the replies that we made, or the conversation that followed. Now, although we paired off with the ladies, I endeavored to persuade Miss Underhill to walk faster, so that Wadsworth and Vickey could the better converse with each other ; yet I discovered that my persuasion was entirely ineffectual. Perhaps Miss Underhill liked to hear the sound of his voice.

We were, though, presently diverted by the most mortifying news ever given to the country. Newsboys were running up and down the streets, shouting out that Floyd and Thompson had robbed the National Treasury ; and I am sure that there was no man, North or South, of all the thirty millions, but felt ashamed. Even the agitators of secession were horrified, beyond expression, to learn that two of their important leaders must ever stand the brand of thieves. Cobb, Floyd, and Thompson were the perpetrators ; yet they walked the streets as usual, and not an officer interrupted them.

Nor was this the end of the shame. Wherever we looked, wherever we walked, these boasters of ruin, these worthless politicians thronged the Capital, to spit their virus in the face of good-natured, honest people. You could not walk alone, nor could you accompany a lady in the streets but profane oaths saluted your ears and these from the men that would presume to destroy a nation, and found another. And thus it was with us; we longed to leave the street.

CHAPTER VI.

Before going further, I told Jenkins it was essential that he should inform me distinctly whether he married Ann Underhill or not. He then said that he had been telling me as fast as it was possible for a matter of this kind to be related, and to do it in a systematic way. He then went into some further explanations as to the secret of relating a serious incident that had a very important connection with the future misfortunes that befell Ann Underhill and thereupon told me to proceed as follows:

When it was nearly night, I promised to call upon the President, whom I did really pity, on account of his having been nearly deserted by everybody. I had also to complete arrangements for the reception of the Prince of Wales. But yet another more important matter, though yet unknown to me, was to be accomplished that night, and which was to throw everything I had ever done into the shade. And this it was:

On my way down to the Jackson House, I was touched cautiously and quickly on the shoulder, and, on looking around, I beheld Prescott; he was motioning silence, even while he urged me to follow him. When we had withdrawn a little, he asked me to come to the Capitol grounds, where no ear could hear, and he would there unfold the greatest secret plot ever formed by man. "I cannot trust myself," he said, "lest the very air I breathe inform other men." He was pale, excited, and in earnest. Indeed, jest and folly no more mingled in the bombast of politicians. The thunder seemed as if beginning to move the whole earth. Prescott took my arm, and his very touch was unlike it had ever been before. Others passed us, and they too had felt the approaching storm; even like wild men, and fierce with fear and firmness, all coldly gazed one on another. Even so short a while before one could not walk the streets but he heard the oaths and political harangue of Southern fire-eaters; but now, no more noise was there. This it was gave it meaning; that put the seal of certainty on it.

"Believe what I say; question nothing," said Prescott, as soon as we had seated ourselves in a lonely part of the Capitol grounds. "We may be heard, and if so, it is our death. In the basement of the Capitol, where the statues are, I discovered the plot. See! listen! I had loitered there, beneath the caskets' base, in view of Commerce, the while in pensive mood, when rumbling voices caught my ear. I looked; 'twas Rhett, Davis, Cobb, Floyd, Thompson, and others I could not see. So strange to see them there, I dodged my head below the rim, and waited. Soon they were beside me; and there they formed the solemn league, pledging all, soul and body, to God, for the performance. Some parts I caught, and some I lost; a woman's voice I heard, but I dared not move. They do suspect Lincoln's election, and thus provide: All their doings to be in secret; no man admitted, but those known beyond a doubt. That the whole rôle is to be played before the 1st of March; that every office North and South shall be at once brought under their control. They then resolved to meet to-night, to specify their modes of action, and due appointments mark out. When they had concluded, and decided where to meet, I feared for my safety, lest they should discover me. They were then moving on toward me; no more than half a dozen yards distant. I sprang to my feet, and ran toward the lower end to escape at the eastern entrance. They were amazed at first, but soon gave chase. The door was locked, and I could not escape. For a moment I was panic-stricken; the flash of knives was in the darkness, and earnest whisperings rushing forth. Close in the corner I backed, and outward fell a prop, where the workmen had placed it for the night. With a goodly spring, I leaped over the side trench, and made my escape. At once I went and told Scott, and he told others. It is now urged on me to play the spy; to attend their meetings, and there discover more. I am myself so small a man, and not having much strength, I am afraid to do it."

"My dear sir," said I, "I will go with you. We will assume a good disguise. You shall be Governor Wise's son, and I will be Houston's adopted boy." I thus told him how it had been with me when I beheld Floyd and Thompson at the Treasury; also telling him that both Scott and Cass had advised me to keep it secret.

We were not long in arranging our plans of dress and mode of speaking, both of us having been reporters for a long time, were as familiar with the style of language of other folks, as if we knew none of our own. Accordingly, we started for our separate places of residence, to adjust our clothing; but when we came out of the Capitol grounds, near the gateway, we beheld that ever hideous-faced Yancey. Like a sentinel, he seemed, as if watching the face of every man that passed. Prescott tightly gripped my arm, but I, to divert the distended ears of him who followed us, chattered and laughed freely about ladies' hoops and length of trail. In a little while we succeeded; Yancey fell back and retired near the gate once more. It was evident now that the man they had seen in the basement of the Capitol was to be killed, if they could find him. Their very first compact in secret formed was thus discovered, and it will be seen hereafter that every one of them now believed a Judas was amongst their number, and that he had induced Prescott to station himself in the aforesaid place. Suspicion fell heaviest, of course, on Toombs, Cobb, Floyd and Yancey, and so great were the others' convictions, that it was resolved none of these four should ever hold any position of trust in the contemplated rebellion.[*]

I cannot say I was fearless in our projected spy business, for I knew every Southerner would be armed, and that death would surely follow the discovery of us amongst them. And yet, my risk was nothing compared to Prescott's. One thing that made it more dangerous, was the place of meeting; which was, the garret-floor, or dissecting room in the old medical college. They would not trust themselves to meet at either of their private residences, lest the women ascertain their business, and so betray them. In the above place, however, they knew no

woman would enter. They therefore called on the old negro janitor, and told him they were doctors; that they had a body to dissect, and that it would occupy several evenings. They told him also, that the corpse was of a well-known person, and that it must be with the greatest secrecy; that he died with a strange and very dangerous disease; that he himself must not venture near the dissecting room until they were through. They told him they were so much afraid that somebody would get the same disease, that he had better give them the keys of the two upper floors, while he guarded the lower ones himself. So much they frightened him, that he said, although he had carried many bodies up-stairs, he would not carry this one up. They told him, however, that they had a man hired to do it. Then they told him what a vast number of doctors had assembled to witness the dissection, but that they had decided only to admit such as had tickets; a rule he was himself to strictly carry out : showing him a three-cornered blank paper. All of this, however, neither Prescott nor I knew of. Accordingly, although we were disguised very well, when we applied at the college, we were confronted by the negro. He wanted to see our tickets. He told us the doctors were doing something up there, and nobody else must come in, except they had tickets. Prescott asked him where the ticket office was ? "Don't know !" said he, "s'pose on the back of this ; one of the doctors dropped his and I picked it up and saved it for him." He then showed the little three-cornered paper ; it had been cut from some scribbled piece of paper. Prescott detected at once it was the shape that made it all right, and he told the negro that he could tell by the back where the office was, and that we would go and get tickets at once. We then withdrew, it being nearly nine o'clock, fearing we should not get in that night ; but we dreaded more than anything else, that during the present evening some rules and signs would be adopted which would forever after exclude us. Now was our time, before it had taken full form, to get in. In a few moments we prepared our tickets and went in. But what was our astonishment, when applying at the third story door, to be confronted by another sentinel, who demanded, " Who sent you here ?" We knew not what answer to give ; for we saw that our answer would betray us. Yet we knew from the manner he spoke the sentence, it was a hailing sign of a secret order, and that he was new in his office. Prescott thought a

_____

[*] History has since proved that this was true. They were so false that even false men would not trust them.

moment, hesitating, but replied, "I have forgotten the right answer, but I know I was sent by Ex-Governor Wise, whose son I am." "Oh, all right! Is this man all right?" Prescott told him that I was Jim Houston, adopted son of the Governor of that same name. "Go on up," said he, "but remember the answer next time; you should have said, 'I came to dissect the body.'" "Oh, yes!" said Prescott. Thus we passed to the fourth floor, where were two sentinels within hearing of each other. It is needless to say, our hair was on end. We were desperate. The first sentinel said, "What is to be done in the college to-night?" His pronunciation showed us it was also a sign. Should we speak, or should we wave a hand? We knew not. We trembled from head to foot. One thing alone could save us, and that was to presume on the sentinel being new in office.

Prescott said—for he remembered he was to imitate a Southerner—"Damn me if I remember; we had the three-cornered tickets: and then the next was, 'Who sent you here?' 'I came to dissect the body.' And then comes, 'What's to be done in the college to-night?' D—d if I remember; but I know I am ex-Governor Wise's son, and that this fellow is Jim Houston, and that we don't care a cursed damn about these signs and answers, but we came here to play the devil with the infernal d—d Black Republicans."

"You can go up," said the sentinel, laughing, shaking us both by the hands, at the same time telling the sentinel above to let us up—that he could vouch for us. "But remember the answer," said he, "the next time you come; you should have said, 'That body must be buried so that no trace of it will remain in the memory of man.' The next question is, 'Will you be coming down soon?' Your answer is, 'Not till I have so provided against its disease, that no other will ever die of the same, I hope.'" *

"I told you," said Prescott to me, "you and I could never learn that d—d lingo."

"I do know it," said I; "you have not given me a chance," and I also put on an oath. Again the sentinels laughed, and we thanked them. Half a minute more, and we were in the dimly-lighted hall. Oh, what a blessing this was to us!—a few little untrimmed candles only. Eighteen persons were in the room; we made twenty. Three more came in afterward. The meeting was organized; Toombs

* These were the correct questions and answers of the then secret order which organized the rebellion.

in the chair; Davis was speaking; the others were seated on the dissecting tables. Davis dwelt at some length on the impossibility of ever harmonizing the antagonistic principles of the North and South, until one should overcome the other. He said a protective tariff would build up the free States; every city and village in the North would ultimately become a place of manufacture, and consequently of capital. But, on the other hand, free trade alone could develop the wealth of the slave States. Next he referred to the stigma of slavery. He said that we (the slave-owners) were to blame for that. Power and might make right amongst nations. When Great Britain was the most powerful nation, she took from the weaker powers what she wanted, then made a law for it. We can now do what she used to do. We only need put our hands forth, and the thing is done. All the important offices of the United States are ours. The navy is ours, and so is the army. The money is ours, and the best men of the country are ours. Now let us see," he continued, "for we take it for granted Lincoln will be elected; we have four months to accomplish this in. We demand, that, as he is illegally elected, in consequence of being sectional, the constitutional obligations of the States are violated. Therefore some other man must fill the chair; and the present incumbent of that and other offices can decide that, above the vote of the electoral college. I will suppose, for instance," said he, "that within a month we decide upon officers to fill the coming vacant seats. On the 15th of February they are all installed; everything warranting power throughout the whole country is given into their charge. What folly, I would ask, would it be for Lincoln to come here half a month afterward to claim the office of President! You may suppose, however, we shall meet with opposition, feeble though it be; yet that very opposition shall be turned to our advantage; for it furnishes us with a treaty power with each State in which a revision of the Constitution will follow, guaranteeing our rights to slavery throughout the whole country, and forever after apportioning the number of representatives in Congress exactly equal between the slave and free States. We can even demand a revision of the suffrage law, limiting the voters in each State to persons of some considerable income. This will give us a respectable governing class, without the evils of monarchy; and it will silence forever the harangue of un-principled politicians."

When he ceased talking, there were several others tried to get the floor, each one only asking the privilege to suggest one word. Floyd succeeded, however, in making the next speech. He recommend-ed that we pursue a strict line of justice according to the Constitution ; that we ever hold in reverence the high moral character of our Revolutionary fathers.

Slidell spoke next. He understood the thing very differently ; he thought the Southern people of a better stock than the Northerners, and he proposed, ac-cordingly, that the Southern or slave States withdraw from the Union.

Hardly had he said this, when up jump-ed a dozen others, denouncing such a sug-gestion as altogether at variance with their designs. This confusion brought up the chair—Toombs—who decided against any new projects. He said : "We have formed ourselves into a nucleus for a new govern-ment on a new principle for the United States of America. Every member ad-mitted here is sworn to that. We will not tolerate any dissent. Whoever speaks on this floor, must understand that any variance from our purpose is at his peril. Speakers must confine themselves to the fact, that we, ourselves, are the beginning, the preliminary government spoken of, and that the object of our meeting is to determine the manner of effectually estab-lishing the new government."

"That's the talk !" "That's the talk !" shouted a number of others as soon as Toombs took his seat ; and immediately after Cobb presented the following well-known resolutions :

"That companies of minute-men be formed and drilled, to the extent of one hundred thousand men, apportioned in different Southern States according to population.

"That, to carry out this organization, a secret embassy be sent to every State.

"That such embassy be empowered to form branches to this government.

"That it shall be in the power of this government to call from said minute-men twenty thousand, equipped for war, to the city of Washington, to be used for any pur-pose the president and secretary may direct.

"That, as fast as branches to this gov-ernment are formed, they shall send and maintain one member in the general body."

These were adopted by acclamation ; but it was afterward decided that the written signature of every one present should be attached ; and that copies of the resolutions should be furnished to the travelling embassy. As soon as this de-cision was made, Prescott and I began to tremble for our safety ; for we were not certain but some of the men present knew Wise's son and Jim Houston. Besides that, we would be forgers of these men's names. In a few minutes the paper was ready, and three or four of the obscure candles were brought near the desk, or rather dissecting table, and quite a light thrown on each signer's face. Toombs signed it first, saying at the same time, that this was the greatest thing ever done by man ; that he would have even sold his life for the privilege of putting the first signature.

Then came Davis, remarking that he was still watching over the dying body of a great man, but that he christened this infant government with his signature with the greatest happiness ever known to any one on earth. He felt that he was indeed making a covenant with the Al-mighty God. After him came Cobb, Floyd, and others, every one of whom made some remarks. Not one was signing in silence. Should we make a speech ?—walk up before all these men and say noth-ing ? Why, they would suspect us at once. Then, too, Prescott stuttered a little when excited, and many men knew him by that. These fears came upon us with much force ; and as we leaned together, rapidly coun-selling on it, Prescott said he had a notion to make believe he had a fit, and so get carried out by me. I told him his whis-kers and wig might come off ; that we had better come out and blow on the whole concern. He said they could kill us and sell us to the doctors, and no one would ever know it ; that was the reason they had chosen this place. He told me to look at the door ; and there, behold, with sword drawn, stood that mysterious Orsini ! We next observed that nearly every one had on side arms.

Now it takes some time for twenty-three men to sign a paper, especially if each one makes a few remarks beforehand ; and yet the time on this occasion flew faster than ever before. Already were different ones looking at us, seeming not to know us. We were almost desperate. We went for-ward. Oh, if Prescott should stutter ! All eyes were on us. Prescott took the pen, saying, "Though the father set the seal, the son with maddened heart puts down the signature." He signed ; and when they beheld his name, they shouted loudly, "Good on John Brown !" Toombs remarked, "I am indeed so happy to see you ! How you have changed ! I'd never have known you."

Now I came, and I said, "May my god-father rejoice; for his son is at the zenith!" In a moment more I was hailed on all sides: "How are you, Jim?" "Why, what's the matter?" "What's come of your big belly?" Of course, I said but little, laughed heartily, and cautioned them to heed the grand object of the meeting. Now, while I talked thus, Floyd looked at me, and I thought he knew me. I put one hand in my pocket, as indifferently as possible, and seized a huge knife which I had provided, in case of emergency, and I fully resolved, if he said aught, to strike it to his heart, and shout out "Traitor!" and in the melee make good my escape. But he did not; he gradually ceased, and became absorbed in the affairs of the meeting, and more especially in giving in a report of his affairs with the defunct republic. "I have to report," said he, "the transfer of one hundred and fifteen thousand guns to Southern forts in order. Of the sale of forty thousand muskets, at two dollars each, to two depositories South. These muskets were of approved patterns, and cost the late United States Government twelve dollars each. There are still at my disposal twelve hundred cannon, besides a number of other heavy ordnance, and I ask you all what I shall do with them?"

In less than five minutes it was resolved to place them at the service of the minute-men. This was the chief of all that was said or done during our stay, but occupied us until after one o'clock in the morning. Prescott and I knew that when the meeting broke up there would many come to us to engage us in a good greeting, and accordingly we resolved that at the first opportunity we would make our exit. Just before closing, Toombs called attention to the necessity of guarding against traitors. He said that every man should be vigilant, and, if he had any suspicion or imputation to any one present, he should out with it at once. That there had been an occurrence at the Capitol which made it essential to look out sharply. He would also state, without any suspicion or imputation to any one present, that there might be a Judas amongst us, and that that Judas might provide for our entire capture at the next meeting. He proposed, therefore, that the time and place of the next meeting be not made known more than an hour beforehand, and that it be made known by members calling for each other; and that, when a person is called for and can-

not go, he shall not be told where the meeting is; neither shall the person so calling go to the meeting himself, lest he be followed. This would make it positively select and safe. And so his suggestions were endorsed, and he and Davis were appointed to make out the time and place. Toombs then urged every member to subscribe his address; and this, too, was endorsed. The members now went forward and put them down. Says I to Prescott, "We'll put ours down, Thirty-seven J street—that large boarding-house." "Agreed," said he, in a whisper. It did not occur to us that the proprietor of that house might be present. I wrote the names myself. "Why, are you at my house?" said a rough voice beside us. "Certainly," said I. "Why, when did you come?" said he. I answered, "This evening." "Not before I came here," said he; "and I came here since you!" Prescott and I felt that our time was near an end. I almost choked as I replied, "That four-story brick—do you keep that house?" "Which?—oh! ah! are you there? That is Twenty-seven. Ha! ha! ha! Why, do you know what kind of house that is?" "Bah!" said I, and Prescott and I were drawing toward the exit. All eyes were turned on us, and some whispering began amongst the members. Cobb shouted out, "Who brought those men here? How do you know they have signed our compact? Who knows them? Are they traitors?" The word traitor rang all over the house. "Traitors! Traitors!" Toombs called out "Order!" but all was instant confusion. Orsini stepped aside to see some sign from either Floyd or Davis. We started quickly outward, and in a twinkle Orsini's sword flashed. I dodged, and the blade shaved my crown, cutting quite through my hat. Prescott was ahead. We cleared the sentinels at a bound, one of whom snatched at my coat-skirt. Pell-mell they came; the stairs and halls all dark. Quicker than the breath of a frightened dove we were in the street. And our pursuers were locked in the college. The old negro had been asleep in the hall, and when we ran over him he woke and sprang to the door, shutting himself inside, thinking that robbers were about to break into the college.

Thus abruptly Jenkins ends this chapter; but he says there is more of the story further on.

4

CHAPTER VII.

By way of beginning where the last chapter ended, Jenkins says that he and Prescott wended their way to their homes about as fast as could be reasonably expected of them. He then adds:

I was as much puzzled what to do with our information as I was frightened about our personal safety. Our Government was so rotten at this time that there was no one with whom we could trust our secret. Scott and Cass were true to the national Government, but their power was little. Seward, Lovejoy, and others were true, but they had no more power and influence over national affairs than they had over the sun.

Now, when I returned to my room and reasoned on the approaching crisis; when I beheld how entirely one-sided seemed all the wealth and influence of the country; when I remembered how surely the Democratic party of the North would take sides with the slave party of the South, I did really feel that the glory and power of the great republic was about falling forever. If so, what madness would it be for Prescott and myself to tell the things we knew! This, you may be sure, was not a condition to please, nor was it such as would lull me to sleep; and so I rolled and tumbled until I thought it was nearly dawn, when I began to doze; and then, alas! I was aroused by still another dreadful omen.

Voices, strange in that place, yet voices familiar to my well-trained ear, were heard in the hall, and in earnest accents. I knew that they were the voices of Madame Ponchard and Orsini. I knew also that no person had any business in that end of the hall at that hour of the night; and, raising myself cautiously in bed, I listened. I heard her say, "No more! no more! Trust me to do what I say, or in my anger forth shall come the story of the poisoned water."

And then he earnestly whispered, "Why, Madame, by that you became possessed of immense wealth! You would impugn yourself."

"I know my part," said she, "and that you were the murderer."

"But, it was too——" said he; but she cut him short by commanding "Silence!" and the mandate, "Do as I bid!"

This conversation, though almost in whispers, was distinct, yet I had not heard sufficient to gather the thread of their discourse. I then heard a slight rustle outside, but did not hear them depart, though the sounds ceased. I rose, went to the door and looked out, but no one was there; and as my boots (having been placed in the hall in order to have them polished) were still standing there, I could not conceive that the intruders had been there for any purpose of thieving. Again I returned to my bed, but with breathless anxiety. After some moments of uneasiness, I extended my hands outward, and violently rang the bell. In another minute the hotel servants were running to me. I threw open the door, and we all sought to find the said persons, but they were gone. The clerk said somebody ran out of the hotel by way of the ladies' entrance, but we could ascertain no more.

It was now almost morning, but I retired, weary and oppressed, and soon fell asleep. When I awoke it was after sunrise, and I felt considerably refreshed. I remembered now that this was the day of the reception of the Prince of Wales, and that I had many things to do; that I must go with Prescott to see Scott; that I had to re-read to the President his own message; that I wanted to see Ann Underhill and Vickey, and also the Judge. My servant told me the bootmaker had sent home my new boots, and he wanted to know which I would wear. I told him the new ones, and I asked him if the old ones were to be found; and he said, "Yes, I have just polished them." Again I was puzzled about the scene I had heard during the night, but I banished it, for I was resolved to have a good time to-day, whether I was to be killed or not.

Accordingly, I sallied forth, having previously armed myself with a six-inch Colt's revolver and an excellent bowie knife. This was the first day of my life I carried deadly weapons. But the condition of society rendered life as insecure as it is in Christian Italy or Spain. I knew plenty of criminals, but I dared not report them to officers of Government, for they were all in partnership. So, I must need defend myself; and, being withal a man of great physical strength, I felt not at all inclined to avoid a contest, just 'in order that I might see what execution I could do. When I entered the side-room for my breakfast, I ordered the doors opened, for it was quite warm. Right before me, in the ladies' drawing-room, stood Wadsworth and Ann Underhill; she was again at the piano, and he standing by her side. He was certainly in grief for the deplorable prospects of the nation, and she was more serious than common. "Can it be," I said to myself, "she is so fond of him? To all others she is so gay and frolicsome, but before him she is shorn of all the glitter of earthly things. Her accomplishments are gone; her winning speeches are finished, but more gentleness she hath. Oh, what a comment is this on the frivolous show that maidens sigh for! So powerless she droops, when once the genial flame comes o'er her. And he, too; his rhetoric and philosophy, and his foreign travels, are all blotted out. As simple as doves and as harmlessly, do the great and good in tenderness strip themselves to the naked heart; and when once seen, all the world cannot cancel their happiness. They may be crossed and tossed and tried in all ways, but never, never can the sweetness of their joys grow less, or for a moment fade from memory." As I pondered on this, the while beholding the only idol I had ever prayed for, the only one whose happiness I prized as highly as I did my own; and, too, beholding a man that had in so short an acquaintance bound me to him more sacredly than had any other I ever met, I felt that it would matter little whether I was killed in some street affray or not. The darkest of forebodings swept over me. Every way was my ill fortune certain. Not that I would stand in the way of two true lovers. Not that I would kill myself. I would conceal my feelings, or go so far away they would never hear of me, all in order that they might not be unhappy. But whether they do truly love—that was my question, I said to myself, when I was young, reading of love affairs, Why do not lovers ask and answer as they would for a pair of gloves? But I now feel the sacred barrier the Almighty hand has before me. It is a theme on which the tongue cannot come. True love makes us all dumb; it has no explanation. The Great Unseen

moves us as if we were chess-men. If we are stubborn, we fall; but if we go as we are moved, we come to glory. Tears started to my eyes, but I banished them. Why shall we weep? to-day is a festival, to-morrow we die. Shall my death make others grieve? No, 'tis better I live and die a bachelor, for then I am in possession of my whole self, and there is no loss when I am gone.

But while I pondered thus, and thus breakfasted, there came up through the hall Judge Francis. With his fingers clutched round the necks of half a dozen bottles of sparkling Catawba, and his hat set up so trim and gay, he shouted, " Glorious be the day!" and he held up the bottles and winked right merrily. " Once in a while," said he, " the man is bowed down, but ever follows a bright morning's sun, and it has such a face, no thought of grievance enters there. Say, you Mr. Jenkins, some men are happy before they become men, and some are happy about that time, but others do not receive their happiness till the show of silver waves on the wise old head, and then, all the stored-up energies of a long life come rushing in a perfect torrent through his every nerve and fibre. These bottles—you see how dingy they are—I have for five-and-twenty years kept stored away, ever having bound myself that only one thing in all the events of life could induce me to bring them forth. And now, behold, with what pleasurable alacrity I wring their necks!"

I burst out laughing, asking if he was going to marry; and he said,

"What! a man of my age? I would not think of such a thing."

"I thought not," said I; "your gray hairs incline you more to the grave."

"Oh! not that," said he, " for I am yet quite young; so young, indeed, that if there were to be war I venture they would have me on the roll. Do you know, Mr. Jenkins, what a strange thing is love? When I was twelve years old, no higher than to a lady's waist, I always fancied girls of seventeen. Well, when I was twenty-five my fancy went for girls of seventeen also; and now that I am almost a middle-aged man, it still runs on seventeen. Indeed, I think love has more philosophy in it than most men imagine."

When he said this he had come near me, and, looking up, saw his niece and Wadsworth in the parlor, and I thought he was displeased, for he said, " I am sure I care no more about that than you do. But come," and he pulled me after him. When we arrived in the ante-room we met Mr. and Mrs. Edge, to whom he began about his wines. I was anxious to get up to the White House, and took this opportunity to leave them. I met the clerk in the office, and told him to have an eye and ear on the Judge, so he could relate his affairs to me afterward. He told me he would, but he directed me to pass through the verandah and there behold such another scene as I had never dreamed of. I did so. Vickey was weeping, and Prescott, having just left her, was passing down toward the avenue, where the great throng of visitors were wending their way in the most smiling confusion. I stood in this position for a moment, thinking of Vickey weeping, thinking what an eventful day this was to Washington, and thinking of Prescott, now limping on before me. In half a minute more he halted, examined his boot, then returned, still limping. "I have something in my boot," he said, as soon as he drew near, going to the other end of the verandah. I followed near, and saw him seat himself and withdraw his boot. He winced. The thought of a poisoned boot came to mind at once. We then examined the boot, and near the ankle, where the leather is soft, we found injected a small instrument, the size of a pin's point. Could it be this was charged with poison, and meant to be an instrument of death? Certain we were that it was a manufactured instrument. It was pointed at both ends; it looked like type metal. I then told Prescott about the persons I heard in the hall at night. He said he heard nothing of it, but that his boots were also left standing in the hall. Again we entered the hotel, and I rang for my servant, and ordered him to bring my boots. As soon as they were brought, Prescott and I went into the ante-room, and there examined them. Exactly in a similar part of the boot was an instrument identically the same. As we were examining these little weapons, one of them came off at the end, and a bluish water escaped. "Now, I know a man," said Prescott, "can tell us what this is. He is an old man in Mark's drug store, a German, who can tell you the simples and the components of all things. The object of these was, no doubt, to be our death; but my skin, from having been a barefoot boy, requires a stronger machine. Had that point entered the skin, the top would have come off, and this fluid would have entered."

We immediately repaired to the drug store, and sought out the old man referred to. He took it in his hand, then laid it on a watch crystal and readjusted his spectacles. He looked at us with some amazement, saying, "Where did you get it?" We told him the nature of the case made it necessary not to tell at present. "I have not seen one of those in forty years," said he. "They are called King's Capsules. It is an Italian invention, and is an excellent illustration of what degenerate nations busy their brains with. Instead of steam and telegraph, they take to these things." He then inverted another glass over it, stopping the seam with a solution of iron and flowers of sulphur. With a quick motion he jarred the capsule asunder, and the liquid that escaped turned to bright red fumes. "The quarter of that," he continued, "injected in an abrasion of your skin, would produce death in one hour. It is concentrated hydrocyanic acid. You should be given over to the authorities for even having such a thing in your possession." We told him how we found them, and also asked him if there could be any danger of Prescott having been already poisoned; but he said no; that, as it had not entered the skin, nor been broken, he need take no trouble about it. We told him, too, that we had no positive evidence who put them in our boots. We were, of course, somewhat concerned at this attempt at our destruction, and especially so since there was no way of redress. Prescott had been already that morning to advise with Scott about the remarkable meeting we attended the night before; but he had obtained only the same misfortunate suggestion, "No power to do anything. Those in office will do nothing. The President still keeps the Secretary of War in his Cabinet, though he knows he is using the nation's arms for the nation's overthrow." And then Prescott went on. "We can do nothing with them for their resolutions last night. It is a free country. They are free to speak what they will, and they are free to do what they will. Hence there is no treason; but even if there was, there are no officers to try them. So, why shall we grieve or bother our heads about the matter? See these crowds of thoughtless people, flocking here to see the Prince of Wales; how little they dream of the threatening wand waving over them."

Shortly after this we separated, he for his own affairs, and I for the Mansion, where I arrived in a few minutes. The President was waiting for me, and I saw at a glance, as he rose to shake hands, he was pale and fatigued. "Come," said he, after we took our seats at the desk, "you that are gifted in the use of words and the framing of sentences, see what I have penned this morning, in a lonely hour. Perhaps you can set it in a good shape, and give it to the country at large, so they will not torment me with their criticisms for my official conduct."

I took the paper up, and read the following lines, which he said he thought should precede the message:

"O bitter, bitter office of the great,
Why has no hand a star in thee implanted,
Showing the conscience how to steer—to hold
Together all the fragments of a State?
Or is it so, that we are instruments,
And nations perish, sans the will of man,
From the enormity of their own crimes?
Me seems to feel, however squelched this fire
On surface is, spontaneous smoulder lies
Deep sunken in our great republic,
Sooner or late 'twill blow, and burst in wrath
Upon the heads of these incendiaries.
However done: however not begun;
However onced, and by all my acts,
For good or bad, that I do play my part,
Even so by all, and for all time to come
Shall I be cursed by my own countrymen.
I am a target twixt two foolish parties,
Even as if heaven had chosen me for their martyr.
I've struggled hard; my fault is not mine own,
But my country's; they do not understand
The Constitution. All our grief is there,
And there we must seek out the panacea.
For, mark the point, the Constitution is,
And is for. But, if that for be not for,
Which they suppose—these my countrymen,
They are right unright in seeing as they do.
But, when the Constitution is and was,
And is and was for us, while the parties
Both mis-construed it to seem what is not,
Or is not for a purpose, then it follows,
They do not understand it. That's the matter,
So does it follow also I shall write
A message and explain these things to them."

He eyed me for some time, evidently wishing me to say something appreciative of this poetical feat, while I was as anxiously trying to discover some means of withholding it from the public. I had no doubt, however, now about the condition of his mind. But I knew, if I disclosed it to the country at large, it would be a serious misfortune, if not result in the entire destruction of the republic. I told him it was certainly the truth, and but for its arrangement it should be inserted as a preface to his forthcoming message. When I thus encouraged him, he started up: "I tell you," said he, "even yet the country may be saved, if it will hearken to our counsel. I have here a letter from Bishop Hopkins, and here a sermon from Boyden, of Hopedale, Virginia, on the 'Epidemic of the Nineteenth Century; the Sympathy for the Enslaved.' With these and the Constitution the country must stand." I took the productions spoken of, and was about to peruse them, when in came the two reverend gentlemen authors alluded to. Very cordially Buchanan received them, and gave me an introduction. Hopkins at once took up his letter, remarking, "In this will you find all the substance of the dispute; and I have so argued it that I almost persuaded myself black is white. The primeval condition of the black man, the stigma the Creator put upon him when he slew Abel, have I so set down that all parties cannot but see the wisdom of the All-wise Ruler of the universe in giving them over into eternal bondage to the white man. I have shown the glory of God in the elevation of the white man, whose triumphs have been the only contribution to civilization, religion, and liberty. I have here pictured this same white man in his glory and ease, seeking out the degenerate African, and bringing him over here and teaching him to toil, and to behold the beauties of Christianity. I have shown how the black man is to be enlightened; and how, by doing the drudgery of life, he gives the white man time and liberty to ascertain the laws of God. In fact, I have so explained the degradation of labor, that even the men in the free States must acknowledge the blessing of our Divine institution of slavery." And with much pride the reverend father slapped the paper on the desk, and pouted his lips as if the argument was finished.

"Truly has he spoken," said Boyden, "and in the same chain of argument I have here a sermon on the hardships of the owner of the slave. I have shown him, with all the cares of his slaves on his own back, while the slave goes scot free of all concern. The master I have shown with Christian care watching over his slaves, giving his whole life to their service. In fact, I have proved him to be the greater slave of the two; and proved also, that, whoever meddles with his property deserves an ignominious death; and, moreover, that all the hatred against a slave-owner springs from the fact that he can accumulate wealth easier and faster than the man who hires his labor done." And he smiled, as if his triumph must go before the world for all time.

"But have you proved that the poor should be contented with their lot?" said Buchanan. "That too much freedom in this country is what is doing all the mischief? That such ignorant people should not be taught to aspire to liberty till they could understand the Constitution?"

Both the divine gentlemen assured him they had done so, and he seemed much pleased. Soon after this the reverend doctors left us. Buchanan then said he intended to have these sermons both published in every Democratic paper all over the country.* The President then assured me that he felt very much better and stronger than he had for many weeks; and he told me that, since this was the day of the reception, he had concluded to do nothing further about the message at present, signifying that I might leave him. I told him I had important matters to relate to him, bearing upon the condition of the country. "If you please," said I, "we will sit awhile, and you shall hear something terrible." He looked anxiously at me, for he was in a mood to be frightened, and I then related to him all I saw on the previous evening; of the resolutions; the minute-men; the determination to seize the whole Government; and then of our detection and final escape; and of the attempt to poison Prescott and myself. When I finished, I saw he was deathly pale, with large tear-drops in his eyes, and he remarked, "Alas! alas! 'tis done! I am the last that will ever be President of these United States."† He bowed his head on my shoulder and sobbed for a moment, then, raising himself upward, continued: "When I came into office, it was reported that this same party attempted to take my life by poisoning the National Hotel, in order that the whole Government might come into the control of my friend Breckenridge. I never believed it in full till now."

"Then did Providence avert that fell calamity to this nation," said I, "and it now remains, with these warnings before us, that we arm ourselves in time to prevent the nation's overthrow."

"No," said he, "no! No more arming. To arm against these men is but to give them arms. Only one mode can avert the coming storm; we must concede to the slave States their full and honest demands."

This was the substance of all we said about the matter on this occasion, it being high time for me to leave. Accordingly, without much form or ceremony, he having told me that he should not mature

the message until after the election, which was to be in two days hence. I took my departure, carrying orders to the different diplomatic corps about the reception and procession. I then hurried down to the Jackson House, where we were to get positions in the Judge's carriage, as much for the purpose of seeing Mrs. Lucy Tabiatha Stimpkins as for seeing the Prince and Duke. What was my surprise in not finding Wadsworth or Prescott, though we had all talked of going together. The Judge, with new gloves and hat, was promenading on the verandah with Mrs. Edge, talking with more importance than I had ever seen him before. The clerk winked at me, called me aside, and told me this story: "Do you know," said he, "that old fool thinks he is engaged to Miss Edge? And that Miss Edge thinks she is engaged to Prescott? I crammed her," he continued, "that Prescott so understood it, and so did her father and mother." I told the clerk to tell me all about it. "Very well," said he; "I found her in the parlor a little while ago, and asked her when her marriage was to come off. She laughed, and seemed a little surprised. Then, as I said before, I crammed her—told her all the city was on tip-toe about it. She said it was strange, very strange, that she should be engaged and not know it. 'Why,' said I, 'who ever heard tell of a gentleman of high rank speaking plainer than he does? And you have yourself so virtuously answered him, that all the city is alive with your praises.' 'Well,' said she, 'that's not the way I like it, nor is it the way they do in Philadelphia.' 'Why,' said I, 'do you know what Prescott's worth? He is worth half a million.' 'And does he,' said she, 'really call this an engagement?' 'Of course,' said I; 'did he not so express himself to you this morning?' 'Oh, no!' said she; 'he said nothing of love. He talked only of the affairs of the country, and he did so fervently portray the coming downfall, that I wept most bitterly. I never heard such fluent words in all my life, and I was so charmed withal I remember nothing he said. And then, when he went away, I almost sighed that he was gone.' And then I told her that he told me he slept not a wink last night; that, as oft as he began to doze, her own dear form appeared beside him, and he thought the music of her voice came also. 'Now,' said Vickey, 'this is strange—very strange indeed;' and, half weeping, she withdrew. In another moment Prescott came in, and he spoke kindly to her, of the promise of a fair day. Then she said,

* Jenkins here handed me a slip which he had pinned in the manuscript at this place, which is to say, that I, the writer of this invaluable history,—am obliged to shame the name of my country by stating that Buchanan's purpose was carried out, and that every democratic paper in the country published the two sermons referred to ; many of them eulogizing the articles as the ablest productions that ever came from man. Though I do it, it almost draws forth tears of blood. So degenerate is my country. Almost as bad as the British cramming opium down the heathen's throats with their swords' points, and England's home Christians the while, blinded by national gain, lauding the act as a mission from Heaven.

† For several months prior to the termination of his administration he frequently used those words.

pleadingly and prettily, 'Did you tell the clerk you did not sleep last night for those roguish thoughts?' 'I did,' said Prescott; 'and they rest seriously on my heart'—for he thought she meant the affairs of state. Now, when he told her this, the tears started afresh to her eyes, and she, smiling the while, went out, saying, 'You need not speak so coldly.' Prescott knew not what to make of her conduct, and so he asked me. I told him she was in love with Wadsworth, and that her sympathies were perhaps inclined to consider that, if there is to be a national conflict, he may suffer seriously. 'Does she love him?' said Prescott; and I answered I feared so. Thus the matter stands," continued the clerk. "I have made love for them all this morning, and may the graces forgive me for the lies I told." I told the clerk, that if I were inclined to write the history of love and war in Washington, I would hardly dare to tell the truth, lest the perfect parallel of these eccentric affairs might make people call it a novel of the first water. But I hope, I continued, that the Jackson House will not acquire too much notoriety for making ill matches. Before I said more, he stretched himself upward, looking through the window. "As I am a clerk, I do say!" said he, "if yonder does not go the Professor and Mrs. Lucy Tabiatha Stimpkins. Say, I will follow them, to learn the stand they make; you bring on the company. We shall see her prostrate herself before England's king expectant." And sure enough, he started out and after them. I at once started for the Judge, and found him in the out-hall, standing face to face with Vickey. In one hand his hat, and in the other a huge bouquet of flowers. He was bowing, saying, " As often as they perish, you see, I am ready with another, fair accompaniments to the fair. Accept them, and in every tinge of color, in all the mingled fragrance, and in these promising buds, behold how sweet a thing is the passing moment, how kindly and tenderly must we cherish that which from nature springs; for lo, a breath, a careless breath, may soil and blemish it. Take them, though I do envy them their biding place."

"Why, really, Judge," said she, "one would think you are in love, for the many kind remembrances you give me. You almost make me dream of such things myself."

"Ah, indeed, dearest!" said he. "I hope we understand each other, and that the idle talk of common lovers may not find a place with us. We must conduct ourselves in the true path of noble personages."

"Oh, forgive me!" said she, taking the flowers. "I could not be idle-spoken to you;" and she kissed him and ran away, but, ere she went far, she returned, saying, "Now, Judge, I tell you, these flowers are beautiful, and I thank you heartily. With these I shall indeed vie with the Prince's mother, Victoria! Oh, would it not be an excellent joke, when the Prince passes, I toss these flowers to him, with the inscription, From Victoria!"

"Ah! but, dearest, they were culled for thee!"

"But only for a joke, you know. You could easily replace them with others, and then I should prize the second ones higher for having parted with these."

"Really? Why, do you know that over each of these tiny blossoms I have in my dreams seen you pondering to catch my lapsing thoughts, to dive to the mysteries and richness of my heart? And would you toss them away so thoughtlessly?"

"Well, then, no—I would not; I will keep them as happy memories;" and she kissed at the flowers, and playfully ran off.

"Oh, what a treasure she is!" said Judge Francis. "For fifty years I have not known what it was to live. On, on in my grovelling way for half a century, ignorant of the joys of love till the spark is turned to a flame by a rosy, romping girl of seventeen. Glory be to the heavens, to the stars, to the moon, the fates, cupids, and all the blunderbusses of the spiritual fire, to think that the little spark in my breast lived so long without anything to feed upon! But oh, what a rapid growth it has! First it quickeneth the breath when its idol speaks; then it fluttereth the heart, and hot burnings come to the cheek; then to the extreme parts of the person it finds way, and chords in full time all the elements of the thing man, till his aged limbs are quick, his mind vigorous to overflowing, and needs must vent itself in squibs of poetry, and a plentiful vent of flowery romances."

Now, when I saw Vickey was gone, I came up behind the Judge, even while he was speaking, and I told him he seemed to be discoursing on love.

"Oh, no!" said he, "I was just speaking of the growth of this country. What a rapid growth it has had! But, sir, I fear me 'tis near an end now."

Just then the clerk came running in, and told us to start at once, or the procession would be over before we could arrive. So, accordingly, we were soon ready for the Judge's carriage, but neither Wadsworth nor Prescott came. Mr. and Mrs. Edge, Vickey, the Judge, and myself, were all. When we were out on the walk waiting, I drew near to Ann, and, as a faithful recorder of events, I will write down what passed between us, that the world may judge accordingly. She looked at me roguishly, and, smiling, said,

"Mr. Jenkins, you come too near me—entirely too near!"

"Too near for what?" said I. "Cannot you breathe?"

"Don't talk to me; my head aches," said she. But I replied that, to talk was to divert; that diversion was good for headache. That, therefore, I must talk to cure her.

"No, I will not have it cured; I love headache," said she. "'Tis good company when I am melancholy. I wish I had a Prince for a beau, then I would give him headache. You taught me; you aim at the heart, and that makes headache. Now, I pray you, do not stand so near me; people will think I am fond of you. But I have no heart for anything but a Prince. You tease me because you happen so much in my company. Woful circumstance!"

Then I told her, if she was not affecting all this, she could herself step a little back, because she stood as near me as I did to her.

"Indeed, I would not humor you so much," said she, pettishly, "as to step back at your command. I might cherish your regard too much. Anger shall be my study, and you shall nurture it with your presence." Then on the toe of her little shoe she dotted with her parasol, the while smiling beneath the auburn curls that swung round her down-turned face. For the life of me I could say no more, for the rapidity of my thoughts kept my tongue still. "Oh, but this shoe hurts my foot!" said she. "Do you know, Mr. Jenkins, I want to have a game of cards to-night. You shall be my partner, and teach me how to cheat. You shall teach me how to sit silent, so as to hide my hand. When you play hearts, I'll play spades to bury it with."

But before she got further with her run on me, the carriage was drawn up before us and we all got in and started. By this time the streets were filled with people, and we were with some difficulty conveyed down to the open lot opposite the old Methodist church—the very spot, too, chosen by Mrs. Lucy Tabiatha Stimpkins and her husband, Professor Jackson. The former was dressed better than I had ever seen her, but the latter, the real picture of a downeast man, with his long, faded beard and uncombed hair, his clothes rather seedy, struck our attention most. Only a few days married, and yet he was going all to wreck. But no wonder, when we remember what a wife he had. But on this occasion we had no time for philosophy. A loud huzza up the street told us the Prince of Wales and Duke of Newcastle were coming. They had to pass through this square to the street below ere they could take carriages to the Mansion, and of course the crowd was immense. Pretty soon a gang of police opened the way, and the veritable heir-apparent to the throne of Great Britain appeared before us. Quickly now Mrs. Lucy sprang in before a young little man whom she took to be the Prince, but who was really only a servant. She pretended to stumble, and did fall at his feet, crying out, "Save me! save me!" In a little while the young man caught hold of her, and in a blundering manner helped her up. All was excitement; the police rushed to the spot to see that the Prince should not be overcome with joyous greetings. Mrs. Lucy shouted at the top of her shrill voice, right in the face of the chap that helped her up, "Which is the Prince? which is the Prince? You are so young, sir, and so noble in your bearing, you make me bold of speech. Pray you, sir, which is the Prince?" And the chap hesitated, and said, "Why, madam, see, you are in the way!" But she continued right on, "I know he's a thing divine, with huge horns, a donkey's head, and rich robes round his body. Quick, boy! which is the Prince? I'll win a smile, a princely smile, a special legacy to outboast other women with." Again he was trying to say something, but she heeded not. "No, sir, I am not insensible to my assumed satire; your own nobleness has a voice to speak without words. I congratulate you, sir, on your exalted prospects. Here, sir, keep most sacred this, the parting kiss, bestowed by woman, independent woman. In this great republic women are beginning to speak; they are rising above the slave-bound women of your old, worn-out monarchism. Again I kiss your hand, that you may boast that this was done by one whose fame shall reach round the world, even Mrs. Lucy Tabiatha Stimpkins."

"Does not my beauty elicit your protection?"

"Stand back there, woman!" shouted the police. "Make way for the Prince!" and in another moment the Prince and suite were past. Mrs. Lucy was pushed aside, beholding what a fall hers had been; for the police shouted to her, even while she kissed his hands, "That's not the Prince! Let that servant go!" And the servant, too, tore his hand away from her, and gave her a severe push out of the way. As soon as she had extricated herself a little, she said, "O insult profane! What lack of gallantry do men possess! Calls not the modesty of my poor sex for a hand to shield me? O Effeminacy, die! Genial, helpless, modest woman, die! Rude man plants his stern muscle on us, and we are dashed about as beasts. Professor Jackson, how dare you!"

"Why, madam, I have done nothing!"

"I know that, to my sorrow," said she. "Why did you not point out to me which was the real Prince? What is the Prince, that I should not go to him and speak as I would to any one else? Was I not created by the same God? Do I not live on the same planet? But you, Professor—you have been the stumbling-block to the whole affair. I never heard that in our new philosophy the husband was to desert the wife in the hour of danger." He endeavored to excuse himself, by saying that the police kept clearing the track, but she told him she would not yield the point; that, had Jackson stood his ground, the adventure had been a decided success. "But I care not," she added; "the chap I spoke to heard my speech, and I am sure it is as much as he can digest at one time. Of course, he is a servant of the Prince's suite, and he will carry it all back to England, where, in due time, he will discharge it to the utter amazement of English women, who have not yet awakened to their just rights."

We heard no more; the procession was past; the crowd was flying on before, and we ourselves had wheeled round, making way for the President's mansion. Of course, we had not been idle spectators of all that had just passed before us. We had laughed ourselves tired; we had seen the plain, unassuming Prince; too young, of course, to show much signs of promise; and we had seen how he had been seen by American citizens. Yet some darker visions passed before us. One young lady, who, we knew, once hoed corn in the fields, but who was now rich through the prosperous avenues of a republican government, sighed as the Prince passed, "Oh, I wish we had a privileged aristocracy here!" By her side stood a rude Scotch woman, who retorted, "And if we had, your nose would be still at the grindstone instead of here. You know not, young woman, what you sigh for." Then there were plain farmers standing near; and they said, "Is it possible the British people wear the yoke of such a boyish royalty?" Again another retorted, "And why not? They love such a yoke, for it is light, and gives them rest from the muddle of politicians." But now that the procession was over, all were merry, and scampering off in their several directions. Just as we rounded the corner below the church, I heard some one calling, and, on turning to look, saw Prescott. He was beckoning for us to stop, which we did, and he came running up. Tears were flowing down his cheeks, and so hurried was his speech, and withal stuttering, I could hardly tell what he wanted. But he told me for God's sake to excuse myself from the company, and follow him. Ann, who had been till now exceedingly merry, was frightened, and so were Vickey and Mrs. Edge; but Judge Francis asked for some explanation. "Excuse me," said Prescott, "this is neither time nor place for me to explain myself. In due time you shall know all."

I at once dismounted, and followed him, ever remembering the lingering look of gentle Ann. When we reached the avenue, only a few paces, in fact, from where I joined him, he stopped short, saying,

"My cousin, James Odell, is killed—murdered at the Planters' Club Rooms."

"What!" said I, "is it possible?" and he assured me that it was even so; that he had just come from viewing his mangled corpse, and that the inquest was about to take place, urging me to go with him. "They mistrusted," said he, the tears coursing down his cheeks, "it was he who played eaves-dropper at the Capitol. He has been killed instead of me."

No doubt it was so, for the two were alike—as nearly alike as possible. He had been inveigled into a quarrel, and then stabbed. We took a carriage and hastened to the spot called the Planters' Club Rooms, in front of which was already assembled a large crowd of people. In a few moments we were in the presence of the corpse—apparently a young man twenty-five years of age. He was stretched on the floor, a pitiful and horrid sight, except his face, which had all the innocence and beauty of American youth. The coroner's court was already in session. The examination of the body had just been commenced. First the pockets were examined, and in them was found three thousand dollars. What a comment was this! Americans kill Americans, but not for money. Not in all the city was an American who would have rifled these pockets. Oh, most wrongly-imputed money-making nation, what a libel is this on the robbers of foreign lands! And yet, oh, what a boast if in one fell moment man crosses the sacred threshold of public opinion to meet with instant death. But hear ye, ye electors of judges, what a power party has!

Now, when the evidence was rendered, the verdict of the jury was given in these words, to wit:

"That James Odell came to his death by stabs inflicted on his person by sundry gentlemen of the club of which he was a member. The jury further declare that the said James Odell used these words:

"'The Southern fire-eaters are bringing mischief on the country, and if I had the power I would hang every one of them;' which words we deem so offensive, that he met the death he deserved."

This was indeed as shocking as the mock trial of Brooks for his attempt to murder Sumner. It was no law at all, no protection to life, and why not? Because the coroner's jury looked through their party spectacles. What chance had Pres-cott and I, if we should in any way betray what we knew of the secret meetings of the seceders?

As fortune would have it, however, this meeting had brought out Iverson and Wigfall. Even while the foregoing scene was being enacted, I overheard the former say to the latter, that if he would come to his house at nine o'clock that night, he would take him——

Further than this I heard not, but supposed it to be the secret meeting of the seceders. At the time, however, I heeded it little, having the sight of the unfortunate victim before us. The coroner took charge of the valuables, and ordered the corpse to be buried properly, and then the crowd dispersed. While on this subject I will state, that on the following day Prescott and I alone followed the remains, which were conveyed by the grave-diggers to the final resting-place. But yet, though his death was horrid, and our grief without remedy, similar scenes were already begun all over the Southern States. Every paper teemed with notices of men being shot or stabbed on the spot, for expressing their sentiments in the South. Vigilance committees and minute-men had sprung into existence in a day, and were already visiting death on every one opposed to Southern sentiments.

CHAPTER VIII.

ON our way back from the funeral, and when near the railroad station, we saw my friend Wadsworth, who came out to meet us. On his observing our melancholy appearance, we told him of the murder done. "Ah, indeed," said he, "this was a horrid deed. And yet me seems to feel this is but the beginning of a reign of horrors greater than were ever known. Oh, that the people North and South knew each other! Oh, that politicians were blotted from this fair land! Oh, that the South knew the North would not harm their slavery! Oh, that the North knew the slaves were content! But, sirs, blindness, madness rules. They have ears, but hear not; eyes, but see not." So saying, he took my arm and walked into the station, pointing to thirty or forty boxes of goods. "See here," said he, "this is my winter's supply for my slaves. Think you they will rebel against me in order to get their freedom? Here are boxes of hats and bonnets; boxes of excellent cloth, for coats and trousers; and here is one of satin and silk, to adorn them with when going to church, or perhaps to the dance, or may-be to play their pranks with Cupid's bower. Why, sir, should you behold the greeting they give me, and should you know their own love of dependence instead of independence, you would say, Man is foolish to grieve about such oppression. But the vainest and simplest philosophy ever broached by any politician is this mooted secession. Under the General Government we are protected in our slaves; but if the South secedes and forms a separate government, it will never be protected by the North. It is throwing off protection, and making an enemy on the border. As for the grasp at the western Territories, it is the table again of the dog crossing the river with a mouthful of meat; he saw the shadow, and dropped the real to catch that which was nothing."

"My dear sir," said Prescott, "you speak with great judgment. I would that your wisdom were common amongst Southern gentlemen." And when he said this, he extended his hand as a friendly greeting.

Now when they had shaken hands, Wadsworth said, looking at Prescott, "I see you wear a ring of an exalted degree."

"Oh, I found this," said Prescott; "it was in the hall of the hotel where I live. I supposed it was of little value, and belonged to some of the servants; but on inquiry, I found such was not the case." He then took it off his finger and handed it to us, that we might examine it. It was an exceedingly old ring, with sets of precious stones to form an eye, and had many signs engraved on it.

"That ring can be traced to the place whence it came," said Wadsworth, and then I too remarked that I could read the meaning of all the characters.

"Then," said Prescott, "take the ring, for it is nothing to me; perhaps through these mysterious characters you may restore it to its owner."

I then told them both that I believed Madame Ponchard or Orsini had dropped it the night before; and if it had been either of them, I doubted whether they came to it by fair means. Wadsworth then took it, saying that he would undertake to unravel the mystery; that, small and insignificant as it was, this ring had once come from persons of more than ordinary standing among men.

Soon after this we parted, each taking some separate course, and all under promise to meet at night at the Jackson House. This promise I, however, made with a mental reservation, secret in my own breast. I resolved at once I would meet with the secessionists even at the peril of my life. I must say, however, as I left Prescott and saw him turning up toward the observatory, I really felt as if it were doubtful whether we should ever meet again. That we were known to be the persons who entered the college on the previous evening, and that the leading secessionists had determined to kill us or hire our killing, we had no doubt. All they wanted was an opportunity, some sort of pretext; and these were just what we wanted to avoid. For my own part, I resolved to be somebody else, to play a deep disguise. But what should I assume? Whom should I personate? Of course some foreigner. I had it; I would be the correspondent—Clarkson—of the London *Times*. This thought I matured at once, and, to complete my arrangement, went to an old acquaintance and purchased a fine pair of horses and a carriage. Next I got a servant and dressed him in livery, from Steinberg's clothing store. By the time I had this all completed it was near night, and I hastened to make my entree into Washington effectual, by going out of it first. Accordingly, I drove up to Georgetown, and telegraphed to the Jackson House that I, James Clarkson, would be there with my carriage and pair by eight or nine at night, with letters to his excellency, the President; and a letter to Yancey also, asking the proprietor to be good enough to send word to the latter to meet me on my arrival. I then, while in Georgetown, forged a letter from Sir Edward Boyton to Yancey, for I had known Boyton's son, who had been on a year ago to visit some of his friends in America, and who had also passed a short time with Yancey. Thus equipped, and armed in every pocket, I once more set out for the Jackson House, where I arrived exactly at nine at night. Sure enough, Yancey was on hand, and came and very cordially assisted me out of my carriage. My livery servant being too Dutch to tell anything he knew, accompanied the horses to the stable. But who should accompany Yancey to receive me, but Floyd, the man I hated most, and most wished to avoid. Yet I was well disguised. Instead of light sandy hair, I now had jet black; my whiskers were shaved all off, save a bunch on each cheek, English fashion; and my nose I had stained to a cherry red.

I shall never forget how kindly Yancey and Floyd took me by the hand, and with what fervency they welcomed me to the Capital of the United States. They told me I should have put up at Willard's, in order to see the real hotel system of America; that they feared I should not be as comfortable at the Jackson House as one of my exalted position should be. I assured them, however, that I had friends coming in a few days, and that I was desirous of being with them. I told them also that the exorbitant prices of Willard's made me refrain from so great an indulgence.

"That's just like you English!" said Floyd. "You are so very economical. Why, do you know, in this country every one of us must have the very best, even if we become bankrupt next day."

"But, sir," said I, speaking slowly and with some impediment, like a member of the British Parliament, "but, sir, you-a must consider-a that in Hingland we 'ave-a less-a hopportunity to replace-a-a a fortune when we-a 'ave been so 'eedless to 'ave spent it so thoughtlessly-a." Now, when they saw how beautifully I got heedless and thoughtlessly in so close proximity, they were in ecstacies to know if I were not a member of Parliament. I assured them I was not, but that I had often been there. Our conversation was, however, soon terminated; the clerk touched my arm, and signified that I might go to my rooms, and I invited the others to accompany me. Accordingly, after I had given strict orders, English fashion, that my horses must have all the attention and care, and that anything would do for myself, we all marched up to my beautifully ventilated apartments. I then told them, in the same parliamentary drag of unmeaningly-connected words, that they could not suppose any ordinary matter would bring me to this country; that I was almost prepared to tell them about the contemplated dissolution of the republic, and of the projected establishment of a constricted republic on the ruins; that it had always been a thing of pity, for the English to behold the lawless character of the American Government; that it was the most inexplicable of all things, to think that in a country great as this, there were no men of energy and talent to seize the helm of state and wrench it from the vulgar mob.

Now, during all this time I had been frequently touching my nose with my handkerchief, and what was my horror on seeing the red paint in spots all over it. Could it be my nose was turning Yankee? Would these rascals discover me? I kept on the shady side of the gas. Yancey was astonished how much I knew of the project of secession. I told him there were any number of ways the British Government had of finding out things abroad. First, it sends out spies; then, correspondents; then, gas-blowers; then, ballets. "And I am on the second list," said I, "for this new adventure." When I said this, Floyd swore. All my prognostications were true, he said. "This country is about to change its form of government to a limited republic; but here will be no pickings for the British Government. We are now the sick old man; but let France and Britain join on us, and you shall see ——" Then came a furious oath. And even with more fierceness did Yancey speak out. They apologized to me, but warned Britain. Though, when I disclaimed any desire of the British Government to seize this country, or any part of it, and, with some authority, added, "Great Britain only speaks in the cause of humanity." "That's a hit at slavery," said Floyd. "All the Abolition emissaries of the North were taught by Britons."

I told him he was sadly mistaken; that the British Government recognized the theory, that there must be in all countries hewers of wood and carriers of water; and that we, the English people, would sooner to-day see this Government with slavery for its corner-stone, than to see it emanate from a common mob. "This is," said I, "one of the chief things for which I am here to inform you, though unofficially. And you may rest assured that it is the doctrine we will ever maintain—first the Government, then the people."

"And those are my sentiments too," said Yancey. "We have tried universal suffrage; now we shall have it limited."

I then asked him in what way this great desideratum was to be accomplished; and he told me, if I would have the patience to wait a few minutes, he would take me to a meeting of some of the prominent leaders, where I could hear and judge accordingly. And that he would be pleased to have me state before the meeting the probable position the British Government would assume during the troubles which must necessarily result during the important change. Next he ordered some sparkling Catawba, and we sat and drank to each other for a good while; and I, meantime, wishing I had Judge Francis here, to tell us a story of his youthful days.

At a quarter past ten we left, arm in arm, they having previously cautioned me to be silent during our walk. Down the avenue; up L to Monroe Lane, and along the lane—it should be called alley—till we came to No. 76, a dingy sort of high-stoop frame house, where all was darkness. I was satisfied now, if I were detected, I would be killed, and that no one would ever know it; and some fear began to creep over me. Yancey touched the door, and some one inside opened it, when we walked in. All was dark.

"What are your names?" demanded the man in the dark. Yancey told him for us all. The man dashed a lamp in full glare in our faces, saying, "Pass on." And we did pass. The house was an unoccupied one, unfurnished, and everything we touched or did seemed to make a great noise. A dim light came down from above after we got further in, and we found and went up a long pair of stairs, at the head of which stood a sentinel and Orsini, both with swords drawn. My friends vouched for me, and we entered, having left our hats and walking-sticks with the sentinel. In another moment I remembered my name, Jenkins, was engraved on the gold mounting, but I was already in the hall, and knew not what to do. Half turning my head, I saw the rascal looking at my cane, and I feared he would call me to account. But he was interrupted by some one else coming in, though he kept the cane in his hand. At the other end of the room—if, indeed, a whole floor can be called a room—were Toombs, Mason, Cobb, Rhett, and Davis. As soon as we came up, I was introduced as Clarkson, of the London *Times*, and greeted warmly and pleasantly. Rhett asked Floyd if he had any good news to report to-night. "I have," said Floyd. "I have this day sent fifty thousand muskets to the armory in Charleston; also sent a good assortment of munitions of war. But that is not the best of it: I have appointed the Governor of your State to look after it." This was followed by a laugh. In another moment I saw the sentinel approaching, bearing my walking-stick with him. "Are you certain you know this gentleman?" said he, pointing to me. Yancey and Floyd said they were positive. "Orsini says he is a painted man, and Orsini knows paint. Here is Jenkins' cane!" "Ah!" shouted—or hissed rather—every one present. "Gentlemen," said I, "I-a cannot receive-a this pleasantly. Is this the way-a statesmen-a build up new States-a? If you ave-a any doubt, gentlemen-a, of my respectability, I will-a assure you I will do anything 'onorable to convince you-a your doubts-a can be removed-a." This, being a rather parliamentary-constructed sentence, won over to me several voices from the members. But Floyd and Yancey both spoke out, saying they themselves doubted me. Toombs said, "Demand any letters he may have about him. See if they are to Clarkson, and if post-marked England."

"Gentlemen," said I, "I have no letters with me. I hope you will not make it unpleasant for me to remain with you."

"Do you know, sir," said Floyd, "I think you are a spy? Show us some proof!"

"I have nothing with me."

"Whence came this cane?"

"I got it at the tavern; I don't know whose it is."

"Then let us examine your face, to see if it is painted."

"I cannot allow this, gentlemen. You brought me. If I am not welcome, take me home again."

"No, sir; not out of this house, till we know who you are," said Floyd.

They then came upon me, and I treated them with backing toward the door, continually complaining of this indignity to a British subject. In the meantime I had taken my cane to look at it, but with the full determination to use it, and also the revolver and knife, if attacked. The meeting was now nothing more than a row, some for and some against me. Floyd had me by the sleeve; Orsini was at my back with his uplifted sword. I wheeled round, and knocked the sword from his hand. With one bound I went down the stairs, but lost my footing and fell. For a moment all was darkness and despair, made terrible by a wild scream from a female by my side. I was in the cellar; fell through a hatchway, bruised my hand, and was almost unconscious of how badly I was injured. The female passed aside, and darted out through a cellar door into the lane above. I followed, not knowing how soon my pursuers would be upon me. But the sounds of the voices and the running party convinced me they had mistaken my whereabouts, and were pursuing me down the stairway. A few minutes sufficed, however, to show me I had made my escape successful. The next great mystery was, who was this thief of a creature hid in the cellar? Of course, her way of escape had been matured, and if I followed her I too was safe. She ran faster than I had ever seen a woman run before, and I ran nearly as fast as ever did man. Her course was down the lane, across the avenue, and to the grounds of the Smithsonian Institute. Curiosity led me to follow so strange a woman, if for nothing more than to assure her I meant no harm. As soon as she was about fifty rods ahead, she slackened her pace, ever and anon looking back to see if I followed. On several occasions she dodged a corner to escape me, but I always found her course, and pursued. When she entered the Smithsonian grounds, going even toward the Institute, I saw she slackened her pace still more, as if waiting to be captured. I walked briskly till near her, and then slower. It was nearly a full moon, and I saw, even before I approached her, she was at least no beggar, or person of scanty cloth. Finally she halted and faced about, waiting for me, and in another minute I was face to face with her.

"Oh, sir, I beseech you," she said, "if you can imagine a woman's fears, you will pity me, and treat me kindly." She burst out crying as if her heart was broken. "Oh, in God's name, sir, let me go! If there is anything sacred in the name of mother or sister, oh, I pray you, grant it unto me! I am yet a child, and my fears will drive me to death."

All this she said while she was sobbing, and before I was within a half a dozen paces. So, when I halted, I assured her, over and over, that I was no enemy; that I would, on the contrary, be her friend, if it were possible for me to do any good act for her.

"Then are you not an officer?" she said, endeavoring to quiet herself a little, at the same time tossing back her velvet robe, and disclosing to my view her other attire, which seemed of the richest quality. A hood she lifted back, and waving ringlets of light auburn played on her snow-white neck. She was pretty; she was bewitching, even while she stood weeping and nearly overcome with fear. I assured her I was no officer; and then I told her about being at a meeting with some friends in the old house, and about falling through the hatchway. And then I assured her that mere curiosity had induced me to follow her, because it seemed so strange for a lady to escape from such a miserable, deserted house. Now, when she saw I was so frank, she replied, saying, "Your words, sir, have done much to assuage my fears. I would that you knew me as I know myself, or as Heaven knows me; you would lend some assurance to my heart-pangs, which it seems can never heal. Oh, pity me! pity me!"

Said I, "Sentiments like these, madam, cannot emanate but from one deserving honorable pity. If you will be kind enough to relate to me what misfortunate circumstance has crossed the path of one so little able to battle with stern realities, and also to tell me what I can do to extricate you from your perils, you will, I do assure you, find in me a reliable friend."

"I am indeed much pleased with your proffered assistance," she said, becoming calm, and deeply interested in eyeing me from head to foot. "But were I to tell you of the misfortunate circumstances that have crossed my path, you would yourself, man as you are, feel that fate had forever closed the portals of justice to me. My life has not been a happy one; and, were it day, you could see in my

young face such furrows as would tell a sadder tale than words ever painted. Now, sir, I pray you, if you will befriend a helpless, virtuous girl, please leave me. I would retire to the place whence I came; and I must so proceed, that no one will suspect or molest me."

Said I, "My lady, you do impose a burden on me. How can I leave? This would be the greatest burden of my life, to leave you thus sorrow-stricken, with the thought of your probable woes ever haunting me. Can I nothing do that will give you a ray of happiness? Must I myself forever remain ignorant of the mystery that surrounds you?"

She then folded her handkerchief, and sobbed for many minutes. I knew not what to do or to say; but after I lingered awhile, I turned to go away, remarking that, if my presence was not pleasant, I would most unhappily take my leave of one whose strangeness would ever be constant in memory. But when I started, she said, "Stay awhile; I will be calm in a moment." Then she snuffled a little, and cleared herself, and put on some dignity. "'Tis well, sir," she said, "that a stranger approaches me thus, and that I behave as if I were ignorant of myself. You mistake me for some idle heroine, who has, for a love-sick fever, imposed some hazard on her future prospects. Such is not my case, neither do I feel at liberty to tell my grievance without first knowing to whom I speak. For the telling of my woful prospects may bring greater ones on me. Yet I need a friend. Oh, sir, I do need a friend! So long I have prayed God to send me a friend!"

Her dignity again broke down, and she sobbed as before. As soon as she quieted a little, I said, "Madam, I do assure you, if it be possible for me to prove myself that prayed-for friend, you need but give your commands, and I will obey them. Nay, so much I am convinced of your virtue and nobleness, you can impose whatever you will, and I will obey you. Take courage, madam; for, as Heaven witnesses, I will be true."

"Take heed what you swear, man, for there are things you know not of. Would you, sir, to a strange woman—if indeed I am at the age of womanhood—swear to forswear your country's laws?"

"Almost you put me to the test," said I. "Whatever law could interdict your seeming nobleness, seems not law, but violence."

"A friend stands above all things, save Him who formed us. If you cannot be so to me, you are not the meet of my long,

long prayers. Go, sir; I pray you, leave me!"

"No, madam. Now I swear before God I will ever stand at your command."

"Uplift your hand and speak to Him!" she said, as calmly as ever woman spake; and I held up my hand, and said, "God witness!" And then she came to me, took my hand, and, pointing upward, she said, "O Lord my God, receive my humble thanks, that Thou hast sent to Thy heart-broken child a true friend. Aid me, O God, to maintain my trials, and bless this great, good man!" She turned to me then, and added, "Sir, however fair you behold me, and with what freedom of speech you may see I address you, know that I am called a slave; called a negress; called a fugitive, flying from my owner. Five hundred dollars are offered for my capture, and I am sought for by many. Now, my friend, I have but to tell the horrors in store for me, and you will carry me safe to Canada; for I know you would not see one so young and helpless as I am doomed to the fate hovering over me."

I was so astounded I scarcely knew if I were not in a dream; for I gazed full in that snow-white face. Her eyes were large and blue; her lips thin, and a pretty dimple rested in each cheek and on her chin. Her hair was pale auburn, and nearly straight; her person full and round, but she was tall and of upright form. I never heard a sweeter voice, and her hand was so small and soft to the touch—— She could not be a slave! To-morrow a constable may say to me, "Come, sir, help capture my slave, and carry her back, or you, sir, shall to prison for refusing." This noble-spoken girl, who hath all the centres fine of genial worth, and outer form of all, that hath each her several parts compounded into that one excellent being, woman—a slave! Why droops my soul, that but a moment since would have challenged the world in her behalf? A pristine love a moment since, and, Heaven witness, so soon shocked and dead! Even while the same eloquent beauty clings so prayerfully by my side. Away, away, ye cavilling, doubting, carrolers of my peace! She is a woman, fair and virtuous! I will, will be true!

All this passed through my mind quicker than I can tell it; so that, when she ceased speaking but for a moment, I told her she could rely upon me; that I would provide her safety out of the country. Moreover, that I would make myself a special guardian over her until she was comfortably situated. She pressed my hand fervently, the tears fast rolling down her cheeks as she gazed piteously up into my face. It could not be, I thought, from her resemblance to Ann Underhill, that I loved her also; yet, if outward form and a gifted speech show off the heart and mind, why not some noble worth in this poor slave?

"Now tell me," said I, after she had again thanked me for my many promises, "tell me of the misfortunes you have endured, and how you came to this unhappy pass."

"Not yet," said she, "for even now may I be pounced upon and captured. Let us away to some secure place, and I will then tell you all about it, and who I am and whence I came."

"Then," said I, "'tis well we take the train for Canada even now."

"No," she said; "I have a half-sister who will be here to-morrow night. She is out of money. I must wait till she comes. Let me go now to my room in the deserted house, and, if you like, you can call to-morrow, and I will tell you the story of my life."

But I urged her to go to a hotel. She said they had her carte-de-visite at all of them; that she should surely be captured. I then asked her if she were not afraid to go back to that house. "No," she said, "no; I trust in God! See how He has blessed me!" Again she pressed my hand, adding, "Go, now, go, though it breaks my heart; still I have more joy this night than ever before came to poor woman. Say you call to-morrow?" I told her I would, and she said, "God bless you!" She took my arm, and we walked together till we arrived at the intersection of the lane on Pennsylvania Avenue. "To-morrow, at twelve," said I, as we were parting, and she again wept, saying, "God bless you!" And in a moment more she disappeared up the dark lane, and I went home.

CHAPTER IX.

ALTHOUGH the election of Lincoln had been known for a good while, still the counting of the votes of the electoral college had not taken place, and a vain hope was still entertained by some Southerners that some Northern electors might prove false, and yet elect some other President. This was the most doubtful period of the nation's history. The rumor was spread, too, that Scott was wavering, and might join the seceders; in fact, in all the length and breadth of the land there was no public champion for the Union. The hearts of millions were praying that God might give them a leader for the cause of national glory and justice, but all was sullen silence, save the clamoring of the destroyers of liberty. They had it all their own way. Now the electoral votes were to be counted, the die cast, the fall begun. Accordingly, this day was a memorable one. All the leaders of disorder were concentrated in the Capitol, and countless curious spectators filled its every avenue. It was about eleven o'clock when we started. I had for my companion Miss Underhill, while Judge Francis had Mr., Mrs., and Miss Edge. I knew we were all well attired, but the scenes around made it seem as if it were all a dream. I had never seen the streets so crowded. The air was fresh and pleasant, and the leafy trees of the Capitol grounds never looked so splendid. The reveille sounded afar off. They were Scott's troops. I saw a few galloping horsemen. I knew America had few troops, and feared this was the beginning of a mighty revolution. Everybody was full of emotion. Some men, old and feeble, I saw in tears. When we passed the gates one man said, "I fear the great republic is no more." Another, drooping, said, "Oh, that I had died ere this unhappy period!" The bells were ringing, or rather tolling, in parts of the city, adding more gloom to the awful affairs of state. Anon hurried past us the votaries of secession, with muffled-up cloaks a few, and many in rich but scanty attire; and the heinous laugh and grin of demons

rested in complacent triumph in their beautiful faces; for, though devils all, they were Americans. It was the saddest day I ever saw, and every one else, save the secessionists, seemed as if throwing the awful burden of their souls at the portals of Heaven. Not a breath of air stirred; no leaf had motion. When we arrived at the steps of the Capitol, near the lower fount, we faced about to see the vast assemblage. Ourselves saying little, for so solemn was the hour—as if a nation was at prayer; as if Liberty was in the throes of death; as if the voice of twenty millions were in communion at the throne of Almighty God! My companion touched my arm, and we looked aside and beheld Breckinridge; he was with Rhett, Floyd, and Davis. He was one of the candidates for President; he was going in to count the votes himself. Soon we all followed, and in a minute more were standing in full view of the expected scene. It was then twelve o'clock precisely. Pennington called the House to order. Stockton then prayed, the substance of which was, "God bless the out-going Administration. May it close its labors without further violence or more stain of blood. We pray for the President elect. Thy blessing rest upon him; protect him hitherward; guide him with Thy counsel, that he may administer the affairs of state as a worthy example of civil and religious liberty."

The House then sent a message to the Senate, requesting them to enter, in order to count the votes together. I never saw such excellent order. You could have heard a pin fall. When the Senate entered, the House arose to do them honor, and provided them a circular line near the Speaker's desk. Breckinridge, the slaveholders' candidate, being Vice-President of the United States, and President of the Senate, took his seat beside the Speaker. In a moment all was order again. Breckinridge then rose up, saying, "We have assembled pursuant to the Constitution, in order that the elec-

5

toral votes be counted, and the result declared for President and Vice-President for the term commencing March 4th, 1861. It is my duty to open the certificates of election, in the presence of the two Houses, and I now proceed to the performance of that duty."

When he ceased, the House was even more quiet than before; and as he took each sealed package from each State, and broke the seal, it seemed to send a death-like shudder over every person present. He handed the packages to the tellers to be counted. Oh, what a terrible spell now came upon us ! Six thousand of us were present, and we all trembled for the result. The Southern States were under threat, if Lincoln be elected, they would secede and destroy the nation. Even now were they silently praying, nursing their vainglory and hellish glee, for a cause to show their foolish madness. This cause would come of Lincoln's election. Oh, that they could show how ugly they could be, for the seeming menace against their glut in human bondage ! Their prayers were full of curses. They mocked the God of Justice. Might was their king. Like tigers they were, gazing at the tellers, to tell them to say it if they dare. And yet they feared. They had boasted they would ; and conscience—for they were Americans—still swept o'er them. But the blindness of uncertain failure had seized on them ; the rays of national glory were being sealed to them forever. Pitiful creatures ! what a bleeding shame to the great republic ! For your madness to damn your country.

Not less, though, were we prayerful the while. We viewed the tellers in their routine, with our hearts divided. Lincoln was on the side of liberty, and most we hoped he would be elected. But we loved the opposite party—not for its principles, but they too were our countrymen. Almost we hoped against our wishes, and wished against our hopes. We would not enrage our fellows. Yet, with silent pledge, we said to Almighty God, Thy will be done. Give us this day the result of the voice of the nation. Thou hast prospered us, and we know that Thy wisdom will ever guard us. If it be that the voice of the great republic is for Lincoln, so shall we stand trusting in Thy name.

Now, while we thus in silence sat, and much feared, musing in awful mood, the tellers fast told over all the States' decrees, as each State had by parts its several parts proclaimed. Anon this silence ceased. Then Breckinridge, with trembling hand, held up a slip of pa-per, reading, even while he grew deathly pale :

" Douglas, twelve ; Bell, thirty-nine ; Breckinridge, seventy-two ; Lincoln, one hundred and eighty."

Every person present seemed as dead. Even our breath had nearly ceased. Anon a tear from many an eye stole down. No one looked on another. Countrymen—all —the banter forth and challenge taken. But fast the blood returned to Breckinridge's face, and almost black he was with choking madness. " Lincoln has," he said, " the majority of the whole vote. He is elected President. Hamlin is elected Vice-President." He could say no more ; the eyes of six thousand people were gazing on him, and he was the vanquished candidate. We pitied him.' He was the slaveholders' choice, but not the nation's. The law is, that the majority shall rule ; but not so now, thought the vanquished and his adherents. They swore, though not aloud, they would not submit ; and this was the first treason formed in the hearts of men on this continent.

Soon the senators took their departure ; the House meanwhile had risen in due honor. Such was the terrible day—the hour of death. But darkness was over us all ; the country was without Heaven's sign ; like a clash of arms in a midnight battle, the wail and war-whoop was heard, but the end no man saw. " The slave party is beaten ; will it yield to the nation's ballot ? Will it try by arms what it failed by moral power ? And will not the liberty party cringe to them, and plunge the whole in chaos ? " Thus we said, and thus mused, even from the moment the Senate left. Then the busy voice of maddened whispers ran amongst the six thousand people. Louder grew the hum, and order ceased. We turned, amidst the throng that now became a moving mass, and slowly made way beneath the dome and thence toward the upper porch that faces the grounds above the Capitol. Quick now past ourselves we saw Floyd, Madame Ponchard on his arm, and Orsini near, all making way to the open plot beyond, where grouped a thousand men and women, gazing upward. Before we cleared the trees, we were near Washington's statue, and then, in view full of the dim-like sun, we gazed and saw the colors in their brightest hue, the red, white, and blue.*

" See ! see ! " said Floyd, for he and Yancey, and others, were just a pace ahead, and as he pointed to the sun ; " I

* This was seen that day by sixty thousand people.

care not, though Heaven curse, we can, we will disprove such a foolish sign."

And then Yancey said, smiling, "This is God's farewell to the Stars and Stripes. He is with us."

"No, I will tell you," said Madame Ponchard; "for you see there are no stars. This is a new flag for us. The red is a challenge to our foes; the white is a white man's government; and the blue is the menial North." And then they all laughed heartily, turning around to see if others laughed at what they had said.

Not two yards distant was I, my face shaved even as on the previous evening, when I had imposed upon them in effecting an entrance at the secret meeting. They were astounded, but refrained from violence, because I had a lady in my company; though in low whispers they pointed me out to Madame Ponchard and Orsini. The crowd meanwhile became so great that I soon lost sight of them, but again encountered the Judge and Vickey. His old silver spectacles were thrown high upon his forehead, and he was alternately looking at the sun and his fair one, to whom he introduced nearly every one he met. He only introduced them, though, then kept on, as it were, with an interrupted discourse on the planets and on the rays of light. So he says to us, "Ha! ha! Jenkins and Ann—fine day!—Miss Victoria Edge!" and, before we had time to say anything, he turns to Vickey: "As I was saying, the parallax seems as it were to conjoin, and the effect is more or less transmitted to the rays of light within the earth's atmosphere. Just as I told Agassiz in the researches on spherical action—ah!" and he turns to Mr. Holt, "ah, Mr. Holt! strange phenomenon! Shall I introduce you to Miss Edge, of Ohio?" and again, not waiting for a reply, he goes on to Vickey: "If you comprehend me, I only allude to its passage through our atmosphere. Humboldt, you know, seemed to doubt somewhat on this point. Fine day, Mrs. Barrow! Shall I make you acquainted with Miss Victoria Edge, daughter of the great railroad contractor of that name?" and he bows, and good-naturedly turns away, saying to Vickey, "It is indeed, as you may imagine, a pity that our great authors dwelt so little on this subject."

His style attracted attention. Those who knew him not, wanted to; and those who knew him wished to hear him further, and these desires pleased Vickey; for what girl would not love to walk with a man that could so easily attract attention?

"See my uncle," said Ann, "sailing away with that young girl. Don't an old bachelor always act silly? Indeed, I believe a wife is a looking-glass through which a man can learn to see himself."

"Then 'tis better," said I, "some men never get wives, for some are blest in their ignorance of not seeing themselves. Yet I would that I could so see myself——"

"Come," said she, pulling at my arm, "come; I fear this sun will give me headache."

And thus she ever broke off the dialogue that I had so often ventured on. She could playfully speak of marriage, but the instant I took it up she found something more important to talk of. In this instance I was about to bring her to account for her style, when we reëntered the Capitol, and passed under the dome, where were congregated about a hundred people. At the head, and spokesman for the whole, was Rhett. Near him stood Davis; but Mason was skulked aside in listening attitude. "Never! never!" I heard Rhett say. "They may battle us, they may beat us, but never, never can they subdue us.

"The common mob has now outraged the state,
It has made fools of us, and liberty.
Judgment is dead, and vagabonds, foul brained
By the base clamor of stump-orators,
Force on the state their low-bred bullies,
Regardless of all law and decency.
Our nature does revolt at this base stuff,
And we will banish it. So help me Heaven,
We shall despoil the whole, or have our rights.
In God's name Southerners rise to their work;
Uncover this foul thing; disembowel it,
Strip yourselves to the skin, and bathe your hands
In its sweet blood. Snivel and bow who will,
Gentlemen have no choice but to strike out.
Before to-morrow's setting sun my State
Shall rend the bonds; we shall be, shall be free.
The government of Adams, Washington,
And Jefferson was that which we adjoined,
And it is gone, effaced—aye, dead and buried.
Government none has this republic now.
Forsooth a bootman, fresh from the deck,
And smoking with the smell of pork,
His knuckles big with handling greasy barrels,
And such a foot—as flat as any nigger's;—
What! for his very jackass qualities
Made President of these United States!
No, no, no! I am wrong; this pretty pass
Is rational glory. Any ass can be
A President, and we'll go on our bellies
To him, as part of our religious bliss.
Now hark you. I'll go ten thousand, Lincoln
Never reaches Washington. The thing's too dirty,
It will never be stomached by an intelligent people."

He then turned to leave, and many men present shouted huzzah at the top of their voices. Mason, who was downcast, his hands deep-crammed in his pockets, now came to Rhett, and said he would like to talk to him about these affairs, stating also that, as the Government had really ceased to live, it was necessary something should be done to save the country from coming to civil war, and perhaps entire destruction. Rhett burst into tears, saying, "My dear sir, I cannot. I cavil no more. This day I leave Washington, never to return. An ungrateful country has turned the South out of doors. I go now to draw my sword against ingratitude. I shall only hereafter pull down the tottering edifice, to make way for something sound and noble. Go, tell Buchanan this—to-morrow one star shall be ripped from the American flag."

"God bless you! My heart is with you," said Mason, and he shook hands with him. "Tell Thompson and Stephens their doctrine's frail; that, in trying to take the whole country, they will not take even their own States. South Carolina will go alone."

Again they shook hands, each prophesying that war would in all probability prevent them from ever meeting again. Hardly had they separated, both nearly overcome with the affairs of state, when a loud, uncouth laugh directed our attention toward the lower steps. "I tell you they are vanquished. I tell you, Professor, they are vanquished!" and again the laugh rang out, and we distinguished Mrs. Lucy Tabiatha Stimpkins and Professor Jackson. "You see," she continued, "Lincoln's election has knocked these fellows. Thanks to the Harmonial philosophy, this is a triumph of Liberty —a triumph for human freedom—a triumph of the genial power of woman. I well remember when these fellows, not long since, run me out of the telegraph office by their unseemly laughter. Now I can laugh—ha! ha! Professor Jackson ? "

Jackson.—"Indeed, it is the first triumph I have enjoyed."

Mrs. Lucy.—Oh, no, Professor ! the honor is not mine, but my principles. A New York paper has for years claimed that it always elected the Presidents. But now let that editor look, and see what woman has done. To see those fellows, those dealers in human flesh, with tears in their eyes, and whining at the giant power of woman!" In another moment she darted through the crowd, Professor Jackson trying to follow, even while roars of laughter sprang from the throats of thousands.

For my part, I rather enjoyed it, but gentle Ann turned away her face, saying, "Oh, for shame! Take me home, I pray you."

"Why, no," I said; "let us follow a little, and see what more she says." But my companion hid her face with her fan, and pulled at me to go the other way, and I went. I saw other ladies do so too, and I wondered at it, for the men all longed to follow Mrs. Lucy, to hear the style of her enjoyment.

After we came below the Capitol, we looked at the sun again, and the colors were still there—a fact which I remarked to my companion; whereupon she suggested that we should seat ourselves beneath the trees, and await the issue. But I told her I was under the necessity of hastening home, because I was to carry the result of the vote to the President.

"You have never a moment to spare when we walk out," said she. I told her then we would linger awhile if she liked, though she said, "No; when I bethink me, now, I have no time either." And so we started homeward. I often wondered why it was that I did not seize upon the opportunity she offered. When we reached the gate we were met by the clerk, who had anticipated our weariness, and brought the Judge's carriage to take us home. He had the best joke of the season, he said, and he longed to tell it to me in full, although he further said that the joke was not yet fully completed. At that instant Wadsworth came up, and got into the carriage; whereupon the clerk winked to me, as much as to say I should come near him, and leave Miss Underhill to the care of Wadsworth. Before I reflected, I agreed to it; but, I have ever since considered it a very weak thing on my part.

In a little while we were all safely ensconced in the Jackson House. The clerk asked me to wait in the office a little while, and he would tell me the joke he had on foot. Just then the Judge, with the Edge family, came up, and the clerk, seeing them, shouted, "Oh, indeed! now is to be enacted the other part of the joke;" and at that he broke away, and thereupon took the Judge and the Edge family in by another way. I waited a while, to hear what it was that he should be so excited about, and presently I saw him through the scuttle window, looking in toward the parlor. He was laughing to himself fit to kill. This made me uneasy, for I wished also to enjoy what he was laughing at, but still I remained a long while a spectator. Finally he broke away, and ran to where I was, exclaiming, "It's took! egad, it's took! Oh, the best joke!" and he slapped his thighs and laughed heartily. As soon as he quieted a little I told him to tell me the joke.

"I have just completed the greatest feat," said he, and he took me aside; "the very greatest feat you ever heard of. You know," said he, "the Judge is dead in love with Vickey, and believes she is going to marry him. And, would you think it? I've got an old maid dead in love with the Judge. You know Mrs. Edge—kind-hearted old woman! She wonders why the Judge is always round them. So, a week ago, I sat down and talked the matter over with her. I told her the Judge admired her more than he did any woman he ever saw. She believed it—felt wonderfully flattered; whereupon I told her that any of the Edge family was an angel to the Judge.

"'Indeed, do you think so?' said she.

"Said I, 'I know so. He told me he never saw so fair and noble a woman as you. He is tired of fashionable follies. He says that you are not ashamed to own that you once made candles and soap for a living, and he loves you for it.'

"'Well, really,' said she, 'I kind of thought so. I admire him for it, too. But, you know such things must not be talked of. I will tell you,' she added, in a whisper, 'I have a maiden sister, the very picture of me (only, some folks say I was a little—just a little—handsomer than she is), and she has three thousand dollars. Now, what is your opinion? If I send for her, do you think he would take her?'

"'Of course he would,' said I. 'He would marry any one related to you; I know he would.'

"'Well, now, really!' said she, smiling. 'They are just about the same age, only I must say she may look a little older of the two; but then, you know women always get to looking old sooner than men.'

"I told her to lose no time, but send for her sister at once. When this conversation was ended the old woman became so anxious about it, that she immediately wrote and posted a letter to her sister. So now, to-day, while all of you were off to the Capitol—in fact, all the Edges, too, being absent—the old maiden sister came, all breathless and dirt, fearing some of the Edge family were dying, because they had sent for her to come. She is the strangest old creature I ever saw—so tall and thin, and leaned away over, and as harmless seeming as an angel. I don't think she is exactly in her right wits, but it may come from her old age. Well, as I was going to say, you were all absent when she came. I met her at the door, and she asked me for the landlord. I told her I was the man; and she smiled enough to show me she had not a tooth in her head, as she said,

"'Indeed, sir, you are a young-looking man to have a tavern like this. Can you tell me, sir, what is the matter? My name is Peggy Van Dorn.'

"I knew, then, who she was, and I put my hand on my breast, sighing,

"'Ah, indeed, my lady, there's matter enough!'

"'What! are they dying?' said she, and she pulled out her awful long handkerchief, and eyed me with great solemnity.

"'Worse than death, I fear,' said I. 'Did they send for you?'

"'They did, and I hurried with all my might; the trains are so slow I thought I'd never get here.'

"'Well indeed,' said I, 'you might hurry. You are the only hope; it rests with you.'

"She then got her long handkerchief to her eyes, and began to snuffle a little. I told her that none of them were sick, but if she would step into the parlor I would tell her all about it. She at once went in, I having told her you were all off to the Capitol. When she got in she took off her bonnet and laid it down on the floor beside her with much care, frequently stopping to wring her nose and wipe away the tears.

"'You must know, then,' I began, 'here in Washington is one Judge Francis Underhill, of Loudon Heights, the wisest man that ever lived, and the handsomest. He is worth two millions of dollars. Well, now, mind you, you must not blame a man for what he cannot help, nor must you think hard of Washington society for what you yourself might do. You are aware, also, of the beauty and nobleness of your sister, Mrs. Edge, and of her ten thousand pleasing charms. This Judge, this millionnaire, has formed a powerful attachment to her, and he is well-nigh distracted to learn that she is already married. The wisest counsel of this city has been in session, to determine what to do about it, not wishing to see so great a man throw himself away in such a manner. Many of them having been acquainted with you, and knowing the striking resemblance between you and your sister, it has been decided that in this emergency you should consult with the Judge, in hopes that your excellent judgment may devise a means to win his affections away from her.'

"She looked steadily at me a moment, and then said, 'How old is he?'

"I told her he was about sixty.

"'I'm afraid he's too old for me,' said she, and again she wiped her eyes, seeming lost in reflection. 'I am but fifty-one, past since last 4th of July.'

"'That's nothing,' said I; 'you cannot be insensible to the fact you are both at least old enough to marry. You do not wish to live to be an old maid?'

"She shook her head in the negative, and then changed her bonnet over to the other side. 'How much did you say he's worth?' said she.

"'He's worth a million of dollars,' said I.

"'I thought you said two millions,' said she.

"'Well, I dare say,' said I, 'he is worth two millions. It is almost impossible to estimate his wealth.'

"Again she shook her head in the negative, and looked straight out another way.

"'You are aware, also,' said I, 'that there are plenty of instances where men have fallen in love with other men's wives, resulting in the most fearful consequences. I must not name them, but the history of this city is not clear of such stains; and if we go to England, France, and Italy, we find high life full of it. In all countries, in the highest walks of life, the marriages are always planned out by proxy, the persons themselves being merely children to the wise counsels of their best friends. In many countries it has been found necessary to make a law governing the marriages of the heirs of royal and imperial families. In this country, of course, we have no such law; but then, you know, the same thing is done in other ways. We find we must protect the truly noble. You and the Edge family have risen from candle-makers and soap-boilers to be persons of the highest quality. Nobleness is yours by nature.'

"'I have always felt that,' she said, and she seemed to see a ray of happiness beaming on her withered future.

"'It is, therefore, thought meet and proper that we bring you and the Judge face to face, to see if indeed such a marriage might not be not only a thing of necessity, but a pleasurable consummation. He has already given his consent, and longs to be presented to you.'

"I feared I was getting it on too thick, and so I waited a moment to see what reply she would make. Having taken her bonnet up and set it down on the other side, and flourished her handkerchief a little, and brushed away some imaginary specks from her dress, she finally ventured to ask, 'What kind of looking man is he?' and I answered and said, 'One of the most noble you ever laid eyes on. He is, to be sure, rather stout and fleshy, but he is so fair and so fresh, like a ripe apple. He is not tall, nor is he short; and he carries his head considerably in the rear of his abdominal viscera, in real royal fashion. His forehead is so large, and extends so far over the top of his head, you would almost think him bald; but this comes of his princely blood. Such feet and hands! they are like a lady's, so soft and delicate.'

"Again I waited a moment to see the impression I made on her, and she replied that she had read somewhere that opposite figures made even numbers; that, as she was tall, she needed a stout man; that her hands and feet were large, and so she had always admired small ones most.

"Now, while we talked thus, I was apprised the Judge might return any moment, and I might be caught in a rather meddlesome business. Accordingly I assured her that the Judge's mind was made up; that she must take it for granted that every one was expecting her to reciprocate his affection, and never to cast a doubt in the way. 'You have, therefore,' I concluded, 'nothing more to say, when you meet him, than that the proposed marriage is your extreme pleasure. But if you, when you see him, do not like him, you can tell him that you oppose the marriage, and it will end there.' I rose up then to go, and she rose up too, dangling her bonnet by the strings, and with some hesitancy she asked, 'You think he's got the money?' I assured her there was no doubt about that at all, and then told her to keep her seat till I brought in the Judge. She looked both pleased and scared, and complied with my request. Then I sallied out to meet the Judge, and to post him on the part he was to play. Fortunately, I met him near the gate, and called him aside, leaving Mrs. Edge, Mr. Edge, and Vickey viewing the rainbow round the sun.

"'Now, Judge,' said I, as soon as I got him alone, 'I have more to tell you about your expected marriage than you ever dreamed of.'

"'Pooh!' said he; 'about my marriage?'

"'There is no use making long words about it, Judge,' said I; 'I know you and Vickey are dead in love with each other, and I know, too, that a great obstacle is in the way, which will probably prevent you from ever marrying. No joking, Judge; I want a fashionable wedding at our hotel, and I want everything to go off smoothly; but I tell you there is a cat in the bag, and it will scratch like fury if you don't look out.' The Judge thought there might be some truth in it, and he merely told me to go on, to say what I had to say. 'Now,' said I, 'Judge, you know Mrs. Edge has never given her consent, and she is really the master over Vickey's affections. She can, by the mere crook of her finger, turn her daughter's love all over to Prescott, for whom the girl has a great admiration. Now, there is one way in which the old woman can be won over, and that is through her old maiden sister. This is a poor, old, dwindled creature, not worth a pinch of snuff. And yet Mrs. Edge does whatever this old half-witted maid bids her; she looks to her, in fact, as a master, ruling spirit. Now I come to the joke: I put up Mrs. Edge to send for this old maid (so we could have the thing in our own hands), in order to let her see high life in Washington. The maid has come, and is now at the Jackson House. I want you to soft-soap her up—in fact, to court her a little, no matter how distasteful it may be, in order that she may buy over Mrs. Edge's goodwill to us. I have had a long talk with her. Her name is Peggy Van Dorn; and I told her that you and Vickey were in such great hopes that her influence would overcome Mrs. Edge, that she had been sent for for that very purpose. And I promised her that, for her good influence in this, we would all put our heads together and secure a husband for herself in the bargain. She is in great glee, and I do hope we can keep it up; perhaps some fun will come of it.'

"'Now, as I am a Judge,' said he, 'you are the cunningest rascal I ever heard of! But say, you, can we not get up some old fool to marry her? I would enjoy it so much! Why, I can make an old woman like that believe she is a perfect angel. But how could you invent such a thing for such an old person? Oh, you rascal!'

"'Oh, we'll marry her off to somebody,' said I; 'we'll pay her off some way; only you play well your part.'

"'Trust me to that,' said he. 'I'll do such wonders on her affections as makes Cupid tremble for his profession. You leave that to me.'

"We then returned to the carriage, and, with our company, proceeded to the Jackson House. On the way up I told them all of the arrival of Miss Peggy Van Dorn, and of her desire to see them all.

"As soon as we alighted, Mrs. Edge and Vickey hastened in to see her; Mr. Edge went into the office to examine his papers in reference to some new railroad project. With the Judge I lingered outside till the common greetings between the ladies should be over, and then we entered the parlor. Of course, the Judge was introduced, and a general free conversation ensued about the result of the doings at the Capitol. In a little while, however, Mrs. Edge called Vickey, being anxious to leave the Judge with her sister for a moment, promising that she would return to the parlor in one minute. The Judge then told her of his extreme happiness in getting acquainted with the Edge family, and added that there was only one link to fasten, before the chainwork would be completed, which would be the happiest event of his life. 'It seems as though I still have another consent to win, and that is yours.' She was silent, and pulling furiously at the bonnet strings. 'You know, at your time of life, which, like my own, is well-nigh spent, a little encouragement is a thing of great joy. You are yet capable of feeling those warm emotions, and you know, too, that a brighter day awaits your happy decision.'

"I don't believe she knew a word he said, and I thought she had forgotten what I said; so I kept near her back, digging her old ribs, telling her to say, 'I admire you, sir; I consent to the marriage, sir;' but she was so frightened, and withal had so much fuss with her bonnet strings, and I feared every moment some one else would come in, that I was nearly frantic with anxiety.

"'You have been apprized of Mrs. Edge's decision?' asked the Judge.

"'Oh, yes, sir; I—I—' she replied.

"'Well,' said he, 'I trust we understand each other?'

"'Tell him you consent,' said I; and, before she thought, she said,

"'Oh, yes; I—I consent to the marriage.'

"The Judge then took her withered hand in his, saying, 'I say, now, you are a very queen, an angel. I never saw such majesty. You have performed your part like a princess of the royal family of Britain;' and he danced about, dragging her after him in greater glee than I had seen him in a dozen years; and she herself danced a little. Just then Vickey and her mother came in, exclaiming, 'Well, did I ever!' I turned, and told them the Judge was so anxious to meet one that rejoiced in Lincoln's election, that he danced like a child. They then took her out, and I returned to the office."

Thus ended the clerk's story.

CHAPTER X.

SHORT sentences, I said to Jenkins, are easily understood. We can always discover in them the author's meaning. Referred him to many authors, naming even some of our greatest modern citizen writers. But, he said, for his part he liked long sentences the best, and maintained that they left the sweetest and most impressive influence, referring me to one of our great American poets, quoting this beautiful verse :

" I laid on my back and viewed the setting sun,
And, as the radiance faded out,
I sucked the sky to keep it there."

And, as a proof of its elegance, he told me that that poet had been named after the famous cotton mills of Massachusetts simply for having sucked the sky. He smiled in triumph, and, taking up his notes, proceeded as follows :

I had no more time to spare than to hear the clerk's story, but hastily took leave of gentle Ann and Wadsworth, whom I most reluctantly had to leave together while I departed to acquaint the President with the result of the election. This was only a few minutes—at most not an hour—after we were at the Capitol. But what was my surprise, on going to the door of the Jackson House, to behold Floyd. Davis, Mason, Madame Ponchard, and Orsini flying past in a carriage drawn by two spirited horses in the direction of the White House. I determined to be there before them, and ordered my driver accordingly ; being well armed, and fully determined that, if Floyd gave me any justifiable ground at all, I would be a full match for him. In fact, I even hoped that he would shoot at me, or stab me, or in some way give me an excuse for ending his career. It could not be gainsaid that he had bartered himself, and his oath, and his office. He had forfeited still more sacred trusts, and even publicly challenged God to grind his body into dust if he ever again yielded to his former obligations ; that not a vestige of this country should ever be governed by States prohibiting slavery. He revoked all his former life, and now stood sworn the opposite way, even while he was Secretary of War. Davis was more silent and cunning, using him as a cat's-paw to his deeper-laid schemes. Rhett, Davis, and Toombs were, in fact, the master spirits ; while the more profane and weaker instruments, Cobb, Yancey, Floyd, Mason, Slidell, Hunter, Thompson, Iverson, Breckenridge, Wigfall, Miles, and others, were barking bloodhounds sent out to start the game.

Buchanan was waiting in the hall to receive me ; for, though he had heard from the general election that Lincoln was elected, he still clung to the hope that in the electoral college some of the minority candidates might come over, and, through their united votes, beat Lincoln. There was scarcely a shadow of difference between Douglas, Bell, and Breckinridge. They had all run on the slaveholders' platform, only the former ran it blind in deceiving the people. They had merely lent themselves to a pretended difference, but all for a Southern, sectional, slave purpose. Lincoln ran against all these men, and on a platform to settle all the national troubles by a constitutional amendment. He beat them all. The nation decided to amend the Constitution, so as to prohibit slavery where the other party wanted to introduce it. The question was settled. The election made it law in the hearts of the American people. All it needed was execution. Now, this being so, the beaten party would never have hereafter a clue for arguments, whereby they could obtain office. This election made their political death.

As I stated before, the President was waiting for me, apparently very much downcast, and he hardly saw me ere he feebly said,

" Tell me, sir, oh, I pray you, is it true ? Has he indeed the majority of all the votes ? "

" He has," said I ; " it is certainly true ; Lincoln is elected to be the next President."

" That can never be ! " he said ; " no man shall ever be President of these United States after me. What say Davis, Toombs, and Rhett ? "

" Rhett has gone home," said I, " and he gave strict orders that you be informed that, ere to-morrow's setting sun, one star shall be ripped from the American flag."

"I told the people this," replied Buchanan. "They would not go according to the Constitution. They have voted to rob the South of the vast West, and the South will never stand it. That great unsettled territory was as much intended by the Constitution to be for the South as for the North. But this vote has used the liberty of voting the national domain over to the free States. If there be war, the North have themselves to blame. I'll never raise a hand in their behalf. If there is any justice at all, it is all on the other side. Come in; I shall write such a message, and you shall pen it for me, that the very reading of it shall overturn this whole affair. Take my word for it, if there be ever another President for the whole of the States, it will be either Davis or Toombs, Lincoln's election to the contrary notwithstanding."

Hardly had we turned to enter the Mansion, when Prescott came up on a full run, shouting,

"South Carolina has already passed the ordinance of secession. It was passed unanimously, immediately on receipt of the news, by telegraph, from Rhett, of the result of the electoral vote."

We were astounded. It had been suspected, but not to take place so suddenly. Buchanan nodded his head a little aside, saying,

"I told them so; I told them so."

He then took us both in, and we all seated ourselves to weigh the matter at our ease. Just then Davis and Floyd came in, even without any ceremony, the doors being open, and affording a free passage.

"I know the meaning of this," said Floyd, as soon as we were all squarely face to face. He eyed me. "It is the furtherance of that dastardly election; it is a hurried dodge to sway a Christian President from his constitutional obligations."

I told him I was ordered by the President to be here at this time for his special purposes, and that I could hear no personal insinuations. "I know, too," said I, "all the plans and purposes of the secessionists; it is my duty, as a citizen, to inform the President of what I know."

"And how did you gain your information?" said he. "As a spy? Ay, worse! as a British subject—the most abject of all falsity. You have more shamed the name of American than could any living man. Any falsity but this, this base assumption. Tell all you know

of us, and, when it is known that you put on the garb of an Englishman, no American will believe a word you say. A man so mean cannot speak the truth."

Now, I must confess I felt a little shame, and was at some loss for a reply, so suddenly had he blown upon me. Yet I comanded myself a moment, and said that I considered any deception whatever would be justifiable, if it should succeed in exposing such a villainous scheme for extending the power of human bondage by usurping a government founded on civil and religious liberty. "You must be aware now," I said, "that my determinations are not to be baffled by bluster. The whole country knows you robbed the national Treasury. Your name will ever be branded as thief."

Buchanan had stepped aside, scared for his life, and Prescott and myself were in full attitude for an attack. Davis, too, seemed to shrink back, cowardly; but Floyd, thief as he was, showed no signs of fear. He was armed with a bowie knife and revolver; so was I, and so was Prescott.

"Were it not for the place, I would cut you in two," said Floyd; and I retorted that he could take any other place he chose, either by notice or without warning. "Only too glad will I be," said I, "that you may fall upon me in ambush or in public or by appointment. If you have no conscience other than to perjure yourself, I will teach you."

"Oh, gentlemen, for God's sake!" said Buchanan, his knees shaking so he could hardly stand, "will you leave me? will you retire?"

"Only this message have we," said Floyd, "to tell your Excellency, that commissioners are to be appointed to call on you to negotiate for the sale of the forts, arsenals, and Government property in South Carolina, and that they must be received and treated as emissaries of a foreign country."

Buchanan was so frightened he knew not what to say, and stood there trembling, till Floyd and Davis bowed themselves out. "Oh, sir," he then said to me, "if there should be blood shed in this house! If I should be killed! What have I done? God knows I have stood by the Constitution!"

"I think you have not," said Prescott. "You have stood by the South. You now stand by the South. You see them rob the nation; see them plotting treason; see them doing in South Carolina what Jackson stopped them from doing; see the election of Lincoln in a constitutional manner, and you declare it is unconstitutional. You crouch and tremble here, while these common traitors dictate to you the terms you shall yourself subscribe to. In cases of emergency you can call out the national forces, but you creep into technicalities to avoid enforcing the constitutional laws you have sworn to protect."

"Oh, sir, I am in no humor for this. I know I seem so to everybody, but it is not so—I am no child; I can speak; I will show these fellows what I can do. I will never, so help me Heaven! never sell these forts and arsenals. But I pray you both, leave me awhile. I am a little excited—I fear I am."

Before we had time to leave, he had himself withdrawn. In a minute more we wended our way out. When in the hallway I touched Prescott's arm, and with one hand drew forth my bowie knife, remarking, "This had most assuredly been Floyd's death, had he raised a hand on me."

Right before us, outside the Mansion, and near the upper step, was Madame Ponchard. She saw the knife, which I instantly sheathed, and I heard her pat distinctly with her foot on the stone—a signal, I thought, to some one—and I left my hand still resting on the handle of my knife. A few paces brought us to the outside door. To the left, and below, there stood Orsini, both hands in his pockets, and he was apparently in a sleepy attitude. He had been stationed there, no doubt, to stab me; but her signal was to warn him that a witness was by, and one that would perhaps fall on him. Perhaps the showing of my knife saved us, yet this was merely conjecture. We passed out unharmed, and were soon in our carriage on the way back.

"Oh!" says Prescott, as soon as we were seated, "oh, do you know I believe I have found your fugitive? I am almost certain I have."

Now I had previously told Prescott about the slave girl; that I had lost trace of her, although I had searched the city over and over. He then told me that, if I had no objection, we would drive that way, and he would show me the place where he was confident he had seen her on a previous occasion.

Accordingly we proceeded over to the east side of town, down Clay to Montgomery street, and then down Park Avenue. Here we encountered a dusky-looking washing and ironing establishment, where a pug-nosed old woman kept herself half hidden behind poles, tubs, and

clothes. "This is the spot," said Prescott, as he was about halting. "Let us call and ascertain. I am sure I saw just such a person here at the break of day this morning." I told him, however, to drive on, for we would probably only frighten her, and not succeed in getting an interview. He acceded to this, and, after we had passed a square further on, I bid him excuse me; that I would return, while he proceeded homeward; cautioning him, too, that, as it was getting late, he should make good speed, keeping an eye out for assassins.

In a few minutes afterwards I was before the washerwoman, endeavoring to gain the required information. She was Irish, and spoke in exceedingly broad accents, and was stubborn to all my queries, seeming to know nothing about what I meant. She was, she said, an honest, hard-working woman, and hoped that other folks would do the same as she did. She was sure, she said, that I was not such a fool as to think that two persons could live in a shanty as small as hers. I told her I was a friend of the missing girl. What had she to do with that? she said. Surely, if she washed and ironed her clothes like an honest woman, I should not come there and bother her with my tomfoolery.

For a long time I talked with this old woman, who persisted to the last that she never saw nor heard of the slave girl I was seeking. Yet, she betrayed such signs as made me sure she was playing false. I could do no better, however, than reluctantly to turn away, saying, "In half an hour I will pass here again. If the said girl is here, bid her secrete herself where she can see me as I pass. If she knows me to be her friend, bid her speak. If she does not, let her keep secreted. I will never trouble you more." Again she persisted it was nonsense to talk such stuff to her; that I might pass the shanty a hundred or a thousand times if I liked, provided I did not trouble her with my nonsense. I left, and strolled round awhile, and then, in about half an hour, started back. Ere I reached the place, however, and in passing some plaster and boards where the builders had been at work, some one called my name. I turned, and faced the sound.

"It is, then—it is indeed my friend!"

I heard the voice behind the boards, while plainly before me rose up the fair one, bursting into tears. I knew her at once, and expressed my happiness in finding her.

"Oh, sir, pardon me that I act so unbecomingly! I hardly know if this be life, or if it be death; exposure, fear, and hoped-for joys nearly distract me. Scarce I know where I am, and yet too clearly do the vivid scenes appear."

I had gone near her, seeing that she was in fact a little bewildered. "Be calm," said I; "you have nothing here to fear. Let trust in me give you time to collect your presence. Your speech betrays a soul strained to the utmost. If this do continue, your blood will take improper roads, and so derange you fully."

"Yes, yes, I will be calm; but first let me weep. Oh, blessed vent to woman's bursting heart! Oh, sir, that I could waste myself away in tears! I know that God has sent me a friend."

She then caught my hand in both hers —two small and delicate hands, the sight of which, so fair, like swords fell on the boasted name of American, to hew from us at a dash the stain on liberty.

"With me, sir, it is life, or it is death," she continued. "The sea of agony is over-flooded; desperate is my hunger for kind words, and in the surge betwixt two contrary tides I seem the fool. Please, sir, I will not weep long. Oh! oh!" She started, looked up the avenue, and again composed herself. "A sound of common things. You see that carriage? I am half unhinged. Why! did you go to the old place to find me?"

I told her I did.

"No wonder," said she. "I was barred out. I ran away that very night, God knows where—I don't; but I walked nearly all night, and then I came to yonder new buildings, and laid me down on the shavings to sleep. Praise Heaven, I slept so sweetly! I dreamed I flew, with a friend, from my native country—that I was free. How did you find me, sir?"

I then told her it was through Prescott; that I had, however, previously searched all over the city in vain.

"I throw myself all on you," she interrupted. "I know you will take me safe to Canada; that you will shield me from every danger. Oh, sir, if you knew my suffering, you would ever regard my fervency and freedom with due allowance. But come, I will take you to the old washerwoman's shanty, and there relate my ills and threatened barbarous treatment. 'Tis not well we talk long in this place. Have you ever been in Georgia? Oh, we have pretty places there! But cold, cold be the hearts, where summer's radiance ever is; to balance fair majestic Nature's parts, the winter is all in human bosoms. The lily springs where burning suns pour down; and shadows, too, appear cooler and darker there, but not in wild nature. Oh, no; only in man is death! I could tell you such tales of Georgia and Virginia, you would call me mad. Who was this Prescott with you? Do you know he is your friend? Many men, for the reward of five hundred dollars, would betray me."

As she ran on in this way we were slowly wending our way back to the shanty, and I observed that nearly every moment she started and looked about, as if suffering with great fear and anxiety. "And why should I not be?" she said. "Six times have I run off, and six times captured been, bound, and carried back. On the seventh Bruce succeeded, and so will my pursuers. My vigilance is but the desperation of all my powers. Every nerve hath an eye, an ear, an action. Oh, that I could quiet them—that I could still myself to rest! My aching head, my bursting heart, my soul that pleads for power from above!—all in struggle, all grappling for the feeble force I have, each to wield in front extreme its own importance first. 'Tis the grasp of a drowning soul on the sea of life; breakers and foul winds blind me, even while on the furious surge I catch the glimpse of a far-off shore. But no; I gasp, I rouse to see, to feel, to prove each separate sense by another, that I am past all danger, landed clear from the billows, and in my hand the rod of liberty. Then why, whence this shaking form, to gain the world, and quiver still? But dark forebodings come, and imps of treachery steal from every corner; the clank of chains hath its echo in every spear of grass. Oh, my native country! what a chattel am I! A fool that I love thee still!"

Thus she continued, till we had seated ourselves in the shanty, where she was interrupted by the old washerwoman, who accused her that she had said she had no friend—that every one was an enemy—that on no account was her concealment to be divulged. To all of this, however, the young girl gave a satisfactory answer.

It was now quite night, and we had no fear whatever of being discovered. I asked her what her name was, and she said Lizzie; she knew no other. I asked her if the washerwoman knew of the reward offered for her capture. She answered, No. "I took care to conceal that," said Lizzie. "I told the old woman that all the trouble was about a forced marriage. She does not mistrust I am a slave. She says she knows I am some great lady."

Now it happened that, while we conversed thus, the old woman packed up some clothes and got ready to carry them home. I feared Lizzie would dislike to have me stay with her alone, and I signified the same to her.

"Oh, sir, you much mistake me," she said. "Had I no more confidence, you had never found me here. I feel that a Higher Power guards over me. This is my last attempt to fly from slavery—to fly from a new-found master, whose designs I can never forget, for the deep horror of his boasted might. Welcome all hazard! I am resolved. These poor, frail parts, these hands and limbs, given me as instruments of adornment and protection to the spirit within, shall first exhaust themselves to carry me safe to a foreign shore; but when they fail, and all the avenues on earth are closed to me, I will, to keep the soul unspotted, open a vent and wing myself to the imperial throne above!"

She half choked at her own words, drawing a bowie knife, and then smiling in anticipated triumph.

"And this is my vow, when man no more protects me; Lucretia will end herself before Sextus comes. Think not, sir, I speak of you, but of the home I dread."

Now, while she showed this desperate resolution, I involuntarily recollected that her nature was at variance with a large portion of the American women, who, when failing to win their point with man, kill him, and that's the end—so unlike Lucretia's death, that aroused the city of Rome and overswept the kings. And so, too, this poor fugitive had hit the vein that most moves man in her behalf.

As soon as the washerwoman left, I bade her relate to me all her trials and hardships, and to depict more plainly the dangers that awaited her.

"Oh, how can I tell you—how collect myself when thus excited? And you know, too, I have a half-sister, who has not yet arrived. I fear she has been captured, and carried back to slavery. Ever comes before me the vision of her gentle wrists and ankles encased in iron; and I fancy I hear her suppressed sobs pleading in my ear—to help her. She is so fair, so gentle—only fifteen. Such a form as storms the noblest heart, as tempts the ruffian. And she unprotected! Oh, how can I tell you my long misfortunes, while my sister is away? Sit near me, sir, for now it is growing dark, and I need something tangible to remind me I am safe the while." She smiled a little, and looked up with much modesty, adding, "You know you are in Heaven's sight my protector, while I, like a drowning child, catch at the shore in the name of all that's holy."

Now, when she had laid her hand over into mine, she entered upon her history, which I have here in brief set down, to wit:

"When I was about four or five years old, I lived with a planter by the name of Palmer, in the State of Georgia. Of the still earlier part of my life I knew nothing, nor do I know now. I do not know who was my father, nor who was my mother. When I was very young, an old colored woman took care of my sister and me. We called her Mammy, but I never thought her my mother. Until I was nine or ten, I never thought about who I was or where I came from. I was brought up under the belief that I was a negress. I and my sister had more privileges than any other of his slaves. We slept in our master's house, and always ate at the second table. But, as I hinted before, at about nine years of age I began to surmise some on my unknown ancestry. I could not account for my lack of color, though I was despised by the genuine blacks, partly for my whiteness, and partly for the privileges I had. I mean also my sister; for we were treated the same. These surmises about my origin led me to watch the conversation of older folks, from whom I learned that I was a favored slave because I had a nose and hair the very style of Palmer's. My curiosity became greater. For weeks, for months, ay, for years I stationed myself in byways, in chimney-corners, garrets—anywhere, everywhere—to see, to hear, and, in the language of my master, to know whence I came and whither I was travelling. But I gained no information. Only once I heard him tell our mistress he had ordered a teacher for Lizzie and Kate, and that he intended they should be well brought up, and finally sent to France. Of course, I kept this a secret, only I told my sister Kate. The nature of our lives gave us no familiars. We occupied a position between the blacks and our master. My sister and I often prayed, when we laid down to sleep, that God might change us into genuine blacks by morning. We wanted some one to love, to be familiar with.

"When I was eleven, we were put to our lessons under the promised teacher. But this was kept a secret, on account of the law of the State forbidding slaves being educated. Soon, then, our intercourse with other slaves was nearly extinguished. Our teacher was a gentleman, a small, lean man, very pious and good. He it was who taught me first the road to happiness; taught me to subdue my passions, and to trust in a Higher Power. Blessings rest upon that man! He showed me the finger of God, which has ever pointed me to the narrow path.

"At about twelve I was instructed by an excellent artist from Savannah, in cutting and making ladies' wearing apparel; and, according to my instructor's report, learned quickly all the intricacies of changing models.

"At about that time my master was elected to the United States Senate. He had previously held several high positions under Government, but never so high as senator. One term he served, bringing Kate and me with him, as servants to our mistress' toilet; and he then resigned on account of ill health. At his home in Georgia he had much company, and I am forced to believe that his company ruined him. He gambled. Our mistress died. She was the purest and best woman I ever knew. She was a defenceless little creature, and whenever she addressed us, 'twas with such a voice and gentle sentence as only Heaven inspires. This was the beginning of our darkness. Our master mortgaged his plantation, and went to Savannah. Here he lost all his money, and was reduced so low that he moved to a cheap cottage in the suburbs. He had no servants but Kate and me, and the old negro woman who took care of us when we were children. One faithful negro man he brought with him, who now agreed to hire out for the support of our master. But the latter got intoxicated one day, and sold him. That money was soon gone. We had nothing more. One day he came to me, in the cottage, and, taking my hand, said, 'Lizzie, what shall I do—shall I sell Mammy?' I answered him, saying, 'No, master, no; for then would soon come the end. 'Tis better that we work for you. I think I can turn the talents and the culture you have bestowed on me to a good advantage. There are many rich ladies here, who, when they know my capacity to cut their dresses and to adorn their persons, will soon reward me handsomely on your account. Besides, I think Mammy, and Kate and I, and perhaps yourself, would die if we were separated. You cannot be ignorant of the fact, that you are in very feeble health; that you are, in fact, likely to be called at any moment.'

"He burst into tears, and told me to leave him a moment. I did so. In half an hour I returned. He was kneeling down by the sofa, praying and weeping. In one hand was a miniature of his loved wife; in the other was this trifling jewel —see, sir!—a thing, I had heard him say, that had been presented to him many years ago in some foreign country. He ceased grieving only by falling on the floor exhausted. I ran to him, but he was insensible. I took the jewel and miniature, lest some accident befall them, and then hastily summoned Mammy and Kate to help him. After some difficulty we got him aroused and assisted to a bed, when we summoned a doctor. For many days now we were in great trouble. We had not money to buy medicine with. Mammy ironed to earn a little. Our master was very low, speechless. I then went out to get work. Fortune smiled on me. I knew not what to charge for my work, and the ladies I worked for were so ignorant, and, being rich, valued me according to my prices. Consequently I deemed it just—for I was vain of my capacity—to charge at least ten times as much as would any other person. This soon became notorious, which helped me still more. I ceased doing anything myself, only visiting wealthy and fashionable belles. On my arrival they would send for their regular dressmaker, who had to cut and trim according to my direction. Often I got fifty dollars for a single visit. My accomplishments and ease of speech elicited much curiosity, for I always represented myself as a slave, stating who my master was, and what misfortune had befallen him. Sometimes the money was given to me, sometimes sent to my master. One day I was sent for to visit a fashionable actress; but as I knew nothing about that style of costume, I declined going. The next day she called on me. I declined again. I did not like her. She was called beautiful. She repeated her call, but I still declined, hoping within my heart I should never see her more. She had not harmed or in any way treated me rudely, but I felt that she carried an awful fate before her. Oh, that I had never tried to banish these intuitive impressions! Forgive me, sir, I weep when I remember. Well, our little caste in life rapidly improved, but my master long lay in feeble health. One whole year he lay there, my little sister Kate ever by his side, Mammy ever preparing him some of her thousand fancy feats for his nearly-exhausted palate, and I, I am happy to say, toiling to the full support of all. Nay, more, in one year I saved six hundred dollars. My master would not touch this money. Though, when it had been sent to him for my services, he would hold it in his hand till I came to his bedside, and then give it me, ever saying, 'God bless you; save this, Lizzie; I will some day make you happy!'

"How long this course of things would have run I know not, only that Fate changed the scene. In my visits one day to the house of a wealthy and honorable citizen, when I withdrew something from my pocket, this jewel fell on the floor. The gentleman of the house picked it up, saying, 'What's this, young woman?' I told him it was my master's; that it was something he valued very highly, and that always, on leaving home, I carried it in order that it might not be stolen or lost. He eyed me with some suspicion, and then asked where my master lived. I told him. He then put it in his pocket, and went off to see my master. I was nearly frantic, for I feared I would be accused of theft, when Heaven knew with what a loved and honorable purpose I had done it. When I came home my master called me to his side, having ordered all others out. He was then propped up in bed. After asking how I came by it, and why I carried it, and, having heard me all through, he said I had done well. 'Some day that jewel shall be yours,' he said, with some emotion. 'You shall discover something which shall make you and your half-sister happy through life. Should ever any misfortune overtake me, keep you this jewel. How I came by it I cannot tell you at present. But it was first presented to your father. Whenever harm comes near you, tell men that such was your father's jewel, and no man will harm you.'

"I was certainly pleased at this, but feared that, if indeed my master believed in such a charm, he had lost some of his reason. Though I was more anxious to learn something about my own father, and yet I dared not be so impertinent as to ask him more. He bid me take the jewel and keep it till he called for it, and then told me that I should order a feast of simple things that night; that his friends had discovered his whereabouts, and would visit him at nine o'clock.

"True enough, many men called on him, but they were strangers to me. From that time on my master regained rapidly in health. Society cheered him up, but he was a changed man. He drank no more, nor did he ever gamble after that.

"One bright spring morning he called me to him, for he had entirely recovered now, and frequently took a walk or a drive, saying, 'Lizzie, you must go out no more to work. You have been a good girl, now rest yourself by preparing for a journey to the interior.' He told me nothing of his plans, nor of his business. I had seven hundred dollars in gold, which I often offered him, but he invariably answered, 'God bless you, Lizzie, I have plenty of money; keep your own.' I knew then that the gentleman who discovered his whereabouts by having seen this jewel, must have provided him with money. One day, when I was absent, getting things for our journey, the actress called again for my services. My master bid her wait till I returned. Oh, woful day! Dread Fate, why did I stay so long? He, whom I should have guarded, was in the snares of the evil one. Yet I tarried, so heedless of the woful future. Excuse me, sir, my tears are the fruit of untimely joys. But I must tell all. My master smiled on this woman. All men have a failing part, but some are never touched upon it, and so, pass applauded for their virtue. The pure never throw a stone, and the untried are great boasters and full of vain glory. My master was good and great, but even these can be overcome. We excuse those that steal to appease a starving stomach. But who, with a heart of love and tenderness, can feel the desolation of a noble man whose house is stripped of conjugal joys, and not pity him for catching at something whereon to cling in good companionship? I adjusted the style the actress desired, and she paid me handsomely.

"Soon after this my master informed me that he had redeemed the mortgages on his plantation, and that we must return. Oh, how happy I was to get away from Savannah!—To get away from that actress! But I was happy in ignorance. The anticipated horrors came. We had hardly got settled on the old plantation, when my master returned to Savannah, married the actress, and brought her out to the plantation. This was the renewing of winter to my own life. Though I was but a slave, the new wife was jealous of me. But she concealed it well, for she was a woman of great comprehension. I never asked what countrywoman she was, but thought she was Spanish. She was very dark, with dark eyes, and she spoke with so much deliberation on all occasions, though ever saying little, I was positive from the first that she would in some way prove treacherous. But it came sooner than I expected. She ordered a magnificent ball. All the choicest liquors were provided. Guests, the first in the State, were present. That night my master drank. Next day he took sick and died."

For a moment my fair companion could say no more. I read at once her surmise, that her master had been murdered. But she soon went on.

"The widow became the owner of us all. We were all advertised for sale. My beauty and accomplishments were asserted in the advertisements in all the Savannah, Atlanta, and Charleston papers. Can any one conceive the meaning? Can any one know the horrors within my soul? 'Tis now nearly three years since, and yet no minute has passed to give me joy. I was sold, with my sister, to a neighboring planter, where I was kept as lady's servant. My sister had nothing to do. But he announced that he would sell all his slaves at the end of the following year, and this kept me in continual dread. Many men called to see me, and often tried various means to purchase me. I became frightened, and ere the year rolled round I ran away. When seventy miles from home I was seen by an acquaintance, and arrested and carried back. I had four hundred dollars then, having given my sister the balance, with instructions to follow me soon after. They took my money, and never returned it. On the next day I was home again, where I received a severe reprimand, with the threat that I should now be sold without consulting my wishes in regard to a buyer. Again I repeated the attempt, and was again excused with a reprimand. He then changed his purpose, to not sell for still another year. Before this appointed time arrived I had been selected and bargained for by a gentleman from Charleston. The sight of him was almost death to me. His eye had not the mark of avarice, and yet it made me pray for death. It had more terror to me. Under the guise of something else I was bound by a chain to my sister, and taken into Virginia. We loved to go North; slaves always fear going further South. We were then put into the fields to hoe tobacco. In a few days after, when we were at work, my Charleston purchaser came up to us. He was on horseback. I shuddered at his approach, and at the words he uttered.

"'Which do you choose?' said he, after he had smiled and bid us cease our work, 'you are no longer ignorant of my will nor my power. Obedience will give you ease and enjoyment; its opposite will entail upon you toil and sorrow.'

"'By sending me here,' I said, 'you have given me my choice. I pray you, sir, leave me to toil here all the days of my life, and I am content.'

"He then made an oath that he would tame me or be my death; and, bidding my sister and the other slaves to leave, he then attempted to dismount from his horse, but his foot tangled in the stirrup, and the horse ran off, dragging him some distance, and leaving him helpless on the ground. We took advantage, and Kate and I ran away. Several times I have been captured and carried back; but, ere he recovered from his bruises, we ever escaped. For the last year we have been running and hiding. A few months ago we were, near Columbus, Ohio, captured and carried back. My master had entirely recovered, and then paid the captors three hundred dollars. We were so overcome that we were both taken ill. We pretended to be worse than we were, in order to prevent violence. A few weeks since we fled again. At night we were pursued; but we had matured our course, and the place of our meeting in this city. All the advertisements in the papers stated that Kate and I were so attached to each other we would most likely be found together. For that we separated. And now, alas, I fear we meet on earth no more! She has no money, and I know not how she can live. Oh, that she were here! Send her to me, O Heaven, or I must die!" She burst into a new flood of tears, ending thus her story of life in a land of liberty.

In two hours after I had her in boys' clothes, with a short black head of hair, registered at the Jackson House as Joe Travers, of New York.

CHAPTER XI.

"Now Cupid strode up in his bright array,
Even to the side of the great ancient Mars,
And smiled, and tipped his toe for a footrace,
Holding his arrow right to th' other's nose,
And hearts abundant casting in the path,
While Mars, in grim and frowning majesty,
Whetting his rusted sword with thoughts of blood,
Kicked at poor Cupid, falling by the way
On Cupid's battlements—the hearts of course,
And Cupid shot him through. And so, love rules."

THE night passed most unpleasantly to me, for the tale that Lizzie told brought vivid pictures of horrors to my vision. The threat of war, too, brought clouds and darkness and blood and death. The threats of Floyd and Davis sent the frenzied blood to my every nerve: the imbecility of Buchanan enraged me. But these fevers passed.

And pleasantly soon Fancy pictured peace and harmony and love. For, even on the verge of mighty war kind nature comes with gentle consolations; for man's power, exhausted by conjuring evil, is lulled to sleep with visions more than mortal. Yet, when he wakes, how all-forgetful is he!

Thus I moralized till the bright morning came, and then sallied forth. No more the thought of war; no more concerning secession. Hardly had I come down to the office of the Jackson House, when a rough, burly-looking customer met me, with a paper in his hand. Pointing to it, he said,

"I say, sir, do you live here?"

I told him I did.

"Then," said he, "read this. I've lost some niggers."

I took the paper which read as follows:

A runaway slave known as Lizzie, formerly owned by the late Hon. John Palmer of Georgia. Five hundred dollars reward offered for her. Also three hundred dollars offered for the girl Kate, a young sister of Lizzie. They are both nearly white, with light hair, blue eyes, well dressed. Kate is fifteen, and Lizzie eighteen or nineteen. Both are good-looking girls, and might readily pass for white. They have been traced to this city, and are supposed to be here at present. Apply to Wm. H. Russe', office, Jay Street, Washington.

Scarcely had I scanned the advertisement, when, tripping down the stairs came the identical Lizzie, now and hereafter known as Joe Travers—a modest, beardless boy. The fevered excitement was at its flood on my nerves. What could be done? In she came square before us ere she saw the hated face of him whom, more than all things on earth, she dreaded.

She the slave to such a man!

She started, almost frozen at the glance, and then walked away. He, ashamed of his profession, seeing the boy, as he supposed, approach me, took the paper from my hand, and it fell on the floor. So, when the slave started, he was the while scrambling after the fallen paper, and thus most providentially failed to fully see her. Yet so much had he seen, that, when we were again alone, he said, "Had my niggers brothers, I'd swear that boy was one—the very dimples in his cheeks and chin, and the sprightly step—I swear, I would that he too were my slave."

"That boy!" said I. "His father had better hear you talk that way."

"Oh, not for the world!" said he. "I was only joking! And then he asked me to go and drink with him, promising me that he would give me such a description of his fugitives as would enable me to capture them, and obtain the reward; stating also that he had been told that I knew more about the city of Washington than did any other man, and would be likely, in consequence, to aid him in an effectual manner. "I will tell you, stranger," said I, and I wondered the while to see so coarse a man all hung with jewelry. An immense gold chain of choice workmanship dangled weightily on a rich silk vest, the breast of which, being open, showed a splendid cluster of large and small diamonds, so set as to resemble the ice-tipped branches of the wild orange tree. Golden leaves tried to hide the brilliancy, but anon, as the wearer moved, waved aside to show some secret gem. On his fingers were rings. One was of native gold, and rudely made; others, set with choice stones, seemed so rarely carved and chased as it had been a jeweller's lifetime to contrive them. Strangely, too, this man's boots, unpolished, outside the trousers, were poor and common. On his head was a soft wool hat, large in the brim, and seeming to rest on his heavy, dark side whiskers, while the points of a coarsely twisted moustache, like horns, stood far out, displaying a lofty Roman nose piled high up between two as sensual eyes as ever were in the face of man. A little walking-stick with a gold handle he twirled in one hand, between the fingers of which was a half-smoked and badly chewed cigar, and the advertisement I mentioned was in the other. "I will tell you, stranger," said I. "if you will excuse me for calling you such. ——"

"My name is John Russel, sir, descended from the ancient family of that name in England."

"Ah! then, Mr. Russel. In these days it is useless to seek for a run-away slave. They get to Canada by steam, and I hope yours may soon be there too."

"What," said he, "you too talk so?" I made no answer and we parted, he to seek his slaves, and I toward the girls in the parlor. I saw him go to the door. He seemed still to look after Joe Travers. I feared he did. I looked for Joe. Not to be seen. I then went into the parlor. Vickey came to me and asked me for a good dentist. I told her where to go. Asked her if she had tooth-ache? "Oh, no," she said, laughing. She then excused herself, and went out. I was about to leave, when in came Mrs. Edge and the clerk, who seemed very polite to her. He winked at me to keep still; so I sat down, unobserved, by Mrs. Edge. "I know it will make a great difference with her," said Mrs. Edge to the clerk; "her face is so sunken in, and then she can't half eat. I've been telling her so for a long time, but she's so close with her money. Now, she's not like me in that at all; I go in for any expense according to one's station, you know, and I tell her she's getting so old it need not make much difference now no more with her as long as she's got to live."

"Why, certainly," said the clerk; "you have just my views exactly, and so has Vickey."

"And I wish Mr. Edge was the same," said she; "he's gone after railroad contracts ever since we came. His soul is all in a railroad—poor, dear man!—Always into his papers; he hears nothing you say to him no more, unless it is about railroads. Only the other day I called his

attention to our accomplished daughter as she passed so lovingly before us. 'See,' said I, 'what a beautiful train she has;' and he started, and said, 'What road's that on?' for he thought I was talking about a train of cars. Poor, dear soul, he started up, and says he, 'What road's that on?' and I thought I'd a-died a-laughing; and then he got up and went out, for he said it was nonsense to call Vickey's coat tails a train. 'What road's that on?' he said so funny."

The clerk laughed a little then, and he turned to her, saying, "Excuse me, Mrs. Edge, but I am in a hurry, and I will be pleased to hear what you have called me here for?"

"Oh," said she, "yes, yes. Well, what I was going to say is this, for you see I am a plain-spoken, honest woman, and I always speak my mind, and I always think it is best for folks to understand each other as they go along, and then they will always remain good friends. I'm laughing at what Mr. Edge said; says he, 'What road's that on?' But, as I was about to say, you know we don't make much pretensions ourselves—that's Mr. Edge and me—but we have spared no expense on our daughter. She has a finished education. She went to Philadelphia. Every one who sees her knows she's prepared for the best of society and people of the highest rank. Only the other evening I noticed, when a promiscuous crowd was in the parlor, and one of the ladies there said something or other not just according to genteel society, and Vickey spoke right out and said, 'We are taught differently in the high society in Philadelphia,' and that made them all stare pretty straight, I tell you. Indeed she's smart, if she is my own daughter, and I say it myself, and she knows what's proper for a real lady."

"No question of that," said the clerk; "she is the belle at this house at least. Every one speaks of her in the highest praise."

"Just so I say, if I am her mother; and what I was coming at is this—that is to say, I have not decided yet who Vickey shall marry. But I understand that you have been instrumental in encouraging an attachment between her and Prescott, and that's what I was going to speak of, for I could not entertain such a marriage at all. Who is this Prescott? He's nobody—a penny-a-liner! How could he provide for such a lady?"

"Oh, indeed, Mrs. Edge, you much mistake me, I have not been instrumental, only so far as to speak of the virtues of each. Prescott is an excellent man. He is not rich to be sure, but you have yourself told me that you and Vickey did, in former years, work not only at soap-boiling, and candle-making, but in the fields hoeing corn."

"But we have proved ourselves; we are now universally acknowledged to be the very head of society. Judge Francis Underhill, of Loudon Heights, told me with his own mouth he considered Vickey the most perfect lady he ever saw. He is too old to flatter; he speaks wisely. Now, then, shall we turn backward from our attainments to help up this fellow by the way? No, no; far from it. Excelsior, as Vickey says, is our motto. Then, too, you must know that Vickey has many suitors. There is Wadsworth, so rich and handsome. To be sure, he is an owner of slaves, but my mind has changed on that score since we came to Washington. There's nothing like the lowly being contented with their lot. There must be distinctions in society; persons of rank always will hold this, and I don't know as we could make a better choice than in this young man. But there are others. Only this day a finely-dressed man lingering at the street corner, seeing her rare, ladylike appearance, slipped a card into her hand, and desired to walk with her. I tell you, and I make due allowance for my vanity for my own child, but she can say with pride who she will or will not choose. Now, all I have to say is, that I do hope you will discourage this young Prescott off. Indeed, I know you will, for you know he's no match for our Vickey."

"Certainly so, Mrs. Edge. Why, of course I will, rest assured—indeed—Oh, yes!"

"You know," she interrupted, "I'm a little afraid she takes to him a little, only don't say nothing, you know; you understand?"

Again and again the clerk gave assurance that her wishes should be carried out, and then they went out of the parlor, for some one had been calling the clerk. I was about to follow, but the clerk returned alone.

"Oh, I have such a joke!" said he, and he laughed heartily. "Oh, such a joke! Do you know, these fool Edges believe everybody is in love with them. Sure as fate, they believe the Judge is going to marry the old maid, and she is gone off with Vickey to get a new set of false and big plumpers." Again he laughed. "You see, they observed that the Judge was not very attentive to the old maid, and suggested that they ought to fix her up a little. Mrs. Edge got some patent breasts for her last night, and now Vickey is off to the dentist to get her mouth filled up with teeth and plumpers, and the poor old thing is half raced to death with battling the huge pads and hoops and whalebones. Oh, I declare, 'tis an excellent joke!"

I told him I was real sorry for the old maid, and also for Vickey, who were both so innocent and well meaning.

"Nonsense!" said he, "I'll get Vickey to marry the Judge, you shall see. I vow I shall have a wedding at his hotel, somehow or other."

At this instant came a violent scream from the stairs above. We ran; I thought of Joe, the fugitive, and feared she had been detected and captured. I felt under obligation not to suffer her to be wronged to the value of anything by another if in my power to prevent; and with these vivid fancies flying through my mind, I rushed to the spot. Here I was startled afresh, to see, not the fugitive, but my own gentle Ann, reclining on the stairway, pale and helpless. Below her, on the stairway of the lower floor, and leading into the street, was a rude crowd, pushing and jamming furiously to make an exit. From the noise I could tell nothing, nor no word distinguish. Only gentle Ann, almost frenzied, cried out, "Stop them! Oh, for God's sake, save her! O Heavens, is all my labor lost!" In a moment the crowd was gone, save the lingering servants, who, half-affrighted, peered from every corner. "Dear, gentle Ann, what is the matter?" said I, and I raised her up, and she leaned her head over on my breast and sobbed aloud. Again and again I urged her to tell the cause of all this; but she clung fast to me, and seemed as if her heart would break. "Oh, urge me no more!" at last she stammered. "The things whereof I weep I cannot, must not mention. Take me, oh, I beg of you, take me to my room, and leave me! Oh, how can I—how can I?" and I never saw so near a death with weeping. I then took her to her room, even to the doorway, where she turned and warmly pressed my hand, saying, "How lonely, lonely now! I scarce can enter. Leave me, my heart is broken." She then went in, and I came away, not being able to guess the cause of such great sorrow When I encountered the servants, I inquired the cause of the confusion on the stairs, and they told me somebody was taken prisoner—a woman, a young woman, a girl of about fifteen! "Can it be," I thought to myself, "that such was the fate of Joe's sister, Kate? Captured here?" I then remembered that for a week past my gentle Ann had seemed so cast down and sad, and I thought perhaps she had been secreting this fugitive. I made some cautious inquiries accordingly, but gained no evidence to substantiate my theory; but I resolved to linger about the hotel till I could get an interview with Ann, and then ascertain, if possible, the whole mystery. I then repaired to the office to await and to reflect awhile, but was instantly hailed by a newsboy shouting into my face, "Buy a paper, sir? buy a paper, sir? Beauregard in Charleston building batteries. General Scott burnt in effigy all over the South. Davis or Toombs to be made President and installed in Washington before Lincoln gets here." Of course I bought a paper, and I read it, too. The boy's statements were true. Active treason against the established government was on foot. The party beaten at polls had resolved to carry their point by the sword, to place themselves in office. Yet I called it vanity; called it boasting; for I, nor any other man, could be convinced that so great a folly could be attempted by an intelligent people. Some one touched my arm, after I had read and reread the paper for a good while, and, looking round, I beheld Professor Jackson. "Lend me the paper?" said he; and I answered, "Certainly, sir, I am done with it." He looked rather cast down, and his clothes were certainly the worse of the wear. When he had taken the paper, he pulled out one from the ragged pocket of his coat, and said, "I can exchange with you. I am one of the editors and publishers of the Journal of Progress, devoted chiefly to literature." I thought, when he said devoted to literature, he meant it as a pun on the thousands of illiterate pamphlets and magazines that claim the same heading at the top of their title page, and are published in all the cities and towns all over the country, and so I said, "Indeed! Literature is cheap now-a-days, especially in the name. Had Humboldt lived here, he need have taken less trouble. After he had spent thirty years in study, he was urged to prepare some literary work, but he replied, that, as nearly as he could compute the time, he had forty years more to study before he could prepare himself to write on a literary subject, but if the society would wait until that time, he would be happy to make an effort to please them. I wish he had lived in this country."

"Ah, sir," said the Professor, "it was well indeed when man depended on mundane evidence, to ask for time to prepare a literary work; but now, you will, I am sure, admit that knowledge is beginning to be intuitive. Appreciation and confidence is all that is needed. But, sir, a journal like this of ours is in advance of the times. People go in for trash,—novels, picture papers, caricatures. That's the trouble!" and he looked over the paper I gave him, while I glanced at the one he gave me, but I read it not. My mind had other matter; I cared not for literature. Several times I observed the Professor casting glances toward me, and at last he ventured to ask me if I was not a contributor myself to some paper. I told him, not at present. He then asked me if I would not like to take a share in the Journal of Progress? I said, no. He next asked if I would not like to buy him out? Again I said, no. But he persisted, asking if I would not lend money on the establishment, taking charge of the income till I got my money back, with a hundred per cent. profit? "No," said I, "I cannot engage in business. I have retired from all business, save what pleases my fancy. If you want to borrow money, go to your banker." "We have none," said he. "Then go to a broker," said I. "We have been," said he, "but they said they would not lend money on literary establishments. They don't go in for literature. You might as well ask a monkey to appreciate our Journal, as to ask a broker." "Have you not funds enough to carry it on?" I asked; and he answered, "No; we're out entirely. If we could only get started rightly, I am sure it would be a success. I have put all I had in it. I put in a hundred and sixteen dollars. And my wife has put in rather more than that. I am now delivering lectures every night, and so is my wife, for the benefit of the Journal." "Well," said I, "can't you raise funds sufficient?" "No, sir, there is hardly anybody goes to literary lectures. The first night I took in eleven dollars above expenses; but the last two evenings I hardly came out even, and we are getting in considerable of a strait. For economy sake we took a room in a shanty and went to housekeeping, and, if you will believe me, sir, we live on bran bread and water, eating only one meal a day." "You are certainly very persevering," said I; "but if you have not money enough to carry it on, I think the better way is to sell out the whole concern." "We have tried that, too," said he, "but every one says just as you did; they don't want to buy. They think there is going to be war in the country, and they won't invest ; whereas, in my opinion, this very Journal, rightly managed, could avert the whole danger of the country. If I only had my own money back, I would not care."

Just then Joe Travers came in, and I excused myself to the Professor, and followed Joe into the hall beyond, and there told her how best she could avoid her pursuer, John Russel ; that I had not the slightest doubt but he would know her if he came near her, and fairly looked on her. She promised in every particular to follow my advice, but cautiously urged me to go with her to the Quarters, which is the place where slaves are kept preparatory to buying or hiring or sending off when changing owners. That she feared indeed her sister Kate had been captured, for she heard of something to that effect just a few minutes since. I agreed to go with her. I am confident no one heard us talking. We went out the back way. In the garden was the Judge, lounging on a bench beneath the trees. He was sound asleep. Beside him lay a piece of fool's-cap on which was written the following lines. I took the paper ; did not consider it stealing ; he had often taken my manuscript notes himself, and then returned them. I intended to return these. The words he had written were as follows, to wit :

" I go for the girl of seventeen,
Go for the gentlest age of a gentle queen,
  Ere she's fraught with evils taught,
Or cunning made by love's parade,
  In innocence so rare, as never a man can dare,
O so sweet, the girl of seventeen,
O so sweet, so sweet my youthful queen.

Though I flirt with all that's rare,
Never my heart was captured fair,
  But by the girl of seventeen—
Though I dally with the cold unseemly things of state,
Though I've power to unmake and make the great,
  —I throw them all away,
And never do I prattle nor play,
  Never do love but the girl of seventeen.

I'm called the rare and ruin of the past,
With never a heart to love me at last,
But O, a secret, all killing with joy,
Tells me though old I'm ever the boy,
Ever the boy for the girl of seventeen,
O for the gentlest age of a gentle queen.
  Ere she's fraught with evils taught,
Or cunning made by love's parade,
In innocence so rare, as never a man can dare,
O so sweet my girl of seventeen,
O so sweet, so sweet my youthful queen.

When we got outside the gate, we halted till I read it over, and thereupon Joe remarked, " I rather like that old man, sad as I am, for it is so humorous in him to love so young a girl." I then told her about the Judge, and about his eccentricities ; his egotism ; his good nature, and his present love adventure. We were then going toward the Quarters, and I took a

good while in telling the Judge's life to her, but when I finished she heaved a sigh, saying, " Oh, sir, tell me more ! My every breath of life holds upon a thread when you speak of the ties of the human heart. To be so free, to love and never fear the bond by mortals torn asunder. Oh, please, sir, tell me more ! Tell me of this Vickey. Oh, what joy is hers—to feel that even one so old has proffered to the craving of her warm devotion !" I told her I thought it was rather ridiculous for so old a man to suffer himself to fall in love with one so young. " Oh, indeed, sir, it is not. Whoever is not thirsty can wait for a gourd, but the others can dip with a leaf and drink to Heaven's praise. Oh, sir, what pain is it to famish, to be alone in the world ! I do hope she may love him in return."

As we walked along, she frequently asked me if I thought any one could detect her ? and I assured her that with due caution and presence of mind, she might forever pass unknown. She heeded my advice and manifested considerable resolution, saying that she believed she could go even to the Quarters, and if her sister was there, still maintain her composure unobserved. But when we neared the place, at that low spot of ground just in front where the Irish exile sighed to have a house, so the clank of niggers' chains might lull him to sleep, so forgetful that for liberty he had himself rebelled—when we neared this memorable spot, and beheld there assembled some fifty or a hundred people, and in the crowd what seemed to be the fugitive, Kate, marching amidst a throng of police and the curious populace, Joe siezed my arm, exclaiming, " What is yonder ?   See ! a charge in double breast of full a score against that poor, helpless girl. Oh, I cannot, cannot further go ! 'Tis my sister—no, it cannot be ! Oh, what shall I do !" and she burst into tears, holding me that I might proceed no further. Said I, " Be resolute, dear girl, imagine nothing. Look with indifference ; 'tis not your sister, I am sure. At all events study more what you can do, and waste your power less on idle sympathy."

Very soon I saw that she could go no further without herself becoming a mark of observation, and persuaded her to halt by the way until I inspected the tumult. This was the occasion on which I gave her a cigar. She did not smoke, and it was not lighted, but simply held it in her mouth to assist in disguising her as a boy. I then proceeded alone, leaving her standing on the sidewalk. Many persons passed, but no one seemed to notice us. The attention was all on the tumult. I could not tell at first what it was about, but the crowd was very dense, and I saw coming on a full run Mrs. Lucy Tabiatha Stimpkins, and Professor Jackson. I knew then that it was the party with the fugitive, and that a rich scene was about to be enacted. I ran as fast as I could, and when I reached the place, Mrs. Lucy rushed in before the officers, looking, indeed, almost a maniac.

"I protest!" she said. "In the name of Heaven I protest! You shall not re-inslave that child!" and she seized hold and forced a halt. But the officers pushed her aside, saying, "Now we want none of that sort of stuff. Let go. Let go, I say." But the woman said, "Never but by violence. I will hold on as long as my feeble grasp has power, and when that fails I will cast myself upon the points of your daggers. Hew me in pieces who dares! Here! I will bare my breast! Dogs! Beasts! She shall be free!"

"Away, away, foolish woman!" said the officers, and then the owner came forward, saying that whoever claimed his slave was a thief and an Abolitionist. "I want nothing of you, you are opposing the law. Away, away!" And then the crowd surged forward, and the mutterings of many voices made confusion. But soon the woman's shrill voice broke forth again. "Halt! Halt, I say! This thing shall never be! She is no slave; she's white! Carry me, drag me, tear me hence who can!" And I now looked far into the crowd, and beheld Mrs. Lucy clinging fast upon the poor slave, who, though frightened, told me in her fairy-like face she was the identical sister, Kate. The men were endeavoring to pull Mrs. Lucy away, but as often as they tore her hands off she again laid hold. The sympathy of the crowd was with the poor slave, who, all dust, with clothes rent by violence, and her pale auburn hair dishevelled and dangling on her pallid features, wet with tears, and eyes dilated with fears terrible, but now an instrument of contention, pulled both ways as a child between two furious bears. All the while nearer to the Quarters they surged. But yet awhile, and the dire confusion broke; some blows, a squall, a scream. I saw it not, but heard, and then beheld a part and parcel of the crowd tear loose and run. And then an opening. There stood Mrs. Lucy Tabiatha Stimpkins, some scratched and bruised, but worse her clothes the contest held. Kate was dragged off with the flying crowd. Alone stood Mrs. Lucy,

and thus after her vanquishers held forth:

"Now curses on ye, O ye cruel monsters:
And bide ye yet, but this is Heaven's spoil.
Die, Liberty! All that is holy die!
Satan come on, to thee I do bequeath
My countrymen and laws of equal rights!
The right to choose pursuit, forsooth, alas,
A constitution faced for Heaven, but planned
For Satan's vilest purposes. Fly! Fly!
Ye dogs of plunder! Gloat on your fair flower,
Drink deep the sin! Long live the angel girl
To satiate your hellish appetites.
No, never, death! I swear, as I am woman,
Never shall villains walk that sacred road.
She shall be free, or meet her prayer for death!"

She said more, but it was all after that style, and then she turned abruptly away and was soon lost to view. I followed the crowd up to the Quarters. It was a brick house, rather old and shabby. On the front was the following sign:

"Slaves bought and sold here. Highest price paid for fugitives. Guard room; keep a night-watch. Slaves boarded for their owners. Money advanced on slaves. Slaves procured on short notice, and warranted. William Filmore, Esq., proprietor.

Besides this were many posters for "Runaway slaves." "Rewards." "Overseers to go South, wanted." "This house has connection with all first-class slave-traders in the South." "Established eighteen years." "References of the highest respectability." "Fugitives captured." "We keep several first class detectives to ferret out runaways."

I read all these notices before I could make way through the crowd to the house. Heard much laughing. Many of the men joked about the fugitive. The words they said cannot be written. Hard words were also used about Mrs. Lucy. No man cried "shame." I know that if any man had showed disapproval to the dragging of the slave to the Quarters, he would have been shot or stabbed on the spot. One of the officers, the one who most pulled at the fugitive's arm, was a United States Marshal. I did not see him kick her. He gripped her arm so tightly she cried. It was not the Marshal that seized her by the hair. It was an assistant. Heard him say it was fine wool, and he added an oath to his words. She offered no resistance during the foregoing melee; she was pale with fright. She did not moan. Large tear-drops flowed down her cheeks. I could not see her fairly in the crowd. She had chains on both wrists; also on her ankles. She could not go as fast as the Marshal, and that was why he gripped and jerked her arm so cruelly.

In the Quarters she was placed in the front room; could be seen from the street. The window was open; the day was warm. I saw her sitting on a bench. Two others were sitting at her left hand side. They quite dark ; I think they were mulatoes, or half breeds, as they are commonly called. One of them seemed contented ; that one was a man. The other was a woman, about fifty years of age. When Kate was pushed into the room, the old woman rose, saying, " O Lord, my God ! " and she burst into tears. The keeper hit her lightly with his cane. The slaves then sat down and the keeper went out. Many others beside myself lingered in front of the house to look upon Kate. She saw us not. She looked downward ; never raised her eyes toward Heaven. Once or twice she gazed at her arm, now black and blue from the Marshal's grip, but instantly her eyes again fell to the floor. She moved not ; sat upright, pale as death, a beautiful American slave !

While we looked on, Russel came up. He clapped a man on the shoulder, saying, " That's the chalk ! Your money's ready." Some of the crowd set up a cheer for the secession of South Carolina. They said Cotton was king. Many of them boasted that the Government of England would be on the side of slavery; that if the Southern States would found a government, based on slavery, that the British Government had assured them they should meet every encouragement it was possible to give. Many of the crowd gave groans for Lincoln, and for Abolitionists, and then they gradually dispersed. I returned to my companion, Joe. She was still at the lamp-post with her cigar. I feared to tell her her sister was indeed the person, for I thought she would betray herself by crying or fainting. She asked me, " Is it really my sister ? Tell me, for I am dying with suspense."

" No," said I, " it was only a common culprit. A little thief girl."

" Oh, indeed ! really ? "

" Ay, really ! "

" Then I am so happy. Oh, what a burden it has been to me ! and now I am so relieved. Indeed I would like now to see the girl, thief as she is, that has given me so much concern. Come, take me to the prison, I will see the thief, or drunken woman, that I may laugh at my foolish fears."

" No," said I, " a prison is no place for a youth like you, let us return to the Capital."

" Why, now, indeed, you frighten me. It was my sister, and you fear to tell me ? "

" On my word, dear girl, can you think I would wrong one I have sworn to befriend ? "

" Now, I objure you, if you are my friend indeed, tell me if it were my sister ? "

" Why, I am your friend, and wishing to save you, for you might be overcome ; I told you wrongly."

" Alas, my sister ! Poor Kate ! Take me, sir, I honor you, oh noble citizen ! "

I then told her to take my arm, and we walked awhile, she drooping and weeping the while. I knew not how to comfort her ; I had no plan to rescue her sister. After we had gone two or three squares, she stopped short, saying, " No, no, what am I about ? Why do I not go to my sister ? Come, I will share with her ; take me ! " and she looked up into my face, her tears were gone and she seemed resolute. " You see, I am older and grown in more independence, but my sister looks for some one to look out for her. If I go back with her, Providence may show us yet some way of escape, but if I stay here, I know my sister will pine and die. Therefore I must go. Come, take me ! "

" Rather say you will help provide your sister's rescue, and I am not long in yielding. After we have failed in all things, your proposition is still good. Russel will undoubtedly keep Kate here for several days, while he searches for you. During this interval we can counsel on all the plans we may invent. Let us hence now, using our judgment more, and our sympathy less." To this she assented, and we started back. In front of the flower gardens we encountered that ever crazy pair, Mrs. Lucy Tabiatha Stimpkins and Professor Jackson.

" I never heard of a husband," said she to him, " if indeed husband means a woman's partner—that loitered by the way nursing ever the woes of a lost purse. Why have you not followed me ? Were you true to our glorious cause, we would now have been champions in one of the greatest affairs of the age. With my single hand I encountered a hundred men, who were mad with the capture of a fugitive little slave, and full exultant, flying with their game, and boasting of their clutch on the frail creature. But I was overcome. Brute force overrun woman's moral power. And I have to thank you. You were not on hand."

" Indeed, my dear, you much mistake these matters. We are in advance of the age. The tide is against us. In all our adventures we fail. Had I been there, they had murdered us. You, being a woman, was spared."

" Is that indeed your courage in the cause of human rights ? Have you been really lecturing for years on the cause of Woman's Rights, and now, when we put our doctrine into practice, and have almost accomplished the glorious result, do you eternally wail over that hundred and sixteen dollars? Did we not carry the late election? Did we not exult over the Senate, and the members dared not lay hands on us? You say you cannot live on one meal a day; you do not like water and bread. Are you a glutton? Do the temporal things of life most concern you? Now I tell you, I am seriously considering about reducing our food to one meal a week. I have carefully estimated the wear and tear of the human body, and I find it cannot exceed a pound a week. Whoever eats more than that, is not conversant with or obedient to the laws of Nature. If we raise money enough to publish another edition of our Journal of Progress, I intend to have in it an editorial on eating. You shall see then where you stand. Have you been here all day?"

"No; I have been very busy."

"Well, what have you done?"

"Nothing, nothing."

"Professor Jackson! There are four million slaves in this country; do you know that?"

"Yes, I do."

"Well, do you know that the Southern States wish to extend their slave institution, and that to accomplish their purpose they are about to separate from the Free States?"

"Yes, I do."

"Do you know the British Government encourages them in it, in hopes to destroy this nation?"

"Yes, I do."

"And will you sit and remain silent while these evils are being carried out?"

"I don't want to, but how can a man work without tools?"

"Tools! Professor? Had you seen the helpless girl—the poor child I just saw—you would not talk of tools. When I have nails on my fingers' ends, I have tools for such work. When I have a tongue, I am provided. Ay, any power left, I can use it, and will. Come on, let us march hand in hand. I have work aboard. The law, feeble as it is, and in as vile hands as it is, may be used."

"Well, as for this business, I know nothing. But I am sure of failure. It will be a loss of time and loss of money. I think I can do more good going round the country lecturing, than I can in this business. If you will pay me back my hundred and sixteen dollars, I shall like it better."

"Now, I tell you, unless you arouse yourself up to more action, you shall never have a cent. I shall turn you adrift altogether. You shall learn to treat me as a lady, or I will have done with you. So, there now."

"Oh, indeed, I meant nothing! I am willing to do anything reasonable. Only lead the way, and I will follow."

"Come on then, we'll have no more of this."

He signified his entire consent, and they got up and walked off together, her tongue on the continual clatter, but we heard no more.

"Oh, that she is not ashamed!" said my companion as soon as we started on, "to let herself become so foreign to the retiring sweetness of woman, which so charms and pleases all men. And that he is shameless in the presence of such a creature, who has so seemingly entailed grief on him till he has no power to shake her off. Why, now, I thought indeed, where laws protected marriage, marriage was the heaven of a lifetime. Truly, it seems where trouble is not forced on us, we ourselves seek it out and adopt it as a desirable thing to live with. But we, that are bound by others, to others whom we abhor, we have real woe. My poor sister Kate, in all this dread while must loiter there, alone in spirit, thought, feelings. Pondering ever on her horrid prospects. Nothing, save the soul within her, feeds her pleading, bleeding power. Even time must linger to wear her patience out. Oh, my poor sister! my poor sister!"

Again and again she asked herself what she could do for Kate. "Oh, is there nothing I can do? Can I not break open the door and provide her exit? Can I not even speak to her? Shall I desert her now she is in prison? O God, show me what I shall do? Is there no penance worthy of this? Teach me, O my Father in Heaven. Impose upon me that the tearing of the flesh from my arms will free my sister. Take hence an arm, a foot, or shut up my ears, but O, burst the fetters of that helpless child? Give her freedom! O give her freedom!"

I told her she should desist in this idle talk, for it amounted to nothing; urging her to use her judgment only. I knew, too, it would not answer for her to see Kate, for she would be sure to betray herself. "Have you no way," said I, "you can send word to Kate?"

"Ah! Why, certainly! Have I forgotten myself? We had it planned. I am to write on a thin paper, send it her in a piece of tobacco. A glorious thought! See; but no! Well, I can at least comfort her." I was much teased by her excitability, for many people passed us, and some of them frequently turned to look at us. If it should be proved that I was accessory to her disguise, I was safely in for a year's imprisonment myself. Knowing this, I cautioned her every few paces, and hurried as fast as I could to the Jackson House. I was anxious to see Ann Underhill, to learn all about her concealing Kate, and to learn too if she had a plan matured for Kate's rescue. In turn I had resolved to tell her all about Lizzie, or, as now called, Joe Travers. I will not deny that I hoped the similarity of our actions would enlist her more in my favor.

Washington was becoming dangerous for me; men were murdered every day for their political sentiments, if opposed to the slave sentiment of the South. Boasts were common and bets frequent, that Lincoln would never reach Washington alive. At the Planter's Restaurant was an open book on the counter, where men subscribed their names, and the amount they would give to any body who would kill Lincoln. Books of the same kind were opened in nearly all the hotels in Charleston, South Carolina. But this was all called mockery; nonsense; political scare-crow. The threatened aspect called together a body of politicians, nearly all of whom were proslavery men, under the name of a Peace Congress. I was selected as a member of that body, and was now pressed for time in which to accomplish my purposes. The secessionists still held their meetings in the deserted house where Joe was first found by me, and I determined too that Joe, knowing all about the house, should secrete herself on the premises and learn all about their proceedings. Of course, I could not spend much time in trying to free Kate from the Quarters. The affairs of the nation were becoming too serious.

The writer of this most remarkable history is here ordered to say, that the next chapter is already written, and that whoever looks a little further ahead will discover that fact.

CHAPTER XII.

BEING A VERY IMPORTANT PART OF EVIDENCE ENTIRE, THE RELATIONSHIP OF WHICH CAN ONLY BE DISTINGUISHED BY THOSE MYSTERIES OF WHICH THE WHOLE COUNTRY WILL FOREVER REMAIN IGNORANT.

AFTER viewing the heading to this chapter, the writer asked Jenkins if it was selected from Everett, and he replied by way of explanation, saying, " While I was travelling in a country where were wealthy peers of State, a nobleman remarked of a steamer, 'Its confluence is the traverse of two bivalves set in motion, like the mist in the Valley of the Nile, where inundations so frequently interrupt the pleasure of travellers, with which I presume everybody in this age is perfectly familiar;' and this was called an eloquent sentence. It was indeed with some pride that I remembered the literature of my own country. But I want the men and women to read, and regardless of an author's name, give him his due; and I wish to wake up my countrymen not to boast of the things here written, or my blunders, but to show them that wit and humor lives in every head, only it is sometimes lost in the stately style of tasteless authors."

I told Jenkins that he spoke well, but he had not yet told me of the most important part of this history, and that was whether he married Ann Underhill; neither had he told me how it came out with the Judge and Vickey. I never saw Jenkins look so sad; for the manner in which I spoke, made it seem as if I was joking.

" Wait," said he; " I am only telling what was at that time a too oft repeated tale, and which must now and forever be preserved as one of the most prominent incidents connected with the early history of the great rebellion—I mean the mysterious disappearance of Miss Underhill, one of the leading belles of the Capital. At any other time in our country's history, such an occurrence would have created the most intense excitement; but the threatened aspect of political affairs had cast its deep shadow over all other things, and made them comparatively trivial. Still, the sudden departure, the mysteriously secret nature of this lady's whereabouts was only second in importance to all else in the Capital."

First there were whispers about the hotel; then from house to house, until in all the avenues of the city her name became a theme of every tongue. The causes were discussed, and the probable results questioned. Was she dead? Had she eloped? Had she anything to do with the fugitive that was captured at the hotel? Every person acquainted with her told of her beauty, her fame, her fortune. Those unacquainted with her grieved that they had not seen her and known her. Her uncle, Judge Francis, always so cheerful and gay, was now downcast and depressed beyond measure. The joy of many years was now clouded and full of woful suspense. The flower of his life, the theme of his soul's devotion for so many long years, was, without a moment's warning, now gone, no one knew where, and the pangs of a broken heart were his. By day and by night he sat there weeping and saying little, and those who joked him so often before, now respected his tears; for this is one of the most excellent traits of our countrymen.

On the day following her disappearance, the newspapers were full of notices of her. In New York, Philadelphia, and other cities, the papers called for information of her whereabouts, or anything that would lead to information of her. Large sums of money were offered, but nothing came of that. Days passed by, but still nothing was heard. This was the time that the South Carolina Commissioners came to treat with James Buchanan for the separation of that State from the Union, and the whole country was wrapped up in the interest of the approaching ultimatum. We were all of us at fever heat, for the signs of the times predicted the probable fall of a great and good government.

The Commissioners, too, longed for the Presidential reception for the crowning of their pet scheme; the consummation of which would have backset the rights of man for many ages. But even while these were their woful prayers, the President in turn was weeping for the inevitable fall of his party, and this it was that bore so heavily on his soul.

The whole country was in commotion. The storm was seen approaching and near at hand, but, where first it would burst, was the study and whisper of many millions. Omens, signs, and rumors. The South did most their glory boast, and would they fall to with bloody hands? But should they by Lincoln be outdone? Dread deeds, and terrible to the peaceful, great republic. A nation's life or death within the grasp of politicians; for ere our country's fate was settled, thousands and hundreds of thousands must take a soldier's diadem. In the midst of these approaching terrors, how can I give importance to the theme of a single broken heart? How can I show you the eccentric but venerable Judge in tears, forgetful of all around him? And the belle of the Capital, who shall search for our sorrows in the awful mystery of the disappearance?

Now be it known that, owing to my anonymous character, I am now about to reveal one of the most remarkable attempts at human destruction ever planned on this continent.

The attempts to head off the threatened war were so feeble by all our Government officers, that some of us felt justified in anything that would avert the coming storm. To this end it was proposed by Prescott that we blow up the secessionists during their secret meeting. Accordingly, we procured a keg of powder, and put it under the deserted house, but owing to a former faithful promise, I will not divulge who all were accessory to the dread deed. My fugitive Joe was employed, and had a hazardous part to play, of which you shall hear by and by. The fuse was attached to the keg and extended into the back yard, and was calculated for six minutes from the time of ignition until the keg of powder would blow up. The time for ignition was set down at about fifteen minutes before eleven. This was on purpose to meet the railroad train going North at eleven. We had also bribed the door-keeper to let the slave-girl, Kate, out at fifteen minutes before eleven. Prescott and I were to remain in Washington, but the two fugitives, owing to the expected excitement, were to start for Canada. So much for the design, now for the execution. Joe, my fugitive, was horrified when I proposed it to her, but finally did, to all appearance, give consent and even praised the invention. We trusted her implicitly. And she also agreed to remain in an obscure place within the house until just before the explosion, in order to tell us who all were sure to die.

Now, when the night had come, Prescott and I retired near the place to await the awful moment; our fugitive having effected an entrance and secreted herself within the house. She also awaited the result. In a short time strangers to her came in, amongst whom, as I since learned, were Cobb, Floyd, Thompson, and others.

She, however, goes on to state that she afterwards distinguished Cobb, having seen him in the South on a previous occasion. Fearing that she might be detected in her hiding place, and that she might be suddenly despatched as a spy, she had provided herself with a pistol to be used as a signal to Prescott and myself.

In due time the meeting was called to order. Toombs first addressed the members, and, on this occasion, he said he was reluctantly compelled to admit that the firmness of Scott for the Union made it too dangerous an affair to try to change the government of the whole country; but that the South might safely set up for itself, and that, for his part, he was now in favor of hazarding nothing greater than such a design. He then apologized for having, on a previous occasion, prevented other members from advocating the scheme which he now espoused himself. It was on this occasion that a letter was produced informing the members of the meeting that Mr. Russel of the London *Times* would soon visit the Southern States. Davis and Toombs then advised the selection of Squire Larramie of Virginia, and also one Dr. Thornton of the same place to be sent to England to open a direct communication through the London *Times* and *Post* with the people of England, in regard to the rights and demands of the people of the South.[*]

While these harangues were going on, Joe, the spy-fugitive, was watching them, and, in order that she might hear better, she leaned forward a little; for the wind blew through the cracks of the boards where she was holding her ear, and she had not heard all that had been said. Though there were about forty members present, yet Toombs and Davis did nearly all the talking. In thus leaning forward, however, she was enabled to perceive to her chagrin, that the door was guarded by a man with a drawn sword. This person she recognized on the instant. It was Orsini. He was the companion, about a year previous, of an actress in Savannah. That actress was the woman to whom her own master was married. She looked upon him as the murderer of her master, and she involuntarily screamed outright. But having sufficient presence of mind to compose herself, she sat perfectly still. The members of the meeting, however, all started to their feet, immediately mistrusting that a spy was present. They took candles

and went about to examine the apartments. As before stated, she sat behind some loose boards, where the wind was blowing, and she feared that the tumult in the house would cause the persons in the yard to anticipate her escape, and so blow them all up together. Still she was compelled to sit quietly as the candles were passed from place to place, toward every corner, until they approached even to the very boards where she was sitting. But with perfect coolness she blew out the candles as fast as they were thrust behind the boards, even on several occasions, and the person having the light in charge simply said "Confound the wind!" Suffice it to say, however, they all came to the conclusion that they had heard no scream at all, but that it had been the wind whistling, and so they resumed business.

On this occasion Davis stated that it was the determined policy of every one of the members present, that Buchanan should not receive the South Carolina Commissioners. He hoped that not a week would elapse before the batteries of Charleston would open fire on the forts and garrison of Anderson's soldiers. He had heard with joy that Anderson had removed to Fort Sumter, and he considered this of itself an overt act against the South. It was, he said, a menace to the city of Charleston.

Cobb then wished to know what action, if any, had been taken, in regard to the merchant ship sent out by the Government carrying food to Anderson's garrison. Thompson answered, saying, "The Star of the West—our friends are apprized of her coming to Charleston; our guns will be ready for her reception."[*]

About this period of time, also, Toombs, Davis, and others publicly expressed the wish that Southern members of Congress should not all leave Washington. They feared that the opposition might pass laws to interfere with their designs; and urged the Southern members to keep their seats as long as possible. These are the facts in detail, perhaps somewhat tediously told, of the plot in the origin and carrying out of the great rebellion. The opposition to the instigators, and the evidence against them was, at the period referred to, of so small moment that to speak of it in any manner was only to elicit ridicule.

But there were also at this period pa-

* Thompson publicly made these boasts even while he held his Secretaryship.

Toombs in turn said that twenty-five thousand minute men were already armed and equipped in Virginia ready to march at a given signal into Washington. Many newspapers of the country detailed all the above facts, and the facts were believed to be true, even by the President himself, and yet no action was taken by the Government to prevent the coming destruction.

triots—men firm and determined to use every means, no matter how dreadful, to thwart these apparently wicked designs, and amongst these means was the affair referred to of blowing up the house that contained the leaders. And to do this effectually, we had used every precaution; we had waited till such an hour as would surely catch all the chief leaders; and we could even now, while stationed at the fuse with well-tried matches, hear the fierce murmuring of their villainous tongues. Here for two long hours we sat waiting, watching, wearing, trembling, praying, and justifying the deed before God. All the chances did we weigh, whether we should escape, or whether be caught and hanged, and our heartfelt answer was, God's will be done! Yet withal, most terrible were our convulsions of thoughts, counting the minutes of life and death for our well-caged felons. But then came a new mystery; instead of our fugitive returning to us as we expected, she lingered, she tarried so long. We heard the scream referred to; we heard a rustling in the building; could she have been killed? This troubled us; it set us all on fire. An hour passed; Joe came not. Yet another long hour and she had not come. The time was almost up to light the fuse. What should we do? Who can imagine what an awful suspense was ours? We whispered together, still as the midnight air, and we advised, but heeded not. Yet patience gave us victory. Our fugitive approached us, even a few minutes before the fatal moment. Now was our time. By sign and motion all was made ready. The fatal match was lighted; we saw it burn, and then we leisurely walked away. Our escape was good, orderly, effectual. But how long we waited for the explosion! Six minutes! We waited twenty. Ay, an hour! And no explosion. What could it mean? We dared not return. We had no chance. We needs must go home disappointed. Perhaps might be detected and made to suffer, not for what we did, but for what we attempted. Prescott was downright mad. Joe was mysterious, and seemed discomfited. Neither Prescott nor myself mistrusted but she was heart and soul with us. Though now that the failure was manifest, we needs must look about for our other fugitive, Kate; she had not approached the place designated, and here too were we disappointed. For we traced every street, alley, and lane near the Quarters; but could not find her. Thus, with disappointment on all sides, and the fear of detection too, we wended our way back to lodgings,

but not to rest, for the play was scarce begun.

I cannot now, when reviewing these long past scenes, describe with what astonishment and discomfiture I learned on the following morning of the house having been blown up, and of the escape of the fugitive. My plans and schemes and plots were all frustrated. I set about discovering the cause of what was passed, and to devise something for the future. Bearing strictly in mind, too, that I was the chief suspected person and that a price was set on my head. Added to my distress was also the mysterious disappearance of Miss Underhill. My first desire was to seek such information of her as I could best obtain.

To do this, I encountered Joe, who was apparently as much discomfited as myself, and at about as much loss how to account for the past occurrences. She then went on to give me a description of such things as might lead me to discover something in relation to Miss Underhill's whereabouts; and related things to me which made it apparent that she might have possibly, in some unguarded moment, consented to an elopement.

"Only on the evening previous," said Joe, and she came close to me and told me quietly of the apparent attachment between the two. "Only on the evening previous to this," said she, "Wadsworth spoke to her of the beauties of his Southern home, and of his own loneliness. She was attending to all he said. As if to urge him to cure his maladies with some congenial fair one, she assured him any one might be happy with such a home, and almost hinted that the dreams of such a spot had consoled her own lone heart. Yet not quite did either one speak that which I most wished to hear, and which, too, I thought each of them wished to say but dared not. And thus it ran from day to day. At times he spoke of his intended departure, but still he lingered. At times he spoke of the dreadful aspect of the country. He told her that his fortunes were in the South, and if war came he feared his ruin. And then he thought if ruin came, he could not think of entailing that ruin on another. Thus by indirect hints, and by apparent backwardness between the two, I could only discover that their attachment was guarded by serious affairs." Joe was quick at thought, and turning to me, she added: "But see, Wadsworth, you know, is not gone. Now, were he gone, we could be content; for then we could say They are truly eloped. This pair has flown together: but while he is here, and himself overcome by the course of things, all my conjectures are eclipsed; they are not gone together." And so, in fact, it was with us all. No one to whom this fair lady was attached had disappeared with her. Her dearest and best friends, and her most ardent admirers were still in Washington.

Now, it so happened a few days after her disappearance, and when Joe and Judge Francis Underhill and myself were returning from a place where we had been making inquiries regarding recent incidents of Miss Underhill, we came to a corner of Pennsylvania Avenue, where we met, at diverse angles, Victoria Edge and her aunt. There could not have been a better or more opportune occurrence to divert the melancholy of us all. Vickey was gay and joyful, to all appearances; but the aunt was so strange and so seemingly out of place, that we were completely astounded and not displeased with the difference in style.

The Judge braced himself backward a moment on his walking-stick, ejaculating, "Ah, indeed, these happy moments! Never winter came, but smiling summer followed; never sorrow lingered, but bountiful nature sent a joy to outmatch it. Welcome, you who, more than all the world beside, can fill the place of gentle Ann. You, the pride and joy of a broken-hearted old man —the pride, the joy, the reciprocal tie to a heart-broken old man!" And then with a handkerchief all doubled up, he cleared his face. Vickey, not thinking but his address was delivered to her aunt, wist not what to say, but smiling, turned toward the ancient maid, who was indeed the strangest figure. Alack, I must tell you, she had been to the dentist, and her mouth was stuffed with a double set of teeth, and plumpers stretching her withered cheeks to the utmost. Tightly she clenched her jaws to hold the awful contents, and not a word could speak.

"You must excuse her," said Vickey, "she's just got a new set of teeth, and she cannot talk. Meantime I am happy to reply in her behalf and for myself also, that your bereavement has also well nigh distracted me. Since your niece disappeared, I have not had a moment's happiness. I am indeed so miserable I can only add to your own affliction." She then turned to Joe and me and very cordially greeted us. In a minute more we were walking all on together. But as five cannot walk abreast, so the Judge and Vickey got ahead, and in spite of myself I was obliged to be the arms-bearer to the old maid. Joe, in spite of all the horrors and

woful scenes she had passed, now hung her head and screened off the oft recurring laugh. Again and again the old maid attempted to speak, but her teeth and plumpers so stretched her mouth she always failed. Two or three times they got loose and well nigh made their escape from her mouth, but she caught them and crammed them back. People were passing us and continually turning to look at her; and she walked so limpy and slow, so proud of her patent bosom and high-topped bonnet, the latter all tipped and tinselled with gold, and such hoops; my legs tilted them a yard high on the other side. It was the fashionable hour on Pennsylvania Avenue, and even the leisurely promenading ladies and gentlemen of fashion walked faster than we. Those who came along on the other side, from behind, and passed us, having seen the old maid's fine bonnet and fine dress, beneath whose up-tilted skirt hung common flannel half down her wrinkled stockings, turned, when just ahead, to see the face of so strange a woman. Here, behold—they did behold a face like a famished squirrel's full of nuts. Next they looked at me and then at Joe. They were astonished; nudging and grinning all the way. I wished seriously I was at home. It seemed to me that always when I went anywhere, I got the oldest and ugliest girls. The hotel was yet so far off. And then, too, if that mischievous clerk should be watching for us; and he should see me with the old maid? I sighed for an interruption. If only Floyd would come, or Orsini, and challenge me, or if some special messenger should call me. Doomed to walk with the most foolishly dressed old maid; with a face for the grave, and a frock for a flirting girl of fifteen. Fortunately, however, a change occurred, and I was relieved. A man came galloping down the avenue, and seeing me, halted just opposite where we were. He beckoned for me to approach him, and I did so. I had never seen him before, and though under other circumstances I might have hesitated, yet now, being so anxious to get rid of the old maid, I gladly accepted his invitation to proceed in another direction, leaving Joe without any instructions as to what she should do; only saying that I should be at the Jackson House ere long.

At this important part of the history, the writer is obliged to strike off from the main column, to deal with one of the wings thereof. It must be remembered that heretofore this history has been written in subsequent time; the reader has been following the story; but from this point onward, the prospective will bear a very important part. What is to be said now is selected from Jenkins' notes in advance of the place here stopped at, and it begins in this fashion, to wit:

Not long after Ann Underhill became acquainted with Wadsworth, she took to the habit of promenading on the outer porch of the hotel, and frequently alone. Those who are acquainted with this house know that the porch alluded to is very pleasant in the afternoon, and is often the resort of persons of fashion. To see a lady walking there is nothing strange; one would hardly question whether she be in love or in quest of a lover; he would hardly straighten himself up and walk with a brisker step at the sight of her; hardly put the squint-glasses on his nose; hardly pull out his chronometer, or even twaddle his walking-stick against his leg. Thus could she loiter there, as others often did, and scarce a person noticed it. The excitement in Washington at this time was very great; the rebels had made constant threats to take the city, and many of the residents of the place apprehended serious trouble. Many foreigners were in the city, and inasmuch as they were never accustomed to see young ladies unattended in the streets, they could not now, and believe them to be as chaste and holy as angels. American young ladies do not like to have fops turn their squint-glasses full in their faces at every corner. They are little rebels against such impertinence. They are not ignorant of the motives of such men, and know how to judge them. And this is the chief reason that ladies ceased to promenade alone. The prospect of war had brought "men on leave" from foreign navies and armies, and their conceptions of America, formed on the basis of their own countries, had polluted the social air. Many young ladies would not call on their friends, unless attended by one or two companions. So, when cut short the old way, they must seek exercise by some other. Thus it was our gentle Ann took relief on many an afternoon on the outer porch. Vickey had been for a good while engaged in fitting up her aunt for fashionable life, and was necessarily absent much of the time. According to the clerk's story, Vickey fully believed the Judge would marry the old maid; but the clerk had cautioned the Edge family to keep it an entire secret from Ann, lest the latter should break off the match; for the clerk knew that, however eccentric the Judge was, yet his niece

would not tolerate any advantage to be taken of him. She loved him dearly. She was without any other near relative; and he had ever been with her and watched over her. She was his only sister's child, bequeathed to him as the last of the Underhill children. The Judge claimed to be descended from persons of the highest quality, and he ever esteemed his niece as of a superior race. He had provided her the best teachers; he had taken her constantly into the very best society. Of course, he petted her; he had made her his ruler; she was his guiding angel. She was mistress of Loudon Heights. Whatever was required by her, was furnished at once. Yet she was not spoiled. She had good, sound sense. She knew her uncle's eccentricities, his egotism, and his boasting, but she never mentioned them, or, if so, only to please him. She never found fault, never complained; but she pleased him till he made himself as her child, yet she commanded not—for such is woman's chiefest power. Nor had she stateliness nor much to awe with at first beholding; but more by mirth and backwardness calling out all that is noble in man in her behalf; for what man, though he crush the blooming thistle, would not fondly hold the violet and therewith join his heavenly converse? Nor was she silent, nor pleading with pretended faintness of voice; but frolicsome with due demeanor, and ever at a game of harmless mischief, as makes man ever remember and treasure each passing moment. Nor ventured she her wit on persons, nor passed a pun that ever pained another; only on things did her wit and humor tell. And such decorum had she when you spake your sorrows, she seemed to pray to Heaven in your behalf; though mostly is she described as a merry, good-hearted girl and everybody's favorite. Every one who knew her was kind to the Judge, for none would do aught to grieve her. She was likely to become heir to her uncle's estate, and of course had many inquiring friends. Lovers had been after her since she was a child, and, as in her childhood she had valued them, so now the serious part thereof seemed not to disturb her. There had been acquaintances with whom she played in infancy; with whom she danced and walked now in her youth. One of those was a young man by the name of Perkins. The Judge had cautioned her three years before that Perkins was a fast young man, and so she knew it and was cautious. They had been much together when little children, and she knew that he was a brave, adventurous person. Now it so turned out that, when this boy grew up to the size of a man, he became a gambler and a politician, being a wealthy man's son, and not provided with any trade or profession. It was said he came to Washington as a lobby-man—that is, to help at outside pressure to get bills through Congress; that he was paid for such services by large contractors and by railroad companies. Be that as it may, he was often without money, though his father always provided him well. Now it is a principle in society, long established, that such men are always ready to marry any sort of woman for money, and especially if she be young and handsome. This man—if a person of twenty one years be a man—had proposed marriage to Ann Underhill a year since, and had been rejected. Yet, according to his personal appearance, he was an excellent match; and he would also some day inherit a fortune by his own father. He had not openly proposed marriage, nor had she positively denied him. He had merely ventured in the neighborhood, and she had tossed up her hand. He despaired, because he feared her uncle knew too much about him, and he ventured only so far as to satisfy himself that it would be hopeless; though he hoped still, and often came near about her, but not to give offence, for he was an accomplished gentleman. He had noticed her apparent attention to Wadsworth, and he inwardly resolved—at least it afterward seemed so—that by some means or other he would carry off the prize.

Accordingly, he watched her, and often he saw her promenading on the porch as before mentioned, and then he would accidentally, so seeming, endeavor to come there himself. Sometimes he would wait to see if her promenading there had anything to do with Wadsworth. Once he ventured to ask her why she walked there. She told him there was so much excitement in the streets, and so many of those foreign squint-glasses, she could not go out so well as before, and that she loitered here in consequence. But he believed her not. An evil mind doubteth everybody. So he watched her more. One evening he observed her looking over the banister at a lady passing on the sidewalk. He saw the latter toss a paper on the porch, and Ann picked it up. 'Twas nearly night. The lady, or girl rather, who threw up the paper was veiled, and quickly disappeared. Ann turned the paper toward the light, and read it. Her hands fell; she was astonished. She

looked over the side; the person was gone. Again she read the paper, and now pressed her hand on her forehead. Perkins was puzzled, and determined to await the result. In a moment, however, she was gone. He sought her, but was told she had gone to her room. Still he doubted, and lingered near. And, fortunately for him, Mr. Edge came in. He had had much to do for Edge; Edge used him as a pump-handle, in Congress. Judge Francis Underhill was a fine gentleman—very fine for women; but, in Edge's eyes, he was nothing for business. Edge was smart. He could soon find out his man, and he liked those best who would buy and sell. Perkins suited him exactly, because Perkins would sell his word, his honor, his friend, or anything else, to the highest bidder. So these two cronies sat to talk, but sat where Perkins could observe. Long they waited there; talked over all the stocks; all the railroads, the canals, steamships, steamboats, etc., etc., peculiar to politicians and stock brokers. At once, however, Perkins starts, excuses himself, and so Edge goes away. This was Perkins' time. Ann came down; looked at her watch; hesitated a moment, and then went out on the porch. It was quite dark. No one else was there, Perkins mistrusted. Soon, from the lower steps, a lady came up, and, at near approach to Ann, halted, and entered into conversation. No one else heard them, only Perkins—suspicious man!—who had slipped beneath the curtains, and was listening to catch the words. Oh, villainous man, eaves-dropper to such tender ones! Suspicious mortal! A hush, a caution! He heard the words, "Starved—lost—sister—must die!" But he heard no more. This was enough. Sharp man, he knew she must be one of the runaway slaves.

Now stealthily Ann and the fugitive entered the hotel and passed from view. A paper fell as they passed the door, and Perkins eagerly sought and seized it. Now to the light, and thus he read:

"Dear stranger; I am almost starved. I am young, like you, but I am flying for life and liberty. You look so sweet, I know you will befriend me. Please, when it is dark, bring me some bread to this porch, and throw it me. God bless you! KATE."

Perkins knew it all. Three hundred dollars were ready to be picked up, and he resolved to do it. On went his hat, and off he started; but ere he reached Russel's house he thought of the other fugitive, the sister for five hundred dollars. To make the greater sum certain, he resolved to wait a few days, believing that the other fugitive would come to this one. Here now became his special watch, and he was often seen loitering round the hotel for hours, ay, and for days.

Ann was much affected by the tale that Kate told her, and became more secluded and less mirthful. The fugitive she kept in a secret room nearly all the time, only at early morn or in the evening late did she permit her to go out. She had resolved that, as soon as Kate found her sister, she would herself conduct them safely off to Canada. After a few days had passed, however, they both began to believe that the fugitive Lizzie had gone ahead. Ann applied to the Judge for money, and of course he gave it her. She had only to mature some plan of action, and to set it on foot. The two girls often weighed the matter together, and as often formed some new plan of reaching Canada. Finally, though, they fixed upon a time—the evening train of a certain day. But how to travel to excite no suspicion, that was the matter, and thus was their woman's invention planned. They were to travel as mothers. But, not having babies, they resolved to get two monstrous dolls, and have them dressed in the finest embroidery, with long trails; to keep them muffled up, as if very solicitous of the little dears' welfare. Of course, conductors and private detectives would treat them kindly. Accordingly, the dolls were purchased, and Kate entered upon the work of adorning them. Two whole days and nights they provided the things; sometimes so merrily congratulating themselves on the surety of their enterprise. At last the affairs were all completed; they had only to wait for the night to come. But lo! foolish girls, vain hopes! The Old Boy had his snares around you! He had a shrewd instrument watching over you, and that was Perkins. He despaired of the other fugitive coming, and he resolved to make good the first. On a fair morning he sent the marshal, and Kate was taken to the Quarters. Ann was nearly distracted. The toilet was there, and so were the dolls; but gone was the gentle youth with whom she had longed to fly. This was her day of weeping, but not of despair. She saw Perkins when the capture was made, but supposed him innocent. On the afternoon of the same day she saw him again at the hotel, and she resolved to bribe him to get the fugitive's escape. Accordingly, she placed herself on the outer porch, and waited till he came up. He was every inch a gentleman in appearance and style, and, after saluting her, he hoped she had

recovered from the fright in the morning.

"Indeed I have not," said she, "and I fear I never shall. The awe of that moment, and the contemplated horrors awaiting that poor girl, have sent a chill to me that will never, never cease."

"Oh, I do think it was dreadful," said he.

"And yet you opposed it not?" said she.

"I dared not; 'twould have sent me up for three years. Indeed, I abhor such things; but I must preserve my own liberty first, and then to others give it."

"Had you known that girl, and the life that awaits her, you would have saved her."

"I would without knowing her, if I could. But the law must be carried out, and, of course, there are such as would always, for the reward of three hundred dollars, betray a fugitive. But as you have spoken of her and of the life that awaits her, I should be pleased to learn it myself from one who would be pleased to tell it. Perhaps I might yet meliorate her condition."

"No one would be pleased to tell it. No one can meliorate her condition. Money is of little value, and brave hearts are scarce. Her owner will not sell her, or I could save her. She is in chains, and you can do her no good."

"Now, that is strange, you tell me this. Do you remember ever a thing I tried, and failed in? Do you know a thing that money cannot get? Now, I will wager you to the value of a fine bonnet that I can get that girl's chains off before to-morrow morning's sun for one hundred dollars."

"How?"

"Will you wager?"

"I will; and I will furnish the money."

"Done!" said he; and "Done!" said she.

Now, it followed that she told him all she knew about the fugitive, and of their plan to escape to Canada, and he seemed much affected by it, often exclaiming, "Oh, had I known this! Oh, what monsters some men are! Poor, poor girl! But now, hark you! you shall yet carry out your purpose. To-morrow morning shall you start for Canada. I ask no favors; I want no money. It is a most holy cause, and highly honorable."

She believed him; thought he had still a noble nature, and she would fain clap her hands with joy at the coming prospect. He told her to hold herself in readiness on the following morning, before the break of day, and then he left her. She was much pleased; was never so happy before. Thus did she while away the time; having worked herself up to such a nervous pitch about it she had no rest. Poor girl, how simple and childlike in human discernment! Thou hast been talking with a devil. The old maid with the plumpers, whom thou wouldst laugh at, were it not for thy better manners, is an angel. She rises at the early cock-crowing of the morning, because, forsooth, she never learned the fashions. She walks before the break of day to taste the morning air. But hold! ye yet! the future is known to no mortal. There is a purpose in all the habits of man that safely leads conception on to their holy origin.

Perkins resolved to use the other hundred dollars as a bribe, and then to make a stronger and more lasting hold upon gentle Ann. To get her captured with the fugitive, as herself a fugitive, and then to have——

The writer of this great history is obliged to apologize for this abrupt termination to Jenkins' notes on this subject. And he will also apologize for what is coming immediately after, to wit:

Ere the morning came, gentle Ann arose and left the Jackson House. In her arms were the dolls, and she had thick shawls over them. She was too impatient to wait for Perkins, and so repaired to the Quarters, or near there, and watched and waited. Two men, disguised, opened the door, and out came the fugitive. Ann followed, fearing at first, and ever keeping in the rear. When they had walked so she could see them fairly, so she could make sure they were the right persons, they halted, having met a third man wrapped in a cloak. To him the slave was confided, and the other two started, of course for the Jackson House. Ann would have called them, but she was too much frightened, and so stood there. In a little while there was a loud report. The guard ran away, but the slave stood firm. Then Ann came up and greeted her, each well-nigh overcome at so unexpected a meeting. Thence they flew for the railway station fast as possible, or at least fast as two young women with very young babies could. What was their surprise, however, ere they had gone far, to be accosted by a man in deep disguise, and demanded to halt. "I know you!" he said; "you are the fugitives, Lizzie and Kate. Here, you wretches, I will cowhide you?" and he

seized them, and was beginning to handle them roughly, when lo! the simple old maid came near, being even before daylight out to take her morning walk. "What on earth's the matter?" said she. "Here, police! soldiers! watchmen!" and she screamed as if her throat were of brass. The villain ran off. But he had so frightened the poor girls, and had withal thrown away their dolls, that they feared to go to the railway station. Not knowing what to do, however, they ran, and the old maid then got frightened, and she ran too. But she was so slow she soon lost sight of the others. Two men then came, and, overtaking her, asked for the two girls, assuring her that they were friends. She told them the direction, and they pursued. The old maid then went home, and told what she had seen, assuring everybody that she would never take another walk at so early an hour in the morning. The girls ran toward the Potomac, anon beholding their pursuers and again avoiding them. In a short time they neared the river bank, and coming to a rickety old boat, they just succeeded in getting into it and shoving off from shore, when the men, to them unknown, came up. Ann at once resolved to cross the river, she herself pulling on the oars, with a full determination to get on the first train for some indirect route to Canada. She never knew before how strong she was, or what resolution a little fear could give her. But this was in fact a feat of much magnitude, and must result in nothing short of failure.

With what triumphant feelings they shot out upon the river. The discomfited pursuers were amazed. No other boat was there, and the girls felt so completely master of the attempt that they would have shouted to them in derision had not their lives been in peril by the unsafe vessel they were in. But their joy was soon brought to a close. Some idle sailors were passing, and they saw and heard their pursuers beckon to them. The girls put forth all their power, for they next beheld approaching from the shore the sailors' boat, with the two men in it. The sight appalled them. The distance to be rowed was yet very great, and all odds were against them. Not strength, but weakness, came over them, though they pulled with all their might. It was now sunrise, and they were exactly between their pursuers and the sun. Again they heard another explosion, or a not far-off cannon. Kate felt the awful danger to her, and she now seized the oars and took them from Ann, who was astonished how strong the slave was. Their frail boat took a new start. Hope again lived, and for half an hour they sped forward without doubt. But then uncertainty revived. The boat of the stalwart men came after them like a steamer, casting the shining water in flaming wings on either side. The tears involuntarily flooded the eyes of the poor girls as the dread fate began to appear. Nearer came the long-desired shore, but still nearer the never-faltering boat behind. Soon they hailed the girls, who made no answer. They were then near the shore, but the impossible could not be. Kate saw it, and she dropped oars. "Oh, my God! my God!" said she; "I am forever doomed! You see—you see, they are here! Now I will drown myself. I will never be taken alive, so help me Heaven!" "Hold! hold!" said Ann; "Heaven save her!" and she caught hold of her, but she jerked loose, exclaiming, "No, never! Let go; I'll die! Here! if ever you find my lone sister, give her this pin; say it was from Kate, even while the perils of slavery were stripped of every hope, and the darkest crimes of licentious man found refuge in American law. Tell her that my constant prayers to heaven are but the folly of vain hopes; but yet within my breast is a natural flame that burns forever chaste and pure, and so I die!" Ann was then holding her, but the other broke loose, being almost frantic and wild. Then, standing up, she leaped overboard, but did not sink at once. With her mouth full of water, she shouted, "God bless you!" and then she went down. But she could not sink well. Ann was frightened. Both men saw her; they were at once alongside. One of them, the smaller of the two, caught her dress, and they pulled her into their boat. This was the first time Ann looked at their faces; both were strangers. One of them said, "Now for the other!" and he seized Ann's boat. The girls were then only the breadth of a street from the other shore. Ann did not know if Kate was alive or dead, but asked, and one of the men said, "Stop your mouth, girl, or I'll cowhide you!" She was frightened. He did not say she was a fugitive till they got ashore on the other side, and they would not let her speak. The men took a tie rope off the boat, and tied them together. After about ten minutes Kate was able to walk, but she looked more like one dead than alive. The men then ordered the girls to march. Their hands were fastened behind their backs. The men swore fearfully, and, if Ann attempted to speak, they beat her. She knew they mistook her for a slave, but

she had no way to prove herself, and was crying; but Kate did not cry. One of the men said that, before six months, they would wallop such wenches in the streets of New York and Boston. The other said, "It takes us to do it! When we strike out, the world will go with us. The London *Times* and *Post*, and all the nobility, will be with us." And then they would say, "Trot along there, runaway! You'll get it good when you get home!" but they used words that cannot be mentioned, though they were very merry. Ann would say, "I am no slave; I am Miss Underhill, of Loudon Heights;" but they said, "Hush up, wench! we've heard that sort of stuff before;" and then they kicked her. She soon became quite faint, but expected every moment something would turn up to release her. After a while they came to a road, and some people passed them. Ann screamed out to them, and told them who she was, but got severely bruised for it. One of the men said, if she opened her mouth again, he would put the gags on her. This was before they came to the cabin. The cabin is about half a mile, perhaps more. The cabin is a railway station, and is small, with only one door and one window, and a bench in front. They were compelled to sit here, but hardly had taken seat, when they heard a yell near by, and, on looking over the way, saw a crowd of a dozen men hanging a man to a tree. One of the captors said, "There goes another Abolitionist!" and he ended with an oath. A train of cars then came alongside, and halted. The girls were ordered aboard. Again Ann protested against her capture, and assured them of her name; but they would not hear her. "I can prove myself," said she; "I have money. In my pocket is a purse of six hundred dollars." The men all laughed, and one of them put his hand in her pocket and took the money, saying, "I know, now, we're right. The elder of the fugitives had money. This is the person. Not another word now, you ——!" and he thrust them into the cars, swearing at them all the time. He got into the cars also, but his companion did not go with the train. Kate was very ill, even as if she might die. Dark purple sat in round her eyes, and she had lost her senses, for she spoke not, and hardly ever looked at any one. The train then started, but the girls knew not where they were going. They were taken, however, to Montgomery, South Carolina, and put in the Quarters there. Word was then sent to Russel to come on and pay charges and take his slaves; but he

7

was two days coming. In the meantime the girls were kept locked up, and no one whatever, save a simple old negress, ever saw them. There was great excitement in Montgomery at this time. Secession delegates had arrived from all parts of the South, for the purpose of electing a President. Some of them were continually making stump speeches; some declaring that their President would be for the Southern States alone, but others said they were determined to rule over the whole country. They said they would give the New England States to England, Mexico to France, and Central America to Spain. They openly avowed that Squire Larimie was already off to Europe to carry out these plans; that they had money enough to buy up all the foreign newspapers, and that in that way they would rule Europe itself. The people were all enthusiastic. Business of all kinds was suspended; no courts or tribunals were at post. Nearly every day some one was murdered for Abolitionism. Parties of ten, twenty, or fifty men roved about in quest of victims; any one suspected of opposition to slavery or secession was seized, and marched with a tether rope around his neck to the nearest tree, and there hanged. Women became infatuated with the excitement. Seventy first-class ladies formed themselves into a vigilance committee, and often paraded the streets of Montgomery in a body. On one occasion they were jeered at by a cartman, because they interfered with his horse and wagon by their unseemly marching. They at once accused him of being an Abolitionist, and surrounded him. With the lines of the harness they entangled him, and would have slain him on the spot but for his agility. But, when he broke loose and ran, a gentleman shot him. The ball took effect in his neck, and he fell, and expired in a few minutes. The ladies all dipped their hands in his blood, and swore they would not wash it away till every Abolitionist in the country was annihilated. This occurred on the very day that Russel came for his slaves. Many people in the city knew Russel. He was a large dealer in slaves, having a plantation in Virginia for growing them, and often visiting all parts of the South to sell them. He repaired immediately to the Quarters, but no sooner beheld gentle Ann, than he denied that she was his slave. He did not believe she was a negro, but he verily believed she looked like the Abolition wretch that tried to steal his slave Kate. He could not let her out of the Quarters without an order from the constable, and the constable could not do it without a voucher as to who she was. They therefore took a leisurely stroll to consider the matter, and finally resolved to telegraph to Perkins, at Washington, to learn the truth of the girl's story. In a few minutes they got a reply, stating that they were to keep her confined till he came down; that dreadful suspicions were afloat about her. Already was there such vigilance on the cars, and so much watching for Abolitionists, that the cars ran at only half their usual speed. The consequence was, that the poor girls had remained in all seven days in the Quarters when Perkins arrived. The Quarters here were in the suburbs of the city; it was merely a large log cabin, without a window, and having only one door. At one extreme end were the necessary closets, with water, etc.; but the slaves were all unchained, being seven in number. There were five different open spaces between the logs, about the size of a man's arm, which answered for windows. At one side was a plentiful pile of hay to sleep on, but there was no other bedding. The negress kept to feed them passed the food through the open spaces mentioned. Most of the time the slaves sat or lay on the hay, indifferent to any casual observer who might chance to be curious enough to look through the cracks to see them. When Perkins came to look in, gentle Ann was seated on the hay, beside the others. She was pale and silent, her head resting against the rude logs, and her feet drawn up underneath her. She had been stripped of her hoops, and her clothes were in evil trim; her golden ringlets were fizzled and faded, and frowning wrinkles had already seared her fair forehead. She was not asleep, but fixedly gazing aside, and seeing nothing, nor heedful of the noise near the door; but much swollen were her eyes, and her fair bosom still heaved with the latent fire of noble blood. Beside her lay the fugitive, Kate, sound asleep. She had not changed since first her capture, save that she had nearly recovered her health. Long abuse had hardened her. Now, when Perkins came up and looked in the Quarters, and beheld the ruin he had purposely made, he fancied the girl before him would never detect the manner of his mischief, and that, by pretending to be her rescuer, he would be sure to get her acknowledgment in marriage. So, after he had looked in a moment, he said,

"Oh, Miss Underhill! what sad misfortune is this?" She started, and turned

toward him. "Is it possible," he continued, "that this sad fate has come upon you ?"

"Oh, Mr. Perkins, I thank God that you are here," said she, springing up, and running to him. "It seemed no one would ever come, and I am almost dead. Get me out of this! Oh, I cannot live! What horrors I have undergone!" and she made such eccentric ejaculations, that he almost feared she was losing her wits, wringing her hands all the while, and crying at a furious rate. As soon as she gave him an opportunity, he replied very kindly to her.

"Oh, that I could have had your pains and bruises myself!" said he. "Ever since last I saw you, I have been well-nigh distracted about you. Not a day, not an hour, not a minute have I ceased to seek for you. Why did you not await at the Jackson House till I called for you ? And yet I have heaped constant abuse on myself for letting you think of such an undertaking in the first place. Oh, that I had told you to stay at home, and I had taken the fugitive to Canada myself! Can you ever forgive such great neglect ? Oh, I have died a thousand deaths!" and he, too, rubbed hard upon his eyes.

"Oh, sir, grieve not!" said she; "I know it was all my fault. You are a most kind and noble man. I can never repay you for coming so far to rescue me from this cruel fate. Oh, I am so thankful that you have come! Go, please, at once, to the constable, and get me out. May Heaven aid me to repay you!"

Again he made protestations of his own suffering in her behalf; and then, duly assuring her that he would soon get her out, he took his leave. All this while Kate lay asleep, and Ann knew not whether to awaken her or not, thinking it would perhaps be better to go away silently, than to take a farewell of one who was doomed to slavery forever—of one whom she would never see more, and whom she could never benefit. Kate was yet ill from the effects of attempted drowning, and now seemed more of a resigned, heart-broken Christian, fit to be taken to a bed of death, than a slave to work in the cotton fields. But such could not be; for, even while gentle Ann gazed on the palli i, sleeping slave, the voice of the Christian white man was heard in the street, exultant singing,

"Away down South in the land of cotton,
    Cinnamon seeds and sandy bottom, etc., etc."

Perkins soon returned, and in much haste informed her that the story was spread abroad that she was an Abolitionist, and that the constable had kept her there for safety, to herself; that everybody concerned believed she would lose her life if taken out publicly; that she should have some one to vouch for her and take care of her; that as for himself, he was engaged in affairs of state, and did not wish to compromise himself; but that, if she had reliable friends in Washington, he would send word for them to come after her. While he spake thus she was almost frozen with his words, for he kept continually affecting to weep.

"Indeed, it seems to me," she at last ventured in a pleading manner, "that you can get me out, if you will try as hard for me as I would for another situated as I am."

"You tried to save Kate," said he, "but what have you gained by it ? Shall I entangle myself to save you, and be thereby brought, with yourself, to an untimely end ? Nay, say that you demand this risk of me, and I will venture on it. Yet, in all candor, I ask, why I shall be put upon such an ordeal, when there are others with whom you would so much prefer to hazard the fate ? Could I take your place, and send you safely to Washington, I would most gladly do it. But we must not put aside our judgment; we know the streets are all in riot; what shall we do ?"

"Oh, I know not. I do not wish to endanger you. But cannot you buy me out ? Offer the city here a mountain of money—anything—if the authorities will only give me safe conveyance back to Washington. Ask anything, and I will give it."

"I want no money, nor does any one I know of. Nor can I hazard now what I could have before."

"I do not understand !"

"You grieve me. You blame me because I do not throw my life away for you, and, in turn for the risk I run, you offer me money."

"Oh, how much you mistake me! Had I a friend, nay, even an enemy in prison thus, so wrongly, I would wade through fire to open the doors. I would make even my enemy love me for the deep interest I took in it."

"If I could do that too, why, I would."

"You are so strange !"

"Must I then explain ? Yes, though my heart break, I will speak. When I was in some show of adversity, and the evil tongue of others injured me, while you were surrounded by vain flatterers, I was cancelled from my childhood dreams. Now, when the tide of my fortune is at its flood, when I stand at the proper age of virtuous discretion, and penitent for the idles of other days, you, and yourself with a city against you, must knock at the door of my generosity Alas, I cannot, cannot say more!" and then he wept, while she, in much amazement and sorrow, looked on, trying to think what to reply.

"I believe you are truly noble," at last she timidly spake, "and that I have been too neglectful. But oh, you cannot, must not compromise me in this evil plight! How can I live till another come for me? —and if the communication should be closed? You know I am but a child yet before the law. I have a guardian who is master of me. If I disobey him, I will be turned out on the world—with nothing; and, with nothing, I ask you in all candor, what would be my attractions to any man? Now I pray you, that, as I regard you nobly for having come so far for me, that in my heart I feel that I can never repay your kindness, ask no more of me now, but give me my liberty."

"If your liberty were in my hand, I would give it you. But, as to your attractions, with nothing else to aid you, they are more to me than all the world beside; they have usurped my every other joy, and hold me desolate from all things. I know your uncle, and all else you allude to, and I acknowledge your wisdom in the mention of it. But you forget one great affair; which is, that the Government of the country is in a transitory state, and that now is the founding of something new, the very tone of which forbids that ever be the name of Abolition attached to my name. If I go out with you, I am ruined in the affairs of state; if I go not, my fortune and name are built up. One way I will win for certain; the other way I may lose both."

"Why, then, have you come so far to see me?"

"Because I loved you—because I wished to state my position—because I would willingly be branded an Abolitionist, or anything else, and forfeit all my prospects in the new government, for you."

Gentle Ann held down her head, the large teardrops rolling down her cheeks. Yet in all her sadness and fear a ray of eternal light began to appear to her; for the thought of being forced into a promise of marriage made her doubt his sincerity. Summoning all her courage, she at last spake out,

"Oh, sir, I beseech you that you remember my situation! I have told you I could not be neglectful of your generosity if you set me free. If I should be,

why, then I am, in cold ingratitude, unfit so good a man."

"Yet you make no promise?"

"Oh, how can I? I am free to tell you, any man of noble actions might win my admiration. I pray you that you urge me no more."

"What! and leave you?"

"Oh, say not so! Shall I, must I stay here, while you rove so free?"

"Too lightly you weigh your chance of escape. It is at the peril of your life; and if I go with you, it is at the peril of mine also. The roads are lined with vigilance committees; none can pass or repass without military permission. I can send for your uncle, but he may never reach this place alive. I may conduct you safely to Washington; but shall not rather he who is to be your husband run the risk?"

"Oh, sir, I can bear no more!" said gentle Ann, and she sobbed bitterly.

"Think not, dearest," he then began, "that I would compromise you, or bar your liberty to choose. If all my acts are not most noble, I would hold no bond over you. But I ask you in all seriousness, if I am not right in pursuing the object of my love even in desperation? Can so urgent a lover ever do a thing to give you one unhappy thought? I have already a good commission in the new government, and, if you will be my wife, I am at the portals of fame and fortune. I tell you frankly, too, that I cannot act on uncertainties. You are at liberty to choose; your uncle or some of your friends can come for you—that is, if they are not murdered on the way." Coldly now he surveyed the object of his passion; a girl untutored to the craft of gay men.

"You have taught me to fear you," she faintly said in broken sobs; "for, had you sought only my liberty, it would have been a weighty argument in your behalf."

Here she halted, for she cried so she could not speak. He answered her in irony:

"Then I am feared, and my arguments betray an evil design! I hope you will not rue this; and I hope, too, you may be happy."

He then started to walk away, and she began to despair of her situation, and so she called to him, saying,

"Oh, do not leave me! Tell me, will you not indeed do anything to get me liberated without I promise to marry you? You know I must have my uncle's consent."

"I must have your positive answer," said he, halting, and looking back at her.

"But I have not myself to give away."

"Why not? You are now mine; I can take you to church at once; or I can—turn yonder pack against you."

Now, while he spoke, there appeared in the distance the female vigilance committee, together with about one hundred little boys, with drums and fifes playing. Ann knew who they were, for the old negress had before told her about them.

"One promise *will* I make," she replied, "that, if my uncle give his consent, you have mine."

"That is no promise at all. Nor will I urge you more. I would not marry one who is not willing to it, and so I take my final leave."

"Oh, do not go, and leave me here! Say, what would you? What shall I do?"

"Now, indeed, I pity you, and I love you for your consistency. No, I will not bind you thus. I will set you at liberty, and carry you safely back to Washington, and you shall there state my conduct to your uncle; and if he decide against me, I will not murmur, choose whom you may."

"Why, now, that is nobly spoken! Oh, how thankful I am! God bless you!"

"But hark you," he replied, drawing again near the doorway, "it is not as easy as walking in a street. We must have strategy. You are known here as an Abolitionist. Russel has told the people you stole his slave. Now, if you are set out here alone, you will be either murdered, or caught and locked up in some prison till the country is made again quiet, or you may be incarcerated all your life. There is only one mode of escape; I have studied every plan whereby I can get you back to Washington. I will apprise the constable, and you shall be set at liberty just at dusk. I will have cars provided, and then conduct you safely in some byways and unsuspected places to avoid the mob."

"Oh, that is excellent! Now speed the time; make sure every course. Oh, that night were come! How can I ever repay you? Excuse my crying; you know not what I have suffered. But I will tell you all—oh, such horrors as I have passed! could you believe the half? Oh, that I had ever kept under the eye of my uncle! My foolish, foolish undertaking! He will never forgive me—O Heavens!"

Her feelings well-nigh overcame her, for the confidence she felt in Perkins removed her restraint, and her long-pent-up anguish and overstrung nerves now gave way, and, quite exhausted, she sank down on the hay and hid her face.

Have you ever been in Montgomery on a winter's eve, and felt the genial air? Could you an Italian sky surpass, and free from banditti roam in the light of an early evening moon, and treasure evil in one single thought? Have you seen a country maid from home on a lone road, miles away with one man, and never thanked your God you were an American? Or was it possible that virtue and honor were so common here you knew not of them? Possibly you have never been in other countries. Possibly you do not know that the avenues to employment in a republic are a greater incentive to virtue and honor than all the edicts and soldiers of any of the kings or potentates on earth. A republic is a book on the rights of man, and the citizens are taught to read it; but a monarchy is a game of grab-all with a whip in the hand of the mighty. A man that opposes or rebels against the former, rebels against himself, and must be mad. Only destruction could come on such. But the philosophy of all things is fixed, and no man may change them. The vigorous body is neglectful, and foul disorders prey upon its vitals; then stern nature sickens and purges the whole. The surfeit in spots appears, and the wise man trembles; for these are the signals, and the Almighty points at the nation's fall. Treasure it, O ye mighty men of earth, for the law of equal rights amongst men is in the care of Him who rules the heavens! Justice is in the firmament with an uplifted sword; who would not fall, let him behold. It is the guiding star to the mind, and the footstool to the climbing genius. Vain politicians heed it not, but cavil on the meaning of words, and their own ingenuity blinds them. Heaven shall strike them down, and their party with them. They will not heed equal rights before the law, and they shall be ruined. They have long been told of this, and the wisdom of the prophecy makes them fear its truth, and they are enraged thereat. They are mad. They are given up to all manner of profanity and wickedness. They make oaths to Heaven, then violate them, and even Heaven itself do they defy.

Of this party was Perkins. Once planning rebellion against liberty, had fitted his soul for all wickedness. He knew his own impurity, and that no good act of his could ever win her guardian uncle's will. Some things we can forgive in a man, and welcome to his arms our fair ones; but there are others that seal a separation forever—things that make a grave more welcome than a husband.

Perkins was intelligent and sensitive, nor could he brook to be denied. His victim was a heart-broken girl, far from home, in prison, and he led her out at night. She was all joy for herself, but nearly overcome with grief for the poor slave Kate, left bawling in the Quarters, whence the pleadings and prayers were screamed till gentle Ann was lost in the distance. Closely now on his arm she hung, all confident, and nearly crazy with her hurried thoughts, nor noticing where she travelled, till full out in the open country road, by the light of the evening moon, he bade her halt.

"Tell me, now," he spake, in slow and solemn voice and determinedly,

"Tell me, now, has this night no charm
  for you,
To cancel all the past, and bless the future?
Will ever this most glorious scene occur
To you in after time—and me forgotten?"
  Ann.—"Oh, never! never! But why
halt you here?
For now, amid the joys I feel, I fear
A cloud may mar the dear, the beautiful
  scene.
Shall we not go on?"
  Perkins—"Whither?"
  Ann.—"You frighten me!"
  Perkins.—"If frightened now, I fear you
shall be more."
  Ann.—"Why! you will not proceed to
Washington?"
  Perkins.—"No, not at present."
  Ann.—"But you promised me!"
  Perkins.—"I thought so then, but not
now.
             Here I stand,
To be accepted or denied by you;
And all these beauties witness this my vow:
That more I hope to never live in heaven,
Than to deceive so innocent a girl,
And that in all attest I love none else,
Nor ever shall misuse your confidence.
Will you be mine?"
  Ann.—"My uncle, I have promised, shall
know all.
And, if he give consent, you need no more."
  Perkins.—"Out with your uncle! Only
you I ask!"
  Ann.—"Indeed, then, I cannot answer."
  Perkins.—"You shall!"
  Ann.—"Since ever I was a child, and for nearly every day of my life, I have promised my uncle, nay, called Heaven to witness it, that I would never promise any man without my uncle's approval first. Shall I forswear myself?"
  Perkins.—"Promises like those to an uncle or a father are nothing in the sight of Heaven. They are idle, toy-like, children's words."

  Ann.—"Oh, say not so! Who promises before high Heaven, be it even on a pin's head, is not released for all time. Now, I pray you, that as you esteem my feelings, keep me not here, but take me to the station."

  Perkins.—"Never! I am denied. I am scoffed at. I am a tool to help others to their joys, and left to feed on my own bitter thoughts. Your uncle will never consent; nay, though I lifted you from the water's edge, or though from a burning housetop I bore you safely, he would point his finger, and say, Unclean! Had I, with the promises of my fortune, lived in Britain or Europe, and I een the father of a dozen children and still unmarried, the bond of equal rank would not have been yet broken. Here has a sentimental philosophy sprung up, and I would join hell itself for its overthrow. You know what I mean. There is a time when all ceremonies cease, and love can wait for no more speeches. You shall be mine!"

Instinctively now she withdrew her hand from his arm, and he turned to face her. She drooped with fear and trembling, and then with much craft made answer,

"Oh, say not so! for my own unhappiness might ruin yours. Please take me to the station, or back to the Quarters, or where you will, but do not more for which you impugn yourself; for yet you are possessed of a noble soul that may long live in happiness. Too gloomily you view the things whereof you complain, and in too much haste you urge the final course. If not I may be yours, there may be one never knowing to the things you accuse yourself better suited to bless you."

  Perkins.—"You forget—I say you shall
be mine!"

  Ann.—"Why, now, how could that be? for the priest will ask me if it be my wish, and if, perchance, I say him no, what then? I should not be your wife?"

  Perkins.—"You jest; but I will teach you in plainer words, that, if you do not consent before the law, I will not be bound by the law, and yet you shall rue that you fill the place never sanctioned by ceremony."

  Ann.—"I know not what you mean; but I pray you, that, as I esteem you for your kindness so far, you take me to the station. When we were little children together, you would take me by the hand and lead me; are you less gallant now? Now I pray you, tease me no more, for I am sick and faint with long suffering."

She then took him by both hands, and looked up into his face, now so cold and silent. Long he stood, motionless, and then teardrops rolled down his cheeks. Down he hung his head, and she herself saying nothing, for it is in silence the soul reaches up to God.

Perkins. —" O   Innocence   Immortal !
    whence this might,
To shear the villain's craft and long-laid
    schemes,
And purity embolden by its pureness,
As standing here, and powerless I am,
So helpless, and in an angel's grasp.
Never, no, never can you know my heart,
Nor the dread mystery, why you are here ;
Nor aught of all your woes and suffering—
Save that even he you do refuse—is guilty.
I never knew a woman's moral worth,
And was taught evil by my rights in slaves.
Pity me, and forgive. Here is my death,
My life, my liberty, my all in this,
A bowie-knife ! "

He stepped back from her, and swung his hand with the shining steel, while she in terror stood, uplifting both hands and gasping, pale as in death.

        " Now go, I charge you here,
And by this instrument am sworn to Heaven,
Or else you die ! Go, go ! And when you're
    gone,
And only yonder pale moon may witness,
—I'll die ! You are too pure for me, and I
So much admire your nobleness I am dead
To all ambition. Here, on this lone spot,
Will I undo the body organized
Ever with fire ungovernable—ever
The blur and ruin to my own pure spirit."

Ann. —" Though I die, but hear me
speak one word——"

Perkins. —" Silence ! Begone ! I hold
commune with none,
Nor would you feel nor see the work of this
Dread instrument, begone !   I am re-
    solved ! "

Ann. —" I shall not go, God witness, I
    shall not,
Here, I come on the blade, now strike me
    down—
That promised little to so true a love."

Perkins. —" Begone, vain woman ! "

And he pushed her back, and sternly stood clear.

        " You could not be mine
In honor, and in shame you never shall.
I sent you here ; I had you dragged in
    irons,

Even as a slave—and now have led you
    here—
For nothing noble. Go from me, I say ;
One must die—two need not, or the crime
    is yours."

Ann. —" Ah, indeed ! Can no voice of
    entreaty——"

Perkins. —" Nothing ! Begone ! "

Ann. —" O Heaven ! what shall I do ? "

She then cried bitterly, for he was so determined she had no more hope, and, half praying and pleading, she sank down even at his feet. In a moment now the scene changed. A vigilance committee of a dozen men were returning from the hanging of a neighboring farmer, and, turning the bend in the road, came full upon Perkins even as gentle Ann lay at his feet. The persons all gathered around, and in much earnestness looked to Perkins for an explanation. "She is sick and weary," said Perkins ; "will you help me take her to the city ?" and then the weeping, faint-ing girl was raised up. One of the vigil-ance committee exclaimed at once, with an awful oath, " Why, this is that Aboli-tion wretch Russel spoke of ! Hang him and her ! " and then he called her by an evil name. The crowd was inclined to make quick work of it, nearly every one shouting out, " Up with her ! " " Hang her ! " and such like words ; but Per-kins stoutly denied she was an Abolition-ist, and kept the crowd at bay for some time. One of the men then said, " He is an accomplice of hers. I do suspect both are Abolitionists. I would rather hang a dozen innocent ones, than let one Aboli-tionist escape. Let us hang both, and that is the end of it." After some parley, however, it was concluded to postpone the hanging till next day. Gentle Ann was so weak and so frightened she realized little of what was going on. The mob then tied her and Perkins together, and marched them back to Montgomery, one of the pleasantest cities in the South.

Jenkins informs me that it is the better way to say nothing more in this chapter on the above subject, for there are other things of great moment connected with this invaluable record which may be found in the next chapter by simply reading it once over.

CHAPTER XIII.

THE COURTS OF JUDGE FRANCIS.—THE FOUR STYLES OF TELLING A THING.—THE PLOT TO KILL LIN-
COLN; AND THE OTHER THINGS, WHEREIN ARE ILLUSTRATED MANY OF THE HIDDEN MYSTERIES OF
NEWSPAPER ACCOUNTS ABOUT MADAM PONCHARD, PUBLISHED AS SOON AS THEY OCCURRED AFTER
THE WOFUL IMPRISONMENT OF MISS UNDERHILL, AND OF PRESCOTT'S ATTEMPT TO SUBVERT THE
THREATENED WAR BETWEEN THE NORTH AND SOUTH IN ITS INCIPIENT STAGE, BY AN INDIRECT PUB-
LICITY THROUGH SCOTT AND BUCHANAN, BUT WHOLLY ON HIS OWN RESPONSIBILITY AND IN IMMI-
NENT DANGER, AND APPROVED BY THE AFORESAID COURTS.

WHEN I read the heading over, I told Jenkins an excellent scholar could perceive that a few words inserted in it at various places would make it quite plain. "Well," said he, "let him perceive it. We must be diplomatic, no matter what comes of it." I made no more argument, but signified my readiness to proceed. He then handed me a bundle of papers, saying, "These are Prescott's; take them, and write them out." I then asked by what right Prescott claimed notes before our exalted courts. "He has no right," said he; "we granted it him. He had long knocked at the Temple and cast in morsels of learning. We let him in, in order to show him by our wisdom how much he lacked. We put him in the box, and he gave in the following testimony, which, by our court, was pronounced upon. The approaching war had reduced the number of members of our court to a fraction. Prescott had never been in the box before; the Judge scarcely had his old spectacles adjusted, when the former began, and these were his words before the court, to wit:

"It is hardly possible for the people of any period to place a correct value on their own transpiring events, or to conceive the verge whereby they walk so near to life or death. On the morning before Cæsar's death the great Roman empire was all joy and gratitude for the seeming changeless glory and peace that awaited their mighty nation; but yet they were on the verge of a fall that will be awful to contemplate for thousands of years to come. The Trojans hoped and believed in their power and glory, even till they were destroyed. The Lacedæmons, the Carthaginians, and the people of all countries and kingdoms under the sun have boasted of their power and safety even to the day of their fall. For five-and-thirty times has France set up the boast, and every several time come to ruin. Great Britain thought she had hit on the noblest and most enduring form; but her distant colonies have gradually alienated and stripped the parent stem, till, standing there, she is only a helpless show, commanding by the shadow of what was once a great power. In olden times she could raise four hundred thousand men; but in the late war with Russia she could raise but six-and-twenty thousand. Like an old man, she acknowledges not her weakness, nor will she while a crown can hold the helm. She has passed the verge, like an old farmer whose sons have gone away from the old homestead, leaving only a few old maids, as harmless as doves, to mark the fall that has been so gradual as not to be felt by the people. All other nations have fallen by war or by internal dissension and general disintegration; and, strange to say, every nation's fall has been previously predicted by its wisest men, and scoffed at by the general citizens even till the day of trial came; for, what men do wish to believe, though the verge ripens to their every sense.

"But what of ourselves? Is our nation at the verge where all men pass? First the childhood, with only wild nature pleased, and all-absorbent with rural joys. Then the age of admiration and self-love, where the mirror and the boast hold command over all else. Next, followed by the goal of disappointment, and turned to battle with the unruly members within itself, and in despondency commit suicide, or in triumph conquer matchless glory. Who that thinks of these things is not solicitous for the welfare of his country? And who can, in an approaching crisis like the present, stand idly while the poniard is raised to his Cæsar's breast? It is not deserving of praise to fight for one's country, for it is natural; though, when an officer is given a sword, and himself swears to keep the peace by it, and then himself will stand and do nothing, he is indeed a criminal fit for the trap and craft of any design against his life. A very dog in the manger, holding back the guard while murderers plunge their swords and bayonets in the hearts of innocent millions. An officer loving more his party than his country; a man to forswear his oath before God; to set bloody war afoot, and gloat on poor widows and orphans, rather than see his own party turned out of power. What man, knowing such a man to hold the chief office of a nation, would not feel that his country was at the verge of its own greatness? Nor could any one blame a citizen for trying to counteract the evils of so vile and perjured a wretch. Was ever so poor a person put in office? Was ever a Constitution so distorted? Was ever a man of so low a mind raised to so high a station?"

Judge.—" Is your name Prescott?"

Prescott.—" It is."

Judge.—" Well, Mr. Prescott, you are off your subject. You remind me of my ancient French friend, Victor Hugo, and, if you were not handsome, I should banish you also to some lone island. Always, when he begins to tell a story, he tells a good many others first. We want nothing with ancient Rome or Greece, but Washington. If you cannot give in your testimony without running abroad for illustrations, or without ambiguous reference to men in office, you are not suited to this court. If you allude to James Buchanan, say so. If you have any affair between him, Madam Ponchard, and Jeff. Davis, why, say so. We want no Romes here."

Prescott felt the rebuke, and would have gladly shut out the comparison to the French author had it been possible; but remembering that in earlier days, before he had arisen to fame, he had played in the minstrels, and learned to say plain things under color which he never could have without paint, he rubbed his face now to make believe the blush was hidden, and then struck out in the following most remarkable words, to wit:

Prescott.—" Then, now, of a solemn voice I speak, and I speak as my heart moves me. I stand not, sir, on legal forms or etiquette, but use such plain, blunt words as best apply to this eventful period. For, even while gloomy winter overhangs this city, while rains and storms, thaws and freezings alternate changes play, and suns and clouded heavens vie for the mastery; while covered lies the withered leaf of autumn, and budding green in embryo yet is sleeping, wrapped in the folds of fruitful and never-denying earth, and the birds to their holes or to their southern homes, albeit devotional all for the glorious bounties in an early spring, changes far on in the world's history and magnitude of human events are about to be borne into the presence of an unguarded people. The toil of labor for the scene and coming convulse stirreth now in the heart of millions, and the mutterings of its thunders hide all that is on the face of the earth. Like a newly-kindled fire, over which lies endless food for the devouring flames, its yet almost unnoticeable sparks and smoke have more terror to more people than did ever before the threatened war in any age. Millions of people, honest and virtuous, unarmed and unprotected by soldiery, now behold the bloody Mars galloping forth with sword uplift, while bayonets in the hands of millions are pointing to the breasts of countless women and children."

Judge.—" This court cannot receive such testimony, Mr. Prescott. It is neither history nor philosophy;" and the Judge winked at various members.

Prescott was excited, but firm, and thus went on, to wit:

" While many men and women, here in Washington, are engaged in trying to plunge the whole country into war, or, by their threats, to maintain in power the party that has just been defeated by vote, it will be, no doubt, to future generations a great mystery why somebody does not nip the thing in the bud. And it will be, too, no doubt, said, owing to the imbecility of Buchanan, that nothing was done to avert so great a calamity. But such is not the case. There are many men, unofficials, who are knocking at every door, communicating and urging everything possible to arouse a patriotic action, but who as signally fail in every attempt."

Judge.—" Come to the point, Mr. Prescott; this court is waiting for the testimony."

Prescott.—" On a fair winter's day, amid the mixed multitude thronging the streets of Washington, was to be seen one of the busiest men you ever heard of, hurrying hither and thither in the show and fashion, his hands clenching a bundle of papers, his brow all sweat, and snarled with alternate hope and anguish in every feature. He seemed but a boy in step and action, but his fixed features, long experience, and some adversity, marked him full thirty or forty; and his hesitance was like a woman's. He seemed to notice none, and few, indeed, noticed him; but yet he had ventured upon a part in the great national drama that will ever signalize him as the first active patriot of the present period."

At this point the Judge interrupted Prescott, by declaring his style too much like a parson's novel, or the romance of a schoolgirl.

Jenkins then took up the subject, and thus related it himself, to wit:

For a long time there had been threats made by many secessionists that Lincoln would never reach Washington alive; and even Buchanan had said that Lincoln should never be President. Offers for Lincoln's destruction, for his head, for his body and for his skin, were now made in nearly all the hotels of Washington, and in many cities throughout the South. Most of the American people could not—would not—believe the country was at the verge of its own fall. These offers and bribes for Lincoln's death were laughed at—considered merely a political boast, that would vanish by the coming March. Yet the evidence to the contrary was true beyond all question, to persons acquainted with the whisperings and low cunning manifest in all Washington society. Two persons, Madame Ponchard and Orsini, mysterious in all their doings and actions, had weighed the offers for Lincoln's death, and found a profitable balance on murder's side. These, in a remote corner, secluded by some leafless winter trees, in an unguarded moment let fall some strong words, the which reached Prescott's attentive ear. It was late in the evening when he observed them to halt and to prepare to hide something. "See! harken, now, Orsini!" she said in rather audible whispers, "lest some woful fortune turn on us and us betray, beneath these stones we'll hide these scraps, and so hide the evidence to convict us, if caught." "Agreed!" said he, and then, in some indistinct mutterings, agreed they both to keep this spot as the hallowed receptacle of their designs. Prescott watched with eager eye these would-be hired murderers, in hopes, in part for fame and notoriety, but more to thwart so foul a purpose, till they were gone; and then, repairing to the spot, upturned the stones, and, in the broken column of a fallen lamp-post, found crammed certain papers.

It was too dark—being at night—to read or guess with certainty what was thereon, and so, to make all safe, thinking they would return to deposit more or call for these, he returned them, resolved that, with the first gleam of the morning light, he would return and read them. He did so, even while he thought all the city asleep, supposing no one was fool enough to rise so early; but of that anon. The papers were a collection of subscriptions for Lincoln's death, and were so plainly written as to be unmistakable. Hastily he ran over the amount, and found that it footed the enormous sum of two millions. Aside from this, there were others, offers for the heads of many other men. When he had satisfied his curiosity, and safely replaced the papers, he left. Orsini left Washington the next day, and travelled South. For six days and nights Prescott watched the hidden papers, but no one seemed to come near the spot; yet, ere he had gone far from it, one morning at the break of day, he met Mrs. Stimpkins, the famous lecturer and editress. "Ha!" she said, "I'll know now, Mr. Prescott, why it is you frequent this spot so regularly. Are you, indeed, too, conspiring against the life of the in-coming Administration? Are you, indeed, to receive two millions of dollars for simply killing one man? Has man wronged you also? Is, also, man's fickleness your ruin? Know you that you have laid a trap for your neck? Know you that for six days and nights I have seen you come here to count over your expected gains?"

Thus saying, she tightly clenched her long thin lips, and hand over hand rubbed her large knuckles, eyeing him with the fierceness of a very tiger.

"Madam," he said, "you much mistake me. I have been also watching this spot, in hopes to acquire evidence and power to convict the would-be criminals doing this."

For a moment an incredulous smile overspread her half-starved face, the while her eyes piercing still, and she slowly, firmly said,

"So, indeed! Am I to be forever unarmed by plausible stories? Am I to be again balked by the cunning of man? to disbelieve my own senses, and all faith bestow on a race whose every word and action have ever galled me with disappointment?"

He told her he knew not what she meant.

"You don't?" said she, satirically. "Then hark you—I will tell you; and, little can I ask you to believe, if indeed you have found, as I have, all men and women to be false ; but I speak in justice to myself. First, then, I don't believe you ; you are a dough-face, a man to betray the liberties of your fellow-creatures for money. Such is man's nature, and you, bearing the semblance of a man, must be false to human rights. You smile! Sir, I have been many times married—have dived into the deepest recesses of man's heart, and I speak only the things I do know. For gold, for gain, for self in any sense, man, this would-be lord of creation, will sell virtue, honor, love, and kindred. Benevolence, morality, and religion will he use as masks for his selfish purposes. Give him an opportunity to better his fortune, and he will fall in love with a bundle of bones or a bag of meat ; add another opportunity to his view, and he will cast the same bones or meat into a gutter. Give him adversity, and his love is like a snow in harvest, a fancy to melt away ere 'tis seen. Such has been my experience, such my evidence. The joining together of a few hundred dollars has ever been the cause of my marriages ; and my every husband has painted out sure prosperity in the prospect ; but when failure came, a want of congeniality was discovered, and I was cast aside, or perhaps opportunely I cast them aside. Thus have many husbands failed me ; but my last one, the celebrated Professor Jackson, for the most trivial cause, because I limited him to one meal a day, has left me the worst of all, or rather I did not cast him off soon enough. Again I take the field alone, a champion once more for woman's rights. But, sir, Professor Jackson wrongs me still. He lectures on the same subjects I do, thereby even robbing me of my own profession. But I am resolute ; I have learned man's selfishness, though it cost me dear, and I am sworn to make my mark on every man I meet. I don't believe your story !"

"Indeed, madam, you much mistake me," said he, "and much abuse us all. There are strange coincidences in nature. You may have five or seven husbands, and all of them selfish and bad, and yet, were you to take another, he might prove a very angel."

"Sir! sir !" she almost screamed, "would you offer yourself to me? Must here begin another course, to end in failure—to tear hence still another vital part? Oh, curses, curses on thy sex ! Even while you lay hands on a murderer's bribe, you talk of marriage !"

He then assured her that these papers were not his, but Madam Ponchard's.

"Then do I know," she said, "you are false. If 'tis but to curse a woman you lay this trap, if but to send some woman to prison, then you act verily a man's good part. Yes, I believe you ; you are not the villain to murder Lincoln, but still you are a man, and, as such, woman's enemy. Were these would-be murderers of Lincoln men, you would not stir a hand ; but, since 'tis woman, verily how noble you are ! Now, I shall see to it, and, if it be indeed a woman, I swear I will thwart you, though the heavens fall !"

He called her, for, when she closed her speech, she started onward, and he endeavored to tell her the importance of keeping the matter a secret. She would not heed him, and strove to appear as if she had vanquished an enemy.

Prescott knew not what to do, but immediately left the place, and sought me, and disclosed all his discovery, with particulars about a Mr. Russel, of Baltimore, being engaged in the plot.

Our plans were at once submitted to Judge Francis, and we were directed to assume the responsibility of procuring the aid of two trusty officers to make, at the proper time, the arrest of Madame Ponchard and Orsini. Prescott was despatched to Baltimore, to appear before Russel as a man from Alabama or Mississippi, and to convince, if possible, the would-be murderers of Lincoln that he was also in the ring with them, and by this means obtain all the information possible of the numbers and designs of the gang. This affair was managed well by Prescott. On arriving at a tavern in Baltimore, he came across the said Russel, to whom he represented himself as the leader of a similar plot from Louisiana. The bait took exceedingly, and several Baltimore gentlemen were introduced to help mature the plans. Prescott informed them that he was not only acquainted with, but a partner in carrying out the plot. Russel was a crafty man, and had a straight and honest-looking eye, even when telling downright falsehoods, and could so laugh, talk, and fill up the time, that no other could edge in a word. Yet, in apparent candor, like a child fond to learn, Prescott led him on, and some suggestions made that won him to value highly his every plan. In course of time, Prescott asked, then urged, then commanded him to come to Washington, to help consummate the plans for Lincoln's death. To this he acceded, and the trap for his capture and conviction seemed sure. On the following day he and Prescott reached Washington. This was the day on which Lincoln left his home in the far

West for the Capital. Already had Scott the whole city guarded, but the assassins had resolved to commit the murder in Baltimore.

What was our surprise to learn that this same Russel was a member for the Peace Congress, and that he professed such a warm attachment for ex-Presidents Fillmore and Tyler, and that he so honestly believed Lincoln's death would settle all the trouble between the North and South, by giving the South supreme power ever after.

Immediately after Prescott and Russel arrived in Washington, and when they had proceeded a short distance together and then halted to part, they were met by the little thin-faced man Stephens, and Jeff. Davis. The former walked on slowly, but Davis spoke with Russel, and suggested to him, within the hearing of Prescott, that the proposed assassination of Lincoln would not amount to much unless a hundred others were killed the same day; and this, he said, would be the most humane way of settling the matter. Russel replied that the whole of the leaders of the Black Republican party could be disposed of within a week. Shortly after this Prescott left, and so also did the others, each one going his own way.

All the above information was now communicated to the selected officers, and all of us were assigned a part to perform, either for evidence or the arrest. Scott ordered two agents off to meet Lincoln and inform him of the dangers awaiting him, and to plan out some mode of reaching the Capital without passing through Baltimore. On the same day of the departure of these two agents, we had another interview with Buchanan. He was pale and distressed, and, when we told him about the two agents sent to meet Lincoln, he really trembled with rage. "Shall Scott transcend his powers?" he said. "The whole thing is bosh; it is unconstitutional. I know Madame Ponchard and Orsini, and I do suspect this whole thing to be a conspiracy against them in hopes to aggravate the South."

He was inconsolable. We left him fevered with rage, fearing that he might, in fact, betray us, and so frustrate all our intentions.

Now it became necessary to guard the place where the prize papers were concealed, but we needs must guard them in such a way that we could get witnesses and that we remain unsuspected ourselves. To do this, we resolved to open a news-stand near by, and to put the fugitive Joe there as salesman. To this she readily assented, not knowing, however, our object. But I myself had some unpleasant conjectures about her. For several days past she had failed in appearance, looking really depressed and broken down. And whenever I inquired after her anxieties, she seemed to avoid me; seemed as if the spell of her former open-heartedness was at an end. At present, however, I accounted for it by the disappearance of her sister Kate. As it was only for a few days we desired her services, I urged her to brave the task, and in hopes the better to catch the eye of her sister, should she pass that great thoroughfare, she herself seemed at first enraptured.

On the evening of the third day, when I called at the news-stand, she was in tears. It was then about seven in the evening, and she was greatly agitated. No one else was near, and I insisted on knowing all her trouble. She leaned on my arm a moment, and sobbed bitterly. "Oh, say not all," she replied, "say not all my trouble, for it would break the stoutest heart. But come; I am a child—provide me safety at once. I do forget, but I must fly. I am detected. That murderer, Orsini, passed here, and he pointed to a friend even as he passed. He was in company with the actress who married my master."

"What! Madame Ponchard?" said I.

"The lady," said she, "so richly attired, in black, jewelled. Oh, I know she and he murdered my good master. They are now after me. I must leave in an instant. Tell me where to go—what to do!"

For a moment I was shocked and confused, but, on regaining my presence of mind, I told her to wait but a moment and I would call Prescott. She clung hard upon my arm and looked most piteously into my face. In a moment more I released her hold, and she sat down, while I hastened fast as I could walk to the Jackson House. In a little while I found Prescott, and solicited him to come and help provide safety for the news-stand till we could quietly and surely wait on the fugitive's requirements.

What was our astonishment and mortification, though, to find, on our return, that the poor girl was gone! Not a restige of her could we find. No note—nothing. Thinking that perhaps Orsini and Madame Ponchard had returned and had frightened the fugitive off, we now sought for the hidden papers; but here too were we confounded. They were gone! Our object was, as has often been told in the newspapers, to get the would-be assassins arrested, and to keep them so until Lincoln should reach the Capital. But this little slip was likely to frustrate all our designs. Of course we informed the detectives of what had happened, and this in a measure made them distrust us. The consequence was, on the following day a sort of wholesale arrest was advised, and to have Russel taken up at once. Now it so happened that, when the detectives passed near the place where the papers had been hid, our veritable Mrs. Lucy Tabiatha Stimpkins was looking for the valuables, and in a quandary about their disappearance. They approached her, mistaking her, in fact, for Madame Ponchard, though really they looked as much unlike as any two ladies could.

"Madam," said they, "we are sorry, but our duty compels us to demand your presence at headquarters this morning;" and they smiled, and signified for her to come along.

"What fool effrontery is this?" she said, scowling with her deep, sunken eyes, and bracing herself in the most upright position. "Know you that I am woman? Independent woman! Independent! I have, sirs, a duty to perform, and I will perform it though a world opposes me!"

The officers smiled a little, and told her she was all right—it was all very well, but there was a little affair which made it necessary for her to appear at the police court, hoping she would pass along so quietly as not to attract attention.

"Do you know," she said, looking terribly fierce, "do you know to whom you speak? Have the inalienable rights of woman sunken to this low ebb? Is this the sphere of intellectual woman?—to knuckle to man; to go to police headquarters; to go quietly! Quietly! I would, sirs, make my voice ring louder than the thunders. I have felt the tyranny of man, and, sirs, my heart bleeds for the manner in which woman is crushed; but this low degradation shall never come on me—never! never! You may defraud us of the right to vote; you may tax us without letting us hold office, but you shall never tie woman's tongue. Never!"

This did attract attention, and already were a few beginning to collect around. One of the officers stepped up to her and took her arm, smiling, and saying,

"Oh, yes, you are all right; but come on!"

"Hence!" she said, snatching loose. "Begone, inferior mortal! From all that was perfect, was most perfect woman made. But, sirs, you have robbed us of our affections—of our souls; you have turned us into barren skeletons and weazen-voiced orators, and you mock at us for the wreck you have made. But when you say 'March off quietly,' there's the mark, quietly; you have then come to the place where you can go no further. March off quietly! I'll make my voice rattle more than all the devils in pandemonium!"

The crowd began to assemble rapidly, and many of them began to laugh, and this, too, still attracted more attention—the officers following her up gently, and she as violently stepping back and lecturing them, to the amusement of the bystanders. Fortunately, however, in a little while Prescott came up, and, seeing the mistake that had been made, succeeded in setting all right, so that the officers retired, leaving her master of the field. Here she held forth in a speech on woman's rights in earnest; but we cannot relate her speech, owing to more important matter.

It was on the day after the fugitive's disappearance, and immediately after a court sitting before Judge Francis, when I had come down from the Temple, and meeting Wadsworth even at the columns thereof, and seeing him in apparent distress, I halted, and engaged him in the source of his reveries. He had never before, to me, looked so ill—never before so melancholy and downcast. At first thought I inwardly rebuked myself for not having heretofore tried more to minister to his apparent sorrows. Another thing that flashed over me for the moment was, he had talked for a long time past of going home to his plantation; and now, why did he linger still in Washington? With tearful eyes he gazed into mine, taking my hand, in such assurance as sacred made the word of each to the other; saying, "I have waited for you," and he seemed at loss whether to say more. But I assured him, in my gentlest manner, that I was anxious to do him service, and that I could perceive that something more than common was preying on his mind. "You are right," said he; "I am almost distracted. I hardly know whether I am living or dead." With this expression he half turned his face away, so fair and noble, and the tears flooded his cheeks. Drawing a card from his pocket, and cautiously turning it over, and passed it to me, remarking, "You know not how desolate is all the world, with no one to love!" I looked on the card, and, while I read the words on it, I was nearly palsied.

"God bless thee! With no mishap, thy dear one will soon return."

I knew who it was, and, although I stood as motionless as a statue, a torrent of emotion well-nigh caused me to sink to the ground. Oh, that I had never lived to see this—to feel that the dearest one I ever knew had so kindly written to my most excellent friend! Oh, the racking in my brain, the flood of gushing thoughts and strange imaginings! The dread of long mistrust, but long concealed and curbed by my best judgment, had now, in an unexpected moment, had the veil lifted, and doubt settled forever. Visions sad and lonely then spread out before me, and my course through the long future loomed up as mountains of darkness perpetual in the clouds, while my own isolated self appeared in the distant future vainly trying to achieve that happiness which all men covet on earth, but no one has ever attained. "Vain, vain man," I mused to myself, "see you not the higher law, and acknowledge it, that the aspirations and fond desires of the full-grown man are dependent too on the independent will of others, and that yourself in obedience here must find exaltment in the things that goad and murder you!" Bitter, bitter bane this, to an unprovoking man! But why of myself? Thus, in a second of time, I measured a world in thought, and confounded stood, with the little card half hidden by the clouds of mist gathering in my eyes, till Wadsworth, more collected but weeping more, urged me to tell him if I knew some misfortune to her.

"I see it in your eye, your face, and whole expression," he said; "you have ill news for me. Oh, tell me, I pray, what evil tidings make you fear to break it to my sensitive ear? I know your kindness to me, and your gentleness to her. You fear we are separated forever? Oh, speak! why are you silent?"

He seized me by the hand, and earnestly peered into my face; but I was so confused, for his innocent construction of my sorrow overpowered me, that I found no utterance at first, and then he added, quickly:

"You know not what I have been doing? I have searched all the North, and even Canada, but I tell you the newspaper stories of her flight are all false. She has not absconded, but some great misfortune has befallen her. Now I charge you, and you know by what injunction I crave aid in my distress, if you know aught of her that will give me either peace or sorrow, speak it—in Heaven's name speak!"

"I know nothing of her," said I, "and you astound me beyond measure. So much credit has been put in the stories about her having been seen travelling North, that no one doubted. Besides, also, has not the Judge received letters from her in Canada?"

"Those letters are forged!"

I was thunderstruck, and still silently waited while he resumed:

"I traced those letters out. The Judge gave me the said-to-be address, and urged me to go to Canada and see her, keeping it quiet, until such time as we should be married and she could return in safety."

Here was another shock; the Judge had given his consent, and I had never known it.

"The Judge knows not, but believes the letters are genuine. He will die if I unfold the truth to him; but oh, sir, what fate must hers be! Some deep and cursed villainy is afoot. That lady never left Washington, at least on a Northern railway or steamer." He then minutely described all the manner of inquiry he had instituted, and related the sad result. I listened to his adventures, myself much moved by the tenderness of his style, and when he had finished, he gave a lengthened sigh, and pressed my hand warmly, saying, "I know of no one to whom I can so well unfold my sorrows, or who would so much excuse my weakness as you, and for that reason have I cast my history before you. Pray, sir, do not let your sympathies too much my troubles bear, but rather counsel and advise me with what I shall do to regain my life-treasure in that gentlest one of all I ever knew. My day-dreams, my night-dreams, my hours of ceaseless thought have only life in her, and her absence is my living death. Oh, sir, in Heaven's name, tell me, what shall I do? Give me a thought, or a dreamed-of prospect, and I will follow it to the end of the world. For I have fashioned out all conjectures and hopes, and pursued them to the very uttermost end, and failed. Give me some clue, some possible hope, whither she is gone, and I will fly. My admiration for you, and my love for your intelligence and nobleness, have sent me here to meet you. Thus have I loitered near the Temple, that I might eagerly devour your first conjecture."

He then waited for me to reply, and I summoned all my powers to act the noble part; although, had a dozen swords' points pierced me through, I had suffered less than what was now galling me to the very soul. And he so innocent of what was moving me!

"My friend," I said, with some caution, "too much we value things so mortal, and too hastily surmise the coming end. Take less to heart, and more control on the feelings keep, while sterner judgment and time and sure events work out these mysteries. Think you no one else has ever borne such woful loss, and yet controlled and hidden it from even a friend's suspicion?"

Wadsworth.—"Oh, that could not be! When two souls so tenderly love, they will speak though Heaven frowns. Oh, say not that mortal ever so loved fair woman, and concealed it, for it is in the nature of things impossible—impossible!"

"I think 'tis possible—quite possible! Indeed, I have heard it so said, the deepest love in silence lives, and bides the powers above. Know you all the history of this gentle lady?"

Wadsworth.—"Oh! indeed, I know it well. But no, perhaps not all; for so gentle and kind a one has a history in every hour's thought, and since she has passed some twenty years, of course I cannot know it all, though much I trace it back, of what she was by what she is, and so do full acquit myself I know the whole. What of her? For if in anything past you can unravel something leading on to the time present, it may much mystery explain."

"Well, then—for my attachment to you is quite equal to your admiration of him whom you have sought to comfort you—let me tell you of this fair one, who has no superior in this world. She was once a child, and, as such, played as children do, wore short dresses, and at times went out in the sun without her bonnet. Frivolous, this, to tell; but no, you shall hear. Along with her, and with other children, too, was a little boy, called by the others Freckle-face, always in mischief, always teasing all the other children. Only gentle Ann he never crossed, but kindly treated. When she lost her bonnet, he brought it her, and playfully tied it on, and she regarded him well. Anon the other children teased them both, because of their affections, and this nearer brought the primitive loves to each other, till, though in almost infant years, they betrothed themselves. Long they lived so—one, two, three, four long years—and their affection became a type of purity and nobleness to all the neighbors. The par-

ents of each were about equal in rank, wealth, and culture, and much approved the intended marriage. But, as all people are subject to die, so the boy's parents both died, leaving him heir to a great fortune. The boy was taken by an uncle, to be educated and cared for till he came to maturity. This uncle had a daughter, cousin to the boy, who was now set upon by several indirect methods, of which he knew nothing, to be won over to marry the cousin, and so forsake gentle Ann. He was then in his seventeenth year, and needs must remain with his uncle four years, according to the will and testament of his own father. He was forced into the society of his cousin, but no mutual love ever sprang up between them; and, on the other hand, he was told falsely about his dear, gentle Ann; that, as she was only a child of thirteen, she had since discarded him, and taken up with other lovers. He did not believe it, however, but rested his faith in the All-ruling Power above to restore him, some day, to the dear one of his choice. After he had been absent two years, he fled from his uncle's house, and over the mountains of Virginia travelled on foot two hundred miles to see his long-absent love. And he saw her, and they renewed their pledges with more warmth than ever; but were scarcely done greeting each other, when the rude uncle came upon them, and, bidding him remember the will and testament of his father, succeeded in carrying the boy back again to his place of abode. Not long after this the young man—for he was no longer a child—heard that Judge Francis Underhill had gone to Europe, and that the dear one had totally abandoned him. He became depressed and isolated, but at maturity, coming into possession of a great estate, he came to this city, where he again met his long-lost one, but they met coldly. The stories told to each of the other had chilled the love between them, and neither one would venture again in the sacred channel. At times they would walk together, or playfully allude to the days of childhood, but a power more than mortal ever seemed to stand between them. A thousand times did he try to overcome the awful barrier, and a thousand opportunities did she offer, but whether the recollection of the malicious stories told, or whether Heaven itself intervened, I know not; but their broken hearts both felt the loss of a world, and were silent in it. But hers was not a heart of love to love in vain; her charms fell upon one of the noblest men I ever saw— one of the most innocent and virtuous;

and he gave her a warmer and dearer love than the other ever could—and you are that man !"

"In mercy's name, you have torn my heart asunder; you have laid bare every portal whereon lived my happiness! But tell me—tell me of the young man !"

"I am he !"

CHAPTER XIV.

BEING A PART OF THIS GREAT HISTORY WHICH WAS NEVER BEFORE WRITTEN, ABOUT THE SPECIAL DOINGS OF SOME OF THE GREATEST MEN OF THE AGE, AND APPROVED BY THE COURTS OF JUDGE FRANCIS UNDERHILL, OF LOUDON HEIGHTS, AND WITH THE APPROVAL OF THEIR AUTHORS.

I TOLD Jenkins that, although the above heading was quite Congressional, I could not see exactly what the meaning was.

"Why, I'll tell you," said he, "for you must know that every sentence of a great author is weighed by critics, and judged accordingly. We, you know, must have our style. Every one his own way. One man sets out to tell you a story with a beginning as follows, to wit: 'Two mysterious beings were seen at early morning in a boat in the river Thames, in coarse habiliments, in close proximity and earnest attitude, in silence rowing. One was a female figure in the bloom of youth, in the stern of the boat, in a loose old gown in reduced circumstances. The other was that of a male companion, in a drowsy slouch hat, in bending form, with silvery, uncombed locks, in the middle of the boat, rowing, and pulling something that looked like it might be something'—and so on. Now, you know our style would be: 'An old man and his daughter by the name of Smith searched for dead bodies in the Thames. One morning, having found the corpse of some unfortunate, they took it in the boat and rowed down the river'—and so on. The style is everything. The weary man, the business man, the active mind of this age can fill in; give them the points, and tease not with such worthless stuff."

I told Jenkins that the reader of this history would be too much interested in the fate of some, and not enough in the fate of others connected with it.

"I want no Lucy Dashwoods," said he, "for my model. The interest was there kept back, and it made an accidental glory; it was, in fact, an Eva's death to the book, and made it live."

Said I, "Do you suppose you can make a sweet young girl halt here and read Buchanan's politics, or about a peace convention? Would she not be skipping over to see how it came out with the Judge and Vickey, and Prescott, and gentle Ann and Wadsworth and the old maid and yourself? Then there are Madame Ponchard and Orsini; will not the writers of history skip over your love affairs, to ascertain the part they played in the beginning of the great rebellion ?"

"No, indeed !" said he. "If you will be patient, I shall here read you such a chapter as you never dreamed of." He then took up his glass, and smiled. I asked him what he smiled at.

"At wit," said he. "I smile at wit. Only a short time since a man wrote a poem, stating in the preface that he wrote so funnily, that, when he took it to the publisher, the latter laughed from ear to ear, and that all the buttons flew off the poor fellow's coat with laughter. The author then goes on to state, that after that he never dared to write so funny as he could. Very witty, was it not ?"

Being anxious to get on with the history, I urged him to proceed with the translation; and he immediately took up his notes, and began with these very words, to wit:

My position as reporter had made me quite an important person in the estimation of many people. Slave-hunters always came to me, and also to Prescott, to learn all the hiding-places of Washington, and, in fact, of many other cities. Now it so happened, that the man who came down the avenue when I had been gallanting the old maid with her new plumpers, was Russel, the slave-catcher. As soon as we were alone, he began. Said he, "I am a Baltimorean, and live in Jefferson street, that city. Two ladies have taken a house next door to me, and have acted so mysteriously about it, that I do suppose them to be Abolitionists, and that they keep, in fact, a depot for the underground rail-

8

road. My business has been for many years to assist in capturing runaways, and I scarcely ever err in my judgment of people. The stories circulated about, that the fugitives Kate and Lizzie are off to Canada, or are captured and sent home, are all false. I am too cunning for that. I have long heard of you, Mr. Jenkins. You have figured a good many years as a writer; our occupations are nearly the same."

I did not feel flattered by so rough a comparison, but made no answer; for, in fact, he talked so fast I could not. He called a man to take his horse to the Jackson House, and then he urged me to accompany him, having in a single sentence informed me he was a member of the Peace Congress, the originator of the Bureau of Detection and Capture Bill, and that neither ex-Presidents Pierce, nor Tyler, nor Fillmore could claim it. What he was aiming at I could not foresee, nor could I imagine the cause of so great familiarity of words at first meeting. But I soon beheld his mistake; for he, in the midst of his ceaseless talking, informed me that the clerk of the Jackson House had told him I could be relied upon as all right on the secession and slavery questions, because I was an Englishman. He did not even let me have time to deny it, but talked, talked all the time himself, till we neared the turn leading up toward the Patent Office. "Well, I do say," said he, stopping short and looking at a lady who had just passed, and whom I knew to be Madame Ponchard, "if there is not one of my dearest friends! I'll stick by her till doomsday, and I'll learn all the particulars." And then he turned abruptly away, looking back, and saying, "Meet me at the Peace Congress in half an hour, and such things as I shall there tell you, you shall see; for I do suspect we shall have an uphill time of it. You Englishmen are better skilled in the accomplishment of destroying nations, and you shall have plenty of work, my word, as you say in England."

There I stood, looking after him, and he going away and talking every moment as fast as he could. In fact, I pitied him, for his ideas seemed to come much faster than he could talk. But such strange conduct in a stranger to me left me bewildered as to who he was and what he wanted with me. He followed after the Madame, anon looking back to me and shaking his finger and smiling like a horse-jockey. He was a stout, good-looking, middle-aged man, and seemed a man of business and many jokes, and inclined to say everything himself. Of course I was left alone, and a little embarrassed about receiving such treatment from a stranger; but he seemed so good-humored, that I entertained only the best of feeling toward him. Not daring to go back to the Jackson House lest that mischievous clerk should bore me about the old maid, I loitered slowly along till I came to the halls of the Peace Congress, whereat it has been prophesied there shall never, to the end of all time, stand a monument. Near the doorway, outside, stood Floyd and young Wise. They were looking at a photograph; it was of the usual size called carte-de-visite. I did not look at it, but saw enough to recognize it as Madame Ponchard. Floyd wished to avoid me, and he went in the house. Wise seemed suspicious of me, but he remained in the same place. Ex-President Tyler then came up and spoke to Wise, and they both went in together.

The hall was very large, and ingress only permitted to the officials. You cannot imagine my surprise at seeing my stranger friend already in the hall. I had left him following Madame Ponchard, going in an entirely different direction, and now found him as a member of the Peace Congress, safely and quietly smiling at everybody, and propped up near the doorway, ears and eyes for everything present. I doubted, at first, if he were the same man; but he saw me looking at him, and he tossed up his finger, and nodded and smiled as if he had known me for years. Thinks I to myself, this Peace Congress is a curious conglomeration; for I beheld the venerable Crittenden, and others equally honest in their endeavors to compromise the trouble between the North and South, here sitting beside the most rampant fire-eaters of the South. A man near me then touched my shoulder, saying, "Why, have they got Buchanan's statue here?" and he pointed toward the left-hand chair, whither I cast my eye, and there saw, to all appearance, a marble figure like our present President. But while we looked at it, it raised its hand, and my friend said, "What! is it he?" For it was, and he beckoned for me to come over to him. He was as pale and death-like as a corpse. All eyes were now turned on me, and I felt somewhat embarrassed as I went forward. He raised up to receive me, and, bursting into tears, exclaimed,

"Oh, Jenkins! Jenkins! come to my relief!

I am so harassed by these partisans,
Ice would not melt in my most fevered blood.

Think you that I am dead, or living?
For really, there comes such a flood of
      doubt
O'er my palsied vision, I am lost,
And live, alas! but live in reveries."

I was at loss to reply, for the house was
not organized, and I knew every one was
looking for me to say something excellent.
    "I know no man," said I, "since first
      the world began,
That ever had such heads to battle with.
Giants are boxing with a new-born babe.
The which this nation feeds with choicest
      food,
And promises of blood and priceless treas-
      ures,
But the child calls not, and the giants
      crush it.
We pity you—we pity James Buchanan,
Sworn to defend the Constitution,
Though incapacitated for the work,
Not by your own weakness, sir, but others'
      strength."
    Buchanan.—"Ay, that's the point; I
      can't cope with such odds.
I am so tied to the Constitution—
There is the matter—and these court de-
      cisions.
Methinks, sometimes, when I read Justice
      Taney,
That angels might be profited by him,
And made more constitutional in heaven.
There is such seeming random in men's
      minds
Of late, and they shoot out such wicked
      notions
About the Constitution, I do think,
Christian as I am, Satan roves scot free
All o'er the country."
    Jenkins.—"And it behooves us
To guard ourselves, sir, Mister President,
Lest we mistake the devil for true angels."
    Buchanan.—"And how are we to know,
      forsooth, but by
The Constitution?"

And he smiled in triumph, while many
of the ultra pro-slavery men winked and
smiled to each other, and whispered aside,
"That's it!" "Keep him on that track!"
I pretended not to notice what was passing, and was relieved from further reply-
ing by the sound of the gavel.

Ex-President Tyler was made Chairman
of the Peace Congress, and, as soon as
order was restored, he handed the secretary a recommendation, signed by nearly
all the Democratic party of the State of
Massachusetts. This was read at length;
and the document reflects severer on the
American character than anything of the
kind ever signed by a civilized people.
It was while this document was being
read, that the police appeared at the door

with Madame Ponchard. I knew, but I
now think no one present knew, what the
outside row was about. The commotion
in the Peace Congress was greater than I
ever before beheld. We would fain rush
to the door, for Madame Ponchard's arrest
was deemed almost equivalent to a declar-
ation of war; yet we were so intent on
knowing what the document held forth,
we dared not move. Six or seven members left, the balance of us remained.

The document was said to be signed by
half a million people of Massachusetts.
But was it genuine?—that was the question; or was it gotten up by Fillmore, and
Davis, and Toombs, as a make-believe for
peace? It proposed to please the South
by disenfranchising a large portion of the
people of Massachusetts on account of the
color of their skin; it proposed to let
slave-owners bring their slaves into Massachusetts, and to protect them while
there; it proposed to establish in every
township a whipping-post for runaway
slaves; it proposed to pay the slave-
owner for every slave coming into Massachusetts, if not captured; it proposed to
make it lawful to buy and sell slaves in
Massachusetts, if not to remain there; it
proposed to divide all the Western territory, half and half, for slavery and freedom; it proposed to keep up the balance
of power for the slave States, by purchas-
ing or taking by force Central America
and the West India islands; and all that
this great State of Massachusetts asked
in return, was summed up in four words
—Pray don't fight us!

Hardly had this, the most remarkable
document ever signed by a Christian people, been read, when up jumps a little fellow with a whining voice, holding up a
paper not two yards in front of me, shouting out, "Mr. President! Mr. President!
if it be in order——" and he stretched
himself up and smacked his lips, smiling,
and he slapped on the paper with his
hand, "I will read you a brief answer to
that." Again he smiled, and twisted his
lips like a member of Parliament. I saw
the writing, and knew it to be in Toombs'
hand; it was written on foolscap. It was
twenty pages; the substance of it was:
"We, Southern members of the Peace
Congress, have heard the propositions of
Massachusetts, and we reject them, because she does not give as much as we
want, and because we do want what we
are determined to have."

"Like a love-sick belle, never satisfied!"
said a voice in a far-off corner, whither I
looked, and now beheld Judge Francis
Underhill, of Loudon Heights, spreading

himself, and adjusting his old silver spectacles. "'Tis ever the plight of a girl of seventeen. Her ardent lover tells her he gives his whole heart, his wealth, his muscle, his name, his very soul, if she will but let him love her. Then she proudly asks, 'Will you not give more?' Here is a leading State offering you everything—even promising to rob her own citizens to please you. Hardly are her proposals read, when your heir-expectant jumps up, and reads a previously written speech, saying, 'Give us more! Give us a good deal more!' Massachusetts offers to make a heathen of herself rather than have any trouble with you. She is a cowardly cur, and the South is a greedy hog."

Before he said more, the Chairman called him to order, but all the while were others rising, shouting out, "Mr. President!" "Mr. President!" and trying to get the floor. Finally the small man with the whining voice got ahead, and sharply demanded who the Judge was? "An Abolitionist!" "an Abolitionist!" shouted out several others, some of whom roared out, "His niece and he run the underground railroad!" Buchanan then pulled my arm, and bade me sit beside him, saying to me, "Do you think there'll be a row? Oh, for God's sake, I wish I were home!" and he was even paler than before; but I cheered him up, and urged him to remember that, as long as he stood by the Constitution, he was safe.

"Oh, I have had such a time!" said he, in a whisper, and he pulled my head over to him, shaking badly all the while. "Those Commissioners have been to see me! Oh, what shall I do? They might come in here! When I told them I could find no law in the Constitution empowering me to sell all the Southern forts and arsenals, they said I must read it again, and find it, or they would wring my neck. For two days and nights I have read it, and I can't find the place. Oh, what shall I do if this Peace Congress miscarry? Where shall rest the head of the last of the American Presidents?"

I thought indeed the old man's fears had deranged his judgment, and I longed for some interruption, to put a stop to his earnest whisperings. But while he was thus pleading to me, the little whining man was talking about the North agitating the slave question, and hoping they would continue at it till they fired every Southern heart. He was happy to hear they were stretching cables across the Mississippi, and that suspended Abolitionists were ornamenting every Southern forest. He went in for the Union as much as did

any other man; the Constitution was framed by the wisest men in the world, and he revered it. He deprecated secession; it would bring sure ruin on the South. But he was sworn to fight to the last for Southern rights—and for State rights, too; and when he could find no one South ready to fight with him against these Abolition usurpers, he would go single-handed. He would take the torch in one hand and a bowie knife in the other, and wade through blood and fire till he had vanquished the whole mudsill race of the North.

This was Stephens. His braggadocio made the house quiet, for we longed to hear what all he could say; though Buchanan kept continually whispering in my ear, and I heeded little more than the tenor of the speaker's speech. When he ceased, Crittenden presented his resolutions, the substance of which was—all the new States hereafter added on the Western frontier should be slave States, if south of a certain line; or free, if north of the line; that there should be incorporated in the Constitution a fixed law to prevent future generations, as well as the present, from ever interfering with the growth and moral influence of slavery. After his resolutions he made a speech, and we all saw in him the heart of an honest man. He wept while he spake, and Fillmore and others also shed tears. But his resolutions were too much against the North, and not enough in favor of the South. He, too, beheld the inadequacy, and then his good, honest heart gave way. Exhausted, and beholding the insurmountable end, he finished his speech by imploring aid from on High, even while covering his face with both hands, and falling into his seat. And when he sat down, it was like the going out of a lone star in the dark night; he had failed to carry his measures, and now were five-and-thirty millions of people without a ray of hope. Compromise was buried; Mars, muffled yet, but clad in armor, strode o'er all America, and with the craft of long experience; for this was not the end of the Peace Congress, but it lingered many weeks, though as a tool in aid of the fire-eaters. Though we saw the end in the outset, we had not measured strategy with Davis, Toombs, and Stephens. Their craft must hold out a hope, by pretended love for the Union, while their armament was being put in trim to destroy it. Even Crittenden was blinded by them, and made to hope against hope. And far down South did all the newspapers and hired speakers berate the non-conceding terms of the North. Miles was hired for five thousand dollars, and all expenses paid, to lecture South, and to tell the people that the Northerners would concede nothing; and that Massachusetts demanded the unconditional abolition of slavery; and the people South believed him. Cobb was hired for two thousand dollars, for the same purpose, and the people of Georgia believed him. Iverson was hired for six thousand to employ General Twiggs to betray his part of the national army over to the Southern cause, and Twiggs did it; but his soldiers, good, brave hearts, deserted their traitorous leader.

These subjects were discussed in the Peace Congress, and immediately after Crittenden's speech. And these things caused him to fear for the result; and, thus despairing of the nation's cause, he had put forth his eloquence but to bleed his own heart. Not so with Fillmore and Davis. They wept because they beheld the prospective downfall of an old party. So, when the floor was clear, they were ready with threats of vengeance, some of them declaring that a raid of a thousand men could decapitate the President and Cabinet in two hours' time. I saw that Buchanan was excited, and he pulled me over to him again, asking if they meant him, or Lincoln. I told him Lincoln. "O God, I hope so!" said he; "no—I mean, I hope they may not decapitate me, nor Lincoln neither. Is not this terrible —terrible!" and he cried like a child.

"It appears to me," said a voice, "there is unnecessary quibbling here. These are demonstrations denoting anything but a Peace Congress. Do you not behold what unnecessary pain you give his Excellency, the President? These vituperations are, in my humble opinion, at variance with the designs of this Congress, and wholly unnecessary and uncalled-for."

I turned to look at the speaker, for the word *unnecessary*, coming in so often, made me fear I had really gotten into the British Parliament. I did not know the man; he was past the middle age, a little bald, with a flushed face.

"It appears to me, if I may add," he continued, "that an assemblage of this sort is unnecessarily resorting to the *ad captandum* on one side, and quite as unnecessarily resorting to the *nil ad captandum* on the other, and that no end will come of it, unless it is in strict adherence, which it ought necessarily to be in order to achieve the called-for objects."

As he was going on in this style, I heard some one whisper that he was one of the Russels, a correspondent of a paper published in England called the London *Times*. The other Russel was there, but I could see no family resemblance, nor could I imagine what business such a man had in our Peace Congress. He spoke for half an hour, and the substance of his remarks, translated in English, was:

"You are very foolish. We great statesmen on the other side the water have long told you you would come to pieces, and now you see it. We pity you, and are ready and willing to advise you in your distress; and we trust, too, you are such a young people, while we are so old and full of experience, you will heed what we say to you. You may be, to be sure, sixty or seventy years, but still you are very young. We may be only sixty or seventy, but then we are a very old people. You must remember that we once attempted to coerce your colonies, and that we failed. All the colonies, at that time, were not half as powerful as are your present dissatisfied States, and the result is manifest to the weakest mind. Still, I can assure you we are on friendly terms with you both, and should remain, in the contest, your neutral well-wisher."

I then asked several gentlemen if the man was William H. Russel of the London *Times;* but I failed to learn for certain, neither had I any evidence that said Russel had been imported for the secession cause. Stephens told me that South Carolina had already sent over emissaries to England and France, but he said he knew not who they were. When the speaker resumed his seat, my stranger friend then came forward and greeted him very cordially, many of the people expressing their surprise at such a proceeding in a Peace Congress. Tyler did not call order then, but leaned over, talking to Stephens. Many of the people were whispering, or rather muttering with one another. My stranger friend and the last speaker then started for the door. Toombs was about to speak, but at that instant we heard a voice at the door say, "That is the man—arrest him!" I looked out, and beheld Prescott. Two police were with him, and they advanced to my stranger friend, whom they took prisoner. He swore violently, and demanded the reason. Floyd and others then sprang up and rushed for the door. When I started, Buchanan pulled at my coat, and I dragged him a little. "Oh, Jenkins! Jenkins! don't leave me! don't leave me!" he said, and he stared wildly out of the door. "The South Carolina Commissioners are coming! They'll wring my neck! They said they would! It is not in the Constitution. Oh, don't leave me, for Heaven's sake! they will wring my neck!" Had he not been so pale and frightened, I should have laughed; but he clung to me as close as Sancho Panza did to Don Quixote when they heard the falling mills, and I did not know but the like consequences would result from the fright. At that moment, however, Tyler declared the Congress adjourned till next day at twelve o'clock, and he and Toombs and Davis joined arms and walked off together. Buchanan would not go himself, nor let me. I urged him to believe there was no danger; I told him it was another affair altogether, outside the house; but he stared with great consternation toward the door, frequently saying, "It is not in the Constitution. Oh, those Commissioners! What shall I do?" I then started with renewed force, most of the crowd having gone out, the President still clinging to me with one hand, and with the other pointing toward the door in the most abject fear, and I really dragged him out with me. However honored I was to support the American President to his carriage, I felt full as much shame with the burden as did Dr. Johnson with his drunken woman.

"I tell you, Jenkins," said he, as we stood waiting for the carriage, "you cannot imagine the terrors around me. Only a few days ago, that imperturbable Prescott crammed such arguments down my throat, and, sir, sir, he said, if I sold the forts, I would commit perjury before God. Yes, sir; and he did so enforce his views on me, that a deliriousness of mind has made me more the tool of other folks than I was before. Oh, sir, such a fire as he placed me in—God and heaven on one side, and my party on the other; and they threaten me so terribly, that I can neither walk ahead nor stand still for the danger of them." The tears rolled down his cheeks as he spoke, and he had no more color than the driven snow. I then helped him into the carriage, and he pulled me after him, saying, "For God's sake, come in—see me safe home!" and I did so accordingly.

Here the writer of this remarkable history waited for Jenkins to proceed, but, on looking up, beheld him penning this line, "End of this Chapter." "Now," said I, "Jenkins, whether are you to be the author of this book, or am I to be?" And he said, "You." "Well, then," said I, "what literal truth is there in this chapter?" "Things cannot always be in literal sense," said he. "Things plain and simple may be, but things and times of great importance never can be. You will remember Richard the Third said, 'I want a horse—quick!' but the historian wrote it, 'A kingdom for a horse!'"

CHAPTER XV.

FIFTEENTH SITTING OF THE COURTS OF JUDGE FRANCIS UNDERHILL, OF LOUDON HEIGHTS, WHEREIN ARE UNFOLDED THINGS OF AN UNUSUAL CHARACTER ABOUT THE NOW ALL-ABSORBING TOPIC OF WAR AND THE LOVE AFFAIRS OF DIAMOND WEDDINGS WITH A RAINBOW IN THE HEAVENS.

"Now," said I, after I had read the above heading, "now, Mr. Jenkins, that is carrying things too far! One would think you were making a speech at the Tuileries, or fitting up yourself for a foreign minister."

"What one?" he asked; and I told him I knew not who, for I saw that even in my criticism I had blundered. Now it so happened that I had been, years ago, the principal witness at the courts of Judge Francis, and that Jenkins was only admitted to the box at the time of building the new Temple; consequently my words were now constructed into sentences under his approval, which accounted for his greater vigilance.

"All right; go ahead!" said I, and he uplifted his huge manuscript and read off the following, to wit:

The second thing in importance, now, to the contemplated war between the North and South, was the prospect of a diamond wedding. It was in all the newspapers; it was issued from everybody's tongue; but, true to propriety, the names of the parties were withheld. One was mentioned as the wealthiest and noblest citizen of Washington—a man somewhat advanced, to be sure, but still as vivacious and hopeful as a boy of twenty. He was no less a person than the Judge of that mysterious court of etiquette and learning which has so long been the nucleus of men of great wealth and literary attainments; he was one of the oldest inhabitants; he had travelled farther and learned more than any other man. He had been so long and ardently watching over the affairs of the nation, that he had neglected himself; but, just in the nick of time, he had cast his glories before one of the most enchanting, amiable beauties that ever appeared in the Capital. She was also a millionnaire, and of course the envy of her sex; she ruled the fashions; she was the belle, the queen of the city of queens, and her beauty as rich and rare as ever the sun shone on. Thus read all the papers; thus said all the ladies; thus talked all the gentlemen, and rumor and curiosity exaggerated the stories till the like was never seen before in any age. But, strange to say, no one knew who the lady was; no one, save one, knew who wrote the articles for the newspapers, and every one guessed hard and guessed often to ascertain who the noble parties were. A few knew who the gentleman was; but gentlemen were too much engaged about war to attend to such idle matters; and ladies were the more put to their wits' ends because the gentlemen wouldn't. Now, the truth of it was, that ever mischievous clerk was at the bottom of it all; writing all those stories for the papers, concealing just so much as should deceive both the old maid and Vickey as to which was the intended bride, for he would have them both believe they were both alluded to, but both to be the recipient of a different kind of husband. This he did by stating at the end of the newspaper articles, "also two of the relatives of the same parties, and also wealthy, will be married the same day." So craftily had he managed the matter, that Vickey now placed herself on the list of the betrothed, believing, through the clerk's stories, that Prescott was the millionnaire alluded to, and that the other match was between her aunt and the Judge. One thing troubled Vickey, and that was the style of courtship. She had had her love adventures in a small town in Ohio, and out there the lovers courted in closer proximity. For a long time this had preyed on her mind, and she feared that she might, indeed, be the victim of some mistake or ill-fortune; but she dared not counsel with her money-mak-

ing papa, and she had learned so much of fashionable life while in a Philadelphia boarding school, that it were useless to apply to her less-informed mother. One day she resolved to have the matter cleared up, and accordingly set herself about it. Prescott had also taken rooms at the Jackson House—a fact that should not be omitted in a work like this—but he seldom lingered about the place, his arduous duties as reporter calling him hence most of the time. Occasionally, however, he would pass through some of the elegant parlors or drawing-rooms, nodding to one and another, bidding the time of day, passing only a few words, and then passing himself out. Thus he had often met Vickey, often said something pleasing, and often most abruptly left; for, though he was the son of a washerwoman, his contact with his fellows had polished him a little, and his duties had made him abrupt to business. He was sharp to view his friends, and read their character and standing at a glance. In Vickey he saw the heart of a good and virtuous girl; but he saw the vanity and folly of a boarding-school education. Her diction was trained, her affectation assumed, and her position in fashionable life painful to herself. And she, too, felt it all; and felt, too, that a man of so sharp a vision as Prescott could see and know her prison bounds. Of her aunt and her mother she was ashamed, not for any fault of theirs, but because she had drunken at the Pierian spring just enough to unfit her for spheres of high or low, and because she loved them too dearly to break from their ungainly ways. Gradually did this light dawn upon her, and gradually, too, did she become unhappy, and suspicious that everybody noticed hers and her family's greenness. And then she grieved; she grieved that she had ever improved in intelligence, for it was robbing her noble woman's soul of the objects to love. She could speak fluently, for the boarding-school taught ladies to read and speak in public; taught ladies that a bold utterance was learning; taught that the modulations of voice made woman great, commanding, queenly; taught that a smattering of many books could gild the mind, so that it would pass, on the unthinking mortal who should marry her, as the store-house of an angel's literature. But now, alas, she found that the short period of polishing off at boarding-school was but an external polish; and, too, she found that, to be in the society she had entered, she had needed to have been in it all her life, and to have been ever studying with diligence, to make it now a place of enjoyment. Her attractions were not lasting; she could play you on the piano; but could not inform you on the difference between Beethoven and Mozart; she could talk you on the Constitution and our great, free country, but she had never heard of ancient republics—nor did she know Cato from Plato; she could talk you on Byron and Milton, but she could not tell you the difference between *acatalectic* and *catalectic*. She had heard of *iambic, trochaic, anapestic,* and *dactylic,* but she knew so little about them, that, when you talked to her of them, she sat in painful silence, or cunningly talked of something else. And thus it was on all subjects and things whereof fashionable life amongst a literary people abounds. The consequence was, young gentlemen, and even ladies, of genuine worth and information, who were at first attracted by Vickey's pretty face, prettily-set speeches, pretty playing, queenly grace, soon discovered she was only plated ware, plated by a boarding-school; and so, for lack of learning she was cast aside. That is to say, every new arrival at the hotel was captured by Vickey first, but first, too, would she get the cold shoulder, and then, plainer ones, perhaps, became the greater lights and glory. But this young lady had a heart, a good, honest heart, and she had been told that she was accomplished, and "fit for the best of society." People had told her that her voice was a second Jenny Lind's, and she knew no better; to encourage her in learning, her boarding-school teachers had told her that she was excellent, and that all she needed was a little more brass; and so she got brass. But now, alas! she had learned that there were to be found giants in learning and accomplishments, and that she herself, the pampered and flattered, was but the victim of a boarding-school polish. And she grieved; she grieved bitterly. She grieved in particular for herself; she grieved in the burden she had with her aunt and mother. Then she became unhappy; and then she became distant and watchful, nay, suspicious. She weighed too heavily all things, and cast them all against herself. This made her weep; ay, at times she wept bitterly. She thought no one loved her; she thought some of them loved her very ardently. The Judge told her every day she was the fairest queen he ever saw; he was ever telling her what glorious times they would have after their marriage, and she thought he meant her aunt and she and Prescott; but she was too much afraid to try to find out, and she would only answer; "Oh, I shall be so happy! all of you are so attentive!" but it was all so muddled and confused she knew not what to make of anything. Though, as before stated, she finally resolved to have things cleared up; and she resolved, too, that she would inquire from some other than that ever-mischievous clerk. So, who should she apply to but her own intended? But how could she do it? Ask him if he really meant to marry her? ask him if he was a millionnaire? ask him where he intended to take her on their wedding trip? Oh, how could she ask such questions? But then she remembered that her boarding-school teachers had ever told her she needed brass; that brass and a fluent tongue would make all things pass. So, accordingly, she set to work to invent some plan to meet Prescott alone—to break through all barriers, and to throw herself into his arms, with a full protest against fashionable courtships, and to entreat him to court her hereafter in close proximity, in country fashion; that they might look each other in the eyes, and be as tender as they pleased. Now, she knew of no way to meet him thus alone, unless by rising early in the morning, and catching him in the drawing-room before he had finished his morning papers. This, too, she resolved on doing; and after having been for weeks maturing her plans and her set speeches, the morning came on which she was to make the attack. Now it happened, also, that that morning Prescott was late, and that she was herself the first in the drawing-room, and was first apparently engaged with the morning papers. Not long had she been there, when in came Mrs. Lucy Tabitha Stimpkins, between whom there was no further acquaintance than that each knew who the other was. This occurred at sunrise, and Vickey was not a little astonished to see Mrs. Lucy out so early, for she knew the latter lived at least a mile off; so she bade her good morning, adding, "I thought I was the first lady up this morning!"

"Why, indeed," said Mrs. Stimpkins, "I have been up nearly four hours! I have written out an hour's lecture, and walked a mile. But that is nothing for me; though I am astonished to see you up so early. Most people lose the best part of the day in bed. Though I see by your looks that something is the matter; have the doctors ordered you to rise early? You look horrid!"

Vickey shook: Prescott might come in.

"As I remarked in my lecture last night," Mrs. Stimpkins continued, "these hot-beds of fashion destroy more constitutions, and more effeminate woman's nature, than do everything else under heaven. It makes my heart bleed. Pampered pride and foolish courtships, on which, through the fickleness of man, are wrecked more hearts than were ever joined by all the foolish cupids this side of eternity. I'm done with such stuff, and I wish every woman in the land was awake to that higher progression of human independence. How long have you been sick, Miss Edge?"

"Oh, I am not sick; I am quite well, thank you."

"Then you must be in love, for, God knows, you look a perfect fright—I don't mean your clothes, but your haggard face. Don't mind what I say; I am a plain, blunt woman, and have discarded all deception; I speak the truth, and I tell you plainly, by the look of your face you have either had the ague a month, or have been a month crying your eyes out over some foolish man's pretended love. Is it not so?"

Vickey's eyes began to cloud; her head hung down, and her hands picked about excitedly, but she also smiled the while.

"Indeed, you may smile; but, as for me, I am not the smiling kind, nor will you be, when you shall have passed through what I have. I tell you, this world is all wrong; society is turned upside down; progression is hooted at; the same old theories of a hundred years ago are more prized now by the great multitude than are the truths of our newly-discovered harmonial philosophy. It is the disobedience to Nature's laws makes you sick; it is an infringement upon the mental and physical constitution makes you scowl and yawn at the approach of day. It is ignorance that makes all the mischief. The fool puts his finger in the fire, and burns it; the fool sits in the draft, and gets a sore throat; the fool wears tight boots, and gets corns. Look at my shoes, Miss ——." Here she displayed her large feet. "Those are sensible. Ah, again you smile. Well, let us go on a bit. The foolish girl sits wearily at night to pen a love-letter; she dotes on the expected joys; she teases herself with foolish jealousy; she makes herself sick from the tediousness of marriage; but some day she wakes from her folly, to find that she has been a fool. The joys she expected never come; her jealousy is folly, too; for, when she has tried marriage, she is willing her husband may go to the dogs; but she is too foolish to get rid of him, and so she lives and dies a fool; and her folly has burdened her with a world of mental and physical pain. So, you see, when I see a face scarce above twenty, and see its pain deep and deadening, I can surmise the rest. I wish to see a Mr. Prescott; have you seen him this morning?"

"I have not; perhaps he is not forth."

Mrs. Lucy.—"Oh, yes, he is; he is always early. But no matter; I have a good deal to do to-day, and so I must be jogging on. Now, mark you, if ever you take a moment's trouble over man, you will find that you are making a fool of yourself. The dreams of congeniality are all folly. When you marry—but God forbid you ever do!—you will find that your husband is a stick, only a stick, and not worth a moment's consideration. And so I charge you, if any such foolish matter ails you, banish it at once and forever. I was once as handsome as you are, but the husbands I have had have given me much grief and anxiety, and now, behold my wrinkles and haggard looks! Think you I am fair? Could man have ever bowed and sued to win such a face? Could such a face have ever had its surface moistened with tears of tenderness for a man! And is this the wreck they have given me? You think, because I am a lecturer on woman's rights, I am a heathen; but I tell you it is not I that speaks; it is the injury and misery burning in my soul, and my mouth is their vent-hole. You'll come to it; every woman, sensitive and refined, comes to it. Only the dull sluggards of slaves of soggy fat women escape, and they only because they are too stupid to see their own misery. If you have a lover—or rather I should say a hyena—I tell you to drop him; he's false, all false. I know what I say—he's false. Only a few months since, I married a man, a real handsome man, with a beardy face, and all that—I mean no less a person than Professor Jackson, the celebrated lecturer on psychometry and woman's rights, and he, too, proved to be but a stick. He says he lost a hundred and sixteen dollars by it, and now he wants me to return the money. It makes my blood boil! He harped on that hundred and sixteen dollars till I was worn out, and so I turned him adrift. But mind you, we had no ridiculous divorce suit. We married ourselves, and, when we found we were uncongenial, we separated ourselves, and that's the nearest heaven I ever got. But the joke of the matter was, I was no sooner out of the scrape, than up jumps another suitor, this young Prescott, and spreads himself to win my heart. Fudge! He has no money, and wants to ride into fame on my talents. But I am too old for such stuff——" At this juncture Prescott came in. "Ah, Mr. Prescott, I was waiting for you." Prescott bowed, and bid them good morning ; but Mrs. Lucy kept on talking. "The messengers sent on to warn Lincoln of his danger have met him in Philadelphia, and been told by his important Excellency that he don't consider himself in any danger at all, and that he intends to come through on his own account. Now, what I have to say to you is, that last night, after I had delivered my lecture on the Germ of Psychometry, on my way home, it being late, I ran afoul of that mysterious couple for whom we are both under bonds, and this much I abstracted from them by playing eaves-dropper: That sixty men, known as Roughs, from Richmond, Virginia, have gone up to Baltimore with Russel, and that in that city they are to join with the so-called Dead Rabbits and Plug Uglies, and that they are to institute a formal riot, when Lincoln passes through that city, and during the riot Orsini is to stab Lincoln and be borne off by the crowd. The other part of the drama—the seizing of this city and the killing of the Cabinet—you know as well as I do. This information I wish to communicate to General Scott ; but, knowing the barriers against my sex, I would not wish to presume so much as to go in person to him."

Prescott.—" This is most important, indeed. Not a moment must be lost ; but, to make the matter impressive, I wish you to accompany me to Scott, and in your own manner tell it him."

Mrs. Lucy.—" That, too, is my desire ; and knowing your intimacy with him, and your energy against secession, I applied to you at this early hour."

Prescott.—" We should go at once."

Mrs. Lucy.—" On the instant. It is the shaking off of old theories that moves this nation ; and even now does the harmonial philosophy stand out like a rainbow in the heavens."

Prescott.—" I will provide an umbrella ; for the morning looks like rain."

Mrs. Lucy.—" No matter ; I have one large enough for both."

Prescott.—" These signs are ominous, Miss Edge. Let war once get afoot in this unprotected country, and we shall have great work. You look not well !"

Vickey.—" Oh, I am quite well, I thank you ; but the threats against Lincoln frighten me—that's all."

Prescott.—" Oh, is that all ? Well, don't take it seriously ; sadness unfits so fair a

face for the joys in store. Oh, those mischievous newspapers !" Thereupon Prescott smiled knowingly, and he and Mrs. Lucy went out arm in arm. Poor Vickey would have been willing to sink into nonexistence, but motionless a while she sat there, big tear-drops rolling untouched down as pure and innocent a face as ever the sun shone on.

When Jenkins got thus far, he halted, and I looked up. Said he,

" You will need to make a break here."

" How so ?" said I.

" The annals must be uniform," said he ; " keep the horse before the cart."

" What do you mean ?" I asked.

" Wait," said he, " and you shall see."

" See what ?" said I.

Now, when Jenkins saw that he had used the word " see " when he should have said " learn," he bit his lips a little, and then, without making any further answer, commenced again with his monstrous manuscript, and these words he uttered unto me, to wit:

A galloping horseman in military dress was a strange sight in Washington ; but an officer in full uniform, with a sword dangling by his side, made us all look, and watch with anxiety. Americans, whose avocations had ever been in peace, could hardly believe the evidences of their own senses. Yet these things were beginning to appear. Throughout all the South the secessionists had seized the national forts, arsenals, and post-offices. National officers everywhere were committing open perjury, and turning from their sworn allegiance to the nation, and even robbing it, for the benefit of their particular part, a State. They repudiated the doctrine of republics, that the minority shall yield to the will of the majority, and were by their own example instituting a principle of disintegration inimical even to themselves ; it was the principle that, whoever likes not a law, need not obey it ; but still they called it liberty ; like the Indian denuding himself in the city, because he wanted liberty. And so general had this fault become, the treasonable doings down South, that nearly half the nation lost sight of the fact that we had a Government, a Constitution and laws, and the actions of the conspirators were so common, and even so criminal, that the attention could only be aroused by some deed of more than an ordinary character. And one of these occasions is that of which we speak, when who should gallop through the streets of Washington but Iverson, proclaiming the fact that General Twiggs had betrayed the national army over to the cause of the South. This was like the shock of an earthquake in this country. Not that Twiggs, nor his army, was of much value, but the thought of what countryman he was. To him it was not much; for, when he is dead, his infamy is at an end; but the stain on the American name will never die. Our countryman, of high trust in office, had perjured himself—had been bought for five thousand dollars! This was the blow, and it shook the confidence of us all. Now, while this man galloped the streets, himself exulting at the infamy of Twiggs, how could we restrain our indignation, or even sit in calmness, knowing that Buchanan sat cowering, and praying to his party for their forgiveness, inasmuch as he could not, owing to his position, go to the full extremity.

Here Jenkins became so moved that he could not read for a few moments, and the writer of this remarkable history had to wait a little. Jenkins then took another glass of wine; the glass was not more than two-thirds full, and, when he had put it safely down his neck, he ejaculated the following:

Buchanan! Infamy be thy name,
And hatred everlasting to thy kindred;
Followers, thine applauders, and all men
Whoever speak thee well, take them this
    curse,
Whence goodness is, and honored country-
    men
Most justly do full merit to the brave,
That thou, the opposite, for cowardice
And love of party passively played death
On millions, take the milllions' death, and
    die
In torture of their many million pains,
And ceaseless death of mental agony;
And when thou'rt dead and gone, and yet
    remembered,
Be't only to receive another curse.

"Why," said I, "Jenkins, you were his friend; why curse you thus?"

He put up his finger, and then went on:

Aroused one morning by the clash of horses' feet, I beheld Iverson, and heard the story of his joys no sooner, than off I put for Buchanan to acquaint him therewith. I found him in bed, but with some persistence forced my way in, just as he had arisen. He was pale and excited, but I waited not, and so told my story. At first he ejaculated, "Is it possible! Twiggs!" Again I assured him, and again he replied, "Is it possible? Is Twiggs a Democrat?" I told him I knew not, and that I could see not why that should make any difference.

"All the difference in the world," said he; "all the difference in the world! Don't you know, if I do a thing against him I will only exasperate the South? Rather would I flay the other party alive, for then I would pacify these fire-eaters. Toombs told me this. Besides, is not Twiggs a free man? If the Republican party chooses to draw their throats across Twiggs' sword, is that my fault?"

Said I, and I looked him fair in the eye, "Buchanan, you are aware that the national soldiers in Fort Sumter are about to starve for lack of food, and that Scott endeavored to provision them on the sly, but that, through your connivance, the secessionists were informed of that fact; and so, to-day, the soldiers are out of food."

"Don't call it connivance," said he; "it was my extreme friendliness to both parties; besides, it was not me, but Thompson, that telegraphed them."

"Zounds!" said I, "who is Thompson, but your right-hand man? Why do you keep him in the Cabinet?"

I had scarcely uttered the words, when a messenger arrived and communicated the important intelligence that the secessionists had opened fire on the Star of the West, the steamer referred to. Said he, "Mr. President, it is true what I tell you; the South Carolinians have fired on an unarmed steamer that was carrying food to the national soldiers, and the vessel was obliged to put back." Buchanan then sat down and cried like a child; and when I asked him the cause thereof, he said, "Because such conduct will ruin the Democratic party. Had they waited till the fourth of March, they had had cause enough; but now, alas! alas! Why have they heaped this thing on my head? 'Tis thus those Commissioners wring my neck. O my God, my God! what shall I do?" and again he cried as if his heart would break. The messenger and I then turned to leave him, but he called me, saying, "Wait here, Jenkins; I want you to take my message to the House to-day." I told him I would, and I returned and sat down, but the messenger left. Seeing that Buchanan was so agitated, I took up the unfinished message, and began to read it, but was interrupted by the unceremonious entrance of Jeff. Davis, who, laughing, reinformed us of the firing on the Star of the West. Said he, "I laugh, because no longer ago than yesterday I made a speech to prove that there would not be a gun fired on either side. But I see I made a mistake, and I think 'tis laughable."

Buchanan.—" I think it is no laughing matter

Davis.—" Why, no, not the firing, but the speech I made. It will go in history, that the head and front of secession made a speech in Congress to prove all would be done in peace, while even on the day, and in the same hour thereof, the guns of the chivalrous South began the woful thunder."

Buchanan asked him if he had heard of Twiggs' conduct.

"Oh, yes," said Davis; "but that was looked for. It had been boasted at the Peace Congress that it would take place."

Buchanan then asked me to read the message to Davis, and I complied therewith, and thus it ran:

"*To the Senate and House of Representatives assembled:*

"Americans and citizens of this free land, behold! The hour of trouble and the fall of an empire is at your doors. Arouse ye, and heed the moral precepts of your fathers, or perish all. Arouse to the danger hanging over your heads, and your best reason manifest; for the peril of civil war hath sent forth his lightning tongue, and his thunder resounds on the wild ocean. Behold the tenets of the Constitution and the doctrine of State rights, for they are threatened from the great North, and about to be renovated by the imperial South. Hear me, hear me, in Taney's name hear me, for I am the last of the American Presidents. Hear me, O my countrymen, and then judge ye. Certain Commissioners appeared before me, and threatened the nation—nay, the head of the nation. Am I to have my neck wrung for fault of the Constitution? How could I sell the forts, when there is no law for it? How could I protect the forts, when there is no law for that neither? Are not forts built and manned for the purpose of protecting the nation? Was our nation built merely to protect the forts? Nay, verily. It is not in the Constitution, and is that my fault? I have cried out, Peace! and I have showed them my example; but my countrymen are becoming refractory, and are stirring each other up to deeds of blood. But they are freemen, and, although the ascendency of Lincoln is repulsive to many, it is not unconstitutional; neither do I value it a sufficient cause for a general

civil war; and these my sentiments I now reiterate for the twentieth time.

"Therefore, hear ye, O my countrymen, and fight who may. To you of the South, whom more I love than I do my Bible, I proclaim peace; and I do full assurance give, as I am a Democrat, I will not reinforce any of the Southern forts without your consent; neither will I give the soldiers, who are now in the forts, any morsel of food during my term of office, for it is not so ordained in the Constitution. And if said soldiers starve, it is their own fault, for they need not remain so long.

"To you, citizens of Charleston, I warn you not to fire on the national forts in your harbor during my term of office; but if you see proper to build batteries, and to get all things in readiness for that purpose—and though the building of said batteries is not within itself treason, yet the whole thing must be carried on at your own expense.

"To you, my countrymen of the North, who have too much agitated this question, peace be unto you; and I ordain, by this my special message, that you must not hurt the South during my term of office.

"Lastly, my countrymen, pray for me, for the ills I have to bear.

"Given under my hand and seal," etc.

When I had finished reading it—though the above is but a brief of it—Davis jumped up, and, cramming both hands down his pockets, exclaimed:

"Mr. President, that is neither fish nor flesh.* It is the message of a child spoken to babies. Ere another morning sun I shall be President of this country. You may wriggle and squirm for yet a short while, but the inevitable truth, that the Southern people shall rule this nation, will force itself upon the public mind before another month. If there be war, you will be, through all time, cursed by both North and South. Had you been firm to either, you might have saved the shedding of blood; but you have done the worst you possibly could."

Buchanan.—"Why, Davis, why is this? Have I not ever hearkened to your counsel?"

Davis.—"And therefore I curse you, because you have been my tool to carry out my purposes; but now, as I need you no more, you are in the way, and so my enemy. You have been false to your oath of office to protect the national property, and so you are false to the whole country. And

* The remarks here made by Davis are almost identical with his speech in the Senate, neither are they any plainer or more abusive.

now all men shall oppose you and curse you. The sooner you get out of this place, the better it is for you."

Buchanan looked pitifully at him, pale as death, with big tear-drops rolling down his face, but Davis continued:

"Your every action calls forth hate; your every message is so much disgust; your whole life, your person, nay, the clothes on your back, can only be remembered for all time with curses for your last four years of infamy. You are unworthy the name of man, if, indeed, you have the outward semblance; and you are too destitute of sense and cunning to be by will a devil, and yet your imbecility has made you more the tool of the infernal regions than has been any other living thing since the foundation of the world. For God's sake, leave Washington at once; go hide yourself in the mountains, and live the life of a toad; or, better still, tie a stone to your neck and swim the Potomac, that your hideous person may be lost to the sight of man forever. Lincoln will never reach Washington; a grand *coup d'état* is on the tapis, and no man knows what an infuriated mob may do. Take my advice now; go away—go anywhere; but leave at once, or the threat of the Commissioners will fall on you ere you suspect."

Buchanan grew even paler still, and his knees knocked like one about to die of fear. "Oh, Davis! Davis!" he cried, "why this unsuspected blow! Give me a moment's leave. Merciful Heaven! what have I done to merit this? Oh, pity me, sir; you know not what I have passed through," and he sobbed so much he could say no more.

Davis retorted, "I have no pity. I'm not the pitying kind, and, in the language of the ancient chivalry, I love blood more. A man's life is but so much dirt, and, when it is in the way, it must be brushed off. We are done with you, and you are in the way. Some humanity has prompted me to warn you to leave Washington, but the choice is yours. If you quit at once, surrender all the affairs of Government, you may pacify the demands of the injured South; but no less an act of yours will ever subvert the coming civil war."

Buchanan.—"What! before my term is out?"

Davis.—"This very hour."

Buchanan.—"Impossible!"

Davis.—"Talk not of impossibles. Go at once, and we are friends; stay, and we are enemies to the death."

Buchanan.—"O God! what shall I do?"

Davis.—"I must have an answer at once."

Buchanan sank down into a large arm-chair, breathing as if his lungs would burst. "I'll have to stay, though I die!" he gasped, and then Davis sneered, and curled his lip in fiendish anger. "All right," said he; "you are a Democrat, and free to choose what you will; and you have death—for we are sworn that every Northern occupant of this mansion shall die, though it be for years to come. Should war miscarry, or any deed the time defer, still this thing shall be, though we hire a thousand men to ply the assassin's knife." He turned away and strode out without saying another word.

Buchanan was speechless, and I knew not what to say, lest I might give him more pain; but I suggested that that was merely one of the sparks out of a fire-eater's mouth.

"Had you not better go and ascertain the truth of these things?" said he.

Said I, "I will." I then rose up to leave him, but he rose up too.

"Oh, Jenkins! Jenkins!" said he, and he put his arms around me, and really bawled aloud. I kind of laughed a little, and pulled him loose, saying, "Oh, don't; come, now, it will be all right, I hope," and so I released myself and left, just as I saw him fall back into his large arm-chair.

Here the writer of this invaluable history is obliged to forerun the statements, not in imitation of Shakespeare, but because a combination of annals is history. That is to say, that immediately after the above remarkable interview, Jeff. Davis was elected President of the Southern confederacy. A few men had assembled at Montgomery, and formed a plan of combination for the Southern States, and thus put a man at the head of their government; the full plan was, however, to assume the Government of the whole United States. Lincoln was to be killed in Baltimore, and the Virginia roughs were to kill Buchanan, all the Cabinet, and such men as were deemed dangerous to the South. The next day after the murders, Jeff. Davis and his cabinet were to enter Washington, and so assume the whole national affairs.

Now, with this explanation, we again refer to Jenkins' notes, beginning with these words:

But before I tell you more of what I did, let me now turn back to the young girl we left at the Jackson House, so full of tears and disappointment—I mean Vickey. Turning her face toward the front window, to hear what Iverson said, she attracted his attention. He reined in his horse and rode near, while she threw open the window. Searching then in his pockets, he inquired if she were not the same lady who formerly promenaded so much with Miss Ann Underhill, and also asking if she knew one Wadsworth. Vickey replied in the affirmative, and at once brightened up, thinking she should hear good news from poor gentle Ann.

"Tell me," said Iverson, "if you please, where is Wadsworth? I have private word for him, which I am sorry I cannot communicate to you."

Vickey told him she could not tell, and that she knew not how he could be found, unless by applying to one Mr. Jenkins, who was his sincere friend.

"Well, then, tell me where I can find Jenkins," said he.

"Most likely at the President's Mansion," said she. "But pray, sir, have you any news of Miss Underhill? Can you tell me where she is?"

"I would that I could tell you," said he.

"Oh, so much I would love to hear from her—where she is, and how she fares!"

"Perhaps you may, some time," said he.

"Then it must be soon; for if Lincoln and Buchanan, and all the officers of the Government, are to be killed to-morrow, we must pack up at once and leave Washington."

He laughed, and then inquired, "Is there anything new afoot?"

"Oh, sir, indeed there is; but the whole thing has leaked out, and two of my friends have gone down to acquaint Scott with the designs of the conspirators."

Iverson wanted to hear no more. The conspiracy was discovered; something must be done to outwit Scott, if, indeed, that were possible. Iverson laughed again to Vickey, and told her to believe the whole thing was as groundless as a woman's fear, and that not a drop of blood would be shed. "But I forget, I must go find Jenkins," he added, and then galloped off.

Poor Vickey had a world of trouble before, but now she had curiosity to battle with—a thing at all times burdensome to woman; and in her fevered excitement she got up and walked toward the veranda, where she beheld that mischievous clerk calmly smoking his cigar. He was so near by that he had evidently seen all and heard all that had been said, and had no doubt seen her intended husband walk off with that strong-minded woman. He rose up to meet her, and came forth smiling, bidding her good morning, and calling it a very fine day.

"Too well, indeed, Miss Edge, do I divine the cause of your discomfort. But bear a while; heed nothing you see. It is the course of fashionable society. Young men try their intended wives by every possible manœuvre, to see if they are unsuspecting and constant. Prescott is desperately in love with you, but he needs must put you to this severe test. It was for that purpose I was stationed here, and you may rest assured I will tell him you were as joyful and unconcerned as if you cared not whether he returned or not. You see, he fears you are after his vast fortune."

"Really!" said she.

"Of course," said he.

"Well, now," said she, "Mrs. Stimpkins says he is not worth a farthing in the world."

"Certainly. And did she not say Prescott was after her?"

"She did; and she signified she would not under any circumstances accept him."

"Just so; that was their programme. It is done in order to see if you really love the man and honor him, or if you are after money. You notice that ever since his proposal he has kept aloof?"

"Indeed, to my sorrow I have."

"Keep you aloof also. Leave it all to me."

"But how am I to know he intends marrying me? He is so distant, and I tell you, for you and the Judge are the only real friends I have here; but I am at a loss what to do. My mother urges me to fix the marriage day at once, for she is afraid it is not all right. And Mr. Prescott treats me as indifferently as he does the other ladies. Already it is in the newspapers, and every one looks at me so, my heart almost breaks!" She sobbed right heartily, and the clerk bade her compose herself. "You know," she continued, "father says we must leave Washington in a few days, because there will be war, and I don't know what all, on the day of Lincoln's arrival. Oh, dear! oh, dear!" and she renewed her sobbing.

"Miss Edge," said the clerk, "now, if you please, leave the matter in my hands. I am used to this sort of thing, and I am stern in my course. You are excited, and may make a blunder in course."

"Oh, sir, I thank you. You are so kind!" she said, and the clerk replied,

"Oh, I will write him such a letter—no, that will not do; love affairs should never be written down. I'll go talk to him. You should have been married a month ago, and I'll tell him so. Indeed,

I shall tell him he will lose you altogether if he don't look out."

"And that is true, too. But see, my aunt comes!"

In another moment the old maid came in, but Vickey dodged her, and so went out. The old maid held her teeth and plumpers in one hand, and her bonnet in the other."

"Good morning, Mr. Jackson," said she —she always called the clerk Mr. Jackson; "it's a nice morning this morning. Wasn't that my niece, Vickey?" He also said good morning, but told her he did not know who the lady was that just went out. "I wanted her to help me fix up a little, and I thought that was her. These patent teeth and plumpers, I don't know yet how to put 'em in, and I've been to Vickey's room, and she isn't in. She's a darling, good girl;" and away the old maid mosied out.

"Now, let me see," said the clerk, in soliloquy; "I am afraid the Judge will never take that old creature; and I am afraid Prescott will never marry the gay Vickey with all her diamonds. Vickey would not marry the old Judge, that's certain. Now, what's to be done? If I could put myself in Prescott's place, why I'd marry Vickey, that's more certain than anything I know of. But I would not marry her while she is so fond of Prescott. Here's work. I swear I'll marry her. I'll go tell her with all the cunning I can invent, that Prescott wouldn't give a pinch of snuff for her; that he values one of Mrs. Stimpkin's big shoes more than he does the whole Edge family. Then I shall weep for Vickey; if possible kiss away her tears. Tell her how I too once lost an intended, which will be all false, and then I will offer her my mighty heart, which in my own estimation is not bigger than a pin's head. Perchance I'll get her father's fortune. I must first publish myself as heir to some great estate, and now and henceforth wear fine new cloth"

The clerk then went out elated beyond measure, confident that no one knew his intentions. Though his soliloquy was not that of a novelist, but a real one, he had spoken, and he was heard. An ear unused to stratagem, an ear not stationed to hear, but as pure and noble as ever passively received an unholy taught, now caught the tenor of a designed love. The owner was chilled and frozen by the thought that a man for a fortune would prey on so fair and thoughtless a girl, and all horrors traced in tales of fiction came up to shock and terrify. Who was there, at so early an hour? Where was a hiding-place?

There were no closets. Parlors on one side; a hall on another; veranda on another; and an office on the fourth. And yet there was a person concealed—a person nearly starved. For several days a noise had been occasionally heard, but the plainness of the walls dispelled all conception. In earlier days, when room was less a consideration than now, the Jackson House office extended across the hall; but some ingenious landlord saw that, by extending the hall at the other end, and moving the folding doors about six feet nearer the middle side of the large parlors, an additional room could be constructed nearer the yard, which room is now called the bridal room. When the folding doors doors were moved, the opening behind had to be either boxed up and papered or built up with brick and mortar. As it was done by contract the opening was never filled in; so that, by coming from the cellar upward, a small, thin person could stand within the wall, resting the feet on the short ends of boards that extended into the hollow. But a person could not get up into the hollow space without springing the boards upward, and, when once inside, the boards would spring downwards, rendering it altogether impossible for the person to ever get out alone. But as a full description of this accidental trap was published at the time referred to, no further reference need be made to it here. Suffice it to say, in this death-like closet was the fugitive Lizzie, alias Joe Tavers! And now let us see how this thing came about. You will remember that she kept the newspaper stand for a while, and that she very unceremoniously disappeared. The cause of it was, she feared she was discovered. Persons had been to buy papers and had eyed her so carefully that she became frightened; and well for her that she did. She had become identified. She ran to the Jackson House, to hide herself. Here she lingered for some time, in order to see me especially, but, while watching on the veranda, she beheld the murderer Orsini, who ran for her, and she ran down into the back cellar. He saw her go down the cellar stairs, and quickly followed. She ran then into the front cellar for a moment, seeking a hiding-place behind the Judge's wine-barrels, but her pursuer came too quickly on, and she fled up in the corner by the kindling-wood, just as the light from the now groping detective's lamp cast a ray on the space in the wall. It was full twelve feet up, and a huge plank rested on the edge. Up the plank she scrambled with all her power, with the agility of a squirrel, to find alas! that the hole was too small. But no; she felt the boards spring upward. Quick—'twas freedom, or endless slavery! Her head and tapered shoulders passed through—the plank fell—and out went the light in the detective's hand. In a few moments more she drew herself up, through, and stood within the hollow wall. The detective got another light; carefully searched every crook and corner, and finally concluded she had escaped some other way. The servants were all on hand, and were given a full description of the fugitive, and promised, within her hearing, that whoever found her, and caught her, should have a hundred dollars. Then they left—left the cellar, left Lizzie in the darkness; left her in the hollow wall, a beautiful American slave, who now vowed to heaven she would remain, and starve, ere she would more hazard her liberty. But resolutions, like all other things, can be overcome, and so were hers. Three days and nights in total darkness, in an immoveable position, with nothing to eat, with an active mind, a mind awake to all the glories of liberty, had by slow degrees gradually overcome her determination to die, had little by little invented yet other means of gaining a life of freedom. The sounds of voices in the parlors during the day had aroused her feelings, filled her with envy, with remorse, hatred, love, and with a slow, burning fire. Little by little her tiny fingers had picked at plaster, till a hole was through the wall, whither came a ray of light. Then the curious eye sought the outward group—fashion, glory! Lace and diamonds, gold and the genial smiles of a free people in the parlors she then beheld. They, too, were Americans. Only one, a red-faced man, with bald head, who nibbled the head of a gold cane; he had a foreign twang, and he boasted that, in the coming war, his country would at least sympathize with the South. Then she picked the hole larger, but yet no more than the size of a pea, to see if any face she knew. But no; all were strangers. Oh, that she could see a friend, to look once more on one she knew was true, and then with the happy view, to die! Only one person had ever cared much to save her; that was Jenkins, and Jenkins she would see. But would he ever come? Had he ever stayed so long from those parlors before? Might he not devise some way to get her away—to get her something to eat? But day after day she lingered, waiting, watching for Jenkins or for death. So weak, so frail, so persecuted, almost a maniac. Poor girl! And yet to make and to keep slaves like thee, my own countrymen are rebelling against the great republic!

But here I must refrain; history should not have the style of romance or fiction. It will be borne in mind that after I left Buchanan, I sought for Prescott and such others as would be able to give me definite information regarding the expected attack on the city of Washington. Well, as I came down the avenue, and meeting a friend, I halted for a moment's word, when who should gallop up but Iverson, shouting, "Ha! Is your name Jenkins?" I looked round, and when he saw me he knew me, and for reasons which I care not to mention, he dreaded me. He had supposed that Jenkins was some person he did not know, but now he saw me, he was taken aback, he would not tell me or ask of me what he wanted. I saw his embarrassment as soon as I turned round, but he quickly retorted by saying, "I merely halted to say, go, you, and boast of Twiggs!" and then he wheeled his horse, and galloped off. Without boasting of myself, I must say I knew too much of human ingenuity to be deceived by such a turn; and I must also acknowledge I was not a little interested to know what the mistake was. But this I would not perhaps have ever found out, had it not been for the remarkable events that immediately followed at the Jackson House, which, though talked of so much at that time, have never been published till now. The particulars of the whole affair were as follows:

As I was passing through the parlors I heard a voice say "Stay, Jenkins!" At that instant the Judge met me and I said, "Certainly Judge, what is it?" He looked at me from head to foot, retorting, "What is what?"

Said I, "you said, 'Stay, Jenkins!'"

"Then I'm not sober."

"You certainly did!"

"I certainly am a fool."

"Then there is a ventriloquist in this house. I heard those two words once before and not an hour since."

"Tut," said the Judge, "'tis that Mrs. Stimpkins' spirit. The yowl of her voice infects the house, the furniture, the very air. Whoever sees her once, or hears her nasal twang, will ever after hear and see her when he chances to pass the same spot where she has been. These strong-minded women remind me of horrors; as, for example, a person is murdered in a forest, the strongest man will dread to visit the dire spot—on a dark night. Thought, that divine principle in man, beholds the thing in a thousand times more revolting form. So, likewise, is ever the memory troubled by the thought of these misfortunately organized creatures. Once having seen them, we see them ever after; when we are asleep, when awake; in company and in solitude. We first see her in argument; then in the lecture-room; then with a cowhide or a pistol; then married, then single; then deserted; then haggard; a living skeleton or a thing of lust; shunned by true women, hated by true men; sinking into her tomb the most wretched of anything on earth. Nay, verily, God save me from an intellectual woman!"

"No, I understand; you go for the girls of seventeen?"

"Did you see that?" the Judge asked.

"I did; who was it to?" said I.

"Why, how do I know? Am I accountable for every love-sick swain's poetry?"

Now, while we thus pleasantly talked a few minutes, pacing back and forth through the parlor, the clerk came and told the Judge that Mr. Edge wanted to speak a word with him in the office, and so the Judge went out. I followed, passing near the folding doors, intending to ring for my man-servant. Again I heard that voice, "Stay, Jenkins!" The hair of my head stood on end. I was not superstitious, but the voice was that of Lizzie, only it was so hollow and death-like. Almost palsied in my tracks, I halted. "Fear not!" I sat down. "In God's name speak not!" My eyes were flooded with tears, and the blood coursed in torrents to my fevered brain. In a moment more the clerk came in, and began to tell me a new-laid scheme for another wedding; but I heard not. I was more like one dead than alive, and yet I had confidence enough to dissemble before the clerk. Merely saying, "yes" or "no" to him, I withdrew my note-book and pretended to be writing, hereupon he cleverly withdrew. For one or two minutes I waited, but never before did my mind travel so fast.

"Oh, Jenkins!" Again I felt the immortal stroke. "Your poor fugitive, Lizzie, is hid in these walls! Keep still, or all is lost! I am not a ghost, but am hidden here, and am almost dead." Her voice was indeed weak, and I waited in great pain, the blood now almost freezing in my person. "I can't get down. Come into the cellar, and help me. I think, if you help me down, I will die in your arms, for it seems heaven has so ordained it!"

"Oh, I am glad to find you! I will be with you in one moment," said I.

"Oh, do come!" said she; "but come with caution."

I then went down into the cellar, telling the steward the Judge wanted me to examine his wine-barrels. After groping about for some time, I found the neighborhood, and, then, by drawing matches, succeeded in getting a view of the place, or at least of the hole through which she had crept, and the crevice was no larger than my two fists. Fortunately, indeed, for her, or she could never have entered the place but for wearing boy's clothes. I called to her, but got no answer. My matches went out, and I had to go get a candle. Thus provided I again sought and found the place, but my calling brought forth no answer. I became a little nervous, for the thought moved me that her relaxation from secrecy might have caused her death. After some considerable difficulty I erected the plank before mentioned, and then ascended and examined the crevice. Far along, at one end, I touched her foot; it was warm. Again I called "Lizzie! Lizzie! Joe Travers!" but no answer came, and my own blood turned cold as I pressed her little warm foot. What to do I knew not. I pressed against the two spring-boards, but could not raise them up, for she herself was in the way. I renewed the calls, but all was silent. Almost chilled to death myself with the thought that one of my poor fellow-creatures had died so suddenly in so miserable a place, I then came and reflected a moment on what to do. Perhaps she had only fainted away, and, if I betrayed her, on her coming to, she would be again sent into endless slavery. Perhaps she was dead, and I might get myself in trouble by not giving the coroner due notice. Who should I apply to? Not a servant could I trust. Not that blabbing, mischievous clerk. Prescott or Wadsworth? But where find them?

Once more I ascended the plank, and pressed her foot, calling, Lizzie! Lizzie! Joe Travers!" but all was silent. I could not get my finger up to feel her pulse. Down I came, almost dead with perplexity. But what was my horror, the Judge and the clerk were coming for wine! They exclaimed simultaneously, "What, Jenkins!" "Oh, in heaven's name," said I, for I instantly resolved to tell it all; "see you here, what horrors. That fugitive Lizzie is hid in the wall, and nearly, if not quite dead!"

"Lizzie? Why, she's been gone a week," said the Judge.

9

"No matter," said I, "she is here; come, and I will show you."

"Is it possible!" said the clerk; and I now saw in that mischievous face the glimpse of a pure and noble heart. In a moment more the clerk ran up the plank, and called her, but he, too, got no answer. Down he came, saying, "Stay you here; I will go for the old Dutch doctor in Mark's drug-store. He can raise the dead. Fear not, fear not; if she come to life, she shall never be a slave!"

Out he went, and we remained there to ponder on the sad scene. But we were startled by a death-like moan. Up I went again, calling her by name. "Water! water!" she whispered, and then moaned a little. The Judge then went into the ante-cellar, and called aloud for a saw and an axe. Soon now the cellar was full of folks. Then came the old doctor. Then we sawed off the boards; bent them, pried them, pulled them, and finally extricated the pale, and almost lifeless slave girl. We laid her on a straw mattress; the old doctor examined her, but spoke not. Once he held up his hand to us all, saying, "Sh! sh!" Then he ordered us to carry her upstairs and into a quiet room. The curious crowd then dispersed, but we bore her to a dear, sweet room and moistened her lips with water. Serene and calm she lay there, the orphan child, alike our sister in the sight of the Almighty! She was insensible! I fanned her with a newspaper, and on its page I saw, great God! a Southern Confederacy, based on the corner-stone of slavery. In another column was a letter from Wm. H. Russel, eulogizing the Southern cause. And he was an Englishman. But Lizzie saw them not; only the eye of Him who governs all she sought in her death-bed visions! Long we waited with her; long we watched her every symptom. Some little drugs the doctor gave her, and then he ordered not a word to be spoken. How long we sat in silence I know not; but we saw her face take more a living form and her breathing was like one asleep. Then we left; only the old doctor and a negro girl remained with her. On the day following, all the city papers had it published; told the whole story.

Here Jenkins bade the writer to end this chapter, for he assures me that that which follows is so deeply absorbing to the mind that historians will refer to it for a thousand years to come.

CHAPTER XVI.

BEING SO IMPORTANT THAT IT NEVER OCCURRED WHILE THE UNFORTUNATE VICKEY AND THE MISFORTUNATE WADSWORTH WERE SO UNCEREMONIOUSLY AND SO UNCONSCIOUSLY SEPARATED FROM THEIR LOVES BY THE VERY MEANS THAT MOST OF ALL THEY SUPPOSED WOULD LEAD TO THE HAPPY CONSEQUENCE, BEFORE ANY OVERT ACT OF WAR SHOULD BE COMMITTED AGAINST THE NATIONAL GOVERNMENT BY LINCOLN'S ENTRANCE INTO WASHINGTON AND HIS INAUGURATION, NOW THE ALL-ABSORBING TOPIC IN EVERYBODY'S MIND.

The writer here informed Jenkins that the above sentence was rather more parliamentary than Congressional.

"Why?" said he.

"Why," said I, "if parliamentary is derived from the French, signifying talking testament, the above is wilful and plain to be seen. Had you used the word of, instead of in, in the last line, you had made sense out of "all-absorbing," and rendered it ——" But he interrupted, "All right! all right! Begin—begin!" And thereupon he turned to the notes and read the following, to wit:

SCENE IN MR. EDGE'S PARLOR. MRS. AND MR. EDGE.

Mr. Edge.—"Think you this has not been successful?"

Mrs. Edge.—"Oh, certainly—very successful!"

Mr. Edge.—"I am as thankful as I can be. Taking the season through, I can't put it short of sixty thousand dollars; and when I count in the new contracts, I make it upward of seventy thousand."

Mrs. Edge.—"Oh, I didn't allude to money; I only felt worried a little, on account of my sister's coming and spending so much, and not seeing much of a prospect for anything favorable coming out of it."

Mr. Edge.—"Pshaw! that's nothing. Besides, who knows, may be that old rat will stick to his bargain when it comes to the pinch."

Mrs. Edge.—"Why! you call him a rat!"

Mr. Edge.—"The old Judge? Well, we'll call him a cat's paw; no matter. Still I can't complain; the old devil has button-holed many a Congressman to get jobs through for me. I can't be ungrateful to those who help me."

Mrs. Edge.—"Here comes Vickey."
[*Enter Vickey.*]

Mr. Edge.—"I was just saying, I can't be ungrateful to those who help me, and I put you in that catastrophe."

Vickey.—"Category, pa. But what for?"

Mr. Edge.—"Why, you see the Judge takes a Congressman by the button-hole, and you take him by the heart, and between you, you make him lobby the biggest kind of bill through. Nothing like baiting a trap with plenty of cheese. I've stuck them to the tune of at least sixty thousand this season."

Vickey.—"Indeed, have you made so much?"

Mr. Edge.—"I have; and if I take in the contracts, I'll put it at seventy thousand. Enough to buy you a new set of jewelry."

Vickey.—"Oh, of course, enough; but will it do it?"

Mr. Edge.—"To be sure; you shall have jewels immensurate with your services."

Vickey.—"Commensurate, pa. But I have nearly lost all fancy for fine jewels, and, in fact, for every thing else fine."

Mrs. Edge.—"Why, my daughter, how impetuous you talk! We have been discussing on our success, and your pa and I have concluded to give a grand reception, and we are going to pectorate you off in the finest jewels we can muster up."

Vickey—"Why this is news to me! But ma you mean decorate, not pectorate. When did you resolve on this?"

Mr. Edge.—"Just now. We're going to give Washington a histe in the reception business. I'm going to have the old Judge to manage the machine, and you've got to lay the ropes; and I want you to conflumux everything got up by Mrs. Davis or Miss Lane, or any other of these political whangdoodles. We must make our farewell sensation something to mellow down the whole Capital."

Vickey.—"Why, now, that will be perfectly splendid!"

Mr. Edge.—"You see, I've seen a little of this far-off gemilliken, but it's not the stuff. If Prescott wants you, he's got to hit the nail square on the head. We want none of this how-come-you-so kind of courtship. Your mother and I sit slap up 'longside when we courted, and we said the thing we thought. None of your outside leggers-in for us! We're going to show what we can do when we try; and if that suits him, all right—oh, mother?" [*Vickey hangs her head abashed.*]

Mrs. Edge.—"Oh, of course, we go in for the reception, and we will certainly make a big thing of it."

Mr. Edge.—"I know you will, especially if our Vickey takes it in hand. Come here, daughter." [*He kisses her, and bids her set about making all provision for the great event, and she leaves in the greatest apparent joy.*]

We'll follow her. We care little for Mr. Edge; he goes to his railroad contracts; he studies all the rules of economy and intrigue. Mrs. Edge, too, she is burdened about Prescott's intentions; and also about her old maiden sister. She fears her sister will make blunders in fashionable life; she sees not herself, neither does anybody else. And so we leave Mr. and Mrs. Edge a while, turning to the good girl Vickey, whose smattering inception of culture was her misfortune.

The clerk feared the Judge would come in the general parlor, and so he stationed himself near Vickey's private parlor, in order to have his love adventure unknown to the Judge. He had, therefore, no sooner been apprized of Vickey leaving her mother and father's presence, than he fell back a pace, and waited to assail her affections.

"O joy! joy!" said he, as soon as she approached him. "Never fair lady looked on so happy a man! Behold me—look what a wondrous change! Am I noble? Am I vain? fortunate? wealthy? zealous? ambitious? proud? commanding? here mark you my lordly bearing! And so many fools bow down to me. My dear sir! My very considerate sir! Shall I speak to your honor? Oh, isn't it glorious?—to be drunk with joy! to have a fortune thrust upon one; to be one day a clerk, with every guest calling and growling in one's ears, and the bitter-smiling snarl to bear in the name of hired man; and then in a day to be transformed into a very prince of fortune, and feel the soft caress and deep solicitude that the natural nobleness has so long sought for! Oh, Miss Edge, Miss Edge, be joyful! Sing me your sweetest songs; play me your tenderest music! For really I am intoxicated with the happiness of the present hour."

Vickey was a good, unsuspicious girl, and knew not what to make of so sudden a burst of joy; but she urged him to tell her, for she said, there was nothing in man's nature so winning to woman's heart as this capacity to be happy. But he feigned not to hear her for a while, rubbing his hands together, and ejaculating with great warmth:

"Oh, I shall go to Europe—to the royal courts of Britain, France, Germany, Italy! Oh, land so classic to classic ears, I come! The dreams of my earlier days have come upon me like a thunder-cloud in summer, to electrify and set on fire my ever outbursting soul of royal emotion, and I know no quiet, no rest. Come, sing! Come, play! Romp with me, play me your choicest jokes! Say, you, I have just come in possession of my grandfather's fortune. He was Earl of Standburgh, England. I have the title—the money—Four millions sterling! And I shall have a seat in the British Parliament! Say nothing, keep it quiet. But come, I have a word for you, and you know you have received many introductions through me; there are many ladies here, who have become very desirous for my company for the past few days; the very ones, too, who would not deign to treat me civilly as clerk, and now——"

Vickey.—"I thought of that, and noticed something of it."

"And now," he continued, "only to those who treated me well, will I even speak. I will be the lord I am. To those who spoke me kindly, I will be a lord."

Vickey.—"Did I not ever treat you well?"

"Oh, most kindly, Miss Edge—most kindly, indeed. And I admire you for it. I esteem you above all others for your many pleasantries. And for that reason am I come to you, for I have now to speak to you in your adversity." He stopped short and looked down a moment.

Vickey.—"Of my adversity? What do you mean? You frighten me!"

"Of your adversity, indeed. But believe me, Miss Edge, of all I have ever done, to try make you happy here or promote your best interest in good society, I have done it with as noble a heart as ever rested in the bosom of man. When you came here first, I beheld in your matchless beauty—nay, wince not, for as I shall soon be in foreign lands never to return

here, and never to see you more, it behooves me to speak you honestly—I beheld in your beauty, your grace, and naturally royal accomplishments, the charms to win from any source, no matter how exalted, the hearts of many men. In some measure I guarded you, bringing into your presence only those whom I knew to be truly worthy. One by one I have seen them take up with you, and if I found them unworthy, I drove them off. You, poor, bashful creature, fancied they deserted you."

Again he stopped a moment as if weighing the delicacy of his subject.

Vickey.—"You give me great joy. I fancied I lacked in accomplishments, for I was not blind to those apparent slights."

"Not at all; I was at the bottom of it all. And yet not all. And it is that of which I would speak; for as I am a nobleman by title, I will play the part by action. Oh, villainous, villainous man, what vain conceits and crafty measures thou would'st palm off on unthinking woman! Oh, what corruptions and base desires this world's made of! But say, you know how light and trifling I have been; well, I saw your worth and loveliness. I introduced to you some good men that they might win the prize I was unable to support in the glory she was wont. Amongst those men was Prescott. The rest you know,—only this, that he is false! He says he would not marry you if you were owner of a mountain of diamonds. He says, moreover, he was only taking his wag off you. I declare it makes my blood boil. For a mere song, ay, for a song, I would go shoot this fellow. By heavens! that he should so badly treat so fair and innocent a woman! Excuse, I weep with madness. But these things shall not be known in Washington. It is published here you are soon to marry, but fortunately this villain's name is not in the papers. But now come you a little aside; it shall not be said you were jilted. You shall marry another, and that other shall pass as having been the one."

He rested here a moment to give her time to speak, but she merely replied,

"So vast and varied have been your points of converse, I am bewildered; I know not what to reply to so fair and good a man."

"Then let me suggest, for you must ascertain that of which I speak. Go you to Prescott, and ask him if he intends to marry you. If he say no, then remember, that in that same hour of your adversity, there is in waiting for you the hand, heart, fortune, title of one who will ever love and protect you with a most sacred and holy care."

She leaned her head on his breast, and cried bitterly, saying,

"Oh, sir, I have no one to love me. For weeks and months I have suffered a world of pain, of anguish."

He patted her a little on the back, stroked her black curls, kissed her on the forehead, and pretended also to weep, and to comfort her.

But just at that moment the old doctor came along, having returned from the sick fugitive, whom he declared to be very much better, and desirous, he said, of communicating something of importance to Miss Edge. Mr. and Mrs. Edge then came in, and the clerk put off in short order, leaving Vickey to dry up her tears as best she could. In a few minutes she was off to see the fugitive, and to hear her story of so much importance. The clerk, was, however, much elated with the prospect of marrying the heiress, believing that with one more interview he could have it all fixed up. Though, in passing along the hall, whom should he meet but Judge Francis, who had another bouquet of flowers stuffed under his vest, and ready with a well-timed speech to meet the same fair one.

"Oh, clerk," said he, "is it you that capers ever at the door of Miss Edge's parlor? As I am proprietor of London Heights, I do say you have the fairest girl I ever saw."

"Indeed, I'm in no favor there; but I'll venture, with a fortune in my hand, I would make you tremble in your boots for her."

"Tut!" said the Judge; "I'm old enough to be her father; but do you know, I think you have some knowledge of the affair between us?"

"Not at all," said the clerk; "what is it?"

"*Entres nous*," said the Judge, "I'm engaged to marry her, and the happy hour is appointed here. Do you see—and I trust you will mention it to no one—the last time I saw her, which was last night, I urged her to appoint the time; but she said she was resolved to leave it all to her intended husband. I named to her Sunday next; but she said she would decide nothing herself; that she had given away her heart, and she felt as if, in so doing, she had given away the world. Thereupon she took a fit of crying, and seemed to feel so badly about it that I urged her no more. Now you see I have it all my own way, and so I appointed Thursday night. It is here written down, and you

shall carry it to her, for she is tenderly affected by it."

Having said this much, the Judge withdrew a paper, and handed it to the clerk, and these words were upon it, to wit:

"Dearest of all on earth, your intended has consented to your desire, to appoint the time for our marriage, and herewith names next Thursday evening. I have waited about the office and general parlors all day, to meet you, and to make the appointment to you in person. But your gracious majesty has not been seen, and I am obliged accordingly to send it by my excellent friend, the clerk. I would add also, that I took my usual pretended nap in the garden to-day, watching your window to get a glimpse, but I watched in vain. Some important affairs of state call me hence this night and to-morrow, and perhaps longer; but as soon as I do return, I will call. Till then I remain as usual, your ever loving   JUDGE."

"Oh, how fortunate!" exclaimed the clerk, "she will be so delighted! And to think I, the clerk—why, it is excellent! I tell you, Judge, I never heard of anything that pleased me so well."

"Come, now," said the Judge, "let us into the bell-wing, and crack a bottle of Catawba;" and so, laughing, they walked off together.

Here the writer of this invaluable history was interrupted by the entrance of our friend, a translator, who very cordially greeted Jenkins, whereupon the latter held up his finger, and motioned silence. I saw in his face that some serious matter was brewing in his soul. "Speak!" said I, "speak, Jenkins! Go on with the story."

But he smiled not, only looked at me as if words were too small for his vast emotion. At last he spoke out:

To me he had no kindness done, but yet he had me won. I mean Wadsworth. We were as like as very brothers. Both young, both tall, both brave; but he the more melancholy. For, indeed, he had more cause; his heart was bigger. Of all that between us passed, no matter. But we kindly changed canes. Mine was very crooked and large, his was like a whipstock. But now he had the larger, and I the other one. Had you, in a lone night, seen him, you had sworn by that ungainly gold-headed stick he was me. Now it had been resolved by divers persons that many men should die on the self-same day that the fatal knife of Orsini should pierce

Lincoln's heart in Baltimore. Amongst the doomed I was myself marked out. Behold you now, that near the river's edge my priceless friend had, by long research, traced the course of gentle Ann. Here, at times, in melancholy humor he came to muse and dream of her, who, he had heard had been drowned in crossing the river. Unguarded, alone, he seats himself on the bare ground, and so, amidst tears and the dim light of the waning day, traces first the ripples where all is gloom and death, then visions noble grasp from the heaven above, whither time our sorrows soon must heal. What all' he feels, what little speaks, it matters not. A stealthy tread from behind approaches more silent than the whispering leaves, and deadly. Crouched, hatless, and with a devil's grin, a very bludgeon uplift, Orsini springs, and falls the blow on poor Wadsworth's head. Falling then, and his innocent blood for me flowing—he was cast into the river! Orsini ran, nor man nor woman knew yet who he was. But all things conspire against sin, and Heaven has so ordered it that even walls, trees, and dumb earth bear evidence. Though suffice it here, on the day following all the newspapers announced that a supposed murder had been committed; that the body had been dragged into the river, and had been most probably carried away by the tide. The knowledge came to me, and I knew by the cane and hat who the victim was. So I mourned. I mourned as I had never before mourned. But more of this anon. For the present we must turn to that mortal saviour of the republic—Scott!

Swiftly now did he despatch Colonel Lamon and Fred. Seward to meet Lincoln, and bring him through to Washington in disguise. They met Lincoln in Harrisburg. They cut the telegraph, and started, passing through Philadelphia at night, and, taking a sleeping-car, rode through to Washington unknown and unsuspected. A carriage was in readiness, and conveyed Lincoln to Willard's Hotel. Here it was I first saw him; and I own that, when I looked at him, I feared for the great republic. However honest he appeared, he was, evidently, very short of being the owner of a giant intellect; though his qualities were more the type of an American, more the manner of man that Americans love, than any other that was ever made President. He was not a Kentuckian, nor an Illinoisian, nor Southern nor Northern, nor Eastern nor Western, but an American. His aspiration and love were not for a county, nor for a State but for a country. So unlike Toombs, Yancey, and Davis, who loved more a clan than the great republic; who reversed the order of national progression, by setting States and factions against each other. The one was unity, power, and glory. The other was division, weakness—death!

One was a terror to foreign powers; the other was inviting them to feast on our funeral. For herein is the philosophy—if a State can secede, so can a party; and if a party, so can an individual; and there is the end; for no law could be binding. The national Government must command, and each State be dependent; for, even as three men do build three houses conjointly, the one in the middle shall not pull his part down without the consent of all. Such a man would be a criminal, and the other two should punish him. 'Twas thus that honest Lincoln spoke, but in homelier phrase. His style was weak; character he had none. He was a blank sheet of paper whereon the nation should write its will, and he was an honest judge, to sift and do their full desires as fairly as if he were God's decree. He was an American. Pomp he had not, nor command, nor explanation. Reserved, wise with his little wisdom, and so inviting strength from all his countrymen that loved their country, and not dividing them by his self-esteem or arrogance. God never made a better man for such a season. Was he weak—'twas just enough to make the nation feel its own need of doing; was he slow—'twas just enough to fire the nation with speed; was he conscientious—'twas that silenced his enemies; 'twas that that made the nation exacting. Thus he seemed when first I saw him, and he seemed always so afterward, nor did he ever prove otherwise. To forerun this history I must add, he was a stick of circumstance; the happiest choice, the wisest placed, and as noble a type of an American as ever God made. Now he had come to Washington —come to be inaugurated President of one of the wealthiest of nations—President of five and thirty millions of people.

He had come unknown, unexpectedly to the secessionists. Scott did it. This little thread, this little nucleus was preserved by Scott. Oh, Scott, immortal Scott! While all the nation slept, thy vigilant heel stunned the viper's head. This little act all hell o'erawed, and the devils South, dismayed, in silence stood. This was the first balk the great rebellion had; but even as villains more by craft than bravery win, so now the secessionists yet another fatal plan marked out, which was, that inasmuch as Lincoln had foiled

"Orsini sprang, and let the blow on poor Wadsworth's head."

them in Baltimore, it was threatened that he should die at his inauguration. But more of this anon; suffice it here, Lincoln's arrival spread like wild-fire. People meeting at the corners stopped to tell it, and neighbors went to tell one another. Never was such another time in Washington. Private citizens, ay, the commonest man and child was drunken with excitement, was conscious of the near advent of the awful day. Not a moment's peace or rest had any man, and the highest in office were taxed with terror, were prostrate, were weeping in despair. But most who suffered was Buchanan. He had not only a dread for a great war, and fear for his own life, but his conscience, even his small conscience, had at last turned against him, and was now battering his thin soul to atoms. Like a timorous woman when the ship's on fire, he could only wail, and ask every passer-by what the prospect was. And if passers-by came not frequently, he would sally forth and halt by the way to ask any one he chanced to meet, "Are you sure where the commissioners are? Do you think they will carry out their threats? Oh, that Lincoln's time would come! Welcome 4th of March! Oh, sir, I never thought it would come to this, or I had left my party! I cannot pray. My God, who will pray for me? Is there a man in America can pray for one so neglectful as I have been? Through me, hundreds of thousands of men shall die. Countless widows and orphans—O heavens! how can I ask forgiveness? The Constitution was made to hold the nation, but I let it bend, and now, alas, it is broken! Pity me, pity me, ye gods! I am mad, I am mad! Say, you sir, if Lincoln comes, will I not be in less danger? I think so. Oh, indeed I think so! They would not wring my neck."

Thus would he go on whenever he found a person to listen to him, hoping thereby to gain a little sympathy.

Now, if you please, we shall refer back to the Jackson House, and you shall hear of such a strange adventure as no man could invent were he not to follow true history.

As the Judge and the clerk returned, I met them in the hall. "Ha, Jenkins!" said the Judge, seizing me by the arm, "I'm so glad to see you! Come up—come up!" He always said so when he took any one to his private drawing-room. It was not up, but on the same floor. His whole suite of rooms were on that floor. He had occupied the same rooms for up-ward of twenty years, save the time in each year he spent at his plantation, London Heights. The furniture of said rooms was twenty years old, much mended, and out of fashion. He never took common folks to his drawing-room—only dignitaries, save on special occasions. When he told me to "come up," I knew it was for some important purpose, though he showed little, if any, excitement. He did not pull me, but rather walked with me, one hand resting on my arm and the other on the clerk's shoulder. He is very fat and short; I am tall, and so is the clerk. We could look each other in the face over the Judge's head. The clerk winked at me to keep mum, and at the same time motioned the paper to me. As we thus marched toward the drawing-room, and while the Judge was assuring us of the quality of his newly-opened wine-barrel, we met that almost ever-present Prescott, who had told us on many occasions that he was preparing himself to write history, so that the name of Prescott might go down to future generations.

"Ha, Prescott!" said the Judge, "come up; I will unfold to you such matters as will make a greater history than you ever dreamed of."

"Things are getting warm," said Prescott.

"But I say they are getting hot," said the Judge; "and yet you don't know the hottest part of it. Come up."

We went up. This drawing-room was furnished just as it had been twenty years ago, save the wear and tear. To me the Judge shoved up an old arm-chair, saying, "Jenkins, to you the chair of honor. Sir, the greatest men of America have sat in that chair. The last who occupied it was my bosom friend and companion, Henry Clay. I shall never forget that occasion. It was soon after his defeat for President. Webster sat yonder, on that slap-jack stool. Some less important friends had seats here also. After we drank awhile, Clay leaned over the table —so—taking my hand and Webster's in his, and he said: 'My esteemed friends, this is the finale to my ambition. Long have I labored to attain the Presidency, to carry out these great principles; for I see far in the future, after I am dead and forgotten, that the clash of factions will ultimately come upon our fair land. There are, afar off, now kindling two small fires, which will some day envelop this nation in flames. I have labored a long while to pave a new road whereby we could all walk over the devouring element. But even my own State would not hear, nor can the populace of many States believe in it. Though they will some day learn, and my only prayer is, that future generations may learn by these things that reason and justice should guide them in voting for any party. Now I leave for Ashland, and to Washington return no more.' These words," continued the Judge, "were the last words he ever spake in that chair; and he spake with that tone of voice, that, hearing once, is ne'er forgotten. People ask me to repair my furniture, to trade it off and get new stuff. Ha, the gods! I'm made of better mettle. Sit you here, Mr. Prescott," and, suiting the words, he then placed us all comfortably, and we, almost jointly, thanked him for such exalted kindness.

Now, as you are aware, the left-hand side of his drawing-room is next the lattice-falls of the outer porch, where a large window opens out into the vine-covered corner. Hardly had we got stationed in the room, having only taken one turn at the wine, when we heard a sepulchral voice from some person out on the porch, and, ere we got an insight to the Judge's story, we found ourselves in a listening posture to catch the words of the outsider, whom we mistrusted as Buchanan. His speech ran as follows:

"Weak, weak device! most paltry, paltry part!

This is more foolish than the others.

Ignoble now, but noble when devised,

And so each scheme some failing finds at last,

Though seeming first so fair to reconcile.

What next? Did ever thief devise excuse

That seemed to others just? There is the rub.

Others judge us, and with their own judgment.

Were't not for this; but no—no matter now.

Life is a scene of ceaseless trials,

And we must fail, or nature death would lose.

From low estate have I worked my way up,

And many rubs and jeers and insults borne,

In the vain hope that, when I reached the top

Of my ambition, nothing more would grate

Or gnaw on my too sensitive nerves.

But now, alas! alas! they come, like flies

Round a strong-smelling carcass, and I'm hot;

By thousands stung, by millions hated, shunned.

Their varied adder-tongues are darting forth

At every turn—but some are worse than others.

At first I did indulge those common men,

To hear their speech to please them; they were sugared

Over at first, but gradually sour'd,

Till now their every word is biting acid.

That Davis turned! My God, it cannot be!

But most that biting Prescott do I feel,

O Death, where is thy sting or victory,

But to stand off and goad me with long life?

I am but rubbish, feeling most myself

The curse of my own worthlessness.   O Death—

But what of death? I'm so unfit to die,

And, not having the soul of prayer in me,

I'm cursed by earth and heaven for all I do."

We thought we knew the voice, and Prescott whispered, "Buchanan!" Though, when the speaker mentioned Prescott, we all turned to look on him, and he listened with renewed vigilance, almost breathless. After a little while the voice on the porch became inaudible, and Prescott spoke out, saying, "I never knew where the money came from, nor why it came; but I will know now," and with a rush he threw open the window. There sat, as we thought, Buchanan, pale and weeping.

"We have heard your soliloquy," said Prescott, "and I now demand an explanation."

Buchanan sprang up, shouting out,

"No—no, sir. Dare you insult me! I made no soliloquy. What do you mean?"

"Sir," said Prescott, "we have heard such words here as move me with no common feeling."

Buchanan.—"What impertinence is this? I sought out this retreat, where, in days long gone by, I did so often sit with our friend here, the Judge. Here I come to forget the cares of office—to find a moment's rest; nor can I imagine why my solitude is disturbed."

"Say you not you spoke in soliloquy here?"

"Never! I never did so foolish a thing in all my life."

Prescott.—"What say you, Judge—were those words Buchanan's?"

Judge.—"Perhaps he was asleep, and dreamt aloud?"

Buchanan.—"No, sir; I never dream such stuff. It is all malice and slander. I am an innocent, long-suffering man, and I curse the day I was ever made President. It shall be said I was the death of the Democratic party, and that's what's killing me. What do I care for you or your mother? Must all men be slandered, merely because they have some fault?' Pray, sir, cast nothing more than my sins upon me, for I have that which you never felt—a conscience."

"Well spoken," said the Judge; but what more he said none of us knew, for at that instant were heard out of doors countless voices shouting out,

"Lincoln has come! Lincoln's in Washington! He ran through in disguise!"

Buchanan said, "Thank God, I'm safe at last! I have preserved the great republic, and can now hand it down to my successor in all its integrity and glory. Heaven save me till I get out of Washington, and the devil take the country then."

When he spoke so irreverently, I remarked ironically, that all the country would thank him for his well wishes.

"What! you, too?" said he, and he glared at me as if he were indeed none too sound in mind, and in fact I almost doubted if I had not mistaken the person. "I had thought," he continued, "that at least one man would continue true to so devoted an adherent of the Constitution."

Said I, "I buy no friendship, and, if I must speak plainly, I know why you absent yourself from your Mansion. You have no longer a face for your faults, and timorously hide from those you suffered to betray you. I am as grieved to turn against you as you can be by it; but I am aware you had solemn warning from Scott, Seward, and Cass. Had you sided with them, your any blunder had been excused in consequence of their eminence and patriotism; but you chose to aid and abet those who repudiated patriotism, those who violated their oaths of office, and you knew it at the time. Ay, you not only knew it, but you made me write messages to excuse it."

He made no reply, but curled his lip, trembling from head to foot. This was the occasion on which Prescott spoke, and the following is an abstract of his famous irony, which soon became the household words for millions:

"You have preserved the Union in all its integrity and glory. You have preserved freedom, for you have given men freedom to build batteries for the destruction of Sumter and Pickens. You have given Anderson freedom to surrender or starve. You have left Lieutenant Slemmer free to behold his enemies erecting abattis and breastworks, and mounting cannon for his destruction. You have preserved the custom-houses and post-offices, by giving them over into the hands of secessionists. You have given Floyd, Thompson, Cobb, Toombs, Davis, Iverson, and even criminal Yancey, freedom to abuse the sense of the Southern people by their falsehoods, that the North was about to make a raid on slavery, and you never gave them an official contradiction. Hand it over in all its integrity and glory! Your official inaction and reticence has left the people free indeed—but free with blindness, with madness. Politicians have run away with the Government, and the people are free to cut each other's throats. Why, indeed, should you sigh for the 4th of March—why long for a full retirement? Behold you not how many millions will weep? See you not those rivers of tears from a grateful people, whose liberties you have preserved? Oh, I wonder not that half insane you wander here, to ruminate on your coming praise and glory! 'Tis too much for a common mortal."

"Sir, had you not a heart in it, you could never speak so cruelly. Your part you paint so well, I remember now no excuse. But oh, sir, such threats and abuse as I have had from the other side! God knows how earnestly I have tried to go by the Constitution!"

He sobbed violently even while he spoke, and then, with some apparent madness, started for the door, and escaped outward.

"Zounds," said the Judge, "I almost question whether that be Buchanan or Buchanan's ghost. Or are we drunk on my new wine?" Thereupon we shook ourselves to see, but we decided that we were sober. Just then a delegation arrived from Scott, demanding my immediate presence.

Thus was our affair with the Judge broken up, and we tasted but a glass of wine, nor heard his great secret. For my own part, I hurried off to Scott, who greeted me cordially, and briefly informed me that I was to go to Montgomery forthwith, as it was necessary to have some definite knowledge of the expected attack on Washington.

Here Jenkins closed this chapter, intimating that, as everybody knows about gentle Ann being in Montgomery, it is not necessary to mention anything new before it occurs.

CHAPTER XVII.

"THAT'S a long sentence," said I.

"Yes," said Jenkins; "that's just the mystery of this great book. You can find a Cicero and a Bacon on its every page, with now and then a little sea-room for Quackenbos."

"All right," said I; "let it pass." He then turned to the translator, and asked him to read to me from the notes, stating that he wanted a day off, and he then added, "We must finish the book to-morrow. Five days are enough in which to write a book. Otherwise it will be a long time ere we are done writing the Courts of Judge Francis Underhill." At that he left. The translator then took up the notes, and read as follows, to wit:

The excitement in Washington knew no bounds— —

"Stop!" I said; "substitute for 'knew' the word 'had,' and let it pass."

He smiled, and read on:

Life and property were no longer safe. Every man was suspected to be a spy, either for the national Government or for the rebels. Scott had found a man to join him in the preservation of the country—Joseph Holt, now Secretary. By their management a slight hope had begun to be entertained throughout the country that the national Government would be maintained till Lincoln's inauguration. The rebels, on the other hand, were beginning to fear that their golden opportunity would pass unimproved. At first they designed usurping the whole national Government; next they resolved upon establishing a Southern government, and of reducing the Northern States to provinces. Now, however, they had evidence that to secede and establish a Southern confederacy would be all they were able to accomplish. To do this effectually, it was necessary that Washington should be captured and destroyed. It was described by the Southern newspapers as a "nest for the Northern scum to congregate in."

Scott and Holt, on the part of the nation, had but a small army, and were obliged to do what they could unknown to Buchanan. For this purpose a vast number of private detectives were despatched to gather in all evidence of the conspirators' designs. Thus it was I was despatched to Montgomery, again in disguise, again to outwit the men who had heretofore outwitted me.

I shall never forget the look Scott gave me ere I took my departure. I told him I knew not what disguise to assume, nor how I could possibly escape with my life, were I to undertake this adventure.

"Life has nothing to do with these things," said he. "It must be done, and I know no fitter man."

The next day I arrived in Montgomery. But as the following is taken from my report before the courts of Judge Francis Underhill, they are substituted here, as being entirely satisfactory to everybody.

Judge.—" What took you to the prison ?"

Jenkins.—" An order had been issued by the rebel government offering a full pardon to all the convicts who would enlist as soldiers. It seemed remarkable that a government just established by such boasting men should, in the onset, fill the rank and file in this manner. I went, with others, to see if the convicts would volunteer. The prison had three apartments ; only one was opened. Thirty-one male prisoners were let out, and they all volunteered. I was curious to know who the convicts were in the other parts of the prison. Some one said there were some women and some political prisoners still left in. The crowd all left then, and I also left, for I wanted to see what disposal would be made of the newly-made volunteers. This was on the 24th day of February. Two days previous to this Davis had issued an edict declaring all vessels in Southern harbors foreign vessels. Duties, embargoes, and press money were demanded, and Southern customhouses were established in a day. A chain-cable was stretched across the Mississippi, so that not a vessel from the North could pass down without first halting to pay duty. Volunteers were therefore in great demand, for there were already upward of a thousand prominent points in the South needing a military force. But the place most likely to engage in battle was Charleston, and to this place a vast army was being concentrated. The convict volunteers I speak of were started off for Charleston in less than two hours after they were liberated. They were mustered into a regiment called ' Bloody Dogs.' The regiment left Montgomery at fifteen minutes past six in the evening. Nearly all the town had come to see them off. It was here I heard Russel compare the army South with what the North would be likely to raise."

Judge.—" Can you give his words ?"

Jenkins.—" Yes, sir. He pointed to the convict volunteers, saying to Davis and Stephens, ' Those are the lads for soldiers ! Always give me your devil-may-care man for a good soldier, and for a great army give me men that have known and acknowledged their superiors. It is this, gentlemen, that puts you ahead of the North. Up North there is no authority. Even little boys are taught liberty in the North, and many of them think nothing of arguing and disputing with even their own fathers and mothers ; so that, when they have become men, it is impossible for them to ever be soldiers. They would not obey their officers. On the other hand,

the nature of your Southern institutions has built up a class of superior men, who will be most cheerfully obeyed."

Judge.—" You know those were his words ?"

Jenkins.—" Exactly, only I have culled out the useless words. He also wrote a letter embodying the same, and it was published at length in a newspaper called the London *Times.* It was called a very ably written letter, with much philosophy in it."

Judge.—" Was he drunk when he spoke or wrote those sentiments ?"

Jenkins.—" I think not. Some said he was a little mad at the North, because, one Sunday, he went shooting birds in Illinois, and was fined for it ; on which occasion he spouted rather violently about his august position, when before that Court in Illinois he delivered to the magistrate these very words, to wit :

' You Western suckers, you, how dare you presume to assume to make and establish and lay down laws on morals, and religion, and virtue, and observing Sunday, as no proper and good day on which to shoot birds ? The meaning of the word England is law and gospel, and whenever we go outside of England, we mean to take a little recreation in worldly sports, and pastimes, and amusements, and hunting birds, and shooting ; and, sir, it is the height of presumption for any country in the world to presume to assume to make and establish and lay down laws for government of the Sunday conduct and pleasurable amusements of one of her Britannic Majesty's most honored subjects. Morals out here in Illinois !' These, his words before the court, which were considered by the London *Post* to be excellent argument, and such as would be likely to arouse the American people to higher notions of liberty, were here laughed at. This enraged him, and hence the sentiment before mentioned, regarding Northern degradation."

Judge.—" What were the replies of Davis and Stephens when this neutral correspondent made this comparison ?"

Jenkins.—" They said nothing, but smiled, and winked to each other on the sly. They then walked off together, but had not gone far when the despatch came announcing Lincoln's arrival in Washington. Davis threw up both hands, saying, ' My God ! can this be true ?' Stephens merely said ' Damnation !' I apprehended no more demonstration that day, and did not, therefore, follow after them. They went toward the Exchange Hotel, where they sojourned. I conversed with many people, and became almost convinced myself that the destruction of the American Government and the substitution of the slave confederacy would be accomplished in a grand, jolly spree. It did not look, from that standpoint, as if any formidable opposition could be raised against the new government. It was no wonder at all that everybody became an enthusiastic Confederate. The leaders kept the people blind on that subject—kept them intoxicated with excitements."

Judge.—" But what of the prison, Mr. Jenkins?"

Jenkins.—" I was coming to that. When the crowd dispersed, I walked leisurely along, without any design. It was then nearly dark; you could not distinguish your friend more than twenty paces. When near the prison, I sat down to rest, and to reflect on the awful affairs approaching the country. Not long had I been there, when I saw skulking along, behind the old rubbish of brick and stones, a form that seemed not much larger than a fox, and yet I was sure it was some person. It looked like a little girl with her clothes closely tucked in about her. Up, down, round, off, it was gone. What could it be? Had I rushed up at once, I had discovered all about it; but I lingered long in astonishment, and then got up and followed slowly after. Nothing of it could I discover, nor could I see a place of exit, unless the thin little creature had passed into the walls of the prison. On coming over, however, near the wall, I observed a small opening that led into a vacant and half-finished cellar, where some builder had no doubt not long since designed erecting a habitation, but had abandoned it on account of the coming war. I sat down to muse again on the varied woes of our fair land; and while I sat there, seeing, passing and repassing, the fine, noble young men who were hurrying forth with swords and muskets, preparing to battle alike noble young men of the North who esteemed them as brothers, I could not but weep for the abuse of their minds. They had been told that the North were bound to destroy slavery, and hence their fury. Even intelligent America must fall by politicians' lies. Then I remembered my friend Wadsworth; and the fair, gentle Ann. I almost wept, for I thought them both dead. And, in musing, I thought Heaven sent me sweet sounds to still my deep emotions. For, like the gurgling water in a cavern, hollow, sweet music lived as in depth beyond, and nestled in echo most sublime 'neath the prison or in the rugged walls around. I thought my melancholy had some respite found, but then again I thought I heard a voice—the voice of gentle Ann! And lo! I never wept so much, or more suspense suffered. Breathless sat I there, and gushing tears rolling down my cheeks—the voices were so low and sweet. Must I burst this silence, and madly rush to the awakening scenes of my vivid fancy? Reason most commanded, and I burned even while the tempest held. Again the sound of that voice, and then a long silence—like the fevered suns, when seldom comes the life-like air, and I perishing there, but could not move. First in minutes treasured, then an hour, then two, three. But no, not more than three; for then I heard a stone, as if falling, and steps secretly passing, gliding like a zephyr. Quick I start and downward look, in the low, rude aisle, amongst rubbish; climbing, mounts the little thin form—and out on the plain speeds from my sight. Again I was alone, but, after some hesitation, went down into the excavation, and found my way to the prison wall—a thing of brick and logs, and rudely shaped. Here I found a crack, and, hesitating some, seeing nothing in the darkness round me, I knocked against the opening. What followed, hark, and you shall learn.

"As in the dark night the timid sparrow lone sits trembling for the danger near, herself her frailness knowing, and her little spirit enduring the awful suspense of uncertainty—so, in the confederate cell, sat our sweet, our gentle Ann. Watchful, weary, with imagination wild, to start at even a cricket's sound, and the long-haired, snarling faces of confederate soldiers seeing in the shadows, hearing their hiss and scowl as they roared out to her sensitive ear, ' Abolitionist!' And thus she thought, but spoke not: 'Give me a trial! Give me into the hands of any justice! Go to Washington—nay, at my expense hire you a hundred witnesses, to prove me good or bad; pick you of those who most do hate an Abolitionist, only let them ascertain who I am, and I am content with your disposal.' Thus, at times, she had spoken to the curious crowd gazing at her, but the only reply she ever received was, ' Abolitionist!' Then came the ' Ladies' Regiment;' and, when they looked in, they said, ' Ha, jailer, let her out!" and they whetted their butcher-knives on the ground. Some of them mimicked her weeping, and others said, ' We know Perkins. He gives you a good character.' But this was irony; for Perkins, having professed to join the confederate army, was above suspicion. He had accused her, on the evening when they were both taken prisoners. He told her, on that occasion, that if she would marry him, he would not only liberate her, but return with her to Washington; but that, if she denied him, she should stand accused. This was before they were put into prison, he having obtained the privilege to speak to her privately. But she answered him, saying, 'Accuse me!' 'Then will you suffer, and perhaps die!' said he; 'but I shall volunteer, and so be liberated. You will be hanged for an Abolitionist, if no one protects you.' 'I know that One will save me!' she said, and she pointed upward. 'Indeed!' he said; 'now for your purity and faith I curse you!' and he turned to the crowd, saying, 'Seize her; she is an Abolitionist!' She was caught in the act of running away with a slave. I was with her because I loved her fair face, but the foulness of her heart has turned me against her. Take her, and cast her in prison.' The crowd then bore her to prison, but Perkins started for Washington as fast as he could, to get a written consent from the Judge to marry her. The crowd of people then brought the slave-girl Kate before her, and they asked her if this young lady was an Abolitionist, and if she had tried to run away in her company. The slave girl answered, 'Yes; she tried to run away with me, but we were caught.' They took them then to prison, and gentle Ann was put in a lone cell. But Perkins was no more 'around. Though, as in all human affairs, God hath so much His Spirit implanted, the trumpet of Divine power had sounded to the bottom of that slave-girl's soul. In a short time she, herself a prisoner and a slave, was taken to the cotton-fields, but only to fly again for freedom, and to repay the godlike attempt for her own liberty by gentle Ann. For such is nature. Coming now by stealthy means to the prison where gentle Ann was bound, she espied through the crevices in the cell—and so, at night, unobserved, the nearest part approached. Tapping lightly, lest at the hour of night the sparrow die for terrible fear, she announced her name and mission. 'I am Kate, the slave girl. I have again run off, but I have come for you. Tell me—for you are wise—what I shall do to liberate you?'

Almost like death the words had fallen, and the fair lady most her very life suspected for its transit into heaven. For this was the first kind voice for many, many long weeks. Leaning then close against the wall where was found the crevice, she timorously asked if it were indeed her own dear Kate. Of this she was assured, and then an interchange of thought went on, till Kate proposed to go to Washington for assistance. For this journey she had no money, and many difficulties were before her. She would be obliged to walk all the way, and to live by begging her bread from the slaves by the route of her passage. She might be captured as a runaway slave, or even as a spy. But she resolved upon the task, even though gentle Ann reluctantly gave consent that she should risk so much. The two girls then kneeled down, the one in prison and the other out, and they prayed for that guidance and protection which Divine Wisdom alone can give.

Thus left our Kate for Washington—to see and to tell the Judge all about his niece; but ere she left, she provided a little slave-girl to visit the prison nightly, to see if anything could be done for the comfort of gentle Ann. This little creature, ere the hour of locking up slaves, would steal across the vacant lots, down by the way mentioned before, and, with three gentle knocks on the door, call to the crevice the fair prisoner, and at times putting through the crack in the wall some choice food which had no doubt been stolen on her account. Thus from day to day watched and waited the acused Abolitionist, without proof or trial—for how could it be otherwise? Military always supersedes civil courts on political prisoners. But one course was left whereby she could hope for succor—could Kate reach Washington, find the Judge, and he get here before war actually commenced.

Many days the slave had been gone, and the prisoner was almost despairing, her only comfort being in speaking to the child that brought her something at night. As for the day, it brought only the hiss and scowl of 'Abolitionist!' or the wretched yearning of the 'Ladies' Regiment' to butcher her. She knew her weakness, and hence her fear. Those ladies had threatened over and over again to come on the sly and kill every Abolitionist in the prison. Ann watched for them at every moment, day and night. Her visitor gave three knocks—loud, soft, loud. Who gave not these knocks, must be an enemy, a would-be murderer."

Judge.—"How, then, came you, Mr. Jenkins, to an understanding with her?"

Jenkins.—"As I said before, I knocked on the wall, but I knocked on the wrong place, and I knocked four or five times instead of three."

Judge.—" Well, what was the result ? "

Jenkins.—" There was no result. I then knocked louder than before, and a good deal more. Some one seemed to sigh within. ' Will you tell me who is in this cell ?' I asked. All was silent again. In another moment I knocked louder and harder. Again I heard the sigh—a deep, heavy sigh—and again I spoke, saying, ' Tell me, poor prisoner, who you are, and what fate awaits you. I am no enemy, but a friend. While sitting just above here, on the embankment, I thought I heard the voice of a long-lost and dear one, and I now knock on the prison-wall to satisfy this burning thought, to learn at least who it is that has another such sweet voice.' Long I waited for an answer—so long, indeed, I almost feared I had been speaking to the barren walls. Just then I heard a slight knock from within, with the question, ' Who is here ?' I was certain I knew the voice, but I still used discretion, saying, ' One from Washington, a friend to Judge Francis Underhill, of Loudon Heights. I was a schoolmate of his niece. She is lost, or perhaps dead ; but I thought I heard her voice in this prison.' ' Oh, is it possible !' said she. ' To know of this ! To know of this. What could have severed that divine chain whereby I was bound, and now reverts me back to it ? Verily a pledge to Heaven, though by children, is watched over and cared for by God Himself !' Said I, ' It seems, indeed, as if I had been sent by Providence ; for, must I tell you, though my heart breaks, our friend Wadsworth is no more !' ' Oh, say not so !' ' I would it were possible to say otherwise.' This was all that was said for some time ; I heard her crying, and I was myself much moved, for I felt I was venturing on the most hallowed scene ever known to mortal. After a while we so far conversed as to make some amends for the long-lost love between us ; and I assured her I would rescue her at once from prison, and conduct her safely back to Washington. With these assurances from me, and with a thousand tender thanks from her, we parted, I to the jailer, she to solitary——

" To be brief, I found the jailer, and opened my business with him at once. His name was Randolf, and he looked so carelessly gotten up, I involuntarily compared him, in my mind's eye, to a tow-string half twisted. He was a little intoxicated, and his conversation was a volume of oaths, with a few chance words in it. The word ' Abolitionist ' was, from his mouth, an island in an ocean of oaths, whereon he strove to manifest the bitterest hate that could be invented. To this man —if, indeed, such profanity could emanate from a man—I spoke in this wise : ' The prisoner is not an Abolitionist. I have known her from infancy up ; she is mistress of Loudon Heights. There are belonging to her uncle's estate two hundred slaves. She has been falsely accused for some other purpose ; she is indeed an estimable Southern lady.' Over and over did I repeat this to him, and he ever answered me with the word ' Abolitionist !' ever joining thereto the usual oaths. But I continued, denying with all my ability that she was now, or ever had been in any way, an Abolitionist. At last he ventured to suppose my statement true, wanted to know what I would do with the prisoner, and how, above all things, she could be gotten out of confinement. Said I, ' If I were jailer, and your daughter confined under a false accusation in my jail, I would liberate her, trial or no trial.' ' I have no daughter,' said he, swearing worse than before. And then he twitted me on the fact that I had not treated to the whiskey. Hereupon I took the thought that my liberality might turn to advantage, and accordingly I took him into an inn near by, and gave him a good many drinks. Now, after we had taken much whiskey, and discussed the troubles North and South pretty freely, and had each of us told many humorous stories, he told me that we had better return to the prison ; ' for,' he added, ' if I get much drunker, a fellow might, on the way to the prison, drop fifty dollars into this pocket, and take this key out of that pocket, and so liberate a prisoner, and I would never know how it was done.' We got up, then, and walked toward the prison, and fifty dollars went into his pocket, and immediately thereafter the key came into my hand. By some means we got separated then, and I reached the prison a little before him. Strange to say, the mistress of Loudon Heights was there waiting for me, and she came and leaned on my shoulder, and cried piteously. I said many kind things to her, and she repaid me only with weeping. Soon after this we lifted up our feet, and stood on something, and it carried us very fast. It was something that was leaving Montgomery, and might have been a freight car. But the funniest of it was, the next morning the Montgomery papers noticed the fact that a prisoner endeavored to escape last night, but was captured by the citizens, and hung. I wrote those notices, to put people off the track ; I had done such things before."

Judge,— "Now, Mr. Jenkins, you have done well; but hear me at the other end, and then take note."

The Judge then adjusted his old silver spectacles, and told us this story, to wit:

"Scott kept me on the run. It was Judge this and Judge that on everything. My opinion, my knowledge, my advice must forerun everything that was to be done for the preservation of the great republic. In fact, it reminds me of Mrs. Howard at the ball, being teased to dance, 'Here, Sal,' says she, 'hold my baby, till I trot that fellow through with the yellow breeches.' I had to save the nation, and needs must trot these fellows through with yellow breeches, only I had no baby, but something else, as you all know, of much more value. Now, as I am a Judge, and as I hope to live to see established a high protective tariff, to make every village in America into a Sheffield and a Birmingham, but the weight of these great affairs had somewhat told on my too sensitive nerves; and it seems to me now, when I remember it, with the rebels in arms five thousand strong organized to come from Harper's Ferry on the day of Lincoln's expected inauguration, while on that same expected eve I should venture that great change in life which I can never mention but in awe; for, though I am not old, I am not young, and it seems that the approaching affairs were more terrible than ever before one man withstood. For you see, one might upset the other. If Washington be taken, and sacked and burned, as they do things in war, what kind of jubilee can we have that night? I tell you—for you are not unacquainted with my expected adventures—with these weighty affairs to bear, what more could harrow the soul, to hide them in oblivion? Now drooping, but still in haste, the man absorbed in 'proaching war, and betimes forgetful only for the fairest of the fair, I had a niece, and, though she was the purest and sweetest that e'er the sun shone on, I was forgetful of her. Alack, my frenzied brain! Torment me not, O ye harrowing swords of justice, till this I do confess! Forged missives, not like her hand at all, were given me, to teach me she was in Canada; and I believed them —for I was mad. I read them not. Oh, fool, fool—cruel fool! My niece? Had I, in mine own expected joys, forgotten the mistress of Loudon Heights—scarcely took a thought where she was? But blind deviltry will out. 'Say! say!' some one spoke to me as I hurried up the Avenue, and, turning, there I beheld that villain Perkins. 'Say,' said he, 'your niece is in prison down south for Abolitionism.' I was thunderstruck, but silent; but he went on—oh, the cold villain! 'The letters you have received are all forged. She is locked up. I can free her, but I will not, unless you give your consent for me to marry her. Neither will I tell where she is. She sent me to you for your consent, and told me to say that she prayed in God's name she might lie in prison as long as she lives, if you refuse us.' This was the sort of stuff he put on me; and he spoke so fairly, looking me so tenderly in the eye—for a snake may own a passive eye—and I was confounded with the burden of my own thoughts. Reluctantly to this villain's plea I did consent, and we drew writings on it, whereby I portioned out for them quite a fortune. Soon then he left, and I mused with much unhappiness on what I had done. I was almost distracted; for, though one be slow to passion, it is more terrible. Days passed, but time was out of joint. I hoped Heaven might avert the dread fate to my dear niece. One day a young lady, with a negro servant in attendance, accosted me on the street, saying, 'Excuse my forwardness, sir, but is not your name Judge Francis Underhill?' I told her 'yes,' and she immediately replied, 'Then, sir, I am sorry to say your niece is in Montgomery jail for Abolitionism. She sent me to see you, and to tell you to come to her assistance, as she is in great distress.' I was more astounded than ever, and much pained with the uncertainty of what I heard. To know if these things be true, for a moment I prayed to Heaven—and you know it comes tough for me to pray; but the lady, seeing my embarrassment, continued: 'Make no doubt of my words, but haste you in silence to her assistance, or she must die. I am the slave girl Kate, with whom she ran off. She told me to come right to you, and make a clean breast of it, and you would not only understand, but protect me. I have no servant; this one I brought as a disguise; she is also a runaway.' I feared some trick was being played on me; I am naturally suspicious about some things, and I replied, 'My niece is too fair and too gentle to be spoken of in this manner. Whoever plays a joke on her, knows not the sacredness of a pure heart; and as for myself, in God's name, trifle not with me about such a woman!' 'Sir,' said she, 'as I am living, I tell the truth. Behold you this fine apparel; think you it is becoming the slave girl Kate? Now see, what a stock is here!' Saying this, she so spread her dress that I saw she had on rags underneath. 'Fine ladies, who sport a servant, generally wear better underclothes. As for me, this servant stole a dress, and so made me a lady.' She was so pert, and did so prettily turn her head, I could not but remember the wife of my late lamented friend, General Andrew Jackson. His wife, when a girl, was a little spoiled pet, and her father opposed her marriage with Jackson. One day, after he had admonished her for some time, she said, 'Now, father, do you know I think you are a mighty smart man, and a good man, but you are nothing 'longside of Andy Jackson. Bet you anything he'll be great, some day.' I always, as the old General used to tell me of her, tried to picture out what kind of a girl she was; and as I am Judge of Loudon Heights, I had made her in my mind's eye just like this snub-nosed beauty. I could hardly believe she was an American slave, nor could I doubt, in case of war here, but the British Government would take positive side with freedom. I had seen the slave-girl Kate, but in common duds she was common; now she was in a nice frock, and looked a chirp little queen.

"Having satisfied myself with her story, I ordered her and the servant to the Jackson House, and immediately started for Montgomery. How I met you on the way, you know quite well. My poor niece, weary, sick, and disconsolate—she that was so mirthful and sweetly wild, to come and fall in my arms like one at the brink of death! Do you know what she said? 'Oh, uncle, forgive me! I was so little acquainted with the world!' And then, after a while, you know, she said, 'Girls of romance are girls of inexperience.' Everything she said made me think she was dying. But most I was moved when she said, 'Take me back to Loudon Heights.' This had been her home, where I had watched over her as if she were a tender flower. Poor, poor, dependent girl! Who would not love dependent woman? But her grief was too quiet. Something within was sapping her lifechords. Perhaps she loved Wadsworth: for I know, when I told her he was dead, she turned pale, and her eyes, though filled with tears, had no motion. 'How far is it to Washington?' she said, after a pause; and I knew she was weary for the small conception I had of her fall, bursting heart. Nor did she know mine. Nor do any of you know. I have given Perkins a bond, and he may come here to demand her, to torment her to death. We have her safe in Washington, but this

thing works hard on my too sensitive nerves; for I shall not refuse him but by this heavy forfeit."

Here the Judge exhibited the duplicate bond, and then sat down; but as the reader of this history will be curious to know the particulars of my own affair with gentle Ann. I will here state that, ere we had reached Washington, an understanding was come to, whereby, on the eve of the inauguration, we were to be made man and wife. So, therefore, when we had, in the court of Judge Francis Underhill, each one given in his evidence, I had nothing more to do than to inform the Judge it was all right. This being the end of the sitting, we were all soon engaged in congratulating one another on the apparently happy issue, and then, as soon as the Judge had given the following charge to the jury, we dispersed:

"Gentlemen of the Jury: You have now the case before you. We may never meet again, and I charge you to govern yourselves accordingly. To-morrow is Inauguration Day; I cannot be with you. Since the days of Thomas Jefferson I have been the hey-day man on these great occasions. You know the peril of that office. I must hold Lincoln's hat while he is sworn in. It is to be on the portico of the Capitol. Buchanan and Lincoln will be taken in a carriage from Willard's Hotel. The members of our court will be the honorary guard. Two thousand seceders are armed with knives and pistols, to mix with the vast assemblage, and then to fall on us and murder us. Scott has an army so portioned out he can sweep the streets at a given signal. Five thousand seceders are expected from Harper's Ferry. They are already crying out for vengence, because Lincoln was not killed in Baltimore. This is their desperate day. Though it is to be inauguration, they are resolved to make it disorganization day. If we fail, the nation perishes. If Lincoln is inaugurated, all will be well; and, to glorify that great event, I will myself, on the evening thereafter, so astonish this court by what I shall do, that all the country cannot contain your joy and merriment. But look you well to it; to-morrow we shall have some rich adventure."

Now it so happened that none of us knew for certain that the Judge was contemplating marriage on the next evening; and, being gentlemen, we dared not be inquisitive as to exactness, though we were much interested in querying one with another, to ascertain his meaning. For my own part, I took his arm (not he mine, as many of the newspapers had it),

and we walked down from the Temple together, on the way to the Jackson House.
Not far had we gone, when whom should
we meet but Professor Jackson, who stood
shyly at the roadside for lack of good
clothes, and called to me as we drew near,
saying,

"How are you, Mr. Jenkins, and Judge
Underhill?"

We halted a moment, and he advanced
to shake hands, holding his knees close
together, for he had a rent in his trowsers
that made us look another way.

"Excuse me," said he, "I understand
you have been to Montgomery, and I
wanted to make some inquiries about
matters and things down South."

"Certainly," said I. "Proceed."

Said he, "Do you think there will be a
conflict? Do you believe the South are
really mad enough to carry this thing to
a trial of arms?"

"I do," said I. "The South is all in
one fever of delusion. Their political
leaders have persuaded them that the
whole North—twenty millions of people
—are determined on the extinction of
slavery. Those leaders told the truth of
about half a dozen leading Abolitionists,
but their hearers credited it for twenty
millions. No longer can reason approach
them. A conflict is certain."

"I'm not so sure of that," retorted the
Professor. "I have here a project which
I think would end the matter without one
drop of blood being shed." Saying this,
he displayed to our vision a circular, reading. "Professor Jackson, the celebrated
lecturer and psychologist, being on a
travelling tour throughout the South, will
deliver a course of lectures at ———"—
(here was a blank to be filled in)—"whereat he hopes to convince the people that
their entire ignorance of psychological
laws is the chief and only cause of all the
trouble between North and South. He
will also show them the beauties of the
Harmonial Philosophy, and appeal to that
higher quality of the human soul, the congeniality of the sexes, and point out the
only true road to happiness. The Professor has also a project for establishing a
great national library, in Washington, and
a general publishing house, where men of
limited means may obtain aid from the
Government to have their knowledge set
before the world, thereby eradicating the
ignorance and low passions of which we,
as well as the people of all other countries, are afflicted. These famous lectures
are divided into a series of four. Ticket
to one lecture, ten cents, or four tickets
for a quarter."

"Cheap enough," said the Judge.

"Dirt cheap," said I.

"The question is," rejoined the Professor, "will it pay? Is the South prepared for exalted lectures of this sort?
You have been down South; now, what
is your opinion?"

"Oh, excellent!" said I, nicking the
Judge's foot.

"Just the thing!" said the Judge, and
he nicked my foot a little; "a very fortune to a man of courage."

"Oh, I have the courage!" said Jackson, "and I believe I have some ability;
but, do you know, I am rather short to-
day. I sold my newspaper stand, but it
took every cent of it to get these circulars
printed. If it would not be asking too
much, I would like to get a loan of two
dollars of each of you. I would go at
once to Montgomery, and begin my course.
As soon as I shall have paid all necessary
expenses, I will remit it to you."

"The best thing in the world!" we
both replied, and thereupon opened our
purses and gave the poor fellow two dollars each. Just then that woman, who
was always on the street, came up—I
mean the veritable Mrs. Lucy Tabiatha
Stimpkins—and she saw us give the
money.

"Guess you are satisfied now!" she
sneeringly said to the Professor. "You
thought you could do better for yourself
than I could do for you; but it is nowhere
laid down in the Harmonial Philosophy,
that a husband shall have aught but what
is the wife's. I don't begrudge you those
four dollars."

"Mrs. Stimpkins," said he, "I have
done you no harm. Why is it I can't
walk the streets of Washington but I
meet you, and that you must tantalize me
at every turn? You caused me to lose
one hundred and sixteen dollars, and that
ought to satisfy you."

"I caused you! Must you ever harp
on that hundred and sixteen dollars?
Now, if ever you mention that again, I
will have you searched, and I will take
every cent out of your pockets."

He looked a little scared, and he sheep-
ishly said, "Eh?"

"What circular is that?" said she, and
she took it and read it. "I could make
money out of that, but it is not in your
breeches to do it."

"Eh?" said he.

The Judge and I turned to go away,
but pretended to be inattentive, lingering
a little.

"Professor Jackson," said she, turning
square before him, "give me half the

profits, and I'll join you in that. And more, too—I'll repay you every cent of that hundred and sixteen dollars."

"Eh?" said he; "you nearly starved me once."

"There, now throw that up," said she. "But I don't care; you may eat as many meals a day as you like, and I'll do the same."

We heard no more, for we had gone too far; though, when we got a hundred paces off, we turned to look back, and we saw them starting off together, as a living illustration of an independent woman, a dependent man, the Harmonial Philosophy, and the congeniality of a foolish theory.

That night the Judge and I sat alone, with our sparkling Catawba before us. He told me then all about his engagement with Vickey—to be married on the following evening; but owing, he said, to the great disparity of their ages, they had kept it almost a total secret. But, as you are aware, I heard little of what he was saying to me, for on that same evening I was myself to be married, and, at present, my intended was very ill. In fact, I hardly know if it be possible to pass a more tormenting time; that ever-incessant thought, marriage, rising in a thousand aspects, crowding off every other thought as chaff before a hurricane. The Judge, however, talked well and talked incessantly, till about midnight, when some one tapped at our door. I opened it, and there stood Kate, crying. I urged her to tell the cause, and, after she quieted a little she said,

"I wish you would come to my sister. She is indeed very ill."

I looked at my watch, saying,

"Fear not now, poor child; the fatal hour is past."

We then got up and followed her to the room. Lizzie was propped up a little, and the old doctor and the clerk, and a Mrs. Owens, were standing near. She then tossed up one hand, signifying for me to approach. I did so, and she spoke and said:

"I have much to thank you for. I shall not live to enumerate them. I shall die before the morning sun is here. Some things I must tell you." We then gave her a little water, and she asked to sit up in bed.

Said I, "You must not talk of dying. You are only discouraged."

"The life-blood is blocking up in my veins and arteries. In some parts I am already numb. Treasure what I say, but do not interrupt me. Madame Ponchard killed my master. This jewel I stole from her. She is young Wadsworth's step-mother! This jewel was given me by my master; he said it was once my father's. Take them, and keep them as long as you live."

I took them, and read, on the one she said she stole from Madame Ponchard, "S. N. Wadsworth, P. Miss. 67;" but some of it had undoubtedly been erased. I knew also that the other was a part of the same jewel found in my hallway. Said I to the Judge, "This must have been young Wadsworth's father. And this Madame Ponchard is indeed the Italian stepmother."

The Judge said, "She was suspected of poisoning the National Hotel; but in this lenient country she got off scot free, because she was a woman."

Again Lizzie went on, saying to me:

"Do you remember the place you chased me to, in the Smithsonian grounds?"

"I do," said I.

"The exact spot?"

"Ay, the very spot."

"Well, go there to-morrow; I will be dead then. Even where I stood, beneath a flat stone the size of your hand, you will find something which will astound you beyond measure. But oh, sir, as I shall be dead when you have found it, speak, nay, think gently, and blame not this bursting heart." She then let go my hand, but looked quietly at me a moment, adding, "Heaven bless so good a man!" Tears started to her eyes, and she asked, "May I kiss your hand, before I die?" Next, she called, "Kate, my sister, come here!" But Kate was crying bitterly, and the doctor told her to come. Now, when she had come to her side, Lizzie said, "Take comfort, Kate; these men will endeavor to have you never a slave again. Oh, that I could know, before I die, that you shall be free! I pray for war, for, in the conflict, justice will arise. If the national Government is too weak, Great Britain and France will join in crushing out these cruel slave-owners. Oh, glorious England! The friend of the bond, I know that thy dogs of war will be let loose on our vile oppressors!"

After resting a moment, in much pain, she again went on: "Remember, Kate, modesty and virtue are woman's holiest gifts. Remember it. Of Miss Underhill, who has taken so much on herself for you, I know nothing. I have never seen her. They tell me she is too ill to come to my room. This is the hardest blow of all. O Heaven, can I never see so sweet and dear a face!" Here she sobbed out violently, whereupon some one suggested that Miss Underhill was not so ill but she might be brought in. "No, no," said Lizzie, "I see her now; my soul comes and goes at the beckoning, and I see in the distance as if near by. Come, now, I am nearly done. How numb my temples——"

This was the last she ever spoke; for, even while sitting there and speaking, she smiled, and died.

On the following morning I repaired, with a sad heart, to the place in the Smithsonian grounds she had designated.

Beneath a stone no larger than my two hands I found this most touching note, safely sealed in a bottle:

"To whom God showeth this:—I am a fugitive slave, and must soon die. Here, on this spot, even where lies this small stone, I met a true friend. He did all for me that man could. He planned the destruction of a band of conspirators by intent to blow up the house where they assembled. I was employed by him to bear a part; but, O my God, I proved him false! I could not do the just but horrid deed, and so I cut the fuse. The conspirators all escaped, and I behold that they are about to destroy the nation. I have prayed for forgiveness, but I am dying with despair. And my true friend, to whom I was false, is so noble I cannot even mention my own perfidy. Heaven knows I wish I were dead.

"LIZZIE."

Poor girl, her woman's heart overleaped justice. And she died in remorse, without my knowing her awful agony. Pass on, poor soul; sad tears shall be our lessons to teach us the good heart of a true woman.

I saved the letter, but was never able to unravel the mystery of her having buried it in the place referred to, unless it was indeed because she visited the place in remembrance of having there found a friend. Scarcely had I got back to the Jackson House, when I met Russel, the owner of both fugitives. He was weeping because of Lizzie's death: he had been up to view her corpse, and he seemed much broken down. Judge Francis offered to buy Kate, but Russel said he no longer cared for Kate, now that Lizzie was dead. Thereupon he gave us, for her, a bill of freedom, and he departed for the South.

CHAPTER XVIII.

BEING OF THINGS WHICH DID NOT OCCUR TILL LONG AFTERWARDS, AND WHEREIN, OWING TO THE NATURE OF THE STUFF, IF INDEED IT CAN BE CALLED STUFF, THE ORIGINATOR OF THESE NEVER-BEFORE-HEARD-OF NOTES WAS TEMPTED, FOR A HEADING TO THIS PART OF THIS GREAT HISTORY, TO SUBSTITUTE THESE MOST REMARKABLE WORDS, TO WIT, THERE IS SOMETHING IN THIS, AND IT HAS SADNESS AND HUMOR MORE THAN I EVER SAW IN SO SMALL COMPASS.

AFTER the translator read me the above heading, I ordered him to wait a moment, till I ascertained, if I could as a learned man, who Jenkins meant, but the translator replied, "Cervantes and Shakespeare."

"Well, then," said I, "it is at fault."

"Why so?" said he.

"Because, if Sir Walter be not in, Scotch critics will condemn it."

He laughed a little and was about to proceed, when who should come in but Jenkins himself. Said he,

"I am too excited about this great work, to enjoy myself at any other thing till this volume is done."

We then told him to come in, and sit down, and he did so, whereupon I ordered my men-servants to bring up from the wine vaults another basket of sparkling Catawba, the which, when it had come, we drank freely of; for it is of that peculiar quality which sobers a man when he hath too much natural fire in him, and it makes everything look drunk but the man who drinks it. When we had thus quenched our thirst, Jenkins, having examined how far we were, began the mystery of his notes to unfold.

Whether Lincoln was to be inaugurated or to die, those were the questions in Washington. Knots of conspirators clustered near every corner; every boot concealed a bowie knife, every vest a pistol. Cautiously and so silently were the tongues at work, and such oaths as those seceders swore against this great republic, against the law of freedom, and so gently were they tapped on the shoulder by foreign emissaries, that breathless stood the whole of one of the most powerful nations on the globe. It stood in fear and trembling, seeming to have no head; but the consciousness of right inspired the people to believe a way for safety and glory would be pointed out by the finger of Almighty God. Only an answer to the prayer of so many millions could shield the coming President from common slaughter. As terrible as for Daniel to enter the lions' den, was it for Lincoln to mount the steps of the Capitol; and more, for the lions were God's subjects, but the seceders had repudiated Him, and sung His name in blasphemy. They had defied Him. They had covenanted with one another that, ere the 4th of March, Davis should be installed in Washington. They had armies everywhere, and were armed; but the national Government had been sold by James Buchanan, and now stood there penniless and unprotected. Yet, no, not unprotected. Scott was there, and Holt—instruments and nuclei, whereto the Almighty would build up the most powerful armies ever assembled. But they took not His name in vain, nor party nor schism sought —only the rights of man by God's will. And there they stood, invincible Scott and honest Holt. They saw that morning sun, that 4th of March, and felt a higher approval than by the tap of a foreign emissary, or by the puff of an adventurous correspondent. But their position, and ours, and all men's who loved the great republic then, was mocked at by nearly all European governments. What! ten millions of conspirators, and Scott and Holt to dare oppose them! Only a thousand men to guard Washington, against the threatened approach of thirty thousand rebels! Surely Heaven is in this, or Southern chivalry is a coward—why didn't they come, and not blow so? There was the Capital, defenceless—why not take it? Who held them back? Verily, not Scott and Holt with a thousand men. Why, when Cæsar fell, he had a guard, an army, a million strong. Were those conspirators bolder than these? Lincoln goes unguarded; yet not so, his shield is from Heaven. Conscience pricks those conspirators, and they have not heart to butcher a lamb. And why all their bluster and fury? Washington is like a city on fire, but it burns out. The people rush to and fro; they cluster here and there; whisper, pass on, and point to the Capitol. Men do clench their jaws, and do feel for their concealed weapons, all expectant, to hear the bloody deed is done. Scott and Holt calmly wait the rising sun, that never-to-be-forgotten brilliant sun, their troops at times galloping up and down the streets, and the bugle in far-off places denoting solemn tidings for the coming hour. Both Scott and Holt were calm. So unlike Buchanan. He had that day thrice his wrong clothes put on. His trowsers the wrong side before, and his vest inside out. To the window he often ran, shouting to himself. "O God, if only this day hold out! But if it miscarry, and Lincoln is killed, good Heavens what shall I do?" Again he would return, and sit down, burying his face in his hands, saying, "God knows, I have stuck to my party, if they do tear me in pieces. I've stuck to the Constitution, too. Oh, those Commissioners." Then he would sob awhile, and then again look out of the window, really wearing himself out with bodily fear and a stinging conscience. He had ordered, for several days past, that no one should be admitted into his presence, except such as came by invitation. From affairs of state he had entirely withdrawn, existing merely as rotten debris of the government he had destroyed, and his own rottenness was a stench to his nostrils, his conscience a coal of fire to a perjured soul. Thus moaned and groaned, thus pined, feared, and trembled the great politician that was, this shadow that is. But, shadow though he be, he must, for form's sake, hand over the sceptre to the great rail-splitter. Thus it was I came to him; thus I paid him my last visit—to lead him to the Capitol to get rid of him. And thus, too, I found him, weeping and wailing, "Oh, Jenkins, is it you, dear? They told me never more you'd cross my threshold, dear. But, safe at last, you are come, and the morning's come, and Lincoln too is here. Heaven knows, who says I suffer, flatters me with little knowledge of my pain. I'm wild! I'm mad! Tear me off here an arm! These shrivelled legs crush up! Such pain would be comfort. I'll knock this breast in pieces! Oh, I know what it is to suffer! This day a man told another, I was the death of the Democratic party. I pray Heaven it is not so; but if it is so, may God never give me another happy day." I observed his vest was on wrong side out, and urged him to change it, for it was near time to start. He then changed it, but he put on his gown, and I urged him again that he should wear his coat. Said I, "You know, Cæsar was killed in a gown. I pray you, wear your coat." He then pulled it off and put on his coat. Said I, "Your valet has not looked after your toilet this morning." "Why so?" said he. "Why," said I, "your shoes are not polished, nor are they laced." "I suspect my valet," said he, "of having left the Democratic party." He then tried to stoop down to fasten his shoes himself, but he could not bend so far. Said I, "These things would try any constitution." Said he, "What! is that in the Constitution too?"

I saw that he was not of sound mind, and so I then tied his shoes with my own hands, for which he looked very grateful. I told him I considered it an honor to do such service to so true a Democrat. This touched him a little, and he burst into tears, saying he had not had any one speak so kindly to him for many long months. I knew that in a few short hours the country would be rid of him officially, and I cared not to harass his troubled mind with further censure; but I did not, as many of the newspapers had it, caress him for any purpose whatever. I spoke only as I consider any one ought to speak to another in distress, and it was merely my speaking to him in this manner that made him whimper and cling so close to me. Neither was it at the Mansion, but in the carriage, before we reached Willard's, that he said to me, "Now Jenkins, stand by me. For God's sake, stand by me at the Capitol! you are so large and powerful, and I am such a feeble, nervous person. If there be a row at the Capitol, for God's sake pick me up, and run away with me!" I told him I would, and he replied that I was the only one, he believed, in America, who would turn a hand to save his life. He said, also, that he hoped the country would be more grateful to Lincoln than it was to him; but he still thought the time would come when his administration would be revered. We were near Willard's ere he ceased talking, and then he turned quite round in the carriage, and looked back toward the Mansion, crying, "Can these things be, and all the horrors of a four years' strife at end? Fare thee well, thou hole of hell! Farewell, farewell—a long farewell!"

In a few minutes we were in Willard's, in the presence of that man of destiny, Lincoln, who received us with a hearty laugh; but as I had many things to arrange I left them together, in company of a few friends, and hurried off to find the Judge and members of our court, who were to have entire charge of the etiquette of the inauguration. On arriving at the Jackson House, I found no one I was acquainted with, and, so, to reflect a moment, I sat down on the outer porch. In an instant my attention was directed to persons ensconced behind the lattice shades. No mistaking it,—it was protestations of love on the part of some man, and the tender doubts of some young girl. As often as he praised her beauty and loveliness, she would sigh, and reject it as proof that his attachment was from an immature season. Of course I was too much of a gentleman to look in, and I must not listen to other folks making love; but my curiosity so far mastered me, that I raised up till my ear stood opposite the opening in the window, and then I discovered it to be the clerk and Vickey. "Then why," she gently remonstrated, "did you so deceive me, in saying you were heir to such great possessions?"

"Because I loved you," said he. "I saw that you had a good heart, and I determined to win you. If I took a bad course, it was my head, and not my heart at fault."

"But that was deception," said she.

"Certainly; we all deceive one another in these times. The young man pretends to a fortune; the young lady pretends to education and accomplishments, the young lady with half a dozen years at a female college kept by an overgrown egotist, gets a smattering of French, German, music, and gets also a diploma for having a finished education, albeit she has not read Henriade nor Tasso but in the translations. Penelope, Homer and Quintilian are fools to her; but her parents would palm her off on a gentleman as an accomplished lady. Is this not deception?"

Now, when he began to talk in this style, she cried bitterly, for she felt that she merited the rebuke. But he continued: "If this deception is just, why shall not a man make believe he has a fortune? Anything for getting the best of the bargain. The lady wants a husband more elevated than herself, and he wants a wife wealthier and more accomplished. Anything to win on. A few dashing tunes on the piano, or a loud set speech at a lady's feet. Miss Edge, I am done with this sort of stuff. I am only a clerk at a thousand dollars a year. You have, or will have, a large fortune. If I were to marry a really accomplished lady, I could not support her; if you were to marry a proper gentleman, you would be in constant pain by the society he would take you in. Think you, would you enjoy your husband having with another woman a little chit-chat in French on Fénélon and

Lamartine? Bethink you, they make quotations from Virgil, and ask your opinion! Would you hold up your boarding-school diploma? Now, enough of this; I would not see you weep. I am myself no scholar; but my place here has shown me those who were; and I admonish you, as I am a true friend to a good-hearted and innocent girl, never think of using your accomplishments, or your father's money, to catch a husband your much superior. I have tried to make you comfortable at the Jackson House, and I have seen, too, how frequently you have been mortified."

For some time I heard no more, and I knew not but they had both left; and so, thinking I was losing much of the time in which I ought to be getting the court together, I raised up, and looked into the parlor. There she sat, and there he sat, and both looking another way. Every little while she passed her handkerchief upward. Whether to wait and see the result, or to go about my own business—those were the questions. Pretty soon, however, I saw him rise and stand before her, but she turned her face away. Said he, "Have I abused you?"

No," she answered, faintly.

"Shall I thus abruptly leave you, weeping?"

"As you like."

"Bid me what you will, and I will do it."

She gave no answer.

"To-night," he resumed, "you give a reception, and you are to marry!"

"What!" she whispered, looking up.

"Not to Prescott. I know all about it. To the Judge."

"Ha!"

"Ha! I know, 'tis not all a joke. You call it a joke, and so do others, but the Judge told me all about it."

"Oh, sir, do not trifle thus."

"I am not trifling. I tell you, though, I know all about it; and I tell you, too, it is the most foolish thing you ever undertook. He is old enough to be your grandfather. I always thought it was nonsense, till this morning, when the Judge gave me a card."

"A card!"

"Ay, a wedding card; very pretty indeed of you to invent these covers!"

Here she straightened herself upright—and she is very tall and thin; but ere her astonishment had gone further, he gave her the card. For a moment she perused it, and then she cried out, "Oh, why am I thus abused?" and she cried piteously. He asked her what was wrong about it,

and she, sobbing, told him there was no truth in it whatever. The clerk assured her it was true. She denied it; said the Judge was engaged to her aunt. The clerk told her it was in the papers. She said it had been in the papers about Prescott and herself. Thus they discussed the matter, explaining and complaining, till he, seeing she was partly recovered from her blues, bade her remember that he must go to the office.

"Now," said he, "you see they have been using your name as if you were a stick. Your father and mother half believe you are engaged to Prescott; but Prescott knows nothing of it, nor did he ever make pretensions of love for you. The Judge, on the other hand, professes to love you, and you have returned it. You accepted all his presents, and you have boasted he was to give you a large present on your wedding day. So, you see, I know that it is all true."

"It is not true!" she retorted sharply.

"What! not true that you will marry the Judge?"

"Most certainly not. I never thought of such a thing."

"Just so; and yet in your innocence you favored his every advance."

"Oh is it possible! Has it come to this?"

"Well, you have gone so far now you will need stick to it."

"I won't!"

"But you must!"

"I will not! Those old silver spectacles!"

At that they both laughed right heartily, but she hushed quickly, for the thought was so unpleasant to her taste.

"Why," said the clerk, "I am really very sorry for you. The guests, to-night, will all say you have treated the Judge badly, to have encouraged him and then thus denied him. There is only one way in which you can avoid shame and an ill name by this. You will be hooted at by every one in Washington. You can elope with me, and save your honor. Nay, start not; I mean what I say. You are a dear, good girl, and about my own equal in the general getting up, and I will make you an excellent and appreciative husband." She began to pull and twist her handkerchief at a furious rate, and then he went to her, and took her hands in his, adding, "Don't mind what I say, but judge of my former conduct if I will not be kind and dutiful. I may have much mischief in me, but I assure you my heart is as warm as anybody's, and pretty much the same size. I know you need some one to love you, to speak kindly and fondly to you. Pray you, let me be that one."

I could not hear what she said, but she leaned over on his shoulder, and cried and clung fast to him and I was afraid they might turn round and see me looking ; so I dodged down a little, but I heard him kiss her. Soon after that he took a hasty leave, having conducted her to the door, and bade her meet him again at the same place, in two hours hence. From this I concluded they had promised an elopement, but I had no evidence when it was to take place. Not being disposed to waste more time in looking after them, I immediately started in search of the Judge, whom I found in the garden, on his lounge, sound asleep. Beside him lay a paper and pencil. He had evidently been writing, but fallen asleep at it. On the paper was the following :

"To the tall, fair girl with the shining black hair ;
To the dear, sweet girl with the hazel blue eye :
Come, haste to the garden ; come, haste to the wedding ;
A vacuum in store and love running o'er, Is waiting for you."

Evidently his mind was turned, or he had been reading Tennyson, and I ejaculated, "Ha, Poet Laureate !" Thereupon he awoke, and I admonished him it was time to go to the Capitol.

"Indeed !" said he, moving his spectacles and brushing up his thin hair, "I slept so little last night. Let me see, what is the programme? Ah, I remember. I am hey-dey man. Come on."

So, accordingly, we went, he having told me that Scott had despatched Prescott to Charleston to report on the threatened rebellion. I did not like to tell the Judge what Vickey said, nor did I consider it my business. If she would not have him, he would find it out in due season ; and if she and the clerk eloped, that was their matter. Now it was so arranged between us, for we feared a collision of arms on the part of the rebels with the law abiding people, that we made no exertion to have ladies attend the inauguration, choosing to let them come or stay away, as best they might decide for themselves. We had, however, decided to have thirty-four carriages representing thirty-four States, and each one carrying a beautiful lady, to precede the President's carriage, and to alight and assemble on or near the portico of the Capitol before Buchanan and Lincoln made

their appearance. To obtain the aforesaid young ladies, we had already spent a week, and, now that the time was up, four States were unrepresented— South Carolina, Georgia, Mississippi and Arkansas. Not but those States had plenty of pretty representatives in Washington, but there were few who would accept of wearing the red, white and blue, unless, indeed, we chose homely, scrawny-necked ones. One lady, a beautiful girl from Georgia, by the name of Emerson, we finally coaxed into the programme ; but after she was dressed, and about to start, her mother, then stopping at the Washington Hotel, caught her on the steps, and tore the dress in pieces. The girl's father, however, replaced it with another, whereupon the enraged mother rushed into the house for a pistol, vowing she would rather see her daughter die. The father, though, took care of the girl, and after a while the old woman got over it. The one we got to represent Arkansas was a lean, crooked-shanked old maid, with a coffee-colored face, and such a mouth as made you think of the Mississippi river. For Mississippi State we were obliged to take a little hunch-backed widow, deaf as a door nail, and she grinned incessantly. But for South Carolina there was the rub. We had raced in vain all over Washington ; we had offered five presents—everything we could think of—but only one lady from that State would agree to go. She was a lump of a woman, so fat that her eyes were almost hid from sight, and her dark, grizzly-looking eyebrows grew clear across her forehead, which forehead was about half an inch high and broad as your two hands. A dirty, sweaty-looking mustache she had, and a fatty-like wrinkle hanging down from the corners of her low fat nose ; a double chin a hand-breadth deep, and such a sickening scowl I never saw on woman. Now, on the morning of the inauguration, we received from said beauty the following letter, directed to the Judge and the members of the court of etiquette :

"Miss Sowsy begs to decline her engagement. She thinks it is incompatible with her dignity to longer wear the red, white and blue.

"LILLIE SOWSY."

What was to be done? We had not a moment to lose, this despatch having been received just as we came out of the garden. As every lady was to carry a flag with the name of her State on it, the one from South Carolina would be the most observed of all. After a little consultation, we concluded again to go and see Miss Sowsy, and urge her to it. We did so; but what was our surprise at seeing her with a Palmetto flag, and hearing her say, "Anything but this is Abolition."

On our way back we fell in with Mr. Palmer, of Charleston, and told him about it.

He said his daughter would go, provided we could get a dress ready in time.

It was then a quarter past eleven o'clock, and I urged the Judge to go at once and see the young lady, while I would proceed to have in readiness not only our own carriage, but those bearing the young ladies. Thereupon we separated, each to his own duty; but I neglected to state that we had agreed that, if there was any difficulty about getting the carriages, we would take the ladies in a triumphal car. On my way back to the Jackson House I observed many of the people wore pins and plates engraved palmetto. It was almost impossible to get through the crowd, nearly all of whom were men, the gentle sex thinking, no doubt, a collision would occur at any moment. When I arrived at the Jackson House, I had only fifteen minutes left in which to get the Judge's horses and carriage in readiness and drive to Willard's. We were, accordingly, in much haste, and frequently being annoyed by having to seek for remnants of harness and bridles. The carriage had not been used for many weeks, nor had it been oiled, and it now squeaked and squealed and barked most horridly, and some boys had been cutting stone-slings out of the carriage cover, so it looked like a riddle. Finally, however, we got in readiness; but the Judge had not come. Here was a predicament. He was so fat and so old, and he walked so slow, he might not be here for an hour. I then came out and looked down the avenue. It was one solid mass of human beings. Their meaning and purpose was doubtful, and much to be dreaded. Again and again I pulled out my watch, and I was in intense agony because the Judge came not. Only a few minutes, and I must be at Willard's. I thought perhaps the Judge would go in Palmer's carriage. I could wait no longer. Mounting now the carriage, with only my driver and footman for companions, I started on at a rapid rate. On nearing Willard's, I decided to dispense with so many carriages for the ladies of state, but to pile them into the triumphal car in advance, and in rear of the two Presidents. In a little while the state ladies made their appearance, all showing more or less nervousness on account of the importance of the occasion. In vain I looked for a representative for South Carolina. In vain I looked for the Judge. Whispers and jeers, but low and derisive, went up from the vast assemblage, that South Carolina was not there. Over and over I surveyed the ladies, but all to no purpose. Many of them were the fairest that man e'er laid eyes on. Miss Hendricks, of Missouri,—Lord, what a sweet and noble face! Her ringlets were like pure gold, and her large, blue eyes had in them an angel's purity and love. Her form, so noble and full matured, now adorned and adorning the red, white and blue. Miss Haslett, of Michigan, a brunette grace, with two and thirty jet black curls a yard in length, hiding half the rotund chest now swelling like a bird affrighted, as downward some she meekly held her blushing face, at times her heaven-lit eyes glancing o'er the crowd around. Miss North, of Massachusetts, whose jolly, fun-loving eye all things turned to jokes and merriment; whose smile a dimpled chin and cheek did envy but to strive, as proudly, with a coquettish air, she now and then tossed up the red, white and blue. Miss Hawthorne, of Pennsylvania, an unconscious beauty, not light, not dark, but rosy and life-like, innocent of all things around and child-like, whose heart no room had left for independent thought, and made her thus the most perfect counterpart of man; made her like a fair flower, innocent of her own beauty and sweetness.

And so it was of all the others,—all so many beauties, only from the seceded States we had to take them as we could get them. And those were pretty fair, only the lean one from Arkansas, and the little widow of Mississippi. The lady for Georgia would do, but her mother had scratched her face some. For South Carolina, though, there was no one present. May-be the Judge would go direct to the Capitol with her. It was the only chance, the only hope. The time had come, we must start. I now sent a messenger in to announce to Buchanan and Lincoln our readiness to receive them and conduct them to the Capitol. They were soon at the door, and, although it was supposed they had no guard provided, yet such was not the case. Scott had for the occasion two hundred picked men in citizen's dress, well armed with private arms, who were to proceed before, behind, and, in fact, all round the carriage, to the Capitol and back again. They were provided with white ribbons concealed, which, in case of a row, were to be uncovered, and the men were to sail into everybody and everything that displayed not the color. In a few minutes now the Presidents came down and entered their carriage, Lincoln getting in first, and Buchanan taking a seat at his left hand. Many of us smiled at this little innovation, but were startled by a slight hurrah from some one near the carriage. I looked and there beheld Orsini ! It was as if a viper had sprung out of the earth. In an instant did civilians crowd him back, and those civilians were the picked guard. Again and again did I inwardly thank Winfield Scott ; for what man else could have invented so great protection with so few men ? As yet, however, the public knew it not. We had all heard it said, over and over, that Lincoln should never reach the Capitol alive. But words cannot tell the flight of thought, nor can it show the checkered fear and emotion at such a time. We saw Orsini, and we expected thousands of men on the instant to run into bloody riot. Upward, and where a fair view was had, stood Madame Ponchard, waving her handkerchief. In the vast assemblage did two voices cheer ; but ere the sound had passed around, the triumphal car was under way. No more now we feared till near the Capitol. But here, too, had Scott provided for any tumult. Thus we moved along, and thus to the portico, passing by the way full sixty thousand men. On the grounds, above and below, all round the Capitol, were assembled such a concourse of people as were never before in Washington. More than half of them had come to see the portico washed with Lincoln's blood. More than half of them were armed with bowie knives and pistols, with their hands resting on the concealed pockets. Yet amidst this vast assemblage had thousands and thousands of fair women come, to see and to be seen, trembling for their lives the while. Close around the Presidents, and everywhere that danger most appeared, were Scott's two hundred unknown vigilants. No one, save Scott, knew their number or authority, but they were each a man among ten thousand, powerful and resolute, men who felt that they held the great republic on their shoulders and no one apart his own life valued. And yet, withal, another side this adventure had, and full of danger. Davis and Toombs had more than the two hundred, and better armed, but untutored for the deed designed. For this is God's will, a criminal never weighs the chance of failure but with a mortal instrument. They thought in half-concerted riot to kill the President. A woman, Madame Ponchard, and her consort, Orsini, two common assassins of foreign birth, for hire, were to do this great deed of state ; and the planners and perpetrators, Toombs and Davis, afar off, to escape uncensured and free, to ultimately fly to the Capitol as the chosen rulers of the nation. So now, as our unornamental pageantry neared the portico, that same mysterious woman, and that same oft-accused and oft-released villain, Orsini, must needs rush to the front, waving the stars and stripes, both bent on the treacherous deed. Again that unthought-of two hundred press them backward, as calmly all as if it were a time of prayer. Now, merg forth the four and thirty fair ladies, virgin emblems of the independent States of the great republic, bearing each her flag triumphant—but no—South Carolina is not there ! Over and over we read the flags, and over again we bleed at the thought that a star is gone ! Fifty thousand eyes look for that flag—ay, a hundred thousand eyes ! A murmur begins to arise—such a half-suppressed murmur as was never before since the foundation of the world. It was the midnight hour of human liberty. Come at once, or freedom is dead ! Come, and long lives the great republic ! But oh, the terrible hour, the second that measured more than the lapse of centuries. Coming here are now the Presidents, and a moving discontent makes manifest the fell omen. Tears of disappointment stream from countless patriot eyes, while the opposite, the foes of freedom, now smile and curl their lips in goading triumph. But lo ! What sound is that, and greetings ! They move —make way, and on the portico fall back ! —the flag is coming ! South Carolina ! South Carolina ! Now look the eager eyes, to see what lady this temerity has. Then, tall, and fair, and smiling, comes the maid of seventeen—our sweet Victoria ! Few, so very few did know her, and they thought she was a South Carolinian. She was clothed in red, white, and blue, and so prettily bore her little flag that only in her praise sang all the crowd ; yet sang, but breathless held their voices while they surveyed her queenly beauty, and praised her from their very souls as an angel, a symbol come at the final hour to marshal peace and liberty. Now here it was, and at this trying moment, Douglas spoke. He had been obliged to take the Judge's place, to act as hey-dey man ; and close to my side had all the while remained to be prompted in the part he must fulfil. The Judge had been to Mr. Palmer's, but the daughter would not go. She snubbed him ; called him an old fool; told him South Carolina was out of the Union, and so sent him off. But inasmuch as he had the appointment to furnish the ladies and manage the etiquette, he had no other way left but to call on Victoria, and persuade her to relieve him in this great hour of distress. Accordingly, having, as he passed Mrs. Hamil's silk store, provided himself with a quantity of red, white, and blue silk, he hastened to the Jackson House, where he found Vickey crying severely about the clerk, and the Cupid exasperations between them. She told the Judge she was crying because nobody would take her to the inauguration. Hereupon the Judge exhibited the silk, and expostulated much on her appearance, and so struck a bargain at once, whereby she was to go as a South Carolinian. She was in just such desperate state of mind as makes a woman do anything; and so, between madness and love of adventure, at once assumed the part. Dashing on the colors in more profusion than any other lady would be clothed, she and the Judge and Mr. Edge hastened on foot to the Capitol, and, as before stated, just arrived at what was likely to have been a fatal moment to the Government. Thus coming on the portico, where she expected to be merely as any other of the number, was a signal for greetings she little thought of. South Carolina was really the only State of much interest, and her representative was the very queen of queens. The eyes of the many thousands were all turned on her, and she in turn looked on them all as innocently happy as if she were in a Philadelphia boarding-school. I knew her, and so did some of my friends, and we were all afraid she would speak, and so betray the whole thing; but this showed only how little we knew of the capacity of a green country girl under excitement. Scarcely had she ventured forth, her father and the Judge standing near, and many of the people exultant over her coming, while many, even enemies to the country, were captivated with her beauty, when Douglas stepped forth—to hold Lincoln's hat, and to make some preliminaries preparatory to the oath of office.

"Again are the representatives," said he, "of our several States assembled, as tokens of love for the principles which have made you (to Lincoln) the people's choice. To you (to the ladies), the fair representatives of these United States, I assume the responsibility of bestowing a nation's thanks, and a nation's love. To you (to Vickey), the gentle representative of South Carolina, may the incoming Administration be the inspiration to peace and quietude to your State as yourself over us all holds command, by purity and nobleness of purpose."

Here he halted a moment, and she thought he wanted her to reply, and so she said,

"Our hopes are manifested by myself being here. I would not speak in public; but I love my State, and more, I love my country. This, I do presume, for American ladies, will ever be their highest joy; while noble hearts their lords maintain toward the great republic, to ever decorate their persons with the red, white, and blue." She then smiled, and waved her little flag, striving hard to hide her deep emotion. But as firmly did the people control theirs, for her voice, by its sweetness and purity, had rendered her sentiments most sublime, and to be treasured as one of the most comprehensive and feminine speeches on record. It was a sentiment to make man manly, and this is a rare sentiment in woman's public speeches.

Baker, of Oregon, then came forward, and introduced Lincoln, and thus ran Lincoln's inaugural, to wit:

"This is an occasion of painful joy and solicitude. We all do know the questions upon us. We are all countrymen of one country. But we can never separate. A man and wife may separate and go away, but we must remain, even if separated. If we make ourselves aliens to each other, still we gain nothing. Friends can make laws better than aliens can treaties. Suppose we go to war; after many of us have fallen, the question would still arise. I am called by the people, according to the laws of the country. Only will I execute those laws; and the Constitution shall be preserved. The property of the Government must be protected. In your hands, my countrymen, is the issue. The Government will not assail any State, or the laws of any State. If you assail the Government, that is your matter. You take no rightful oath to destroy our country, but I take one simply to protect it. We are friends. Passion may have strained the cords of our affection, but it must not break our ties of national brotherhood. The chords of memory, from every battle field, from every patriot grave, to every living heart in this land will sing in chorus for this Union when touched by the angels of our purer nature."

Hereupon Taney came forward, bearing the Holy Bible and Constitution, and directed Lincoln to lay his right hand on them, and to raise the left to Heaven, and they repeated these words,

"I, Abraham Lincoln, do solemnly swear before thee, Almighty God, that I will protect the Constitution, defend the national property, and execute the national laws for the term of four years from this date. Help me, God, and make me righteous to do Thy will."

Such was the end. The vast concourse of people were in confusion, every one turning his own way, every one expressing opinions on the occasion. But the secret guard still kept on duty, still kept beside Lincoln and Buchanan. The former firm and much overcome by the trying scene, the latter pale as death, and trembling, ejaculating to himself continually, "O dear! O my God! O Heaven! My God! My God! Oh, dear! Oh, dear!" At times he would look toward the people as if lost to comprehend what was going on, and then again he would look downward, in the most mortified melancholy that ever man exhibited. Twice or thrice Lincoln spoke to him, but got no answer, only heard the low wailings and sighs of the almost dying politician, who, like a miscreant, now fully beheld the crime of his imbecility. He realized, at last, that of all the five-and-thirty millions of people, not a single one would ever more mention his name but in shame and hatred. He realized that he was not a man ; that he had been discovered to be merely a bogus piece of worthless flesh and bones, with none of the spirit or soul of a genuine mortal. Thus, in agony and shame, did we lift his trembling form into the carriage, to take the last ride he would ever take at Government expense. Downward, though, he held his head ; he knew no more where we were taking him, nor of what was passing, than does the delirious maniac, when all things seem as devils for his torture. He had had his day, and this was his last. North and South both said, " 'Tis good, this is his last." Farewell, Buchanan ; thou wert a whale in the ocean, and we took thee for dry land ; but thou didst dive and leave us at the mercy of the waves. Good for thee that we laugh at our folly and some the fall assume, or we had

harpooned thee ! Away, imbecile **President** !

The writer of this great work here halted a moment, for Jenkins became too excited to continue ; but when I told him Buchanan was gone now, he said, " No, not yet ! One other view of him you shall yet have, and then he is done."

In a little while Jenkins reverted to the history as follows, to wit :

On our way back we changed the programme, all of us accompanying Lincoln to the Mansion, when we alighted, and rather unceremoniously made ourselves quite welcome. Lincoln shook hands with the girls, and was quite humorous ; paying no more attention to Scott, Holt, or Seward, than to any one else. Now, although the day was so fair, it was chilly, and Lincoln called a colored chap and ordered him to tell the cook to fire up, or we would all come down in the kitchen. The cook was a Southern man, and, having heard much said about Lincoln's greenness, and having been used to the words " fire up," which means, down South, to pass round the whiskey, what does he do, but, filling a two-bushel basket with choice bottles, comes right before the new President, saying, " Here you are, here's fire for the whole Mansion. We've run the machine pretty fast down in the kitchen to-day, and, considering as when a fellow gets anything new he must 'wet it,' we saved this lot for your Excellency." Down he threw the basket, and we wondered what Lincoln would say ; but he was never at a loss for a word, and he said, " Oh, excuse me sir, it is the outside we would warm. For four years, terrible as it may seem, this house shall indulge in water." He did not laugh, nor was he moved more than had he been looking at the moon. But the joke is told to this day in the kitchen of the White House. The next chapter will be after this ; but as this is the last chapter before the last except one, the last word of this one shall be last.

CHAPTER XIX.

NINETEENTH SITTING, WHEREIN IS GIVEN THE EVIDENCE, WHICH HAS BEEN HERETOFORE WITHHELD FROM CERTAIN PERSONS NOT NAMED, IN CONSEQUENCE OF THE FEARFUL RUMORS PERVADING WASHINGTON, AND THE SHAPING OF THE END OF THE FIRST PART OF THIS REMARKABLE HISTORY.

WITHOUT waiting for an explanation, the writer of these annals informed his informer that the above heading was sufficiently confused to be mistaken for an emanation from that great philosopher who compared Paris to a wheel full of fishes.

"Why," said Jenkins, "that's not confused at all. Fishes swallow one another, and they turn round and get swallowed in turn; and so if they turn round they are like a wheel."

"But why," said I, "does it apply more to Paris than to any other city? For the people in all civilized countries live on one another."

"The philosopher did not say so," said he; but ere I had time to speak further on this weighty matter, he took up his notes, and thus began, to wit:—

[*Scene.—Court of Etiquette and Moral Philosophy. Judge Francis Underhill of Loudon Heights, in the chair; various members of the court assembled; Jenkins in the witness' box; papers in hand, reading despatches. Judge has his spectacles thrown up on his forehead—his old silver spectacles. Time, late in the afternoon.*]

Jenkins.—First despatch from Charleston: "The soldiers in Fort Sumter are starving. The rebels will not let in provisions. The soldiers petition the rebels not to fire, for in three days they—the rebels—can take the fort without resistance. Soldiers seventy-five strong, men all told. Rebels twenty thousand strong, all told. Rebels won't wait; want a spree, to spill blood. Ladies in Charleston circulate a petition for signature, to be presented to Lincoln, praying for no coercion, and warning him that their chivalric twenty thousand will assuredly attack the seventy-five men if he dare to raise his finger in menace, or to bring them food."

Second despatch, from Montgomery: "Beauregard is considered by the South as the greatest of American generals.

Bragg ranks next. They talk of eating up the whole nation."

Third despatch: "Lord Dundreary, the notorious correspondent, has just completed a letter to the English people, wherein he says the Southern people all wish they had an English Prince or Princess to rule over them. It is unknown whether he wrote it from malice or ignorance."

Fourth despatch, from the South, West, and North: "The Mississippi river is being fortified by the rebels for upward of one thousand miles in length. Rebel armies are assembling on the frontiers of all the slave States. All goods being sent South must prepay a duty. Custom-houses for that purpose are established in Philadelphia, New York, Cincinnati, Chicago, and St. Louis. A secession paper is published in Philadelphia called the *Palmetto Flag.* The so-called Democratic papers all over the country embrace the cause of secession. Mayor Wood, of New York, urges the city to secede."

Fifth despatch: "All the frontiers of Virginia, even in sight of the city of Washington, are being crowded with rapidly concentrating rebel armies."

Sixth despatch: "The national Government as yet is doing nothing for defence. Lincoln organized his Cabinet in a day. All is in harmony on our side."

Judge.—"Whether this comes to war or not, it is yet peace; and we, the Judge of this court and proprietor of Loudon Heights, are resolved to have a good time while we may. Just as I said to Lincoln to-day, while I held his hat at the Capitol, we have too much pleasure in this country to be meddling with war. What more, Mr. Jenkins?"

Jenkins.—"I thought Douglas held Lincoln's hat?"

Judge.—"But that blow of Wood, to talk of New York seceding! Will he be remembered with adoration?"

The Judge wiped his spectacles. I saw

he saw I had seen, and wished the court meddle not about the hat. Nor did I presume to disturb the harmony of the court, and was favored by one of the most fortunate incidents that ever occurred. The report of two or three pistol-shots on the street started every member in the temple to his feet. Judge Francis adjourned at once, and we all rushed to the door, where, in looking down the Avenue, we beheld some two dozen persons in citizen dress, surrounding Madame Ponchard and Orsini. They were prisoners, and the people bound them with a rope. We then came down from the portico of the Temple, halting near the pillars thereof, till the Judge charged us all to be in readiness for any summons he might from the nature of events be obliged to issue. We then shook hands, little thinking what would intervene before we assembled together again. The Judge and myself then walked together to the before-named crowd of citizens, but the other members went another way; for several pistols were fired, and many of us feared we might be shot. The citizens said to one another, "We know these two persons, Madame Ponchard and Orsini, conspired against Lincoln's life; we will have them lodged in prison until the facts are examined into, and, if they are guilty, they must be punished; nor can any man pardon them for such an offence but Lincoln himself." Yet some few others said, "Nay, let them go. If you harm a hair of their heads, this city shall on the instant be laid in ruins." The captors were, however, much more numerous, and they marched off with the prisoners, even though many knives and pistols were used on them. In a little while they reached the prison, and the two prisoners were put in and secured. By this time, however, the citizens had increased in number to upward of three or four hundred. A large majority were undoubtedly in favor of retaining the prisoners, but a forcible rescue was threatened all round. In this predicament—for civil law was nearly powerless—a number of men went to see Lincoln, to lay the case before him, and to urge him at once to declare martial law in the District of Columbia, and to caution him on the dangers that would otherwise arise. Now, when they had come to the President's Mansion, it was closed against them, and hence arose the saying that Lincoln was so glad of his election that he got drunk. But this was false; for, as stated in the previous chapter of this invaluable history, Lincoln had made it a law for the White House, that,

during four years, any one could indulge in water as much as he liked. What he was doing, though, that he would not receive the above-named committee, this deponent knoweth not. He knew, though, that the committee resolved to follow the matter up, and that, by careful research, they discovered that he would most probably visit one of the richest of American citizens. As soon as this was ascertained, some of the committee went their way, but others of them waited in the grounds of the Mansion; for not only Madame Ponchard and Orsini were to be feared, but many rebels, made mad by Lincoln's success so far, now declared openly that they would not raise a hand to keep an assassin's knife out of Lincoln's heart. In this state of affairs Scott ordered a small guard, disguised a little, to keep a distant watch over the new President, and the consequence was, friends and guard were alike suspicious of one another, and of known rebels. The arrest of Madame Ponchard and Orsini was really a dangerous proceeding, not so much on account of Orsini, but Madame Ponchard. The American people had been taught so much charity to woman, that any crime she could commit was forgiven. Women could defame the pulpit by preaching holiness, even while in male attire their wantonness boasted pride to have no shame; they stalked the clinique and dissecting room, and, like parrots, learned a choice of words, not for good, but love of notoriety; they clamored for their right to do these things by public harangues which they called speeches and lectures; and these, their bad examples, were seized upon by women of lower grade, who, for notoriety, would horsewhip or shoot a man. Yet, were she arrested and tried, she was always acquitted; nay, she was applauded and encouraged in it, for it was her right; for suppose she horsewhipped a man or shot him—poor, dear thing, it pleased her! Suppose she studied medicine in order to practise sin with good skill; no matter—poor thing, she wanted to! Suppose she vented her grievances in the rostrum, calling it a lecture, poisoning the happy daughter's dreams of the future, by sowing there the leprosy of her own perverted thoughts —no matter; 'tis a free country, and the poor, dear thing had a right to do so! Thus had woman attained a right, wherein she was sapping the foundation of all that is pure and holy between the sexes, establishing a preëminence for herself that obliterated all law, that gave her the fullest liberty to any crime. It was almost impossible to punish her. No matter what the crime, people everywhere, and nearly everybody cried out, Shame! if she were even arrested to be tried. Thus it was when Madame Ponchard was taken. The rebels made capital of it. They called it Lincoln's attack on the women. And because a few men kept guard round the Mansion, the rebels said he was a coward; that he stayed at home, and sent out vigilants to capture women. These stories were seized upon and sent by telegraph all over the country, and the opinions of newspapers in far-off cities were returned to Washington with such exaggeration as pleases best the fancy, to move more than ever the latent fire now kindling there.

Now it is a good thing in a republic to have a judge to suit you; for, if you are on his side, he'll be on yours also, and, no matter for what you are bound up, he can give you an injunction or habeas corpus, and set you free in an instant. 'Tis a blessed thing to be a judge, or to be on the judge's side, and for this reason look out whom you elect. 'Twas so in Washington. The secession party had their judge in Washington. The vigilants knew this; knew that, for the asking, he would have the body of Madame Ponchard. But they selected one of their number to go to the judge and take him out riding, and so it was arranged.

Now, with this brief statement on my part, I will revert to the Judge and myself, which is to say, we separated, he going directly to the President's Mansion, and I following the beforementioned crowd of people engaged with Madame Ponchard and Orsini.

CHAPTER XX.

THE MARRIAGES—THE DISPERSION—THE FLIGHT OF MADAME PONCHARD—THE RECEPTION—THE FALL OF FORT SUMTER—THE CALL FOR SEVENTY-FIVE THOUSAND MEN.

Miss Underhill had now been back some time, but was still quite unwell. The torture had been hard for her, and yet her own remorse was harder. The thought that she had been engaged in such a foolish adventure mortified her feelings. This made her backward and diffident. Mostly she kept her room, and did converse but little. None of us ever mentioned her adventure. We forgot it. We remembered only that she had been on a long visit, and that we had no joy while she was away. In distant strains and on distant themes we conversed; and of all the guests at the Jackson House, only the Judge, myself, and the slave Kate knew what had been, and why so long away our summer flower had ceased to bloom. Yet there was one so close and intimate—I mean Vickey. So kind and true this girl waited near, and all wants supplied. I almost wept that Vickey was so good; for, for her vanity and greenness I had valued her so low, and now must I so much her naked, pure heart acknowledge, I almost did wish it were not so; but most I grieved that society could so spoil and spot such an angel-like creature.

My part I can never write, of what I said or did, or of what to me was said. The mistress of Loudon Heights was the purest and best I ever knew; and with this belief, I assure you, words can never be of light character. Ignorance of things around may lead to mischief, but not the heart will. Listen, and you shall hear. But let us back.

About daybreak there did appear before our servant a man so lean and tattered, with sickly cast and melancholy, not one above a thousand had noticed him. With voice from sickness hollow, and full of woe, he thus began:

"Tell me, sir, is this where Judge Underhill lives? Scarce my sight this house can compass, for long I have lain in a dark room, and am some bewildered. Judge Underhill, does he live here, sir?"

Surveying him from head to foot, our servant thus gave answer:

"Yes, sir; the Judge lives here, and so does his niece. Shall I ascertain if he is at home?"

In some confusion the invalid rejoined, "Did I mistake you, sir?"

Servant.—"No, sir; the Judge lives here. Shall I ascertain if he is at home for you?"

Stranger.—"That part I understand, sir; but what said you of his niece? She is dead!"

Servant.—"Why, sir, then she has died

since breakfast. I carried breakfast to her door this morning, and, if I am not blind, I saw her smile right merrily at the sight of it."

In pensive mood, and almost choking with emotion, the pale man gazed on his informer, speechless, and sat himself down. To and fro the servant walked, as if, perchance, he thought this were a poor relative, or a culprit abashed, and seeking audience with great and good people. And so, to give him further hint that this was no time to call, he thus went on:

"Miss Underhill and her uncle are both quite busily engaged. Report has it that she is to marry this night, and I am inclined to believe so; for, even while I stood with the breakfast things, I saw such dazzling robes of white, and such golden head-gear, I am myself convinced. I don't think they would see company."

Almost the stranger froze, but spoke not.

Servant.—"The Cabinet, and, I believe, the Presidents, are to be here, and the foreign ambassadors. The Judge is a man of great wealth, and very eccentric, and he has presented his niece, for the occasion, some costly jewelry and service in silver and gold. Mr. Edge, the great railroad contractor, is tendered the freedom of the house, and his daughter, to blind the public from believing the marriage is to be, calls the event her reception for this season. But we, the confidential servants of the house, know and understand these sort of things. We have been there before."

Again in silence walks the servant, again in silence almost dies the stranger, nor words—for the wild torrent of thoughts was rushing there—could come to rescue. At last he asks:

"Can this be the same—Miss Ann Underhill, of London Heights? Was she not long since supposed to be dead?"

Servant.—"The very same. Oh! ay, she was smitten after a planter down South, and her uncle sent her off till the chap should leave."

Oh, burning, burning thoughts, that now in deadening blast swept through the pale man's fevered brain; and yet speechless sat he there, trying to master the flow of grief. The servant saw, but seemed not to notice it, for he, too, was an American, and delicate in feeling; but he mistook the cause, and deemed him a poor relative, who, by the marriage, must lose something of the old bachelor's estate, and thus he tried to comfort him:

"But the Judge will never give them anything. The young man is rich enough.

I only wish I were a forty-second cousin to the Judge; his niece might go, for the old man can be wheedled into the good graces of anybody who will try. A thousand or two is nothing to him—only take him on the soft spots. A rich old bachelor must be flattered; you must drink his wine, you must call him and all he has the all that is worth having. He, having never been caressed by a wife, falls in love with you, and so gives you his money."

"Who is his niece to marry?" ventures now the stranger, with as much indifference as he could master.

Servant.—"The grandson of one of those would-be Virginian rulers, whose speech-making and writing made his name notorious."

The stranger knew, for everybody knows that to this day it is a saying, "As Jenkins says, notorious shall ever be the name of Jenkins, and the things that Jenkins says."

So still they were, you could hear the ticking of a watch, as the servant paced to and fro, as the stranger, speechless, sat there. But it must have an end, and so, in time, this was concluded.

Stranger.—"Sir, I am that Southern planter. My name is Wadsworth. The things you tell me are more than I can bear, for I cannot weep like other men. I thought this lady dead, but I am glad that it is not so. You seem to be a man of much discretion and good feeling, and when you tell me she is to marry another, you almost murder me with the sound of your voice. The man she is to marry is my best-loved friend. Alas! so isolated I have lived, I never had many friends. My life has been one continued scene of trial and deprivation on the ground of affection. I have lived where, and by travelling from place to place, the fruit of my love has had no recipient—till, alas, I crossed this beautiful flower! To tell me that she was sent away, till I should leave, oh, what a dagger is in thy words! Is my nature wrong? And are all the parts whereof I am made unsuited to the world, that all persons do shun my love? Oh, tell me not that this is so, or lo, in fell despair, I rend in pieces the earthly part that gains no favor!"

Tears came not, but, heaving high his breast, as one of noble spirit unfairly tried, he much smothered and awhile in silence weighed the matter.

"Say, my friend," he then resumed, "provide me a room adjoining the ballroom, where I can view the evening's doings, but tell no one that I am there concealed. I will see all this gaudy display, and see the marriage, and, if I deem it true that she loves him, and he her, I will rejoice that I saw so good a wedding; and on the morrow I will quit this city. Oh, fear not, sir; I have plenty of money, though I am in rags. I have been confined in an obscure hospital, daily writing letters to my friends the Judge and Jenkins, but, getting no answer, I did suspect foul treatment; and so, having regained a little strength, I climbed over the walls and ran away."

Thus they struck a bargain, and the servant sent him to the room, to the pantry where the scuttle window looks into the ballroom. Now, some servants betray confidence and let their fellows know their bonds in trust; but this one was an American.

Peggy Vandorn, Vickey's aunt, was sick. The Judge had not courted her for a long time, and she was heart-broken. The patent whalebone and straps did not work well on so old a form. Her ribs got sore and lame. Gaiters did not well in place of thick shoes; her feet were galled. The bosom pads had heated her, and her skin was smarting with prickly heat. The false teeth and plumpers had stretched her mouth so much that it was all cankered; and thus, in great pain, she denuded herself of the things of fashion, and went to bed. She was sick. She got thin. She was thin before, but now she got much thinner. She got so thin that her false teeth lost their suction. She could not keep them in her mouth. She felt that they were a useless expense. So were the pads and the whalebone. She and Vickey concluded to take them all back—the whalebone and pads to the store, and the teeth to the dentist—and try to get the money back. So they went, the poor old maid and the gay young belle. But they failed to get the money back. So they told it—told how badly they had been treated. Many people heard of it, heard of their foolish, penurious conduct, and so they were laughed at. Only a few did not laugh. These were the Judge's friends. The Judge was a good man, although he had many foolish eccentricities. His friends resolved to cure and to prevent his foolish adventure. Thus they conspired against him, to be his friend, for they reasoned and said to one another, "This Edge family, however educated, and however kind and true, are possessed with notions too low to ever pass long in good society unscathed. Therefore we must prevent the marriage."

On the morning of the day in mention,

a carriage and pair of beautiful bays approached the Jackson House, and was driven to the stables. The carriage was mounted with pearl and silver, and the harness was studded with gold. No one seemed to know whose they were. The driver would not tell, and it had no other occupant. Every one supposed it was the Judge's, and that, ere midnight, he purposed bearing hence in it his young bride. The melancholy and non-committal character of Vickey made many believe she was engaged.

In a separate room some friends of the Judge now held counsel with the clerk—that ever-mischievous clerk—and they told him Vickey did not want the Judge, but that now was his time, to take her in the extremity of trouble, and she would elope and marry him. And they pointed to the carriage, assuring him that they would make him a present of that if he would thus cut out the Judge. The suspicious clerk feared it was a trick—feared they did not own the carriage. They told him to encounter Vickey during the fore-part of the evening, and that they would have the carriage at the door, which he was to tell her was his own, and a present to her. Thus they persuaded the clerk, and he in turn assured them.

But at about that same hour of the day the Judge called on me to say that Vickey had agreed to elope with him that night; that her father would undoubtedly oppose the match, and she had herself proposed the elopement. The Judge was calm then. He never seemed more calm. Thrice he took off his old silver spectacles, wiped and readjusted them, and I knew by his earnestness to clear them of every speck of dirt that he was at that time perfectly composed. Said I,

"If it is your will and hers, I am with you."

Said he, "I have said."

I then told him I thought a man of his wealth and position should not elope,

"But, you see, she's under age," said he, "and, if I wait, she may back out. Better strike while the iron's hot."

To this we both agreed. I am sure it was a perfect understanding between us. He did not say he had purchased the carriage, but he told me it was for that purpose, and he asked me only to witness his departure, not to urge Vickey in any way, and I was then to return into the ballroom and publicly announce the elopement. No hour was set down, only it was agreed to be in the forepart of the evening. He told me where they would drive to, who

11

"The old maid wouldn't wear her false teeth. She was taking them back to the dentist."

would marry them, and by whom I should send word to them of the effect produced in the ballroom. We then talked over some matters in relation to myself and his niece—matters that I do not care to have inserted in this history, although I state that most of the newspaper accounts of this whole affair were without truth, and were merely the guessings of those busy-like penny-a-liners. One thing, however, was true—that at about five o'clock I called on Lincoln and invited him to be at the Jackson House at about eleven at night, and that I told him that most of the officials in Washington were to make an informal call at that hour at that place. I did not tell him to keep it secret, or to make believe it was an accidental call. But it is true, too, that when I called on Lincoln, he was eating a dish of mush and milk. It was then he told me of the story of the log-rolling, which was no story at all. That is to say, as all Western men know, at a large log-rolling the men frequently divide themselves into parties of six to ten men. He was eating his mush and milk at the time, and he said the secession of those States put him in mind of a log-rolling where the men got drunk, who, instead of piling up the logs, divided themselves into groups for the purpose of pulling them down. "Now," said he, "I am captain of this log-rolling, and I am not drunk, nor can you make me drunk on mush and milk. I don't see any difference between thirty-five drunken men at loggerheads—speaking of log-rolling—than I do with thirty millions of people at war. There is just as much danger at a log-rolling as there is here; and the position of the captain of the one and the President of the other is exactly the same. Through my specs they are just the same size. If those fellows at Charleston pull down our heaps, we'll knock them. You see, the clearing is fenced, and the corn is sprouting, and whoever pulls down the fence will let in stray cattle. Did you see Russel's letter—about the South sighing for a foreign prince? By heavens! let them open the gap to foreign cattle, the fur will fly!"

He set down his bowl with firmness, and then shook his head good-humoredly. "Jenkins," said he again, "I'll come to your wedding to-night; only don't keep me waiting, for I must run the machine on double time for a while."

I thanked him, and then left.

Now it was arranged by Mr., Mrs., and Vickey Edge that the house should be opened at exactly nine o'clock. The two former had, by degrees, come to the con- clusion that no one was to marry Vickey or the old maid, but they were resolved to make this the greatest reception of the season, partly, no doubt, in spite, to show how gorgeously they could do things. To do this effectually, a suitable line of etiquette officers were appointed, to superintend the invitation cards, the dress, the wine, the toasts, the music, and all things belonging to a magnificent display. To Hon. James Hamilton was awarded the honor of devising the cards, which for neatness were never surpassed in this country. The coat of arms, which were a soap-boiler, candle moulds, and railway, were so arranged that, at a casual glance, you would call it the American eagle; but it had a deeper significance: for round the edges, the name Edge was arrayed in gold and diamonds. The dresses for ladies were optional with reference to material, but the trail was specified, and so were the neck and the extent of lace. Gentlemen were to wear coats of either pure black or pure blue, and must be either wool or silk, and not mixed. White gloves were to be presented at the door. The music was to begin at fifteen minutes before eleven. The wine had been left entirely to the Judge, to be provided as he saw proper.

Now, as all persons are aware, a ball, a reception, a wedding, and a funeral are always behind time; so, on this occasion, everything was two hours out of joint. It was nine o'clock ere the Judge had ordered the barrels to be tapped. It was half-past nine before the house was lighted. A few carriages came, and the guests also. One couple, a lady and gentleman, were seen to leave. No one knew who they were. They entered the magnificent vehicle seen during the day, and were now gone. In came the guests; the place was soon one sparkling scene of gold and diamonds; but the lady Vickey, who gave the reception, came not in. Messengers were despatched to her room, which was locked, and from which often and often came the answer, "Tell the guests I will soon come down." And so the guests were told, but she came not. The committee waited at her door, but the same voice answered, "Tell them I am coming this moment," and they went and told it. But the house was all in confusion; it was looking like a farce. Informal introductions took place; the time for music was now come, but what should be done? In the hall, through the hall, out and in again went the Judge, his old silver spectacles stored high on his forehead. Mr. and Mrs. Edge, arrayed in all their glory, were alike confounded at the conduct of Vickey. To all their coaxing, to all their scolding, came that only answer, "I'm coming in a few moments."

But the guests could not wait; they must dance, and so they danced. But Edge became passionate; he declared he would burst open the door if Vickey came not forth. The door was opened. Vickey was not there, only a little girl she had hired to repeat those words. To all their questions she was non-committal. She knew nothing of the belle of the evening. Mr. Edge became enraged. "Give me the keys," said he. "Go, tell the clerk I want the keys. I'll search every room in the house. Off! off!" He made everybody his servant. Everybody ran for the clerk, but no one found him. The clerk was gone. Whisperings now went round, and rapidly, of the elopement. Mr. Edge was astounded. Could his daughter elope with the clerk of a hotel? Mrs. Edge knew there had been foul play. Their daughter had been forced off. Thus they raved, and thus were the assembled guests astonished. The Judge became agitated, but he remembered that it might all be a trick, and so he told them all. "'Twas just as he once remarked to Daniel Webster: a young girl of seventeen is a slippery thing —too slippery for a king. I'd never trust a girl of seventeen."

But now, as came the midnight hour, and merriment went on, in came a messenger, and told us all that Vickey and the clerk were married, and that they craved pardon and the right to return to their presence as man and wife. By deceit the messenger was ordered to tell them to return, and all would be forgiven, and so he left. Now, about this hour, when, in fact, were assembled there the highest officers of state, even Lincoln and Scott, the sad announcement was made of the beginning of the battle of Fort Sumter. Full particulars were expected in a few minutes by Prescott himself, who was announced to have arrived in the city with despatches to the President. Mixed, now, was the pleasure of the hour, and all were horror-stricken. Yet the saddest part is not told.

In another part of the Jackson House, arrayed in snow-white lace, was the lady of my choice, the dearest, purest, and yet the saddest fair one I ever knew. At eight in the evening we were to have been married in the orange parlor, and to have attended the reception soon after. At that early hour only a dim light was in the hall. The guests of the affair were already waiting us, and I was awaiting the approach of gentle Ann, when, in looking down the dim-like hall, and observing a lady in white, I heard a violent scream, and saw her fall against the partition to support herself. I rushed to the spot, and, turning to the gaze of her fixed eyes, there beheld at the window the face of Wadsworth. Scarce could I move, and my head was giddy from emotion. Fixed she was, and so was Wadsworth. I took her hand, and, turning to him, exclaimed, "My God! Wadsworth, is that you?"

"Oh, sir!" he said, and burst into tears; but poor, gentle Ann could bear no more. Even at my feet she sank down, and no syllable uttered. "Come!" said I to Wadsworth, "come!" I could say no more. But he came, and we raised her up, and put her on the hall sofa. I then left him with her, and ran to the orange parlor and briefly told what had happened, and they were all sympathy and kindness, coming even every one of them to where she lay. In a little while she revived, and looked up, and recognized us, holding one of my hands and one of Wadsworth's. Said I to him, and I took his other hand, "By the laws of Heaven this is your wife. We thought you were dead. I renounce all claim to her, though, in so doing, I lose a world. You are more noble, and she loves you more."

Now, when I had thus spoken, the persons present were greatly surprised, for they knew not of Wadsworth's love nor of hers; and when they beheld him in such evil plight, so ragged, and so pale and sickly, they mistook him for a very common person. But, though he was much overcome by the scene, he tremblingly replied, even while the fair one, her face and eyes downcast, drooped between us:

"Of all my life's bitterness this is the bitterest hour. Were it not wicked to wish to die, I would so pray Heaven!"

The clergyman, who was to have married us, then said,

"God's will be done!"

I then withdrew a pace and halted a moment, when thus Wadsworth explained:

"Long have I been confined in a private hospital, but all my letters to friends appear to have miscarried. I know not how I came to the hospital. I have been told I was nearly killed by somebody, and thrown into the river. Somebody rescued me and put me in the hospital. Gradually my senses returned, and so, too, my strength of body. At early dawn this morning I escaped from the hospital, and came here.

I heard then that this lady was alive, and to be married this night. The man of her choice was the best and truest friend I ever found. I wanted to see them both, and then, when I knew they were married, I would depart forever. I am here for that purpose, and I pray you, reverend sir, perform that service, even though by it you be my death!"

"As I live," said I, "that shall never be! I know you are both true and noble, and so much I value your peace and happiness, I will forfeit mine own."

Clergyman. — "Now Heaven witness, these are Nature's noblemen, and this silence of hers is woman's greatest power. Say lady, which of the two is your choice?"

But all was silent; none of us knew what more to say. After a moment, however, the clergyman spoke and said:

"Might it not be well to postpone the matter for a few days, till you have all had time to consider the great importance it may have on your coming lives?"

"No!" said Wadsworth. "No," said I; "this must be settled at once. This ennui cannot, must not last."

Still she held to Wadsworth's hand, and the clergyman, seeing this, said,

"Is it your will and choice that this man be your husband?" and she said, "Yes!" The clergyman then said to Wadsworth, "Though informal it be to ask you afterward, I now ask if you choose her for your wife." And he said, "I do!"

Clergyman. — "Then, in the name of God, I declare you married — man and wife!"

We then all went into the orange parlor, some of the ladies assisting gentle Ann to walk; and when we were got inside, we called the Judge, and he came and wished us all much happiness. Wine and cake was then served, and I am sure I never felt happier in my life. In a little while, however, the Judge and I withdrew, both of us nearly distracted with the sudden and unexpected turn of affairs. The Judge sympathized with me; told me, he feared I concealed the grief I had within, and assured me over and over that it was the most unaccountable. And as for himself, he said he never did, nor never would trust a girl of seventeen.

While the guests were agitated over the news from Fort Sumter, in came Vickey and the clerk, some of the Judge's friends having kept him entertained elsewhere for fear of trouble.

Mr. and Mrs. Edge met Vickey at the door, and the clerk introduced her as his wife.

Mrs. Edge. — "Your wife! You scoundrel! How dare you run off with my child? She's under age. Girl, go you to your room! To-morrow we return to Ohio. You have disgraced the name of Edge. Ungrateful girl!"

Clerk. — "You sent word that you would acknowledge the marriage, and forgive us."

Mr. Edge. — "I did not, nor do I now."

Mrs. Edge. — "I am bewildered with shame!"

Clerk. — "But we are married; I can claim and hold her."

Mr. Edge. — "And if I portion her only one dollar, you would not have her. I am master of my own house. Go to your room, daughter; and see you, sir, only one condition will change my will. After one year of penitence, if she wants you, it shall so be; but if not, this marriage shall be null and void."

He then marched off with his daughter, but the clerk followed also. Now it was soon after this that I met the Judge, and, as before stated, heard him say, "The girl of seventeen is a slippery thing," etc.; and it now became my turn to offer him sympathy, but he repudiated it. "I tell you," he said, "the whole thing was a joke on my part. I would have showed you the whole plan of it, but thought I'd better only make the assumption. Oh, no; the clerk owes it all to me." Hereupon the guests began to smile, but were interrupted by the entrance of the vigilants, who immediately told Lincoln that the secession Judge had liberated Madame Ponchard and Orsini, and that they would soon be here.

"You see," said Lincoln, "I must declare martial law."

But before another word was spoken, came Madame Ponchard and Orsini. Wadsworth stepped forward and laid hands on Orsini, saying, "Murderer! 'Twas you who tried to murder me."

Orsini withdrew a pace, and Madame Ponchard sprang in between them.

Wadsworth started and gazed in astonishment, exclaiming, "Good Heavens! my stepmother."

Quicker than it can be told, there was now a flash from a pistol in Orsini's hand. Many men rushed forward, and Madame Ponchard and Orsini were in an instant ejected from the house. The excitement was now at the highest pitch. The evening's entertainment was spoiled, and we were all about to disperse in confusion, when who should come in but Prescott.

"Ha, Prescott," said Lincoln, and he and Scott drew near. "What of the battle of Fort Sumter! Out with it at once."

Prescott. — "Oh, sir, it is true indeed.

Twenty thousand rebels fought and beat seventy-five soldiers. Even at the dawn of day their batteries burst forth, to try the nation's power. On Sumter's parapet like hail the fifty-pounders fell, all red with the fire-lighted dust as the crumbling wall gave way. The Union men long remained in silence beneath the certain ruin; but when Canning's Point and Mount Pleasant shot forth their deadening thunders, our brave men came forth and answered to the battle. Anderson first, and, in support, Snyder and Doubleday, and next the three-and-seventy men. Each as a target stood, each for safety midst the fiery balls and bursting shells his trust had placed in Almighty God! Now toiling at the huge cannon, sweating and faint with toil, those few men the whole nation's battle fought. Beneath them, behind them, all around them was an ocean of powder, and over it and through it fired the rebels their red-hot shot, and it burned not. The floating battery, the forts around, and the far-off batteries, thus for six-and-thirty hours, all day and all night, the roar of battle held; while, suffocating with smoke, and all the woodwork of Sumter on fire, our men, muffled in wet cloths, still to their dangerous call stood forth. But on the far-off places around was the most sickening sight of all. Ladies sat on the housetops and on the distant hills, exultant at the unequal battle, waving their fairy-like hands at the prospect of blood! Thus fought our men, till all things round them were shot away or on fire, and then the rebels came and took the Fort. Even Wigfall, who much had boasted in Congress of what he could do, now came and tore down the nation's flag." Thus ended Prescott's story, and Scott burst into tears. Lincoln turned quite round, saying, "As you say, General, we'll try if we can fight. Call me out seventy-five thousand men!"

THE END.

www.ingramcontent.com/pod-product-compliance
Lightning Source LLC
Chambersburg PA
CBHW020007030726
47500CB00002B/483